
★

The second he turned onto the road, he recognized something else. Headlights flashed, a horn blared and the Jeep roared out of the darkness. The driver had done the same thing Owen had done with the truck earlier—just sat and waited for him to come out.

Owen stomped on the gas pedal and the Toyota leaped ahead, burning rubber. At least there was no longer a truck blocking his path. He sped down the winding asphalt road with the Jeep's brights glaring in his mirror.

Afraid to slow down, Owen whipped the Toyota around curve after curve. Just as his headlights picked up a pie tin painted with the number 2, he heard an earthshaking rumble. He rounded a tight turn and came face-to-face with a wide yellow truck that took up half his lane. Before his foot could reach the brake, he hit the truck head-on.

★

"...a first-rate crime novel."

—*Booklist*

Previously published Worldwide Mystery title by
JOHN BILLHEIMER

HIGHWAY ROBBERY

DISMAL MOUNTAIN

JOHN BILLHEIMER

TORONTO • NEW YORK • LONDON
AMSTERDAM • PARIS • SYDNEY • HAMBURG
STOCKHOLM • ATHENS • TOKYO • MILAN
MADRID • WARSAW • BUDAPEST • AUCKLAND

For:
Anne Regina O'Leary, Clyde P. Craine, Tom Parker,
John L'Heureux, and Ellen Sussman.
An apple for the teachers.

DISMAL MOUNTAIN

A Worldwide Mystery/September 2002

First published by St. Martin's Press, Incorporated.

ISBN 0-373-26431-3

Printed in U.S.A.

Acknowledgments

This is a work of fiction. Names, characters, places, and incidents either are the product of the author's imagination or are used fictitiously. Any resemblance to actual persons, living or dead, events, or locales is entirely coincidental.

Every work of fiction reflects some matters of fact. I am indebted to a number of people who helped me get a few facts straight. These include Jan Austin for reflections on hospice care; Jim Billheimer for construction particulars; Bruce Burgess for mine workings; Gail Boyer Hayes and Denis Hayes for environmental insights; Dr. William Rogoway for oncology details; and Dr. Howard Sussman for pathology procedures. Any blame for misstatements in these matters belongs to the author.

In the interest of spreading the blame, I also wish to acknowledge the contributions of the Wednesday Night Pizza and Literary Society, whose members include:

Harriotte Aaron	Melinda Kopecky
Sheila Scobba Banning	Amy Mar
Bob Brownstein	Laura Nugent
Anne Cheilek	Catherine Pyke
Scott Ennis	Steve Skaar
David George	Ellen Sussman
Ann Hillesland	Anita Wahi

These members have generously set deadlines, shared insights, rooted out excess verbiage, and offered opprobrium. Without them, this book would have been later, longer, and lewder.

Characters in the book quote two poets without attribution. The line "Too much truth is uncouth" comes from Franklin P. Adams's *From the New England Primer,* while "lipstick on a corpse" comes from Bob Henry Barber's *Cold Knob, Reclaimed.*

Finally, I wish to express my appreciation for the encouragement, support, and valued assistance of my agent, Ruth Cohen, and my editor, Kelley Ragland.

He had been to touch the great death, and found that,
after all, it was but the great death.

—Stephen Crane, *The Red Badge of Courage*

PROLOGUE

Thunder on the Ridge

LIZZIE NEAL BALANCED her shotgun on the arms of her rocker and rested her thin wrists on the base of the barrel. In the hour she'd been waiting, the rocker had slid backward about five feet down the dirt turnout, leaving a matched trail of parallel tracks etched in the red clay. Now the rocker had lodged itself against a knobby root. Unless she moved the chair, she couldn't rock anymore. But at least she'd stopped sliding backward.

Dark thunderclouds had formed behind the ridge to the west, shutting out the setting sun. April showers, moving into May with no flowers in sight. Lizzie squinted to try to make out where the ridge left off and the clouds began when lightning flashed, outlining the serrated edges of pines at the ridgeline. A thunderclap followed, and she drew her woolen shawl tightly around her shoulders.

Throughout the day, she'd heard thunder of a different kind as they dynamited Dismal Mountain. It made the hairs bristle on her arms just to think about it. Imagine leveling a mountain just to get a place to put a shopping mall. It wasn't enough that they strip-mined half the state for coal. Now they were lopping the tops off of mountains just to get a level place to put Space-Mart and Sears and the same stores you could find in Charleston or Barkley or Contrary or half a dozen other locations.

But that wasn't even the worst of it. The worst of it was, they were about to dump the debris from the mountain right here in Doubtful Hollow, where the Neals had lived for generations. Her father and uncles had fled Ireland just after the turn of the century, when a plot to kill the king had gone bad. They'd fanned out here in the hollows of West Virginia, some of them changing their names to Neill, O'Neal, or O'Neill as a kind of pitiful disguise. ''As if the Crown cared,'' her father, who had kept the original spelling, had said, "about a pack of plotters who lacked the wit to see that half the pistols they'd planned to point at the Guy Fawkes Day Parade had been brought in by informers." As if a lifetime of picking coal out of the hollows of West Virginia weren't a worse punishment for a little hotheaded pub talk than any the King of England could devise.

But the Neals and their kin had settled Doubtful Hollow, and mined it, and populated it, and now it was all going to disappear. Lizzie had refused to sell her place, but enough of her relatives and neighbors were willing to move to give the land butchers a toehold. And that was all they needed. They'd bring the mountain to the hollow, dump truck by dump truck, and fill the creekbed until it choked with debris and dirt and shale.

The dynamiting had started yesterday, and the first truckloads were scheduled to arrive in the hollow tomorrow. They were, that is, until she'd threatened to make an issue of it and meet the first dump truck with a shotgun. That had gotten their attention. The idea that an eighty-five-year-old woman might hold them off with a shotgun had made front pages all across the state. Which was only half of what she'd hoped to accomplish. She didn't really expect to stop them, but she could at least show the world what they were doing, make them do it in broad daylight, maybe even make the prospective tenants of the shopping mall think twice about what they were getting into.

But it looked as if they weren't even going to do it in broad daylight. After all the publicity, she'd gotten a phone call that day saying the first trucks would be coming in after dark tonight. The caller didn't give his name, just said he was a well-wisher and hung up faster than a nun answering an obscene phone call.

She didn't know what to make of the phone call, but she couldn't ignore it. She certainly wouldn't put it past the bastards to try to sneak their loads in at night. So here she was, with the sun disappearing and a storm moving in, sitting with a shotgun by a creekside road, not so much to stop the dumping as to make sure they didn't start in a place that could eventually cover her land. That was the other half of what she wanted to do. They hadn't been able to buy her land, and she was sure-God going to see that they didn't bury it.

She'd had her niece Ruth's boy, the one with a Ph.D. from Cal Tech, work it out for her. Given what they stood to take off the top of the mountain, if they started dumping downstream from where she sat, they could easily bury her property, and the hospice as well, by the time they were done. It was her job to see that they started dumping upstream from the lines her rocker made in the red clay.

But not too far upstream. If they started dumping too far upstream, they'd bury the Neal family cemetery before they were done. The bastards at Mountain View Development had laughed at her when she talked about burying the cemetery. Turns out nobody in the family ever bothered to get the rights to Cooter's Knoll, where eighteen monuments marked the graves of her father and mother as well as various uncles, aunts, and cousins. The Knoll had been too rocky to plow and too puny to mine, so they'd planted the one crop nobody expected to harvest.

Because nobody was working the Knoll for crops or coal, the Neals never bothered to stake a claim to it. So the mall developers weren't too concerned about burying the Knoll as part of what they called their "land reclamation project." "What's twenty more feet of dirt to a corpse that's already under six feet of it?" they asked. They did offer to replace the gravestones after they'd added their twenty feet of reclaimed dirt, or even to relocate the remains of her relatives before they started dumping.

But to Lizzie, the answer was much simpler. Just stay the hell away from the Knoll with their dump trucks. Ruth's boy had worked that out for her, too. So long as they started dumping between where she sat and a spot about a quarter-mile up the nearly dry creekbed, the developers should be able to move their mountain without burying either her house or the family cemetery. She'd marked the spots on a contour map, taken it to the developers, and talked till she was blue in the face. They'd just smiled and nodded and chewed their pencils and said they'd "see what they could do." She'd dealt with enough bureaucrats in the WACs, the Red Cross, and hospital HMOs to know what "see what they could do" meant. The last time she'd gone, the developers had lost her map. Lost her map! She was just a dotty old woman to them. Nobody they needed to listen to. Well, now she was a dotty old woman with a shotgun. She imagined that might improve their hearing.

The road was pitch-black now. She could barely make out the tree line on the other side of it. The trucks could come from either direction, so she'd stationed Bobby Ray, her nephew and nighttime driver, a quarter-mile upstream at Cooter's Bend. She'd ridden with him to the Bend, shown him where to park the van, and then had him drive her and her rocker back to where she sat waiting. Bobby Ray wasn't the sharpest knife in the drawer, but she could count on him to do what he was told. It worried her some to have him sitting alone in the dark with a shotgun, but all he had to do was see to it that any dumping took place somewhere between the two of them. That was all either of them had to do. She didn't expect the truckers to put up much of an argument.

She wondered, not for the first time, whether the land was worth all this fuss. Even if she saved her own plot, it wouldn't be the same when the developers finished dumping. They'd kill the creek, and there'd be no more Doubtful Hollow. There was still the hospice, of course, but she wouldn't be around to run it much longer, and Bobby Ray couldn't run it without her. Besides, he was only about ten years from retirement himself. The land was her birthright, but there was nobody to pass it on to. The loved ones she was beholden to were all under markers on Cooter's Knoll. Of her kinfolk's youngsters, the ones with any gumption, like Ruth's boy, left the state as soon as they could. The others, the ones who stayed, had sold their plots to Mountain View Development at the first knock on their door.

She'd left the land herself once, to be a nurse in the World War, but it was sorrow, not love, that brought her back to it. Lightning flashed again along the ridge, followed shortly by a thunderclap that echoed through the hollow. There was a way to tell how far away the storm was by counting off the seconds between the lightning and the thunder, but she couldn't remember how to convert the seconds to miles. Sean had taught her as they lay in the attic of the makeshift field hospital at Cassino, watching the German barrage in the distance, treating the war as their own personal fireworks display. She might not recall the details of the lightning-to-thunder distance conversion, but she remembered the attic vividly.

As she'd gotten older, her memories had telescoped overtime. Those most vivid remained clear, regardless of age. She remembered Cassino, the rough nap of the bare mattress, the musty smell of the attic, the fiery flashes of the German howitzers, as if it were yesterday. But she barely remembered yesterday. Some of her patients at the hospice were like that, hoarding a few memories that they replayed over and over. By the time they died, they seemed to collapse their whole life into a single memory. She imagined that must be what it was like to die, whittling everything down to one memory so strong it blanked out everything else. She already knew what her last memory would be.

The thrum of a heavy motor downshifting came from the creek-side road. Lizzie clutched her shotgun and stood up, nudging her rocker backward. The chair slipped off the restraining root and began rocking, sliding downhill toward the creek. She steadied it, stopping its backward slide, and returned her hand to the barrel of the gun.

Wide-set headlights swept around the curve and caught her in their glare. She moved her finger to the trigger. The truck skidded to a stop in the turnout not fifty feet away from where she stood. She leveled the gun, then lowered it when she realized the vehicle was too small to be carrying much of Dismal Mountain. It was just a small blue pickup, carrying what looked like a load of garbage bags.

The pickup's passenger door slammed and a slim woman wearing blue jeans and a denim jacket came toward her. "Land sakes, Aunt Lizzie," the woman said. "What are you doing out here?"

Lizzie shielded her eyes against the headlights. It was Cora, her cousin Anna Mae's eldest daughter. "Heard they were going to start dumping tonight." She wished she had someplace to hide the shotgun.

Cora crossed her arms and shook her head slowly. "You can't stop them."

Lizzie tried to shield the shotgun behind the folds of her print dress. "Don't expect to stop them. Just want to get their attention. Make them pay some mind to where they're dumping."

Cora's husband Donny Lee leaned his shock of red hair out the window of the pickup. "That shotgun'll get their attention for sure. It's a powerful negotiating tool."

"I didn't bring it to negotiate."

"They gave us a fair price," Cora said. "More than fair."

What's a fair price for a birthright? Lizzie wondered. But to Cora, she said, "I don't doubt it."

"Won't get more than a hundred grand for your land, even with that shotgun," Donny Lee said. "That's the most anybody got."

Lizzie bristled. "I told you. I ain't out here to negotiate."

"We just stopped by to pick up the last of our belongings." Cora gestured toward the bed of the pickup, where several black garbage bags tied with different colors of yarn sat on two soiled mattresses.

Lightning flashed across the ridge, followed closely by a thunderclap. A gust of wind caught the red bandanna around Cora's neck and blew it up against her cheek. "Storm's coming," she said. "They won't start dumping tonight. Let us drop you somewhere, Aunt Lizzie."

"I'll be all right. Bobby Ray will pick me up if it gets too wet out."

"You sure?" Cora asked.

"Get on back in here, Cora," Donny Lee said. "Lizzie's not going to budge. There's a real gully washer on the way, and I don't want to be unloading this truck when it hits."

Cora took a last look at Lizzie and trudged back to the pickup. The mattresses in the truck bed bounced as the pickup bumped from the dirt berm onto the pavement and disappeared around a bend in the roadway.

Mattresses, thought Lizzie. The one memory she would take to her grave would be lying with Sean on the bare mattress in the attic of the makeshift Cassino hospital, fingers laced together, thighs touching, watching the German barrage retreat. She returned to her rocker and flexed the fingers of her right hand, trying to make a fist. Arthritis kept the fingers from closing on her palm, leaving her with a bony claw. If she shut her eyes and tried very hard to close her fist, though, pressure from the bone deposits that locked her fingers open made it seem that there was another hand in hers, keeping it from closing.

Lizzie smiled at the memory of Sean's hand in hers and of the rawboned country girl who had first pronounced his name as "Seen" when it appeared on the chart at the front of his cot. He'd laughed through his bandages and gently set her straight, but the other nurses wouldn't let her forget it, calling him "Seldom Seen" when he'd recovered enough so that the two of them could sneak off regularly to the mattress in the attic.

They had a month together before Sean was well enough to rejoin his unit. By the time he left, the converted hospital was so full of cots you couldn't move without jostling a wounded soldier. His letters came regularly, no more than two or three days apart. When a week went by without a letter, she knew in her heart what had happened. She had to write his parents to find out for sure, but she knew.

Lizzie flexed her fingers against the arthritic pain and returned her hand to the shotgun barrel. After the war, she had stopped off in Dublin to visit his parents, and they let her spend the night in his old room. His father was sour, embarrassed to have her there. But his mother had practically collapsed her lungs with hugs. They gave her the quilt from his bed and a book of poetry from his nightstand. Yeats. Another mad Irishman.

A sharp crack echoed down the hollow. Then lightning flashed and thunder rolled over the ridge. It took her a few seconds to realize that the first thunderclap had come before the lightning, not after it. By that time, she'd heard another sharp retort closer in. Gunfire. Lizzie bolted up from her rocker. Her shawl slipped from her shoulders and caught on the barrel of her shotgun. Another shot rang down the hollow. The gunfire was coming from somewhere near Cooter's Bend, where she'd left Bobby Ray.

Lizzie untangled her shawl from the gun barrel and began a fast walk down the road. Her arthritis wouldn't let her knees bend enough for a run, so she hobbled stiff-legged, bobbing back and forth like a broken metronome. A quarter-mile, she thought. It couldn't be more than a quarter-mile away. Was that thunder or more gunfire?

The road wound and stretched. The shotgun grew heavier in her arms. She wanted to stop and rest, but she didn't dare. She never should have left Bobby Ray alone with a gun. Another thunderclap sounded, but it was beyond the ridge. She hurried on, dreading the sound of more shots. When she heard none, she found more dread in the silence.

Lightning flashed, illuminating the curve in the road that marked Cooter's Bend. The first thing she saw beyond the bend was a dump truck, nose-down in the creekbed, its headlights reflected in the lapping water. The truck's chassis was so long that its rear wheels still clung to the roadway above. The sudden drop into the creek had jolted the truck's load of dirt forward, shearing it off and spilling it over the cab.

Bobby Ray paced back and forth in the roadway, limping in a half-circle around the rear of the dump truck, giving it such a wide berth that he was barely illuminated by its taillights. He held his shotgun in both hands as he paced, jerking it up and down and talking to himself. He was so engrossed in his interior monologue that he didn't notice Lizzie until she called out his name. Then he hurried to her, chattering nonstop.

"They shot at me, Aunt Lizzie. I didn't shoot until they shot at me. They had no call to do that. They shot at me, so I shot back."

Lizzie took her nephew's shotgun, saw that both barrels had been fired, and then put her arm around him to lead him back to the dump truck. She sat him down on the rear bumper, saying, in the softest tone she could manage, "It's all right, Bobby Ray. You did just fine. You just wait here while I have a look at the folks in the truck."

"They shot at me first," he repeated.

Lizzie left her shotgun with Bobby Ray and used his empty gun, butt-first, as a cane to help pick her way down the weedy slope to the cab of the truck. The driver was alone in the cab, slumped over the steering wheel behind a shattered windshield. Half his face had been shot away. More out of habit than hope, she checked his pulse. There was none.

Bobby Ray came down to help her back up the slope, keeping his eyes off the truck. When they'd made it back up to the road, he said, "Don't expect he's still alive."

"Not with half his head gone. My Lord, Bobby Ray. What happened here?"

"They fired on me. Not once, but twice. I was just standing by our van. They got me in their headlights and fired on me."

Lizzie walked over to her white van. It was covered with road dust and a few of the painted letters reading DOUBTFUL HOLLOW HOSPICE were peeling, but there were no bullet holes that she could see. "Looks like they missed both you and the van. How far away were they?"

"They stopped at the head of the turnout there. Got me in their headlights and started shooting."

"You keep saying 'they.' There's only one body in the cab."

"Maybe there was only one. Seemed like more when I was ducking for cover."

Lightning flashed and thunder rumbled along the ridge. Bobby Ray flinched and trembled. Lizzie came to a decision. She handed Bobby Ray his empty shotgun, retrieved her own, and slipped the shells out of both the barrels.

"Now give me your gun," she said to Bobby Ray.

"My gun?"

"Just give it to me."

Bobby Ray handed over his shotgun and Lizzie jacked her two shells into the chamber. Then she handed him her empty gun.

"Now take the van down, pick up my rocker, and bring it back up here."

"Right now?"

"Right now. If anybody asks, you were down there the whole time."

"Down there with you?"

"No. Not with me. I was up here at Cooter's Bend. All by myself. You brought the van up when you heard the shooting."

Bobby Ray stood stock-still. "I brought the van up," he said, slowly, as if he understood each of the separate words but couldn't make sense of their combined meaning.

"You brought the van up," Lizzie repeated. "Just like you're going to do right now. Only for heaven's sake, get a move on."

Bobby Ray laid Lizzie's empty shotgun behind the driver's seat and drove the van onto the roadway and around Cooter's Bend.

Lizzie watched the van disappear. She knew she'd have to explain it all to Bobby Ray again when he returned. She only hoped she'd have the time to do it before anyone came. She fingered the trigger of her nephew's gun. She knew they had tests that could tell from your hands whether you'd fired a pistol. She didn't know whether the tests worked for shotguns. Just to be sure, she aimed the gun at the treetops and squeezed the trigger.

Lightning answered the blaze of the gun and a thunderclap smothered the sound of the shot. A sudden breeze ruffled her gray hair and billowed her skirt. That last thunderclap had come right on top of the lightning. The storm was almost on her.

ONE

The Return of the Native

THE LIGHT COMMUTER PLANE was buffeted by so much turbulence that Owen Allison found it difficult to read, so he watched the terrain below through the bouncing window. The West Virginia landscape was crisscrossed with tree-topped mountain ridges, as if God had wadded up his plans for a level forest and tossed the crinkled remnants into the Ohio River valley. Late summer leaves and late afternoon shadows obscured the winding roadways and other signs of civilization in the hollows below the ridges. One rounded knoll, a reseeded and reclaimed strip mine, lower than the surrounding peaks, looked like a pale green sombrero from the air.

The plane lurched toward a tiny airport set precariously on a lopped-off mountaintop, and the pitching and tossing of the descent caused Owen to shut his eyes and clutch his armrests. His mother would be down below, waiting, with some secret she'd found impossible to share over the phone. There were certain words she couldn't bring herself to say. In her lifetime, she'd survived scarlet fever, buried a stillborn child, and fed hot meals to divers dragging the river for her husband, but she still used code words for anything the least bit unpleasant. Owen guessed that the unspoken word behind her current concern was cancer, probably a recurrence of the colon cancer she'd fought off five years earlier, but all she would say on the phone was that she'd had a tiff with her doctor and it would be best if he could come home for a bit.

The plane bounced twice on the runway, swerved, and then righted itself, drawing a round of applause from the other four passengers. Owen opened his eyes and scanned the glassed-in airport window for a sign of his mother, but the glare of the setting sun off the windowpane made it impossible to see inside.

As Owen stepped down from the plane, Ruth Allison appeared

in the terminal doorway, clutching a pale-blue cardigan around her shoulders. She looked frail to her son, but it might have been the severe way she'd swept her gray hair back into a tight bun, or the way the oversized cardigan dwarfed her hunched shoulders.

Owen crossed the tarmac and hugged his mother, then took her by the hand and led her to the long aluminum bin that served as a baggage-claim area. "I've got a surprise for you," he said as the electric cart hauled the baggage wagon up to the bin.

The kennel was the last piece of luggage to be unloaded into the bin. Owen opened it and a small black-and-white dog burst out, tail wagging, and stood on its hind legs, pawing the air in front of Ruth.

"Oh my land, you've brought Buster," Ruth said. She bent and gathered the excited animal into her arms. "But you still don't cut him like a poodle."

"Those frilly cuts don't suit his name or his personality." Owen had brought the dog because he didn't know how long he was going to be needed in West Virginia, and he didn't want to leave it in California for an indefinite period. He could see from the smile on his mother's face that it had been exactly the right thing to do. Ruth had kept Buster for two years when Owen was working for the Department of Transportation and living in a succession of Washington, D.C., apartments. When he'd severed ties with the federal bureaucracy to restart a consulting business in the San Francisco Bay Area, he had reclaimed Buster, causing separation anxiety in both his mother and the dog.

Ruth hoisted Buster to face level, nuzzled his nose, and then carried him to her blue Toyota, which was parked in a handicapped space right in front of the airport. She handed Owen the keys, saying, "It's getting on toward dark. You better drive." It was the first time in his memory she hadn't insisted on driving on her home turf.

As Owen loaded his garment bag into the trunk, he saw his mother snatch the blue-plastic handicapped symbol from her rearview mirror and stash it in the glove compartment. When he slipped behind the steering wheel, she had Buster in her lap, scratching his stomach.

Owen fastened his seat belt. "How are you feeling, Mom?"

Ruth concentrated on Buster's stomach. "Let's not talk about me. The doctor will see us first thing tomorrow."

The dog lay on its back, pawing contentedly at the air. "I'm surprised you didn't leave Buster with Judith," Ruth said. "Every-thing's all right there, I hope?"

Judith was Owen's ex-wife. Like cancer, divorce was another word foreign to his mother's vocabulary. "Everything's fine. But she's traveling a lot." He started to add, "And I don't know how long I'll be staying here," but thought better of it.

"I keep hoping you two will get back together."

"We're working on it. You'll be the first to know if we do."

"Better be quick about it, then."

Owen slowed the car and looked at his mother. "Is there some-thing you're not telling me?"

Ruth looked out at the passing birch trees. "Nothing that won't keep until tomorrow."

Owen wound his way down the mountain road and picked up a brand-new freeway that had cut the travel time to the local airport in half for anyone who could stomach the mountaintop takeoffs and landings. The freeway replaced a meandering series of roads that followed creekbeds and old rail lines deep into the heart of coal country. To straighten out the new right-of-way, the Highway De-partment had gouged wide swaths through the mountains, so that drivers were walled in on one side or the other by exposed cuts that left horizontal seams of shale and sandstone stacked as high as fifty feet under a fringe of oak and sycamore trees.

The rugged, ribbed texture of the exposed sandstone, washed with occasional rivulets of stream water, often had the feel of a massive sculpture. When Owen pointed this out to his mother, she stared at the passing wall, frowned, and said, "It was lots prettier before they cut into it and took the trees away."

Ruth rested her head against the passenger window, and Buster slipped from her lap to the floor of the car. Owen saw his mother's eyes close, and they drove in silence through the twilight. When they were only a few miles from the exit that would take them home to Barkley, Ruth stirred and said, "Better prepare yourself for a shock."

Owen rounded a curve and came face-to-face with an enormous cut in the mountainside just beyond the Barkley exit. The cut created a sandstone-and-shale wall as high as a ten-story building. At the foot of the wall, workmen were constructing a series of long, low rectangular buildings. Dwarfed by the arching wall behind them, the buildings looked like the molding on a gigantic knickknack shelf.

Owen took the freeway exit and pulled off the road onto the construction site, parking under a large sign flanked by two white-ribbed columns. The sign announced:

MOUNTAIN VIEW CENTER
FUTURE HOME OF
SPACE-MART
HOME DEPOT
REXALL DRUGS

Blank spaces under the Rexall Drugs letters suggested that the shopping center wasn't fully subscribed.

"My God," Owen said. "They've sliced away half of Dismal Mountain."

"That's the shopping center your Aunt Lizzie was fighting. Still think the sandstone looks like a Nevelson sculpture?"

Owen had to duck below the windshield to see the top of the cut. "The way Aunt Lizzie described it, I thought they were just going to lop off the top of the mountain, like they did for the airport."

"They wanted the parking lot level with the freeway."

"But they've sliced the mountain right down the middle." Owen tried to envision the shape of the mountain before they'd blasted away the front half. "That's bound to have created more fill than Lizzie was expecting."

"A lot of things didn't work out the way Lizzie expected."

"I couldn't believe that clipping you sent. She really shot a man?"

"She was protecting her property. She says he fired on her first."

"What does the sheriff say?"

"He's not saying much. I was hoping you'd talk with him. You and he worked well together last time you were in."

"We didn't exactly work together, Mom."

"Don't sell yourself short. Whenever I see him, he always asks after you."

"I'll talk to him. Does Aunt Lizzie have a lawyer?"

"I suggested Judith, but Lizzie says Guy Schamp is all she needs." Ruth shook her head. "Guy's older than Lizzie. There's still time to talk to her, though. Her trial's two months off."

"She's not in jail, then?"

"No. They waived time and set bail so she could go on running her hospice. It's a good thing. I may be needing it soon."

Owen glanced over to see if his mother was making a bad joke. Even as a boy he'd understood that Aunt Lizzie's hospice was a place where nobody ever got well. "Don't talk like that," he said, easing the car away from the construction area.

"I told Lizzie you were coming in. She wants to see you."

"Good. I'd like to see her."

"She always liked you."

Owen guided the car under the freeway to a narrow two-lane road along a creekbed. "I always liked her, too."

"Will you be able to stay until her trial?"

"I'm here for as long as you need me."

"What about your risk evaluations?"

"My work'll keep." He'd just finished a job helping the California Department of Transportation assess the earthquake readiness of their highway bridges. Between his own tardy billing and the state's slow payment schedule, he still had three months' pay coming. Of course he wasn't likely to generate any new consulting business while he was in West Virginia, but at least he'd have enough income to keep him afloat.

The winding road meandered past a series of small houses wedged between railroad tracks, a creekbed, and steep, tree-covered slopes. Dresses and faded denims hung from makeshift clotheslines in front of several of the homes, alongside card tables holding toys and tools, propped-up pictures of Jack Kennedy, Elvis, and Jesus Christ, and hand-lettered YARD SALE signs.

"A lot of yard sales for a Tuesday evening," Owen commented.

"Hard times for miners right now," Ruth said. "There's a temporary injunction against mountaintop removal for strip-mining."

A man wearing an undershirt and paint-splattered shorts stopped folding his yard-sale card table to watch them pass in the early fall twilight.

"What about the underground mines?" Owen asked.

"They're still operating. In fact, the state's producing more coal than ever. But they've mechanized so many of the mines there's not enough work for the miners."

"I guess a mine's gotta do what a mine's gotta do," Owen drawled in his boyhood twang.

"It's not funny, Owen."

"I meant it as irony, Mom. You remember irony."

A hint of a smile formed around Ruth's mouth. "Didn't that go out when wash-and-wear came in?"

Owen glanced at his mother. It was as close as she'd come to smiling since the baggage attendant had unloaded Buster.

The hill crested, and they began seeing a few isolated homes set on cleared knolls or half hidden at the end of steep driveways. Satellite dishes and separate garages marked the owners of the homes as solid citizens who would donate their used clothing to Goodwill, miner's relief, and church rummage sales rather than hang it in their front yards for passersby to purchase. As the slope leveled out, houses began to accumulate, paved side streets sprouted, and a road sign announced:

WELCOME TO BARKLEY
IF YOU LIVED HERE,
YOU'D BE HOME NOW

I did live here and I am home, Owen thought. Four blocks beyond the sign, he turned into a cul-de-sac and pulled up in front of the two-story frame house that had been his boyhood home.

The second the car door opened, Buster leaped from Ruth's arms and made a beeline for the house, where he rooted under the front porch and emerged with a tennis ball that had turned brown from neglect. He brought the ball back to the car, laid it in the street, and nudged it with his nose so that it rolled to Owen's feet as he unloaded the trunk. Owen picked up the ball and bounced it high off the concrete porch steps. Buster scurried under the airborne ball, caught it before it hit the ground, and returned it to Owen's feet.

"If you start that, he won't let you stop until he's worn you out," Ruth said.

Owen bounced the ball off the steps again and Buster repeated his retrieving act. "We've got nothing but time, Mom."

"Isn't it nice to think so." Ruth took Owen's briefcase and carried it toward the house. "Bring your suitcase in when Buster's finished with you. You can have your old room back. It's good to have you home. Both of you."

THE TABLE IN the examination room was empty except for the doctor's nameplate, which read J. BAKER MORTON, MD. Owen and his mother sat side by side on stiff green institutional chairs. The wall they faced held two posters showing cross sections of male and female torsos with all of their organs exposed.

Doctor Morton looked to Owen like an overweight elf who had been drummed out of Santa's Workshop for being too large and too serious. When he talked, he lowered his head and appeared to be addressing the fingers laced across his stomach. From time to time, he would peek out over his bifocals just to make sure he still had an audience. His voice was a low, expressionless drone that filtered through a walrus mustache, and it seemed to Owen that he must have given the same talk a thousand times before in exactly the same words.

Owen's mother sat impassively at his side. She must have heard the speech at least once before, but Owen, hearing it for the first time, struggled to sort through the medical terminology and the dry drone to understand what was being said. His mother's CA-125 levels were abnormally high, and a CAT scan showed a growth on one ovary. Given her history of colon cancer, the growth was almost certainly malignant.

"You're sure it's malignant?" Owen asked. He wasn't surprised by the statement, but he wanted to interrupt the doctor's speech, just to slow the droning flow of information.

The doctor's expression didn't change. "I'm sure. Of course, if you'd like a second opinion—"

"That won't be necessary, Doctor," Ruth said. It was the first time she'd spoken since Doctor Morton had entered the room.

"Surgery is indicated," the doctor continued, "followed by aggressive chemotherapy."

Owen absorbed the technical details of the chemotherapy until he felt he had to interrupt the drone again. He asked the one question he needed to have answered: "What are the odds on a successful outcome?"

The doctor raised his head and his voice lifted half an octave. "There's been some success with the procedure. Since there don't appear to be any extraperitoneal metastases, I'd say a twenty-percent chance of surviving at least five years."

The doctor was trying to sound positive and upbeat. But to Owen, who dealt in probabilities daily, it was a death sentence. "A twenty-percent chance," he echoed. "Of survival."

The doctor nodded.

Owen took his mother's hand. She barely reacted. He asked the next obvious question: "And without surgery?"

"We'll make your mother as comfortable as we can. But I really think you should try the operation. We need to remove the growth as soon as possible."

"Then why haven't you?"

The question seemed to take the doctor by surprise. He peered over his bifocals at Ruth Allison, then looked back at Owen. "Your mother says she doesn't want the operation."

"Please don't talk about me in the third person," Ruth said. "You make it sound as if I'm already gone."

It was Owen's turn to be surprised. "But Mom. Why not operate?"

"You heard the doctor. All that fuss. More surgery. A hysterectomy. Chemotherapy. Vomiting. Diarrhea. For a twenty-percent chance of success."

"Against a hundred-percent chance of failure if you don't operate."

"I just don't want to be a bother to anyone."

"Oh, for Christ's sake. You're not a bother. Either way, you're not a bother." Owen turned to the doctor. "Define success."

The doctor clearly wasn't used to questions. "Excuse me?"

"If everything goes well, what kind of a life can Mom expect? Will she be fully functioning. The way she is now?"

"Oh, better than now, I should think," the doctor said. "The pain will have gone away."

Owen looked at his mother. "You didn't tell me you were in pain."

"You think I'd go to the doctor on a whim? It comes and goes."

"Mom, you've got to have the operation. Even a slim chance is better than none. Think of it as buying hope." Owen couldn't imagine facing the future with no hope at all.

Ruth didn't respond.

"You must have gone over this with George. What did he say?" Owen asked.

"Your brother has troubles enough of his own."

"Your brother gave her the same advice you just did," the doctor volunteered.

"Then I don't understand what's holding you back," Owen said.

"Is there anything we can do to improve the odds?" he asked the doctor.

While the doctor considered the question, Ruth Allison said, "There's prayer. We can pray. But I can do that without your knives and chemicals."

"But prayer with surgery is likely to produce a better outcome than prayer without surgery," Owen said. "Why not give God a better chance to help?"

"God sets the odds," Ruth said.

"That's easy enough for him," Owen said. "He knows the outcome in advance. We mortals aren't that lucky."

"The growth is fairly well isolated," the doctor said. "I should think that improves the odds that the surgery will be successful."

"Mom, do this for me. And for George. Please."

Ruth held up both hands in surrender. "All right, bring on the knives and needles."

The doctor smiled, nodded, and scribbled on several sheets of paper, which he handed to Ruth one at a time. "Take the top form down to the lab for a blood workup. Give the blue one to my desk nurse so that she can schedule surgery. Tell her to make it as soon as she can next week. Then sign the bottom sheets and bring them in with you when you come for the operation."

Owen looked over his mother's shoulder as she glanced at the forms and stacked them on her lap. He felt exhausted and helpless. He was convinced that surgery was the right decision. If the doctor was correct, though, the right decision might not make much difference.

While his mother was having her blood work done, Owen visited the hospital cafeteria. He fed two quarters into a vending machine, punched in the code for his selection, and watched while the spiral mechanism brought a Milky Way bar to the front of the machine, where it stopped just short of dropping into the delivery tray. He swore and smacked the front of the machine with his open hand, but the candy bar stayed stuck in the delivery mechanism. He pulled hard at the COIN RETURN lever without getting his money back and was about to smash his forearm against the machine when he looked around to see if anybody was watching and saw a white-robed nun approaching.

"May I help you?" the nun asked.

"The machine's gobbled my money without delivering my candy

bar," Owen said, thinking the nun was a part of the hospital administration.

"A Milky Way, was it?"

Owen nodded.

The nun stepped between Owen and the machine, crossed herself, kissed the crucifix on the rosary attached to her belt cord, closed her eyes, bowed her head, and joined her hands in prayer. Then she rubbed her fingertips together and delivered a sharp karate chop to the side of the machine.

The candy bar thunked into the delivery tray.

The nun stepped aside. "The Milky Ways always hang up like that. The trick is knowing where to hit it."

Owen laughed and bent to pick up the candy bar. "Maybe you ought to fix the machine."

"Are you kidding? I get a lot of converts with my little 'Miracle of the Milky Ways.'"

"Then maybe you ought to rig the Hershey bars to hang up as well. You could double your chances at converts."

"I'm not sure God would approve of such trickery."

"It's not exactly loaves and fishes, is it?"

"To make it work, I'd have to spend my day lurking around the vending machine." The nun crossed her arms under the folds of her white robe. "You don't recognize me, do you?"

Owen studied the nun's face for the first time. Something about her gray-green eyes was familiar, but he couldn't place them in his memory.

"Maybe this will help." The nun removed her white headpiece and ran her fingers through tight red ringlets.

Owen stared at the red hair. "Kate. Kate O'Malley."

She held out her hand. "It's Sister Mary Perpetua now. But you can still call me Kate."

Owen covered her hand with both of his. "I haven't seen you since that disastrous night in Milwaukee. I had two tickets to a Harry Belafonte concert and was going to treat you to a plush dinner."

"And your roommate's car broke down."

"And we walked to a movie instead."

Kate nodded at the candy bar in his hand. "And dined on popcorn and Milky Ways. We saw *Cabaret*."

"A terrific movie." Owen shook his head. "But I still can't watch it without wincing. I was mortified. I really wanted to impress you."

"Oh, you did. A literate engineer who could quote me poetry."

"When I got back to Marquette for my senior year, you weren't at Cardinal Stritch anymore."

"I was marching to a different drummer."

"I found out." Owen remembered pounding his dorm wall in frustration.

"I know. I still have your letters."

"You never answered them."

"I'm sorry. The order was a lot stricter then."

An older nun passed by and glared at Kate. She laughed, smoothed her hair, and replaced her headpiece.

"So you came back to West Virginia after all," Owen said. "Have you been nursing here ever since the convent?"

Kate smiled. "Actually I'm an M.D. The order has three hospitals. I've cycled between them. But I've been here at Saint Vincent's for the last five years."

"An M.D., not a nurse." Owen shook his head. "I just can't keep from embarrassing myself with you."

"I had you at a disadvantage. I've gotten to know your mother. And your great-aunt. I help out at her hospice. If I hadn't known you were coming, I wouldn't have recognized you either. I like the beard, though. It's very becoming."

"You must know Mom's doctor."

"Baker Morton? Yes. Of course I know him."

"How is he?"

"Bake? He's the best you'll find. Your mom's in good hands."

"I just thought..." Owen hesitated, wondering how to phrase his reservations. "Well, you know. His bedside manner leaves a lot to be desired."

Kate skewered him with her eyes. "And you wondered why, if he's any good, he's stuck here at this hick hospital?"

"I didn't say that. I worked here once, you know. The summer after high school."

"Then you know we've got a lot of top-notch personnel. Doctors like it here. They don't have to deal with a lot of hypochondriacs. When miners come in from the hollows, they're really sick. Any hospital would be happy to have Bake."

"He didn't give Mom much of a chance."

"I'm sorry." Kate put her hand on Owen's forearm. "How are you with death?"

It was the first time anyone had said the word "death" out loud. Owen realized he couldn't imagine what it must be like to face it. "I'd rather not find out."

"In my job, I see a lot of it. Sometimes it can be a welcome release."

"Mom doesn't seem to need a release."

"Not now. But she may. Let me know if I can help."

"Help with what?" Ruth Allison asked. Neither Owen nor Kate had seen her approach.

Kate's hand was still on Owen's arm. He covered her hand with his and she released her grip. "Mom, I used to date this woman. At Marquette."

"My goodness, Sister," Ruth said. "You never told me."

"I didn't make much of an impression," Owen said.

Kate put on a sour face. "That's not true at all."

"Give me another chance," Owen said. "Do they let you out for dinner?"

"Lunch is better. Just call me here at the hospital."

"We'll be back on Tuesday," Ruth said. "That's when they've scheduled my operation."

"I could use some company then," Owen said.

"Tuesday's good," Kate said. "That's my day for administrative details. You'll be a welcome relief."

As Owen backed out of the hospital parking lot, Ruth shifted in the passenger seat to face him. "So you know Sister Mary Perp."

"She was Mary Katherine O'Malley when I knew her. She went to Cardinal Stritch College. I had a real crush on her my junior year, just before she left for the convent."

"Hard to compete with Jesus."

"Never had a chance. I couldn't master that resurrection stunt of his."

The corners of Ruth's mouth twitched. "You shouldn't blaspheme."

"Made you smile, though. Almost."

"There aren't many nuns left. The staff calls your Sister Mary 'The Great White Hope.' She's in line to take over the hospital when Sister Regina Anne retires."

"I thought Saint Vincent's had been bought out by some corporation."

"The hospital's part of a conglomerate. But the nuns still run the professional staff. Sister Mary will make a good head nun."

"She gave your Doctor Morton a real vote of confidence."

"Oh, I never doubted him."

"Then why'd you drag your feet over the operation?"

Ruth looked away. "I've seen friends go through it. It's so debilitating. You shrivel up, lose you hair, can't do for yourself."

"That's not the picture your doctor painted."

"Some surgeons can't see past the cutting." Ruth ran her hand through her hair. "Guess I better get a few hats."

"I've got an old Cincinnati Reds number at home. One size fits all."

"No thanks." She reached out and put her hand on his arm. "I'm glad you're home, though. There are a lot of other things you can help me with."

Owen covered her hand with his. "That's what I'm here for."

TWO

Patient Impatience

"THE PATIENTS JUST aren't dying fast enough." Vern Embry pointed an ink-flecked finger at the computer printout he held over the desk of Willis Grant.

"Vern, boy," Grant said, "you got any idea how callous that sounds? What if some of them sisters you keep the books for heard you talking like that?"

"You know what I mean," Vern said. "The drop-off in room use is just too great. I can't make ends meet anymore just by over-charging the terminal patients."

"Now that's something else the good sisters wouldn't want to hear."

Even seated behind an oak desk long and smooth enough to support a shuffleboard game, Willis Grant looked more like the foreman of a construction crew than the CEO of a major holding company. He wore a short-sleeved dress shirt that strained against his biceps and was tight enough around the collar to cause a little fold of skin to puff out over the knot of his yellow polka-dot necktie. Either the tight collar or his disposition gave his face a faint pink tinge that always seemed to Vern to be just on the edge of a red-tinted rage.

"Nobody knows but the two of us," Vern said.

"I don't hardly need to tell you we'd best keep it that way." Grant ran his hand through the naps of graying blond hair that clung tightly to his bullet-shaped head and nodded toward the printout. "What do you propose to do about this month's shortfall?"

Me? Vern thought. How'd this get to be my problem? Saint Vincent's had never had any cash-flow troubles until Mountain View Enterprises took it over and used the hospital's good credit to borrow forty million dollars, which Grant turned around and gave to Mountain View Development as front money for a shopping center. Instead of pointing this out to Grant, Vern said, "I was hoping maybe Mountain View Development could start paying back a little of its loan."

"Well now, Vern, that's just not going to happen this month. Soon's we get the shopping center open and some tenants paying rent, this little problem will go away. But we've had a rough winter and a wet spring, and the contractor's a little behind."

"You said last month we'd for sure have some tenants fronting cash by now."

"Now, Vern, I control a great many things in this county, but the weather ain't one of them."

Grant leaned back in his chair and held his beefy arms out as if he were about to embrace the empty air. "Look at it this way, though. We're all family here. Saint Vincent's Hospital, Mountain View Development, they're both sister companies under Mountain View Enterprises. It's like as if you loaned money to your sister. Or your wife. And she's just a little slow on the payback. You know she's good for it, though. And she's family. So you're not going to shake her down over one or two late payments."

It's more than one or two months, Vern thought. It's been over six months since the first payment was due.

"Especially your good wife Minna, God rest her soul," Grant continued. "I know how you felt about her. The way you fiddled the dates on her insurance application so her melanoma wouldn't show up as a precondition. That was an act of love if ever I seen one. And it took guts, boy. I'm telling you it took some guts. That's how I knew you'd have the stomach for our little accounting adventure."

"I thought we'd only have to stretch for a month or two."

"One month, three months. What's the difference? It's working. You add an extra night and a few services to the bills for terminal patients. We're just replacing the money the hospital's little business drop-off has cost us. I'm telling you, it's a stroke of genius. Lots of times there's no survivors to check the bill. And when there are, there's a good chance they're so grief-stricken they don't look twice at it. How long you been goosing the accounts, anyhow?"

"Six months."

"And has anybody caught on? Anybody?"

"Not so far."

"Course not. Survivors don't have to pony up the money. It's the insurance company that pays. You just have to keep backup records that'll satisfy the auditors."

"I can get past the auditors. But the longer we do this, the more likely somebody's going to catch on."

"Vern, we go through this every month. Nobody's tumbled to it yet, and nobody's likely to. And if they do, all you gotta do is apologize like mad, back out the overcharges, and..." Willis wiggled his fingers like a teacher coaxing an answer from an slow student. "And...?"

"And blame the computer."

Grant nodded. "And blame the computer. That's exactly right. Look here, Vern. It's not like this is something new and different. You stay at a hotel, they always add a little extra to the bill for a movie you didn't watch, a phone call you didn't make, or something extra from the mini-bar. Hell's bells, you know that."

Vern nodded, even though he rarely stayed in hotels, and the Motel Sixes he frequented didn't have mini-bars or pay-per-view movies.

Encouraged by the nod, Grant continued, "And car companies can't sell you a new car without they hit you for some overpriced and useless undercoating."

Vern nodded again, even though he'd never bought a new car in his life.

"And then there's the phone company. You ever really count all the four-one-one calls they're charging you for?"

"They charge for those?"

"Hell, overcharging's just a part of doing business. It's as old as the Romans. They even had a phrase for it: 'Cave a lot emptier.'"

In response to Vern's blank look, Willis explained, "Means check all them little tiny numerals under the fold of the scroll."

"But what'll we do about the hospital's cash flow?"

"Way I see it, until the shopping center opens, we got two choices: Either jack up the overcharges on the same old stiffs, or find some new stiffs to stiff."

Vern tried not to recoil at the word "stiffs." "I don't see how we can charge more than we already do."

"What about drugs? They pump a lot of drugs into the near-departed. Hell, I hear they have to flush the morphine that hasn't made it into the system when the heart stops pumping. You make up charges for a night's stay. Why not do the same for drugs?"

"Oh, no," Vern shook his head. "No. No. The drugs are monitored. There's a whole system of checks and account logs. It's not like room charges, where the auditor might not even look at the backup data. We'd never get away with it."

"Then I guess we just need to find more terminal patients."

"How can we do that?"

"Well, so far you're only overcharging folks that die on our premises."

"I don't see how we can charge extra for the room if someone dies at home."

"You're not following me, Vern. Lizzie Neal siphons off lots of our dying patients to that hospice of hers. I'll grant you, some of them don't have insurance. But most do. And damn few have any close kinfolk, or they'd be going home instead of to Lizzie's."

Willis Grant leaned forward onto his desk, and words seemed to cascade from his mouth like water over a waterfall. "Hell, it's a perfect setup. Just tack an extra day or so on the stay of those patients we lose to Lizzie. I'll guaran-god-damn-tee you they'll never notice it. By the time they leave us for Lizzie, the reaper's already got them by the gonads. If you just hold off on the bill for a month or so, they'll either be dead or next door to nirvana and so plowed on morphine they'll never notice a few extra charges."

Vern found himself swept up by Grant's enthusiasm. "I suppose it might work for a month or so."

"Oh, it'll work. It'll work. Slicker than snot on a doorknob. We only need a couple of months. Hell, Lizzie's hospice won't last much longer anyhow. She'll go on trial soon, and what I hear is she's got about as much chance as a blind pole-vaulter on a muddy track."

"And if she goes to jail..."

"There'll be nobody to run her hospice. Our own hospice wing will fill up with her charges. And her charges will be our charges, if you get what I mean."

"Our death rate will go back up."

"By God, I love it. I really do. It'll keep our books balanced until the shopping center opens." Grant picked up the computer printout on his desk and handed it back to Vern. "Don't just stand there, Vern boy. Get on back to your office and charge ahead. Hell, charge two heads. Charge as many heads as you need to keep us in business."

BACK IN HIS OFFICE, Vern Embry sorted through the records of terminally ill patients who had recently left Saint Vincent's hospital for Lizzie Neal's hospice. He quickly found a dozen whose hospital stay could be lengthened without much danger of detection. He knew one man, an ex-UMW organizer, had already died, leaving no heirs. He set the records aside, resolving to check the local obituaries to see how many others in the group had already passed on. Strictly speaking, he knew Willis Grant was right. They didn't have to be dead to be overcharged. But Vern felt there was less likelihood of detection if there was no chance the patients would review their own bills.

This had started out as a game. A heroic effort to save the sisters' hospital from bankruptcy until the shopping center got on its feet. At least he saw it as heroic for the first month. As Saint Vincent's occupancy rate dropped and the fabrications mounted, he stopped seeing it that way. It was fraud, pure and simple. It was fraud, and he could go to jail if anyone caught on. But he was in too deep to stop. His only hope was that the shopping center would open soon and be the success everyone anticipated.

"What have I gotten us into, Minna?" he asked, silently addressing the picture of his late wife on the desk. "We never could have paid for your last year of treatments without insurance. I don't know how Willis Grant knew I'd fiddled the eligibility, but he did. And now he's holding it over me."

"Vernon, do you have a minute to spare?"

The question startled Vern. It had seemed to come from the picture of his wife, who was one of the few people who called him by his full first name, Vernon. He was momentarily disoriented until he realized that another person who regularly called him Vernon, Sister Mary Perpetua, had cracked open his office door and was peeking around it.

"I'm sorry," Sister Mary said. "Am I interrupting something?"

"No, nothing." Vern stood quickly and stuffed the records he'd weeded out into the top drawer of his desk. "Come on in."

Sister Mary entered, followed by a thin, elderly man with hollow, sunken eyes who was wearing bib overalls. One strap of the overalls was fastened to the bib with the largest safety pin Vern had ever seen.

Sister Mary turned to the hollow-eyed man and said, "Mr. Akers, this is Mr. Vernon Embry. He's responsible for all our billings. Why don't you tell him what you told me?''

The man fished in the pocket of his overalls for a piece of paper that had been folded over several times. He unfolded it and held it out to Vern. "It's about this here bill. For the night I lost Sunny Joy."

Vern's heart sank. Someone had actually checked their bill. He held the statement, which was etched with grime at the folds, by opposing corners as if it were contagious and asked, "What about this bill?"

"Well, that there bill says Sunny Joy spent the night in a room at your hospital. But she never did no such thing."

Apologize, Vern thought. Just apologize and blame the computer. The man didn't look too sharp. But Sister Mary Perpetua was standing there watching him, with her arms crossed and her hands tucked inside the folds of her white robe. "I can't imagine how that could happen. Perhaps she only spent a part of the night. Even if she only had the room for a few hours, we'd have to bill you for the entire night."

"Never spent the night. Nor any part of it. Sunny Joy got run over and Doc Kessler took her right straight to the operating room. She never made it. Never had a chance."

"Well then, maybe Doctor Kessler assigned her to a recovery room after the operation."

"Either I'm not talking too good or you're not listening too good. Why'd she need a recovery room if she never recovered? She died on the operating table. Never had a chance. When I carried her in, there wasn't a whole bone in her little body. Afterward, I took her straight home for burying."

Vern felt that he shouldn't cave in right away, that he ought to put up some small resistance for the sake of Sister Mary. "Well, I'll certainly talk to the doctor and the duty nurses who signed the room sheet to try to get to the bottom of this."

Akers's deep-set eyes misted over. "She never had a chance."

Vern refolded the bill and handed it back to Akers. "I assure you I'll look into it and will amend your bill. It's probably just some computer glitch."

Akers's shoulders shook. "Not a friggin' chance." He brought his hand up to cover his eyes. "Excuse me, Sister."

Sister Mary moved forward and put one arm around Akers's quaking shoulders.

Vern felt as if he were losing control. "Mr. Akers, I'm very sorry about your wife, and I'm sure—"

Akers's hand left his face and dropped to his side. "My wife? My wife's been dead for years."

"But I thought—then who's Sunny Joy?"

Akers squared his shoulders and drew himself up to his full height. "Sunny Joy's my dog."

Vern looked from Akers to Sister Mary, who didn't seem fazed by this piece of news. He grabbed the bill back from Akers and pretended to examine it, trying to think how he might destroy the evidence he was holding. Finally he asked, "Sister Mary, you knew about this?"

Sister Mary nodded.

"How in God's name did we come to be operating on some dog?"

"Not just any dog," Akers said. "Best damn coon dog in the county. At least she was till your doctor run her over."

"As I understand it," Sister Mary said, "Doctor Kessler was returning home from an emergency call early in the morning."

"Same morning I was running my hounds," Akers said. "They was hot on the scent with Sunny Joy in the lead when the doctor took a curve too fast and wiped her out. Never expected to see any cars that early in the morning."

"There was no time to locate a vet," Sister Mary explained, "so Doctor Kessler brought the dog back here and tried to save her."

"She was just too broke up," Akers said. "She never had a chance."

"All right. All right." The unfolded statement dangled loosely from Vern Embry's hand. He lifted it and asked, "But how did the dog show up in our billing records?"

"It was the drugs," Sister Mary said. "They needed some sort of a record to account for the narcotics they used to sedate the dog. The nurse in charge treated it as a hit-and-run accident."

"And the system took it from there," Vern said, failing to mention how far he'd pushed the system. "I'll just keep this bill if you don't mind, Mr. Akers. Rest assured we'll adjust it to omit the hospital stay. In fact, why don't you just forget about it all together and let us handle it at this end?"

"'Preciate it." Akers shook both their hands as if he were pumping well water and left the room.

Sister Mary waited until the office door had closed behind Akers, then shook her head and said, "My God, I just don't understand how that could happen."

"Computer error, most likely," Vern said. He felt a thin trickle of sweat under the arm that held the bill.

"Someone mixed up the patient's records, you mean?"

"Or miscoded them. Or maybe someone on the afternoon shift saw the workup and just assumed the patient would have used a room."

"It just seems so bizarre." Sister Mary reached out and took the bill from Vern, who had to fight down his impulse to hold onto it at all costs.

"But what I don't understand—" Sister Mary said slowly, pointing at an entry on the statement. "—what I *really* don't understand is how we could have charged the man for grief counseling."

The trickle of sweat under Vern's arm turned into a torrent. Akers's bill was one of those he'd embellished beyond the room rate. He tried his best to control his voice and ask, "Grief counseling?"

"It's right here on his bill. A hundred dollars for G-Con. Mr. Akers thought it was some sort of drug. I saw no point in enlightening him."

"My God."

"How could that happen?"

"There'd have to be a backup sheet for that kind of charge," Vern said.

"How could there possibly be a backup sheet for grief counseling for a dead hound dog?"

"Let's just have a look." Vern checked the bill, stepped to one of his file cabinets, and opened the middle drawer. "Green sheets are volunteers, pink sheets are social workers, and blue sheets are nurses."

"I know, Vernon. I know. I help out with the paperwork on Tuesdays. Remember?"

Vern leafed through the pink sheets until he found the one he'd planted in the audit trial. "Here it is, Patient 854023. One hour of grief counseling." He screwed his lips into a pretend frown. "I can't seem to read the signature here."

Sister Mary looked over his shoulder at the sheet. "How can this happen?"

"Probably a foul-up with the patient numbers. Maybe the nurse that wrote up Sunny Joy's hit-and-run took a duplicate number. Or didn't bother to report the one she was using so that it wouldn't be used later."

Sister Mary frowned. "We've got to find out what happened. This sort of thing just can't continue."

Vern closed the file drawer. "Look, Sister, why don't you let me worry about it?" He took back the offending bill. "I'll find the foul-up and fix it. In the meantime, we've taken care of Mr. Akers."

"Thank heaven he came to me."

And thank heaven you came to me, Vern thought. "It just goes to show that old saying is right. You know, 'Cave a lot emptier.'"

Sister Mary gave him a blank, uncomprehending stare.

"It's Latin. I think," Vern said.

"'*Caveat emptor?*' Is that what you mean? Let the buyer beware? I'm surprised to hear you say that, Vernon. That's not the way we run this hospital. Or if it is, you've really got the Latin wrong. The appropriate phrase would be '*Kyrie eleison.*'"

It was Vern's turn to stare blankly.

Sister Mary translated: "Lord, have mercy on us."

THREE

Notions and Potions

AUNT LIZZIE'S HOSPICE was a two-story brick house in a grove of oak trees set back from the winding creekside road. When Owen was a boy, the house had left an indelible impression on him, right alongside the brooding frame house of Norman Bates in *Psycho* and the lightning-struck castle of the evil queen in *Snow White*. Seen through his adult eyes, the hospice looked a little run-down, with the fading bricks leaning against a one-story frame addition, but it still had the same power of association. It was the place people went to die, the last home they would know on earth.

While the house had aged visibly in the twenty years since Owen had seen it, Aunt Lizzie hadn't. At least not noticeably. She waved at Ruth and Owen from the white wooden porch, and Buster jumped from the car and ran up the steps to meet her, tail wagging all the way.

Lizzie bent forward at the waist to stroke Buster's ears as he pawed the air in front of her. She was wearing army fatigues, combat boots, and tinted aviator glasses, and the two gold bicuspids that bracketed her rows of even teeth glinted in the sunlight as she smiled. "This here's the same doggie you left with Ruth a while back," she said as Owen helped his mother up the gravel driveway. "Reckon I know what you're looking for, little fella."

Lizzie walked to the end of the long porch, where she picked a worn tennis ball out of a patch of geraniums in a window box. On the way back, she circled around a patient in faded blue pajamas who sat, motionless and alone, at the end of a row of rocking chairs. She nodded to the patient and bounced the ball off the top porch step into the driveway. Buster took off after it, catching it on the third hop, and brought the ball back to Lizzie, arriving on the porch at the same time as Owen and Ruth.

"Good to see you, Owen," Lizzie said, holding out her hand.

Lizzie's hand felt like a bundle of brittle sticks. Owen held it loosely, trying not to show surprise. "Good to see you, too." He nodded toward the new addition. "Business must be good. Looks like you've added a few rooms."

"Did that about five years back. Me and Bobby Ray. Couldn't make do with just the beds in the house. Folks was dying to get in." Lizzie speared Owen's shoulder with her index finger. "Then, of course, they was dying to get out."

Owen started to laugh, then glanced nervously over Lizzie's shoulder at the patient in the rocking chair.

"Oh, hell," Lizzie said. "It's sure no secret. Most of my guests know they won't be leaving here vertical." She raised her voice and shouted back over her shoulder at the man in the rocker, "That so, Lucas?"

The man rocked once and said, "Excellent day, Lizzie."

"See? He couldn't hear me anyhow." Lizzie bounced the tennis ball down the driveway and watched as Buster jumped off after it. Then she took Owen by the arm. "I'm glad you stopped by. I'd like to walk you down to the old creekbed, show you where they dumped most of Dismal Mountain. Something about it's just not right."

Buster brought the tennis ball back and nudged it toward their feet. Ruth kicked it back into the driveway. "While we're here, we ought to talk about your trial," she said. "Owen's wife is a crack-erjack lawyer."

"Ex-wife," Owen corrected.

"You need to work on that," Ruth told him.

"Don't need her help," Lizzie said. "My old friend Guy Schamp's a lawyer. Besides, its an open-and-shut case. Man was shooting at me, and I shot the son of a bitch. Wouldn't need no trial neither, except they say I was the only one doing any shooting."

"Guy Schamp's been retired for over fifteen years," Ruth said. "At least think about getting other legal help."

"What do you think, Owen?" Lizzie asked. "Would I get along with your ex?"

"You'd like her, and she's a fine lawyer," Owen said. And she'd like you, he thought.

"I've already talked to her," Ruth said. "She's willing to work for free."

"That's quite a family discount," Lizzie said. "I couldn't let her do that."

"I had in mind a trade," Ruth said. "I might be needing accommodations soon."

"Mom, you don't know that," Owen said.

"I said 'might,' didn't I?"

"In that case, maybe you'd like to come inside, look around," Lizzie said. "Better leave Buster out here, though, in case someone from the Accreditation Board stops by." Lizzie toed the tennis ball so that it rolled against the slippered foot of Lucas in the rocker.

Buster followed the ball. When Lucas made no move to pick it up, the dog barked sharply once. When Lucas still failed to move, Buster picked up the ball, rose up on his hind legs, and deposited it in Lucas's lap.

Lucas picked up the ball in his left hand and raised it overhead. His pajama sleeve slipped down to his elbow, revealing a Marine Corps tattoo on a bony forearm. He rocked forward, catapulting the ball off the porch.

Buster catapulted himself after the ball, retrieved it, and returned it to Lucas's lap.

Lucas's lip turned up in a lopsided grin. He said, "Excellent," and threw the ball off the porch again.

"That'll keep them both busy for a while," Lizzie said as Buster followed the ball down the steps.

Inside the hospice, the maroon carpet that Owen remembered from his youth had grown threadbare. Bright yellow tape along the carpet marked the edges of the stairs and corridors for patients with impaired vision. The sliding oak doors that once led to the living room of the house were topped by curved wooden letters that spelled out the words NOTIONS AND POTIONS. Past the doors, in the center of the room, an assortment of clothing hung on racks over well-worn pairs of men's and women's shoes. Along the walls, long tables held a hodgepodge of framed pictures, shaving kits, books, hand mirrors, hats, and other personal items, all bearing small colored dots marked with prices ranging from fifty cents to five dollars.

"We're the last stop for most of our patients," Lizzie said. "Folks that can't pay leave us their clothes and effects. Even those that have insurance contribute to the ongoing rummage sale." She picked up an army camouflage hat that matched her outfit and pulled it down over her gray braids, tilting it at a rakish angle. "Keeps me in the forefront of the fashion parade."

"That explains NOTIONS," Owen said. "What about POTIONS?"

Lizzie waved her hand toward a table holding boxes of patent medicines, herbal remedies, lotions, deodorants, cosmetics, and small jars filled with colored liquids. "By the time they get to us, most folks are off everything except painkillers, but lots still want to take something else."

"Looks like you get a lot of call for laxatives," Ruth said.

"Your really strong painkillers, like morphine, cause constipation," Lizzie explained. She led them back to the inner corridor, and Owen became aware of a smell that he could classify only as the odor of overripe fruit. An open lift descended from the second floor, carrying a balding man with a supermarket basket full of soiled laundry.

When the lift reached the first floor and the waist-high gate opened, Lizzie addressed the balding man, saying, "Bobby Ray, you remember Ruth's boy Owen."

Owen nodded and held out his hand to Bobby Ray.

"Bobby Ray's Ruth's cousin Frank's youngest," Lizzie said. "I'm not sure what that makes the two of you."

Ruth smiled. "Second cousins, once removed."

"And twice misplaced," Owen said, completing an old family joke.

Bobby Ray screwed his face into a frown, as if both the arithmetic and the genealogy were beyond him.

"Bobby Ray does all the heavy lifting around here," Lizzie said.

A proud smile replaced the frown on Bobby Ray's face. "That's me, the heavy lifter." He backed the shopping cart out of the lift. "Gotta get this stuff to the laundry. Good to see you, Owen."

As Bobby Ray followed the yellow tape down the corridor toward the new addition, Lizzie said, "Maybe you'd like to see some of the rooms, talk to a few of the patients."

"That seems too…" Owen hesitated, searching for the right word. "Intrusive," he finally said.

"Some of them would love it. They don't get many visitors."

"I don't know," Owen said. "It doesn't seem right, somehow."

"You wanted Owen to look over the landfill," Ruth said. "Why don't the two of you go ahead and check it out? I'll just poke around here a little. Get to know my future neighbors."

"That's not funny, Mom," Owen said.

"Neither is chemotherapy, hon," Ruth responded.

"Owen, maybe we ought to gather up Buster and go for a little walk," Lizzie said.

Glad for an excuse to leave, Owen retreated to the front porch, where he found Buster up on his hind legs, sniffing at a rain barrel.

"Ball went into that there barrel," Lucas explained from his rocker. "Good thing, too. He like to wore me to a frazzle."

Owen snapped a leash on Buster, retrieved the ball from the rain barrel, shook the water off it, and stuck it in his jacket pocket.

"What kinda dog is that, anyhow?" Lucas asked.

"Poodle."

"Don't look like those poodles you see in the moving-picture shows."

Owen scratched behind Buster's ears as the dog sniffed at his jacket pocket. "We'll take that as a compliment, won't we, Buster?"

Lizzie joined Owen on the porch and took Buster's leash. "Let me walk him. It's just up the road a piece and around the bend."

The sight that greeted Owen around the bend made him gasp. Dirt clods, rocks, and rubble were piled high in the hollow between two hills, as if simultaneous avalanches had plunged down both slopes and met in the middle. The roots of an unearthed sapling poked up from the center of the mound, like the clutching hand of a drowning man.

"My God," Owen said. "How far back does it go?"

"Starts on down the road by the old culvert, then goes clear back to the old family cemetery. They uprooted Momma's and Poppa's graves."

"It's a lot more than I figured on."

"It's a sight more than they let on up front."

A deeply rutted dirt road paralleled one side of the landfill. "Let's follow that road," Owen said. "Pace it off, see how far back they dumped."

Owen started down the dirt road, followed by Buster, who was straining at the leash held by Lizzie. About a hundred yards in, Owen looked back to see Lizzie poised precariously on one leg at the edge of a deep tire track, trying to keep from falling by waving her free arm in quick circles like a novice wire walker.

Owen hurried back, grabbed Lizzie's elbow to steady her, and took Buster's leash. He'd momentarily forgotten that the combat fatigues and aviator glasses hid the frail frame of an eighty-five-year-old woman. "I'm sorry," he said. "We don't have to go any further. I can look myself later."

Lizzie shook free of Owen's grasp and took back the leash. "Hell, no. I want to go with you. There's something fishy about this whole crudslide and the way they lied about the size of it. I thought you might be able to figure it out and nail the bastards—the way you nailed Amalgamated Coal."

A makeshift dam constructed by Amalgamated Coal had burst thirty-six years earlier, killing thirty-four people, including Owen's father. In his Ph.D. thesis fifteen years later, Owen had shown that the dam was not only manifestly unsafe, but that a safe dam could have been built for as little as forty thousand dollars. Local lawyers had taken his thesis and run with it, arguing that Amalgamated's out-of-state officials knew the dam was unsafe even when they were pumping sludge-filled water into the lake behind it. Amalgamated's owners agreed to an out-of-court settlement of two million dollars, roughly ten percent of their yearly earnings. At the same time, carrying through on threats they had made before and during the trial, the owners closed down their local mines and reopened old shafts across the border in eastern Kentucky.

The award and Amalgamated's tacit admission of guilt made Owen a hero to half the county. To the other half—miners and people whose livelihood depended on the mines—he was a traitor who had caused the biggest local employer to leave town. Even now, over twenty years after the trial and thirty-six years after his father's death, there were still neighbors who wouldn't speak to Owen and shunned his mother.

"This fill isn't anything like Amalgamated's," Owen said. "Amalgamated had dammed off a running creek. These guys have sized their landfill so that water can still flow underneath when it needs to. The creekbed under there was mostly dry anyhow, wasn't it?"

"Except for a couple of months off and on come flood season. That's why they called it Doubtful Hollow. But that's not the point. Those bastards from Mountain View Development are hiding something. I can feel it. They're just as greedy and stupid as Amalgamated."

"If greed and stupidity were criminal offenses, we'd have to lock up half the county. Nothing they've done here is life-threatening."

"Tell that to the critters that used to live in this hollow." Lizzie pointed out sparse patches of freshly sown grass that dotted the landfill like a skin rash. "They spray that grass seed on with a hose. Pretty soon it'll all be green."

"Anything would be an improvement."

"They call it reclamation. Reclamation, hell. It's like putting lipstick on a corpse."

Owen kept his hand on Lizzie's elbow to steady her as they walked along the makeshift road. They stopped for a moment at a hand-lettered NO TRESPASSING sign, but Lizzie tugged at Owen's arm, saying, "I've lived here nearly all my life. Nobody ever kept me out from where I wanted to be."

"Did anyone else live here? Back here in this hollow, I mean."

"A few families. My grandniece had a little cottage."

"What happened to them?"

"Got bought out."

"For a fair price?"

"More than fair, what I hear."

The rutted road veered sharply to the left as the landfill widened, and Lizzie tugged on Buster's leash to keep him on the road. "Fair price ain't all it's cracked up to be," she said. "Suppose I was to offer you a fair price for Buster there."

"He's not for sale."

"Come on. I'll give you two hundred dollars."

"No deal."

"Three hundred. That's more than fair."

"Nope."

Lizzie jerked the leash, causing Buster to yelp and stand still. "Now, suppose I tell you if you don't sell, you're liable to wake up one morning and find your precious property covered with dirt."

"All right, I get the point."

"It's not my point, exactly. I saw it in a movie once. Jo Van Fleet played an old lady trying to keep from selling her home to the Tennessee Valley Authority."

"*Wild River*. Lee Remick was in it, too."

"That's the one. Early sixties. Van Fleet was younger than I was at the time, playing a woman who's older than I am now."

"Pretty good actress. Pretty good movie."

"She had all the moves down. For acting old. But she didn't

know shit about being old. You only get that one way. By living so long you daresn't even buy green bananas.''

For the second time that afternoon, Owen thought his great-aunt looked her age. "Are you okay, Aunt Lizzie?"

Lizzie patted his hand. "Oh, yes. Just bone-sore through and through. Nothing wrong with me death won't cure."

The roar of an unmuffled motor came from the road ahead of them and a Jeep jounced into view, spewing dust, gravel, and exhaust. The driver stopped just short of Buster, got out, and knelt to pet him. Buster responded by wagging his tail and panting.

"Afternoon, Lizzie," the driver said. "Your pooch?"

"Afternoon, Letch. Dog belongs to my nephew here." Lizzie nodded toward Owen, but made no attempt to introduce him.

Letch stood and dusted off his hands. He was taller than Owen's six feet, and his broad shoulders were barely covered by a black polo shirt that had the words MOUNTAIN VIEW DEVELOPMENT embroidered on the left breast. If his nose hadn't been broken at least once, he might have passed for an aging matinee idol.

"Guess you folks must not have seen the sign on your way in," Letch said.

"Oh, we saw it all right," Lizzie responded.

"But you came on ahead anyhow?"

"Oh, for heaven's sake, Letch. That's my property just a stone's throw away."

Letch kicked at a deep tire track with the side of his boot. "This ain't your property. Never has been."

"I just wanted to cut through to show my nephew how you relocated our family cemetery."

"No need to cut through here to do that. Just follow Possum Break Road on around. The new plots are right off the road."

Lizzie's voice dripped with Southern Belle gentility. "But this here way's shorter, and we wanted to walk."

"Sign says no trespassing. Sign means what it says."

Lizzie dropped her Southern Belle accent. "What's the matter? You ashamed of what you're doing to the land? Afraid people might see?"

Letch seemed more amused than annoyed by Lizzie's anger. "It's our land, Lizzie. What we do with it is no concern of yours. Be happy to give you a lift back to the road if you'd like."

"We made it in under our own steam. We'll make it out the same way." Turning to Owen, she asked, "You seen all you need to?"

"Not really. But it'll do for now."

"It'll do for good and all," Letch said.

Lizzie tugged on Buster's leash. Instead of retreating, the dog stood on its hind legs and pawed the air in front of Letch, yelping happily.

"Nice pooch," Letch said. "Better not let me see it here again."

"Oh, that's right," Lizzie said. "That's about your speed. Threaten a little dog."

Lizzie jerked on Buster's leash again, but he kept pawing the air in front of Letch, hoping for more petting.

"It won't do any good to threaten the dog," Owen said. "You can see we can't make him mind. Besides, your sign is too high up for him to read."

"Just get him out of here," Letch said.

Owen took the damp tennis ball from his pocket, bounced it off the dirt road, and said, "Buster, come."

The tennis ball proved to be more of a lure than the promise of more petting, and the dog trotted toward Owen, who turned and bounced the ball back down the road in the direction they had come. When Buster chased after the ball, straining at the leash, Owen took Lizzie's arm and followed the dog, leaving Letch behind. "Buster's led a sheltered life," he said to Lizzie. "He's never learned to stay clear of cars, burrs, or assholes."

"That Letch," Lizzie said when they were out of earshot. "He's the one we should have shot."

"We? What do you mean 'we,' white woman? I don't own a gun. Never have."

"Did I say 'we'? It's just an expression. Comes from running the hospice too long. Everything's 'we' back there. I'm sorry we didn't get to see all the landfill."

"It's okay," Owen said. "I know a way to see the rest."

FOUR

A Mine's Gotta Do...

SHERIFF THAD READER cocked his head and squinted at Owen with his one good eye. "Lemme get this straight. You want me to drive you around Doubtful Hollow just so you can measure the dirt Mountain View Development dumped there?"

Owen stood in front of the sheriff's wooden desk and nodded. "That's about the size of it."

"And Letch Valence ran you off when you and Lizzie Neal tried doing it on your own?"

Owen nodded again.

The sheriff reached up from his chair and retrieved the Mountie's hat hanging on the coat tree behind his desk. "Well, I don't mind jerking Letch's chain. Or doing your Aunt Lizzie a favor, for that matter. Your aunt took real good care of my momma before she passed."

The sheriff stood, smoothed the few strands of graying hair left on his forehead, and put on his Mountie's hat. "Come to that, I probably owe you a favor for a few of my reelection votes. Solving those Cantrip killings helped to put me over the top."

Owen smiled. "Took full credit for that, did you?"

The sheriff pushed open the door of his office and they emerged, blinking, into the morning sunlight. "If you'd been around when I was running for office, I might have let on that you helped a little."

"Just a little?"

"Well, hell. I was the one up for reelection. You ever run for office, I'll fill out an affidavit giving you full credit."

"Save your affidavit. I'm not cut out for the political life."

The sheriff pointed to the nearest of the three patrol cars in the parking lot, slid behind the wheel, and opened the passenger door for Owen. "I might ask you a favor in return, though."

Owen fastened his seat belt. "What's that?"

"Your Aunt Lizzie's got herself in a peck of trouble. Be good if you could get her to come clean with us."

"I thought she'd confessed to the shooting."

The sheriff nosed the patrol car out of the parking lot. "She did, but parts of her story don't make any sense."

"What parts?"

"Just about everything from 'Once upon a time' on. She says someone fired on her from the dump truck. We couldn't find any evidence of that. No gun. No sign of any shots in her direction."

"None?"

"None. Somebody unloaded a barrelful of buckshot straight up into the trees, but the only other shots we could document hit either the dump truck, the driver, or both."

"I can't imagine Lizzie would fire unless someone shot at her first."

"That's not all. We've got a witness that puts Lizzie over a quarter-mile away from Cooter's Bend just before the shooting started."

"And she got the dump truck and the driver? That's pretty accurate shooting from that distance. Couldn't she have driven to the Bend?"

"She doesn't drive after dark anymore. Besides, the witness says she didn't have a car with her. Just an old rocking chair."

"She must have been at Cooter's Bend when your men arrived."

"Oh, she was on the scene then all right. Her and her nephew Bobby Ray. With a van and a rocker. All ready to confess."

The sheriff turned onto the rutted dirt road that paralleled the Mountain View landfill. Owen took his notebook from his jacket pocket and noted the mileage. "Anything else?"

"There's more, but I better pay attention to these ruts for now."

The patrol car bounced past the NO TRESPASSING sign and wound slowly uphill, with the sheriff straddling the ruts left by heavy dump trucks. As the hollow widened, the landfill spread out to cover the gap between the surrounding hills. The sheriff downshifted in advance of a blind curve and rounded it slowly to find a Jeep blocking the roadway. He hit the brakes and swerved into a rut with a teeth-jarring thud.

Letch Valence stood in the open Jeep, one elbow resting on the roll bar. "You lost, Sheriff?"

Sheriff Reader swung open the door of his patrol car. "Just eye-balling around."

Letch stepped down from his Jeep and peered into the patrol car. Seeing Owen in the passenger seat, he said, "I told this man yesterday, and I'm telling you now, this here's private property. Unless you've got a warrant, you're trespassing."

"Got no warrant," the sheriff said. "I was hoping you wouldn't make me get one. It's a lot of paperwork."

"Better get to it, then."

"I figured you might be a little more understanding. See now, I hear you moved a few graves before you filled this hollow. That's a lot of paperwork, too, but I don't recall seeing any come across my desk."

"Those burial plots weren't properly licensed to start with."

"That so?" The sheriff shook his head and made a tsk-tsk noise with his tongue. "That'll make the paperwork all that much harder to fill out. Guess you better follow me in and get started on it."

Letch kicked at the dirt between his Jeep and the patrol car. "All right, come ahead. I'll move my Jeep. Mind telling me what you're looking for?"

"We're looking for whatever you're trying to hide behind those NO TRESPASSING signs."

"We're not hiding anything."

"Then we won't find anything." The sheriff reached for the door handle of the patrol car. "Now back that Jeep up and let us by. We're wasting daylight."

Letch retreated to the driver's seat of his Jeep. Before turning the key in the ignition, he said to Owen, "See you left the pooch at home. That was a good idea. Stay there with him next time."

Before Owen could respond, Letch floored the gas pedal and the Jeep lurched backward, spraying dirt on the patrol car. He laughed, made a quick three-point turn, and jounced around a curve and out of sight.

"That Letch," the sheriff said. "He's about as subtle as a shovelful of shit."

"What's his story?"

"He and a few rehabilitated ex-cons have what I believe in urban circles would be called 'a security service.' In these less enlightened parts, we call them goon squads."

"Valence is an ex-con, then?"

"Not quite. He's always managed to stay a half jump ahead of the law. He cut quite a figure around here in high school. Star quarterback. Handsome as a movie star. Had cheerleaders falling all over him. Went to WVU on an athletic scholarship. But his football skills weren't enough to overcome poor grades and a couple of rape charges. He flunked out, married money, got divorced over his tomcatting, and came away with some mining interests and enough spare cash to start his security service."

"Sounds like his name fits him."

"Real name's Fletcher. Easy to see how it got shortened. Easy to see how he'd marry money, too. Always had more than enough women hanging onto him. All he had to do was throw the poor ones back into the pond."

The sheriff raised his voice an octave and switched to an exaggerated twang. "My pappy always said, 'If you don't go out with anything but rich girls, you'll never marry anything but a rich girl.'" After a brief pause, he added, "Course, my pappy never married."

Owen laughed. "That explains a lot."

"It was a joke, Owen."

"Oh. Sorry. You should have told me."

"I just did." The sheriff maneuvered the patrol car out of the rut and followed the dirt road, skirting one side of the landfill, which began to narrow as they approached the end of the hollow. Streaks of dark shale could be seen near the tip of the fill, mixed in with the dirt, rock, and struggling seed grass.

"Not a pretty sight," Owen said.

"Right now it's ugly as a scabby goat's ass. But it won't look so bad once that grass and scrub take hold. And in five or ten years, you won't know there was ever a hollow here."

They drove on in silence with Owen sketching the shape of the landfill and occasionally noting the odometer reading. Shortly after circling the tip of the fill, they came to a paved road that wound its way up to a ridge overlooking the landfill and took them back to their starting point.

"Seen enough?" the sheriff asked.

Owen recorded the last odometer reading. "For now. I'd have to check the contour map, but it looks as if they put in half again as much fill as they planned on."

"I'm not surprised. You see that shopping center they're putting in? They took away half of Dismal Mountain. Sliced it right down the middle."

"But they must have known what they were going to do. Why mislead people about the size of the fill?"

The sheriff shrugged. "Doesn't make much sense. Now if they were mining coal, I could understand it. They'd have to post a bond based on the size of the cut and pay for mitigation if they covered more than two hundred and fifty feet of stream with fill."

"Which they did, by a long shot."

"Doesn't make any difference. They own the mountain and the hollow, bought and paid for. As long as they're building a shopping center, all they have to satisfy is the Clean Water Act. That's what those settling ponds are for."

"But why put up NO TRESPASSING signs and post a guard?"

"Maybe they just don't want anybody looking at the fill until the grass grows in. It's pretty ugly now, and folks hereabouts are sensitive to the loss of these hollows. Could be they just don't want bad publicity."

"They can't guard it forever."

"It's not gonna look bad forever. They do a good job of reclaiming these hollows now."

"Lizzie says reclamation's like putting lipstick on a corpse."

"She said that, did she? Hell, the greenies have all the good lines. I recall reading that one in a poem about Cold Knob. You got a few minutes, I'll show you a reclamation job that works."

Owen didn't know whether he was more surprised that the sheriff read poetry or that he supported reclamation. "I'd like to see that."

The sheriff drove back to the main highway, followed it for about four miles, and turned off on a side road marked by a green sign reading COUNTY CORRECTIONAL FACILITY. The road wound upward past a terraced hillside and deposited Owen and the sheriff on a level plateau covered with pale green grass that had grown shin-high and waved in the breeze.

In the center of the plateau, a chain-link fence topped with barbed wire surrounded a square blockhouse built of orange bricks.

"My new jail," the sheriff said. "Two years ago, this plot looked pretty much like those ridges around us."

Owen scanned the tree-lined peaks that surrounded the plateau. "I'd say those peaks are still prettier."

"It's all in the eye of the beholder. When they clear-cut this peak, the developer sold off the timber, the coal companies got their coal, I got my jail, the miners got work, and lots of folks will have warmer houses this winter.''

"What'd they do with the mountaintop?"

"We passed it on the way in." The sheriff left the car and led Owen to the edge of the plateau, which overlooked a green, terraced hillside. "That's it right there."

A doe and her fawn scrambled up the terraced slope to the plateau, saw Owen and the sheriff, and scrambled down again.

"Been two years since I got my jail," the sheriff said. "And none of this is an eyesore. Ground cover's back. Wildlife's back. In five or ten years, the trees will be back."

"So you're a fan of mountaintop removal?"

"Nobody's really a fan of strip-mining. And most of the peaks around here aren't threatened anyhow. But if you run the reclamation right, and they're learning how to do that, you can have your coal and Eden, too."

Owen winced at the pun. "No wonder the greenies have all the good lines."

The sheriff held up one hand. "I know, I know. For a long time, they did it all wrong. I can take you to places in this county where the coal companies dumped raw shale in bonepiles that still burn deep down. Black as a bucket of toe-jam, with a smell to match, but that don't stop the odd drunk from lying down next to the burning shale for a little warmth and suffocating from the sulfur fumes.''

"I know," Owen said. "I got pitched into a burning bonepile over by Contrary. I was lucky to make it out alive."

"Bonepiles went out with the Surface Reclamation Act of Nineteen Seventy-Seven. Since that time, the government's been on the coal companies to do right by the land." The sheriff waved his hand to take in the plateau and the terraced approach. "And they're learning how to do it.''

The sheriff fished in his pocket for a cigarette, lit it, inhaled deeply, and began walking back toward his patrol car. "Don't get me wrong, I give the greenies credit for pushing the government into action against the coal companies. I mean, it's a sin what those companies did to this state, and to the miners, too, before the government stepped in. A hundred years ago, a bunch of out-of-state companies came in and screwed the locals out of their mineral rights. Then they went ahead and screwed the miners, too.''

When the sheriff reached his car, he leaned against the door and took another long drag on the cigarette. ''The miners fought back and spilled enough blood to get a kind of loveless marriage going with the coal companies where each one needs the other. The miners can strike on the first day of squirrel season, but they better not stay out long, because if the mine goes under, they go under. At the same time, the mine owners can't get too unreasonable, 'cause they've got the union to contend with.

''Now, though, we got a new kind of out-of-state agitator disturbing the balance of things. Tree-huggers and shrub-cuddlers, they storm through the state like tub-thumping evangelists, singing the praises of the unsullied mountaintop and the holy hollow and threatening to smite those sinners who want to clear out the coal.'' The sheriff stubbed out his cigarette against the patrol car's front tire. ''Way I see it, the same God that made the mountains and the hollows made the coal, and it took him a sight longer to do that job. If we can cut the coal out without hurting anybody, we ought to be able to do it.''

''You can't tell me those big strip-mining operations aren't hurting somebody.''

''Maybe we ought to take a look at one.'' The sheriff pinched the dead ash off his cigarette and dropped the stub into his shirt pocket. ''Show you something else that bothers me about your aunt's story.''

''What's strip-mining got to do with my aunt's story?''

The sheriff opened the door of the patrol car. ''Hop in. I'll show you.'' He backed away from the prison and worked his way to the foot of the mountain, where he picked up a familiar road that wound its way past a series of small houses wedged between railroad tracks and a creekbed. It was the same road Owen had followed on his way in from the airport. Now that the weekend had arrived, though, the number of yard sales had doubled. Every other home displayed used clothing, toys, tools, and pictures in its narrow front yard. Dour men in undershirts and overalls and women in cotton print dresses sat on porches watching over their salable possessions.

After passing several such sales, Owen observed, ''Looks like pictures of Elvis outnumber Christ by about two to one.''

"Let's hope it's because people aren't willing to part with their pictures of Christ."

"Wishing for miracles?"

"Miracles, atonement, or just a good honest day's work. I tell you, there's no sadder sight in this state than an out-of-work miner."

One of the porch-sitters waved at the sheriff, who waved back and said, "The real sin is, the new tub-thumpers are keeping these miners from working just to protect some shrub-cuddler's notion of a pretty view or a crucial critter. Let me tell you, if you have to lop off a mountaintop to get these miners off the givement dole and back to work, I say lop it off. If that means somer are owl has to forage one ridge over, so be it."

"But you have to draw the line somewhere. You can't lop off every mountaintop and fill every hollow."

"Nobody's trying to lop off *every* mountaintop. Trouble is, the tree-huggers don't want you lopping off any. They've got an injunction says you can't start up any new mountaintop mines. None. Zippo. Claim it destroys the balance of nature. Meantime, more miners are out of work and the coal companies are moving their equipment out of state."

The sheriff left the winding creekside road and pulled onto the new freeway, passing the enormous mountain slice that marked the Mountain View Shopping Mall. "Now there's a development we surely don't need," he said. "You can't touch the mountains to mine coal, but you can cut one in half to build a shopping mall for people who can't afford to buy secondhand clothes from their next-door neighbor."

"What about tunneling into the mountaintop for the coal? Wouldn't that give more miners work?"

"Kills more men, costs more money. It all depends on how much coal there is and what's economical. Hell, there's coal everywhere in these here mountains. They hit a good-sized seam building this freeway. The state wanted to haul it out and sell it as what they call 'incidental coal.'"

"Sounds like a good idea."

"Well, the UMW got wind of it, stepped in, and said, 'No siree. You want to pick up that coal and sell it, you got to use union miners.'"

"Just to pick up what had already been dug up?"

"You got it. Once the UMW raised a ruckus, everything came

to a standstill. The union men on the road crews wouldn't pick up the coal even though it was just laying there.''

"So what happened?"

"State finally figured it would cost too much to get the UMW involved, so they just hauled the coal off to the landfill with the rest of the rock, shale, and sandstone. It's all part of that slope off the side."

"In other words, they treated it like dirt."

"You might say that. If you've got a strong stomach for weak puns." The sheriff fixed his glass eye on Owen. "It's a crying shame, is what it is. People freezing for want of coal, but the greenies won't let you mine it, and the union won't let you pick up what's laying around."

Sheriff Reader left the freeway for a county road that wound around the base of a hill, then pulled off onto the berm at a stop sign. A signpost showed that if they went straight, they would reach Logan, while a left turn would take them back to Barkley. There was no sign showing where a right turn would take them, but a wiggly arrow on a yellow traffic sign indicated that the road wound uphill. Someone had painted a red number 5 just below the arrow on the sign.

The sheriff turned on his two-way radio, and static filled the patrol car, interrupted by a squawking voice that announced, "Curve Four, coming down."

"We'll just sit a spell," the sheriff said. He pointed to the red number 5 on the traffic sign around the corner. "Truckers paint those numbers on signs so's they can communicate with one another. You don't want to meet one of those wide trucks on a narrow, winding road if you can help it. Especially if you're carrying a wide load yourself and might have to back it up."

An earthshaking rumble drowned out the radio static as a dusty yellow truck as big as a house ground to a stop at the foot of the hill. A man high up in the passenger seat nodded to the sheriff as the truck turned onto the county road in the direction of Logan.

"Those babies can carry a hundred tons of rock," the sheriff said. With the radio producing nothing but static, he turned right and started up the hill, winding past road signs painted with the numbers 4 and 3. Just beyond a tight turn marked by a pie tin nailed to a tree and painted with the number 2, Owen heard a steady hum that grew to a screeching roar as the patrol car bumped past a clear-cut area and stopped. They were at the edge of a vast moonscape tended by gigantic machines that looked like rejects from the *Star Wars* epic. In the center of the moonscape, a ten-story crane supported a drag line and an enormous bucket that bit into the crumbling mountaintop. Dust rose from the exposed earth, hung in the air, and covered all the men and equipment, including two yellow trucks being loaded with debris.

"Jesus Christ," Owen shouted over the din. "You could almost fit one of those trucks into that bucket. You can't tell me this doesn't leave permanent scars."

"It may look messy now," the sheriff yelled back, "but it cleans up pretty good. My jail site looked just like this when they were uncovering coal."

Owen coughed and covered his mouth with a handkerchief.

"I'll grant you it's not pretty," the sheriff said. "But neither is heart surgery, childbirth, or sausage-making. The trick is, the sausage makers don't let you see the fixings, just the finished product. When they finish here, they'll put this mountain back so it looks exactly like the one we just left."

"Hard to believe."

"Believe it. But I didn't bring you here to give you a 'before-and-after' lecture." The sheriff pointed past the ten-story crane. "See those two big yellow trucks? Like the one we waited for on the way up?"

Owen coughed again and nodded.

"They're the same as the one your Aunt Lizzie fired on. The same kind she claims fired on her. Now what strikes you about those two trucks?"

"There're two people in each cab."

"Exactly. It's a union operation. Two men per truck. That's the way they run the big rigs."

"But there was only one body in the truck Lizzie says shot at her."

"That's just one of the things we need to get straight."

FIVE

Old Habits

THE SMALL, ANTISEPTIC PRE-OP ROOM was barely large enough to
contain Owen, his brother George, and Ruth Allison, who lay on a
gurney under a white cotton sheet.

George rolled an unlit cigarette back and forth between two fingers and a thumb. "They should have been here by now."

"It's all right, George," Ruth said. "I'm in no hurry."

"It makes you think they don't know what they're doing, is all,"
George said.

Owen was concerned that his brother's worries might increase his
mother's anxiety. "Stop fretting, George," he said. "Statistics show
they don't lose more than one visitor for every three patients."

Doctor Baker Morton appeared at the door of the room. "Those
statistics are out of date, I fear. This year's tally shows patients and
visitors are running neck and neck."

The doctor's green scrubs were rolled into voluminous folds at
his ankles, making him look even more like an overweight refugee
from Santa's Workshop. He squeezed into the small room and pulled
the metal clipboard out from under the gurney mattress. "The physician's handbook recommends that I ask you how you feel this
morning."

"A little anxious," Ruth answered.

The doctor adjusted his eyeglasses and scanned the patient's chart.
"Well, don't worry. We'll have your appendix out in no time."

Ruth smiled. "If you do, you'll have to go back in for my ovaries."

The doctor returned Ruth's smile and snapped the clipboard shut.
"I knew that." He stroked his walrus mustache and affected a per-

plexed look. "Remind me again. Just where are those pesky ovaries?"

Ruth continued to smile. "If we keep telling you, you'll never learn on your own."

The doctor shoved the clipboard back under the mattress. "Just a little doctor humor." He tugged the foot of the gurney out into the hallway. "We shouldn't be longer than two hours. If you want to wait," he said to Owen and George, "a nurse will bring you to the recovery room when your mother is ready to wake up."

An orderly appeared to help with the gurney, and the doctor pulled his surgical mask up over his mustache. Owen bent forward quickly and kissed his mother's forehead. "Good luck. Love you."

He clasped his mother's hand until the gurney cleared the door of the room. Then he stepped out into the hall to watch the cart roll down the corridor. The hand he had held stayed upright and bent at the wrist like a marionette's. He couldn't tell if it was waving or trembling as the cart rolled out of sight.

"That doctor inspires about as much confidence as an umpire with a seeing-eye dog," George said.

Owen turned to walk back out to the lobby. "I've checked him out. He's okay."

"I wanted her to go to the Cleveland Clinic."

"We're lucky she decided to have it done at all."

"It's good you came. She wouldn't listen to me."

When they reached the lobby, Owen stopped and said, "This is as far as I go. I've got a lunch date."

George raised his eyebrows. "My little brother, the fast worker. You'll be back when Mom wakes up?"

"I'll be back."

George held out his hand. "I really appreciate your handling all this. The way things are going with me, I haven't been much help."

Owen took his brother's hand. "It's okay. Don't worry about it." He spotted Kate O'Malley's white robes coming through the revolving lobby door, raised his free hand, and waved to her.

Kate waved back and stopped to talk to the candy striper at the information desk.

When George raised his eyebrows again, Owen explained, "My date."

"You working out some sort of fixation you had on your third-grade teacher?"

Before Owen could answer, Kate joined the two of them and he said, "Sister Mary Perpetua, I'd like you to meet my brother George."

Kate smiled. "Oh, yes. The third baseman."

George shook his head. "That was a long time ago."

"We're just going out for a quick lunch," Kate said. "Would you like to join us?"

As the invitation hung in the air between them, Owen tried to think of a way to snatch it back. George solved the problem by declining, saying, "No thanks. I've got a meeting to get to."

IT WAS ONE OF THOSE crisp, late-summer days when Frisbees and footballs start to replace softballs and bats on Barkley's vacant lots and creekside parks. Owen remembered that he and George were always the last baseball holdouts, tossing balls until the Reds were out of the pennant race and the World Series was over, defending their strip of park against marauding pickup games of football players. With the last out of the World Series, they'd oil up their gloves, wrap them around scuffed baseballs, store them in the bottom of the utility chest, and join the football players. The regret accompanying the oiling ritual was usually short-lived. There would always be other summers.

On the sloping lawn beside the hospital, nurses and orderlies in sweats and scrubs had staked out a volleyball court, while three T-shirted teenagers played keep-away with a Frisbee. Owen watched the skidding flight of the Frisbee as he walked downhill with Kate inhaling the smell of fresh-cut grass and the damp aroma of river air.

Kate tilted her head backward, causing her white cowl to billow behind her. "Umm. Feel that river breeze."

"Air of other summers," Owen said.

"That's Housman, isn't it?"

"I guess it is. I was thinking more about the passing seasons than the words themselves."

"I'm sure it's Housman." Kate closed her eyes and recited:

"...Air of other summers
Breathed from beyond the snows,
And I had hope of those."

"That's the one. If I remember, it doesn't end well."

"Few of his poems do."

"How about pizza?" Owen suggested. "When I worked here, there was a great little pizzeria about three blocks from here."

"Johnny Angelo's. Sounds terrific."

A few heads turned to stare at Kate's white habit as she slid into a corner booth at Angelo's pizzeria. At the counter, Owen ordered a medium pizza with pepperoni and brought a pitcher of Coke to the table. He filled two plastic glasses with the soft drink and tapped the red-checkered tablecloth. "Place hasn't changed since I was in high school."

Kate pointed to a wall covered with framed and fading photographs. "There's a picture of you on the wall there. Your mother pointed it out to me."

"Me and the rest of my high-school baseball team. We were state champs my senior year. Johnny laid out free pizzas for everyone."

"Your mother was so proud when she showed me the picture. How is she?"

"Numb. It's as if she's accepted a death sentence and is just marking time until the chaplain shows up to lead her down the last mile."

"Acceptance isn't necessarily a bad thing."

"It can be if it blots out hope. Last weekend we were out at Aunt Lizzie's hospice. All Mom wanted to do was shop for a room."

"She'd be among friends there."

"I can't imagine what it would be like to have a death sentence hanging over me. To know my summers were numbered."

"You think you'd behave differently?"

"Wouldn't everyone? If they knew they had only a fixed time to live?"

"But you do. Everyone does."

"It's not the same thing."

Kate shook a handful of red pepper into her palm. "What are you? Forty-five? Forty-six?" She blew on her palm, creating a puff of red confetti. Then she touched Owen on his forehead with her drinking straw. "I give you twenty-five years to live."

"I don't feel any different."

"The question is, will you behave differently?"

"If you guarantee those years in writing, I'll order extra cheese on the pizza and replace this Coke with a beer."

"Well, those aren't major changes, but they are changes. Anything else?"

"Can't think of anything. I'm still not likely to floss."

"What about mass? Would you go to mass regularly?"

"Not for another twenty-four years."

Kate laughed. "What if I'd given you twenty-five days instead of twenty-five years?"

"I still wouldn't floss."

"But you'd probably go to mass."

"Probably."

"You're not that much different from the people in Lizzie's hospice. They don't change much, but they do change some. They sort out what's important to them. They don't take a lot of crap. And they find God more easily."

"The closer you get to the afterlife, the more you want to believe in it."

Kate nodded. "You won't find many atheists in foxholes or hospices. You should talk to a few of Lizzie's residents. Especially if your mother is set on going there."

"That's what Lizzie said. But it didn't feel right. Too intrusive."

"Do it anyway."

A college student wearing a sauce-splattered apron brought their pizza, doled out two squares apiece, and left the rest in the center of the table.

"I had my first pizza here," Owen said. "Square, with a thin, crisp crust and Johnny's spicy sauce. I've never been able to get used to round ones."

He picked up a square and bit into it, while Kate applied a knife and fork to one of hers. Suddenly she stopped and held her knife poised and pointed at the ceiling. "Listen."

Over the clank of dishes and the buzz of voices, the jukebox was sending out Frank Sinatra's recording of "Send in the Clowns."

Kate sang softly in a clear soprano voice, "'Aren't we a pair?'"

Owen remembered the first time he'd heard Kate sing, in a student production of *Pal Joey*. "I'd forgotten about your voice. I love Sondheim."

"I thought you were wedded to Patsy Cline."

"They're not mutually exclusive. You turned me on to Rodgers and Hart without weaning me away from country and western."

Sinatra's voice carried over the clatter, searching for the clowns.

"The man's amazing," Kate said.

"Sinatra? Or Sondheim?"

"Both. But I was thinking of Sondheim."

"I knew you'd like him. The year after you left for the convent, I saw *Company* in New York. It blew me away. I thought of you because I knew you'd love it, too. I've seen every show he ever wrote."

"I've only seen *Company* and *Into the Woods* on stage. I couldn't manage more than two trips to New York."

"You really should see them all. Two trips to Broadway in what? Twenty-five years? It's not nearly enough..." He stopped, embarrassed. The woman sitting across from him had forsworn marriage, sex, children, self-direction, and sleep-in Sundays. Missing a Broadway curtain or two must seem trivial.

Kate tilted her head, listening to the last strains of "Send in the Clowns." "I know what you're thinking. I'm not exactly footloose and fancy-free. But there are compensations. I've got all of Sondheim's CDs."

"But that's not enough. You miss the story, the acting, the timing, the flow. Look, I've got most of his plays on videotape. Let me send them to you."

Kate leaned forward. "What do you have?"

Owen started through a mental inventory. *"Sunday in the Park, Sweeney Todd, Passion, A Little Night Music—"*

"Not that awful movie with Elizabeth Taylor?"

"No. Not even Diana Rigg could save that one. PBS aired a filmed version of the New York play with Glynis Johns. That's the one I kept."

"I'd love to see that."

"I've got everything but the Overture. My wife taped over it."

"I know the Overture by heart. It's no big deal if it's missing."

"It seemed like a big deal at the time. At least, I managed to make it one."

"Oh, dear."

Owen emitted a short, rueful laugh. "It certainly seems trivial now. Along with most of the things that led to our divorce." He reflected that even the most painful of the reasons for his divorce, his wife's infidelity, seemed much less significant five years later. "But then," he added, "you probably hold with the Catholic view that there aren't any valid reasons for divorce."

Kate's cheeks flushed red against her white cowl. "I don't know. You made vows to each other. If you decide not to keep them, that's between the two of you. I do think people abandon their vows too easily in this day and age."

"Judith and I certainly did."

"But whether there should be a hard-and-fast law prohibiting—" She stopped, bit her lip, and shuddered. "I'm sorry. I'm just not rational on the subject. My parents got divorced."

"I'm sorry to hear that. I only met your father, but I really liked him."

"So, it appears, did a few other women besides my mother."

"It's too bad they couldn't work it out. In my experience, given enough time, a quick affair can seem almost as trivial as a ruined videotape."

"It wasn't a quick affair." Kate's green eyes glazed over and her right hand trembled. "And it killed my mother."

Owen reached out and clasped the trembling hand. "I'm sorry. I shouldn't have been so flip about my own divorce."

"It wasn't you," Kate shuddered. "It wasn't you."

Owen continued to hold Kate's hand in both of his as the trembling subsided. Her hand felt cold to him, but, he reasoned, that meant his would feel warm to her.

Owen's concentration on the hands in the center of the table was broken by an awareness that a sauce-stained apron was brushing against the table's edge. He looked up into the face of their waiter.

"Uh," the boy began, as if he'd forgotten his line, "will that be all?"

Kate jerked her hand away and hid it under the table. "We've got to get back."

"That'll be all," Owen said to the waiter, who lingered at the table, an audience of one hoping for an encore.

Kate, now visibly under control, said, "Bake Morton should be about finished with your mother by now. We can talk to him before she wakes up."

"Then we better be going." Owen stood and helped Kate exit from the booth. As she squeezed by him, he said in a stage whisper for the ears of the waiter, "We've got to stop meeting like this. They're beginning to suspect."

KATE AND OWEN FOUND Doctor J. Baker Morton smoking a cigarette on the slim balcony outside the doctors' lounge.

Morton inhaled deeply and flicked ashes over the side of the balcony, where they drifted downward toward the asphalt parking lot two stories below. "Your mom did just fine. I'm pretty sure I got everything and it hadn't spread."

"Does that mean she's out of danger?" Owen asked.

"Hard to say. She still needs some pretty aggressive chemotherapy."

"But her odds have improved?"

"Certainly."

"By how much?"

Morton rubbed the back of his neck, causing the surgical mask that dangled under his chin to sway like a hammock. "Excuse me?"

"By how much? Before surgery, you said she had a twenty-percent chance. What are the odds now? Twenty-five percent? Forty percent?"

"I really can't say. Every case is unique. But the operation was a great success. All that we could have hoped for. And your mother should be coming out of the anesthesia just about now."

"I'll take you down to the recovery room," Kate said.

Owen thanked Doctor Morton and followed Kate back through the doctors' lounge into the corridor. Outside the lounge, she explained, "Doctors don't like to think in terms of probabilities with individual patients. They can do it with cases in textbooks, which is where that 'twenty-percent' number came from in the first place. But they can't seem to do it with their patients. It gives people too much hope. Or too little."

"Surely one can't have too much hope?"

"You're a hardcase, Owen Allison. You want to know exactly how long a person has to live, and you still want to be able to hope for a few extra days." She stopped in front of a set of swinging doors. "Your mom's through those doors. Go see her. Get started on those twenty-five years I gave you."

"Where will you be?"

"Today's my day for paperwork."

"I'd like to see you again."

"I'll drop in on you and your mom a little later."

"That's not what I meant. And you know it."

A red ringlet had worked its way out from under the stiff white headpiece covering Kate's forehead. She shoved it back under the headpiece and affected a mock Irish brogue. "Sure, and is it a date you'd be asking me for, Mr. Allison? You know I can't do that."

"Don't call it a date, then. Call it two old friends with a lot in common getting together for dinner."

"I think I'd like that. I'll have to work it out, though." She patted his forearm and shoved him toward the swinging doors. "Now go see your mother."

THE THREE-HOUR time difference between West Virginia and California meant that Owen's ex-wife Judith was still at work when he called from his mother's living room to report the outcome of her operation. "The doctor said things couldn't have gone better. But it doesn't seem to matter to Mom. It's like she's just going through the motions."

"The operation's just the first step. She could sleep through that. She's still facing a rough stretch of chemotherapy."

"She always seemed more worried about that."

"It's likely to be much harder on her." After a pause, Judith said, "Keep me informed. I'll want to come and see her if she gets worse."

"You're just like Mom, preparing for the worst."

"I just want to be sure I see her again."

"She wants to see you, too. She even cooked up some lawyer work for you with my Aunt Lizzie."

"I know. She told me about it. How is your aunt?"

Owen told Judith about the talk he'd had with his aunt and the problems Sheriff Reader had with her version of the events on the night of the shooting.

"Do you think you can get a straight story from your aunt?"

"I can try. But it might be easier for you."

"You're family."

"You're family, too, sort of. And you'd have the attorney-client privilege working. Besides, Mom would like to see you."

"What about you?"

"I'd like to see you, too, of course." Why hadn't he just said that in the first place? "But you know how Mom is. She'd like to see us together."

"We are together, aren't we?"

"Not together enough for Mom. She wants to see one roof and one last name."

"And what do you want?"

"To make sure we don't botch it again." It was the same corner he kept backing into. "What about it? Can you come?"

After a pause, Judith answered, "Not for a bit. I don't think I can get away right now."

"What are you working on?"

"A lot of little things. Some personal-injury lawsuits. A little antitrust work."

"Antitrust is McKenzie's area. I thought you were separating yourself from that."

"He's still the senior partner. He brings in the lion's share of our cases. I have to work with him sometimes."

Owen felt a familiar pang. It was Judith's brief affair with the senior partner in her California law firm while Owen was working on the East Coast that had sealed the end of their marriage. When their divorce brought the affair to light, McKenzie tried to fire Judith. She responded with a sexual harassment suit that had paved the way for her partnership.

"I hate knowing the two of you are in the same city, let alone in the same room." The phone call was starting to remind Owen of the long-distance calls they'd had in the wake of the McKenzie affair, full of recriminations for real and imagined slights.

"Working with McKenzie was part of the deal, Owen. He's the last thing you should be worrying about."

"What's the first thing?"

"Your mother, of course. How are her doctors?"

"They seem pretty good. And they come highly recommended. One of the doctors on the staff is an old friend, so I've got an inside source."

"Doctors always stick together. How well do you know this friend?"

"Pretty well. We lost touch for a while, but it's amazing how much we have in common. We spent the time during Mom's operation catching up and talking about everything from our college courses to Stephen Sondheim.''

"It's a woman, isn't it?"

"What makes you say that?"

"Your voice when you said 'friend.' Like you were going to say 'girlfriend' but decided not to. And you keep dancing around this friend's gender without specifying it. Besides, anybody who'd talk more than five minutes about Sondheim would have to be either female or gay.''

"I was carrying half of the conversation, and I'm neither female nor gay.''

"That just means you were interested in the person carrying on the other half. Is she married?''

"Oh, for heaven's sake, Judith.''

"Well, is she?''

Owen couldn't keep from smiling. "No.''

"I didn't think so. Something's going on, isn't it? I can hear it in your voice.''

"Nothing's going on.''

"The last time you ran into an old girlfriend, you could barely keep your zipper shut.''

"This old girlfriend happens to be a nun.''

"A nun? A Catholic-type nun?''

"One of those.''

The line went silent. Owen couldn't tell whether Judith was laughing or thinking. Finally, she said, "Then what's all this talk about everything you have in common? How much can you possibly have in common with a nun? You haven't been to mass in ten years.''

"I've been taking Mom twice a week since I've been back.''

"Jesus Christ. It must be serious.''

"It is serious. I told you, the doctors don't give her more than a twenty-percent chance.''

"I meant with you and your nun.''

"Serious? Serious how?''

"Never mind. It was a weak attempt at humor.''

"I'm not surprised I didn't recognize it. There's precious little humor around here right now.''

"Then I'd better remind you what Sondheim said about nuns.''

"What's that?''

"Don't get in the habit."

"When did he say that?"

"In the song in that movie about Sherlock Holmes and Sigmund Freud."

"'I Never Do Anything Twice?' That's not what he said. He said he'd get in the habit, but not in the habit."

"See. Don't tell me you haven't been thinking about it. Give my love to your mother."

SIX

Chasing the Dark

OWEN AND LIZZIE SAT at one end of a long metal table in the dining room of Lizzie's hospice. Owen sipped tea from a plain white mug, while Lizzie drank coffee from a black mug labeled boss lady. It was mid-afternoon, and the only other occupants of the room were two ambulatory patients who had parked their walkers on either side of a square table and lingered over dessert while seated at the other two sides.

Lizzie cradled her mug in both hands and set it on the table. "Sister Mary Perp tells me your mother's operation was successful."

"You wouldn't know it from talking to Mom."

"Has she started chemo?"

"Not till next Tuesday."

"That'll be the really tough part. It's good you'll be home to help." She swirled a spoon in her coffee and grinned at Owen. "Sister also tells me you cut quite a figure in college."

"She was the one who cut the figure. I just lapped after her, wagging my tail, like Buster returning tennis balls."

"Must have wagged something pretty good, way she remembers you."

The remark unsettled Owen, as much for the suggestion as the source. He decided to pass it off. "Careful, Aunt Lizzie. We're talking about a Bride of Christ."

"Wouldn't be the first bride fooled around on her intended."

"Well, take it from me, this one didn't."

"No need to get your dander up. I was just trolling for a little gossip." Lizzie's gray-green eyes smiled over her black mug. "The good sister helps out here every Wednesday. We usually eat dinner after. You're welcome to join us."

"Thanks, I'd like that."

"We'll put you to work, see you earn your keep."

A candy striper wheeled a cart carrying used lunch trays and an assortment of clean and dirty dishes into the dining room. Lizzie waved her over, took a large black thermos from the cart, and re-filled her coffee mug. "I see there's a couple of desserts left," she said, reaching for a shallow bowl of custard. "Want to join me?"

Lizzie spooned a sliver of custard from the bowl and held it out to Owen. "It'll surprise you. I won't serve my people anything I wouldn't eat myself."

Owen took the spoon and swallowed the sliver of custard. "Tastes like crème brûlée."

"Told you it was good." She took another custard from the cart.

Owen swallowed another sliver of the smooth dessert and paused with his spoon in midair. "I talked to the sheriff over the weekend. He's got a few problems with the story you told him."

Lizzie's voice dripped with sarcasm. "Do tell."

Owen reported on the sheriff's doubts. The lack of evidence that any shots were fired from the truck, the witness who placed Lizzie on her rocker a quarter-mile away from the shooting site, and the fact that only one body was found in the cab of a two-person rig.

Lizzie pointed her spoon at Owen. "All the sheriff needs to know—all *anybody* needs to know—is that I'm responsible for that trucker's death."

"The sheriff doesn't think you were anywhere near Cooter's Bend when the trucker was shot."

"I said I was responsible," Lizzie snapped. "Being responsible means you take the responsibility. And whatever comes with it. Now I just don't want to talk about it anymore."

"Lizzie, I'm on your side here. I'm not the law. You can tell me what happened."

"Owen, honey, you come from the honest side of the family. If I tell you what happened, you'll feel honor-bound to share it with your friend the sheriff."

"What you're telling me is that you've already lied to him."

"What I'm telling you is that I'm responsible," Lizzie repeated. "That's all you need to know."

"Your lawyer will need to know more."

"We'll cross that bridge when we come to it, if the good Lord's willing and the creek don't rise. For now, how about we talk about something else?''

Owen recognized the firm set in Lizzie's jaw. It was the same one his mother used when closing down a topic of conversation. It occurred to him that the stubborn jaw set was hereditary, the legacy of generations of Irish rebels who stood mute before the soldiers of the Crown. ''I was just trolling for a few facts,'' he said.

''Well, this pond is fished out. Try trolling somewhere else. Like that dry creek they're turning into a mountain next door. Did you and your friend the sheriff find out anything when you visited there?''

''Just that they dumped a lot more land than they planned to.''

''Hell, I could of told you that. It's good to have it verified, anyhow.'' Lizzie shook her head. ''There's more going on than a little extra landfill, though. Letch is guarding that site like it's got diamonds in it, and there's trucks coming and going at all hours.''

''Trucks? Why should there be trucks? They finished excavating the shopping-center site some time ago.''

''Could be that's a fact worth trolling for.''

''Could be. What do you know about it?''

''Not much. One of our patients called it to my attention. The trucks are keeping her up nights.''

''Maybe I ought to talk to her.''

''Best be quick about it. She'll be leaving us soon.'' Sensing Owen's dismay, Lizzie added, ''Owen, honey, if you try to limit your talking to folks who aren't going to die, you'll either pray a lot or have a mighty quiet life.''

Owen shoved his tea aside. ''Can we see her right now?''

Lizzie stood up. ''No need to check with her secretary. I'm sure she's in. Name's Mary Margaret Mason, but everybody calls her Maggie. You'll like her. She's a hoot and a half.''

LIZZIE STOPPED OUTSIDE a door on the second floor and put a hand on Owen's forearm. ''Maggie will talk your ear off if you let her, but sometimes she jumps around like a scratched phonograph record. You just have to nudge her back to the subject every now and then.''

Before Owen could respond, Lizzie swung the door open to reveal a skeletal woman in a quilted blue dressing gown, propped up against a sunburst of pillows with different floral patterns. Wisps of gray hair poked out from under a Cincinnati Reds baseball cap. The woman was alarmingly thin, with clear, intent hazel eyes that peered out over bifocals balanced on a nose catheter.

Maggie made two slow circles with her free right arm to invite them in. Her left arm was strapped to a metal armrest and connected to two long intravenous tubes.

"Right pleased to meet you," Maggie said when Lizzie introduced Owen as her nephew. She waved off Owen's attempt to shake hands and motioned them toward the two visitors' chairs. "I guess Lizzie told you I'd talk your ear off. She tells everybody that. The Mister used to say I could sneak in the last word on an echo. Why, my daughters moved all the way to the West Coast just to get out of earshot."

Owen nodded toward a picture on the bedside table. It showed two thin women with dour, angular faces flanking a smiling, portly woman. "Are those your daughters?"

"Why, bless you for saying so. The two on the ends are my daughters. That's me in the center there."

Owen tried not to show his shock at the contrast between the plump woman in the picture and the emaciated form on the bed.

"Guess you can't see the resemblance," Maggie said. "Well, I told them not to unplug my life supports until I was at least down to a size eight."

Owen laughed in spite of himself. He stopped suddenly when he noticed the shadow of a reclining body in the bed behind the gray curtain that served as a room divider.

"Pay no mind to Sally Maethere," Maggie said. "She couldn't hear us if she was awake, and she don't wake up much anymore."

Owen shifted his chair so he couldn't see the cadaverlike shadow on the partition. "Lizzie tells me trucks are keeping you awake at night."

"Oh, I keep myself awake. As much as I can." Maggie waved her free hand toward a stack of well-thumbed paperbacks next to the picture on the bedside table. "Trying to catch up on my reading. There'll be time enough for sleep directly." She closed her eyes and sighed.

When Maggie didn't open her eyes right away, Owen looked uncertainly at Lizzie, who mouthed the word "morphine."

Maggie's lids fluttered, and she looked at Owen with a gaze that no longer seemed alert. "You have real nice eyes. What do you call that color of brown?"

Owen shrugged, then said, "Hickory." Somebody, he couldn't remember who, had once called his eyes hickory, and it had become a family joke.

"Hickory, dickory, dock," Maggie intoned. "The Mister had nice brown eyes, too."

The fingers of Maggie's free hand stretched as if she were reaching out and then fell limp. "He died, you know. The Mister. Miner's asthma."

"Black lung," Lizzie explained.

Owen nodded. He'd seen the effects of miner's asthma before.

"You want the coal, you go down in the hole," Maggie singsonged. "The Mister kept going down in the hole. And it finally got him."

A dreamy smile covered her face. "That's how we met, though. I was handing out paychecks for Consolidated. Kept books for Big Coal for forty years. Raised two girls, made a home, had a good life. No trouble at all. Except for the shift work. That was the worst. He'd be coming home when I'd be leaving for work. Or he'd be leaving and I'd be coming home. Office shifts never matched the mine shifts. When Consolidated started taking on women miners, he tried to get me to go down into the hole with him. Said we could both be on the same shift for a change. Pay would be better, too. I told him I'd go down in that mine when they put windows in. And that was that."

Maggie took a deep breath and exhaled something like a sigh. "Now we're out of sync again. He's off and gone and I'm here." Another breath, another sigh. "My shift's gonna end soon, though. Sure hope they've got windows where he is."

She closed her eyes again, then blinked twice, stared at Owen, and asked, "What was it you wanted to know?"

It was as if she'd suddenly switched channels.

"Trucks," Owen said. "Lizzie tells me trucks are keeping you awake."

"Oh, they're a blessing, really. I drift in and out. When they do wake me up, I get a little more reading done."

"How often do they run?"

"Most every night."

"About what time?"

Maggie's head moved slowly back and forth against the flowered pillows. "I'm not too good on time anymore. It's well after dark, I know that. Most every night, in and out."

Her eyelids fluttered. "In and out," she repeated. Then she closed her eyes again.

"I don't think she's going to tell us much more," Lizzie whispered. "Best to let her drift." She patted Maggie's free hand. "Thank you, Maggie. We'll be going now."

Without opening her eyes, Maggie answered, "Y'all come back real soon now, hear?"

THAT NIGHT, Owen pulled his mother's Toyota into a dirt turnout across from the entrance to the dumping grounds guarded by Letch Valence. In the time since he'd visited the site with the sheriff, a chain had been stretched across the gravel road leading to the site and a new NO TRESPASSING sign had been added to the post securing the chain's lock.

Owen backed the Toyota as far off the main road as he could, wedging it between two large oak trees. Then he settled in to wait for the trucks Maggie Mason kept hearing. The Reds were playing in San Francisco, and the game's broadcast provided a welcome distraction during the first three hours of his watch. It was the only time he could remember being grateful for the three-hour time difference that kept West Coast games going well past midnight in West Virginia.

The Reds were trying to hold onto a two-run lead with Bonds batting in the bottom of the eighth when a mammoth yellow dump truck, one of those that Thad Reader said could carry a hundred tons, pulled up to the chain barring entrance to the dumping site. A man wearing faded Levi's, a work shirt, and a miner's hat climbed down from the cab, stood in the headlights to unlock the chain, and left it dangling while he rejoined the driver for the trip into Doubtful Hollow.

Even though they left the chain unfastened, Owen wasn't tempted to risk discovery by tracking the truck into the disappearing hollow. If Maggie was right, the truck would return the same way, and he could follow it then.

The grinding gears of the inbound truck would wake Maggie, if she were asleep, and give her a few more hours with her paperbacks.

Owen could imagine her reaching for the stack of mysteries, and he felt an odd connection to the woman in her pain and persistence. He wished he'd brought a paperback or two himself to help pass the time, but he didn't want to show any lights at all to passing vehicles.

The Reds held off the Giants and left the field with a one-run win. To help pass the time after the game, Owen played tapes by Kathy Mattea and Patsy Cline, humming along with the lyrics to keep himself awake. When the tapes ran out, he tuned in to Wheeling's country music station, where a passable baritone, advertised as "the best state senator money couldn't buy," was singing "Country Roads." When the baritone came to the last line of the chorus, he changed the lyrics from "Take me home, country roads," to "Vote for me, Dusty Rhodes." Owen wondered whether the station was obliged to give equal time to the senator's opponents, or at least to John Denver.

Owen silenced the senator with a rerun of the Kathy Mattea tape and was humming along with "Walk the Way the Wind Blows" when the yellow truck pulled up to the main road and the man in the passenger seat climbed down and locked the chain behind them. The truck turned right on Possum Break Road, heading back the way it had originally come. Owen waited until it rounded the bend in front of the hospice before he pulled out of his hiding place to follow it.

He hung back, catching the truck in his headlights only when there was a rare straight stretch of road. When they'd traveled about five miles, he closed the distance between them, trying to read the truck's rear license plate. All the numbers but the last digit, a four, were obliterated by road grime and mud.

Owen slowed and fell back farther, confident that he wasn't likely to lose the truck. It was three-thirty in the morning, and he hadn't seen any other cars on the winding asphalt road. Patches of tule fog began to make their way up from the creekbed paralleling the roadway.

A bright flash glared in the Toyota's rearview mirror, and Owen looked up to see headlights coming on him fast from behind. He slowed and pulled to the right to let them pass.

Too late, he realized the approaching car wasn't trying to pass him. Its horn blared, and the car hit the Toyota's rear bumper with a bone-jarring thud. Owen's head snapped back against the headrest, and his car lurched over the center line. He fought to control the Toyota, fishtailed back into his own lane, and floored the accelerator, trying to put some distance between himself and the maniac behind him.

Flooring the accelerator didn't help. The car behind closed the distance between them and, horn blaring, hit him again. This time, though, the impact was less jarring, both because he was ready for it, and because he was moving nearly as fast as his pursuer.

He took a quick look in his rearview mirror. A Jeep's roll bar was clearly outlined above the stalking headlights. The truck must have seen Owen following it and radioed for reinforcements.

The truck. It was just ahead of him now. Its brake lights flashed, and Owen realized they meant to make him the meat in a Toyota sandwich.

He bore down on the slowing truck, which was approaching a blind curve. He sucked in his breath and swung into the oncoming traffic lane, gambling that no one would be coming from the opposite direction. He leaned on his horn, passed the truck, slewed around the curve, and was blinded by headlights coming straight at him.

A horn wailed, and he swept back into his own lane just in time to dodge the blinding headlights. They marked the first oncoming car he'd seen that morning, and if they'd come a few seconds earlier, they would have been the last thing he'd ever see. As it was, he hoped that the headlights would make the Jeep think twice before passing the yellow truck in his wake. Owen used the few seconds he'd gained to speed away from the truck, looking for some way to leave the main road before the Jeep was on his tail again.

Owen's headlights flashed on a narrow wooden bridge that marked a side road leading up into the tree-blackened hills. He braked quickly, swerved right onto the bridge, and bounced across it. The road followed the creekbed for about a hundred yards before it turned uphill. He downshifted and burned rubber up the dusty asphalt, swung through a hairpin turn, and slewed onto an unpaved road that sent gravel pinging against his undercarriage. He drove as fast as his headlights and the winding road would allow, turning uphill twice before following a rutted dirt drive marked by a rusted rural mailbox into the yard of an abandoned farmhouse.

Owen turned off his lights, pulled around to the side of the farmhouse and parked beside a burned-out Model T. He rolled down his window and listened for the noise of a pursuing vehicle. The only sounds were the sawing of locusts, the steady drip of water into a rain barrel, and the pounding of his own heart. He sat clenching the steering wheel for a full five minutes, until he was satisfied that he'd lost the Jeep. He turned his lights back on, pulled out of the farmyard and followed the rutted dirt drive to the gravel road, when he realized he'd not only lost the Jeep, but himself as well. He had no idea where he was.

What the hell, he thought, finding his way back was no different from finding his way out of a maze. And he'd long ago learned that the rule for getting out of a two-dimensional maze was to "put your right hand on the wall and keep walking." Being left-handed, he always applied the rule in the opposite direction, but it worked just as well, keeping him from doubling back on himself. Now he made a left turn onto the gravel road and edged his way downhill, making every possible left turn, until he found himself on a main road he thought he recognized.

The second he turned onto the road, he recognized something else. Headlights flashed, a horn blared, and the Jeep roared out of the darkness. The driver had done the same thing Owen had done with the truck earlier—just sat and waited for him to come out.

Owen stomped on the gas pedal and the Toyota leaped ahead, burning rubber. At least there was no longer a truck blocking his path. He sped down the winding asphalt road with the Jeep's brights glaring in his mirror.

He saw a familiar landmark and skidded into a quick turn, heading uphill past a yellow traffic sign with a wiggly arrow and a painted number 5. It was the same road he'd been on with the sheriff last weekend.

A road sign painted with the number 4 flashed by before Owen realized that the Jeep's headlights were no longer following him. Maybe the driver had missed the turn. Afraid to slow down, Owen whipped the Toyota around curve after curve. Just as his headlights picked up a pie tin painted with the number 2, he heard an earth-shaking rumble. He rounded a tight turn and came face-to-face with a wide yellow truck that took up half his lane. Before his foot could reach the brake, he hit the truck head-on.

SEVEN

Ass-backward Answers

OWEN DRIFTED IN AND OUT of consciousness. He floated on a giant basketball while seven dwarfs pounded on his battered car with picks and shovels. They sent him down a screaming roller coaster to a bright white room where the countdown numbers five-four-three-two-one flashed continuously on the wall, cycling over and over, a film leader introducing another film leader, and then another and another. Masked men and women in white probed, prodded, and poked at him before rolling him through a funhouse door to a dry creekbed where a succession of yellow dump trucks driven by leering men in cowboy hats covered him with loads of dirt. He choked and gasped for air until the dwarfs returned, dug him out, put him in a wheelbarrow, and marched single-file, whistling and singing, past a white-robed figure in an upright glass coffin.

The white-robed figure called to him, begging him to return, but the dwarfs kept moving, whistling and singing, into a dense fog bank. He tried to get out of the wheelbarrow, but found he couldn't move. The lead dwarf called a halt and they began arguing among themselves, shadowy figures moving in and out of the fog. The figure in white returned, blending with the fog, and took his hand. The fog lifted and he awoke to find himself in a hospital bed, looking up into the face of Kate O'Malley.

"You're quite a vision, Mary Katherine," he said. "A sure sign I'm not in hell."

"Not yet. And not for want of trying." She squeezed his left hand gently. His right hand was swathed in an ice bandage, with a metal splint protruding to protect his thumb.

Owen tilted his head toward his upraised thumb. "Must have been trying to hitchhike there."

"The airbag caught your thumb and fractured it. The bag probably saved your life, though, so it's a small price to pay."

Owen began taking inventory. He moved his head in a slow circle, checked his shoulders and arms, flexed his wrists and fingers. When he came to his left leg, he stopped. It was encased in white plaster from the middle of his thigh to his toes.

"You spun out and wrapped your car around a tree," Kate said. "Your leg's broken in two spots below the knee. But the tree kept you from going over the side of the mountain."

He raised the leg about an inch above the bedding. "How long?"

Kate eyed the cast critically. "I'd say about two and a half feet."

"You know what I meant. How long before it comes off?"

"A month. Then you'll need another month in a smaller cast below the knee."

"There goes the prom."

"There is that, of course."

"I'm not going to be much help to Mom."

"Oh dear, your mother. She's down in the cafeteria. She just stepped out for a minute." Kate glanced toward the door, then back at Owen. "I'll go get her." She squeezed his left hand and said, "I'm just so glad you're all right."

Then she bent forward and kissed him. Her lips were cool and smooth and bore down on his without moving. It was like being kissed by an insistent statue.

A sound in the doorway caused Kate to straighten, red-faced under her cowl. The sheriff stood in the doorway, accompanied by a nurse who appeared to be examining the doorknob for possible defects.

The sheriff grinned. "Sorry to butt in. If you two ladies will excuse me, though, I'd like to talk to Mr. Allison alone."

Kate released Owen's hand and smoothed the top sheet. "I'll just go get your mother. She was so worried about you."

When Kate and the nurse had gone, the sheriff said, "If it's any consolation, you came out of it better than your car did. What the hell were you doing on Blaine Mountain at three-thirty in the morning?"

"Running for my life." Owen told the sheriff about the reported truck movements, his vigil, and the black Jeep's pursuit.

"So you followed a dump truck out of Doubtful Hollow, got followed yourself, and wound up hitting the truck head-on."

Owen nodded. "I'm still a little hazy about the crash."

"That's understandable. There's only one thing wrong with your story. The truck that hit you hadn't been down off that mountain since noon. You couldn't have followed it."

"They're lying. They're up to something."

The sheriff scratched his forehead. "What do you think they're up to? There's nothing illegal about driving a truck on public roads. Or on private roads, come to that, when you own them."

"Attempted murder's still illegal in this state, isn't it? That's what they were trying to do."

"Not according to the truck crew. They say that was their first trip down that evening."

"Did you get their license number?"

The sheriff took a thin spiral notebook from his chest pocket. "Did you?"

"The truck I was following had plates that were smeared with mud. But the last number was a four."

The sheriff flipped through his notebook. "Truck that hit you had plates that ended in a six."

Owen closed his eyes and exhaled. "Shit. Must have been a different truck."

"I warned you about waiting to make sure the road up Blaine Mountain was clear. That's why they put numbers on those signs."

"I was being chased. I didn't have time to wait and watch."

"Chased by a Jeep, you say."

"A black Jeep. Just like the one Letch Valence was driving the other day."

"Did you get its number?"

"No, but it hit me. Twice. There must be some trace of the Toyota on its bumper."

"I'll check out Valence's Jeep. Aside from hassling you, what do you think they're doing that might be illegal?"

Owen shrugged against his pillow. "I don't know. Maybe they're dumping something they shouldn't. Lizzie's patient says it goes on almost every night."

"I'll have a patrol car watching tonight. I doubt they'll try to make a sandwich out of it."

Ruth came through the door with Kate in her wake. She brushed the sheriff aside and hugged Owen. When she pulled free of the hug, her first words were, "What on earth were you doing on those roads at three-thirty in the morning?"

The sheriff grinned. "My question exactly."

"A little legwork for Aunt Lizzie," Owen answered.

Ruth eyed Owen's cast. "Well, it will be a while before you'll be doing anymore legwork. And your hand. What have you done to your hand?"

Owen swiped at his nose with his bandaged thumb. "Youse should see de uddah guy."

"It's not funny," Ruth said. "We'll set up a bed in my sewing room, so you won't have to climb stairs. And I'll postpone my chemotherapy."

Owen slammed his bandaged hand down on the bedclothes. "Absolutely not."

"I won't be much use to you if I'm sick and bedridden."

"I came home to help, not to be a burden. My right leg is fine, so I can still drive. My left hand is fine, so I can still write. My bones will knit. You're the one with serious problems." Owen looked past his mother at Kate. "Tell her, Kate."

Kate nodded. "He's right, Ruth."

"If I'm to get chemotherapy, I'll have to move in with Lizzie. I can't imagine you emptying a bedpan or helping out around the house on crutches with one good hand."

"Do we have to discuss this now?" Owen asked.

"There's nothing to discuss. I can look after you or I can get chemotherapy. I can't do both."

Owen sank back into his pillow. "I'm here to look after you. I don't need looking after."

Ruth turned to Kate and the sheriff. "Will one of you please explain to my second-born son that he has casts on two extremities, that he's lucky to be alive, and that it's going to be at least a month before his bones knit and he can expect to do for himself?"

The sheriff shook his head. "I'm sorry. I only get involved in domestic disputes when there's a threat of violence."

"Stick around," Ruth said. "It may come to that."

VERN EMBRY FELT TRAPPED behind his desk. "You said the loan payback would start this month." He tried to keep the panic out of his voice, then gave up the fight. "You promised me, Willis."

Willis Grant shoved a stack of printouts toward the center of Vern's desk to clear a space to invade with his right buttock. He settled onto the corner with a loud sigh, ignoring the jar of pencils and the picture he'd just knocked over. "Vern buddy, the contractors just weren't ready to let Space-Mart move in. Now, I can't charge 'em rent until they're in the building, can I?"

"You want me to charge patients for rooms they didn't use. What's the difference?"

"The difference is, Space-Mart's comptroller is number one..." Willis raised his thick index finger for emphasis, "alive, and number two..." his middle finger joined the first to form a stubby V, "alert. The patients you're overcharging can't pass either of those tests."

"Willis, we've got to have that loan payment. Even with it, we'll have trouble making ends meet. Without it, it's just impossible. Even since BUBBA Ninety-seven—"

Willis raised the rest of his fingers and spread his palm like a policeman halting traffic. "What the hell's BUBBA Ninety-seven?"

Vern tried to keep his voice level, his eyes focused on Willis. He'd told him before, just about every time they'd had this conversation. But he laid it out for him again, patiently, as if he were lecturing a slow child. "The Balanced Budget Act of Nineteen ninety-seven. Before it, Medicare gave us a hundred percent of whatever we spent on their patients. Since BUBBA Ninety-seven passed, we're lucky to get eighty cents on the dollar."

"Then they got no right to complain if we get that missing twenty cents back by overcharging a mite."

Vern shook his head. "It'll take more than a mite of overcharging to keep us in the black. We need that loan payment."

"You sure you're overbilling all you can? You're not missing any angles?"

"Hell, we even invoiced the owner of a dead dog."

The news stopped Willis cold. From the look on his face, Vern imagined he was considering the possibility of combing the state highways for roadkill to invoice. Finally, Willis asked, "Did he pay?"

"No. And he complained to Sister Mary Perpetua."

"Damn nosy nun. What'd you tell her?"

"Computer error."

"Good. Just like we planned. She buy it?"

"For the room charge. She couldn't see how the computer could be blamed for the grief-counseling bill."

"Grief counseling?" Willis's voice contained a mixture of admiration and incredulity. "Vern, you're out of control. What'd your nun think of that?"

"Most likely that there's a lunatic loose in the billing department. I don't think she suspects what's really going on."

"It's okay then. You can get back to business as usual. Did you do what I suggested and bump the bills on those patients who go from us to Lizzie Neal's to die?"

"A few. I got spooked by the dog thing."

"You got to do better, Vern. Next to the mines, we're the biggest employer around. If we go under, you might as well hang a CLOSED FOR BUSINESS sign on the county line."

Vern wanted to say, "You should have thought of that when you loaned out our working capital," but he kept silent.

"You hear me, Vern? You got to do whatever it takes. We can't let this hospital down. Hell, we can't let the county down."

"I hear you, Willis."

"Good. You keep after it." Willis slid his buttock off the edge of the desk and clamped his hand on Vern's shoulder. "We're in this together, now."

After Willis left, Vern tidied up the printouts that had been shoved aside, picked up the spilled pencils, and returned the knocked-over picture of his deceased wife to the center of his desk. "Good God, Minna," he said aloud to the picture. "What have we gotten ourselves into?"

He took a small tape recorder from his inside vest pocket and switched it off. "Like Willis says, though, we're in this together."

TIME DRAGGED FOR OWEN in the weeks following his accident, as the thigh-high cast severely limited both his mobility and his morale. He'd had casts on his leg before as a result of an overeager slide into third base in junior high and a tendon torn on the tennis courts in graduate school, but they'd never extended above his knee. And there were even some compensating advantages to the earlier injuries. In junior high, Mary Jane Lewis had signed his cast, and in graduate school, his girlfriend had discovered a penchant for pampering that disappeared altogether when the cast came off.

He found few compensating advantages with the thigh-high cast. And his bandaged thumb left him clumsy with buttons, crutches, and keyboards, so he arranged his life to minimize encounters with clothes, stairs, and computers. He lived on the ground floor of his mother's house, wearing sweatpants and loose, floppy sweaters day and night. Although he was able to drive the used Saturn he'd bought to replace the totaled Toyota, the struggle to work his cast in and out of the driver's seat made him limit his driving to a weekly run for groceries and the twice-weekly trips to carry his mother between Lizzie's hospice and the chemotherapy clinic.

Ruth was grim and silent during these trips, and deflected all of Owen's inquiries with the observation that the effects of the treatment were rougher than a root canal but no worse than natural childbirth. She continued to insist on staying at the hospice, and Owen knew from checking with Lizzie that the chemotherapy was causing severe nausea and frequent bouts of diarrhea.

Owen's ex-wife Judith called regularly to check on Ruth's progress and his recovery. When she first heard about his accident, Judith offered to come to West Virginia to help out, but Owen argued that it was more important for her to clear her caseload so that she could be available for Lizzie's trial, which was six weeks away, than to play nursemaid while his bones mended.

The only bright spots of Owen's near-invalid status were Wednesday-night visits from Kate. When she finished helping out at Lizzie's hospice, she would stop by with a take-out dinner and they would watch a videotape of a musical comedy and talk for long laugh-filled hours about topics ranging from canine grief counseling to the Catholic Church's crabbed position on female prelates. A viewing of *Singin' in the Rain* led from talk about Debbie Reynolds' strained perkiness through the Eddie Fisher-Liz Taylor affair and singing nuns to Owen's remorse over his failed marriage and Kate's frustrations with convent life. *Into the Woods* took them from talk of their favorite children's tales (Owen's was *The Thirteen Clocks,* while Kate loved *Charlotte's Web*) to comparisons of their mutual aversion to risk and their regret that they were both, for widely divergent reasons, childless.

The one subject that never came up was Kate's tight-lipped kiss on the day Owen awoke following his accident. It reminded him of the chaste kisses they'd shared in college, but he sensed that Kate didn't want to discuss either their college flirtation or her impulsive "glad-you're-alive" hospital-bed kiss. There was no uneasiness between them, though. Their talk flowed seamlessly, and Owen had the cathartic feeling that he was revealing more of himself than he ever had to anyone.

Although Kate brightened his Wednesdays, Owen had a hard time finding any joy in the other six days of the week. He got a large-scale geologic map of the area and plotted the contours of the dump site next to Lizzie's hospice, but after computing the exact size of the fill, he still couldn't figure out why anyone would want to keep it a secret.

The sheriff had stopped by a week after the accident to say that there were no marks on the front bumper of Letch Valance's Jeep to match the dents in the Toyota's rear bumper. "Course," the sheriff observed, "Letch's bumper looked a little newer than the rest of the vehicle. He claimed he replaced it a couple of months ago after hitting a deer."

Owen emitted a short, sharp laugh. "I'm the deer he hit."

"Well, Bambi, you're lucky he didn't clean and dress you. You know it's legal to dine on roadkill in our fair state."

"Did you try tracking those trucks?"

"I sent a patrol car out four nights running. They didn't see any truck movement."

"I must have scared them off."

"You're pretty scary, all right. So scary they almost made a ghost out of you. Now that would really be frightening."

"They'll start up again. I'm sure of it."

"How can you be sure of it when you don't have a clue to what they're doing?"

"Whatever it is, they're not done. They were doing it night after night, and there's too much fill there." They were frightened, that's all, like a fly hiding in the curtains after a near-miss swat. They'd be back, he was sure, with more of the scraps or waste or whatever it was they were dumping in Doubtful Hollow.

TO HELP PASS the time, Owen started reading mysteries, which he'd share with Maggie Mason during his trips to the hospice to take his mother to her chemotherapy treatments. He'd just emptied five of Michael Z. Lewin's Albert Samson mysteries from his backpack onto her nightstand when Maggie announced that the trucks were moving again.

"Not every night," she said. "But twice this past week."

Owen shifted both crutches to his right hand, fished a spiral note-book out of the backpack, and asked, "What nights?"

"Last night. This morning, really. And two nights ago."

Owen wrote down the dates, then tore a fresh sheet from the notebook and placed it on top of the stack of paperbacks. "Will you keep track for me? When you hear them again, I mean?"

"I'll try, love. But I can't promise. I'm just a mare's hair away from a size eight." She raised one eyebrow and cocked her head, pulling her nose catheter taut. "Or didn't you notice?"

For an instant, Owen didn't understand. Then he remembered her joke about turning off the life supports when she got down to a size eight. Flustered, he tried to reach out to her, losing one of his crutches in the process.

"No need to get your slats rattled." Maggie nodded toward the fresh stack of paperbacks. "I've got these here books to get through at least."

"I've got more at home. I'll bring them as fast as I finish them."

"And I'll spy on those trucks for you just as long as I can. What do you think they're up to, anyhow?"

Owen grasped the metal railing beside the bed, bent his good knee, and retrieved his fallen crutch. "I'm not sure what they're up to," he said, tapping his cast with the crutch, "but they gave me this for trying to find out. I think maybe they're dumping something illegal in the hollow."

"Lord bless you, honey, that's the last thing they're doing."

"What do you mean?"

"Just that you got it wrong end up. Like the man in my supposi-tory joke."

Owen stared blankly.

"You mean I haven't told you my suppository joke? Lord, I thought I'd laid that on everybody." Maggie smiled and leaned forward as far as her catheter would permit. "There was this hill-country farmer, see, who comes out of Mingo County to see a doc-tor. 'Doc,' he says, 'I don't hold much truck with modern medicine, but I haven't moved my bowels in a week, and it's paining me something fierce.'

"The doctor examines the farmer and sends him home with a small tin of suppositories, telling him they'll fix him right up.

"Well, the farmer goes home, takes the tin of suppositories to his outhouse, drops his drawers, sits down, and opens the tin." Maggie sat up straight, wiggled her shoulders, and examined an imaginary tin of suppositories, mimicking the farmer on his privy.

"Then he takes one of the suppositories, swallows it down, and waits for a signal from his large intestine." Maggie aped the farmer tentatively tasting a suppository and checking his bowels.

Owen laughed.

Maggie held up her hand, palm outward. "Don't jump the gun on me. Joke's not over yet." She examined her palm again and pretended to shovel a few more suppositories into her mouth. "Anyhow, the farmer gobbles down the whole tin of suppositories and sits for an hour on the privy, but nothing happens.

"Next day he's back in the doctor's office, complaining. Doctor gives him a big jar of double-strength suppositories, tell him they're guaranteed to work, and sends him home.

"Same thing happens." Maggie smiled, mimicked the farmer unscrewing the jar of suppositories. "Farmer goes back to his outhouse, gobbles down half the jar, and waits. Not a peep. He has dinner, goes back to the outhouse, swills down the rest of the jar and waits some more. Still nothing.

"Next day, the farmer's there when the doctor opens his office. Hands him the empty jar. Tells the doctor the suppositories didn't work, and demands his money back."

Maggie mimicked the doctor's look of incredulity. "The doctor looks from the farmer to the empty jar and back again. Finally he says, 'My God, man. What are you doing? Eating them?'"

Maggie drew herself up haughtily and raised her voice an octave to imitate the farmer's outraged sarcasm. "'What do you think I'm doing?' the farmer says. 'Sticking 'em up my ass?'"

Owen laughed out loud. "That's a great joke. But what's it got to do with those trucks in Doubtful Hollow?"

"You're like the farmer. You've got it wrong side up. Those trucks aren't dumping anything after dark."

"How can you tell?"

"Lord bless you, I worked next to a mine for thirty-odd years. Those trucks aren't coming in full and going out empty. They're coming in empty and going out full."

"And you can tell how? By the sound?"

"Honey, you try hauling a hundred tons uphill. You're going to sound a lot different than if you're running around empty."

It came to him then. He knew what they were hauling and why they were hiding it. And he knew how to catch them at it. He balanced on his one good leg, leaned over Maggie's bed, and kissed her full on the lips.

Startled, Maggie reached up and adjusted her nose catheter. "Nobody's kissed me on the lips since the Mister died."

"Well, they should have."

EIGHT

Embracing Shadows

AS SOON AS Owen got home from the hospice, he called his friend Ken Kaylor in Seattle. An inveterate tinkerer, Ken had designed thumbnail-sized video cameras with transmitters for firemen's helmets years before the TV networks thought of putting them in catcher's masks. He always made Owen think of Q, James Bond's armorer and gadgeteer. The difference was, Ken had a sense of humor. After catching up on business gossip, Owen asked, "Do you still have those cameras we used for tracking the loads on Washington's rural roads?"

"The dark-cheaters? They're around somewhere."

"I need five or six."

"Don't tell me you've got six girlfriends you think are stepping out on you?"

Owen laughed. "Nothing like that."

"One girlfriend with six guys?"

"No girlfriends and no guys." Owen told Ken quickly about the filling of Doubtful Hollow, his late-night chase and crash, and what he thought was happening.

"When do you need the cameras?"

"I was hoping you could get them to me by next week. My big cast gets cut in half then, and I'll be mobile enough to handle them." He paused, hating to bring up the next topic. "There's one thing, though. I can pay the freight, but I can't afford the rent."

"What the hell, they're just collecting dust right now. Buy me a dinner next time you're in Seattle."

"I may need them for three or four weeks."

"Make it two dinners. The wife needs to eat, too."

"If this works, I'll feed your whole family."

"Be careful what you promise. There's another grandchild on the way."

"That's great news. I'll stand by my offer, though. Newborns don't eat much."

"I'll ship the cameras off tomorrow. You be careful, hear?"

"Don't worry, I'll get them back to you in working order."

"The cameras are replaceable. *You* be careful."

THE LAST WEDNESDAY NIGHT before the casts on his leg and thumb were to come off, Owen popped three skilletsful of popcorn on the stove, filled a turkey roaster with the white kernels, and, swinging his cast between his crutches, toed the roaster along the floor to the living room. There he sat down on the couch, lifted the turkey roaster to the glass coffee table, and propped his cast on the table to wait for Kate's visit. She swept in at ten minutes after seven, carrying a pizza from Johnny Angelo's.

"Sorry I'm late. One of Lizzie's patients went into cardiac arrest."

"Were you able to help?"

"Not enough, I'm afraid."

"It wasn't Maggie Mason, was it?"

"No, it wasn't Maggie." Kate slumped back onto the couch. "Funny, I don't even know the woman's name."

Seeing Kate so dejected made Owen want to change the subject. "Did you see Mom at Lizzie's?"

"She was sleeping. Peacefully, it looked like." Kate nodded toward the heaping mound of popcorn in the turkey roaster. "Are we expecting company, or is this a triple feature?"

"Neither. I just didn't want to be getting up for refills once the movie started."

"That's why I'm here. So you won't have to get up. Visiting the sick is a corporal work of mercy."

"That's what I am to you? A work of mercy?"

"That's what you are on my sign-out sheet."

"You have a sign-out sheet?"

"Oh, yes. Just like at the Cardinal Stritch dorm."

"Can't they reach you through your beeper?"

"The beeper connects me with the hospital. The sign-out sheet is for the convent."

"Is there a curfew?"

"Why? Are you really planning a triple feature?"

"No. But next week, I'll have this splint removed." He held up his bandaged right hand. "I'll have two opposable thumbs again. And they'll replace this thigh-high cast with one that ends below the knee. I thought we could celebrate by going out to dinner before the movie."

"It's probably best if we celebrate here. It will be hard to pass you off as a work of mercy if we're seen wining and dining in public." Kate opened the pizza and doled out two slices. "What's tonight's movie?"

"*Cabaret.*"

"I thought it made you wince."

"I never saw you again after we watched it on our last date. I thought if things had gone better then, well…" Owen shrugged and half laughed. "I don't know."

"And what do you think now?"

"I've seen you again. The curse of *Cabaret* is removed." Owen snapped the fingers of his left hand.

"That's a load off my mind."

"Then let's watch the movie." Owen pushed the "Play" button and settled back into the corner of the couch. Kate sat on the edge of the cushions, leaning forward, and Owen found he could watch both the movie and Kate's reaction to it from his corner vantage point. She smiled at Joel Gray's antics as emcee and sucked in her breath when the camera panned downward to show that the cherubic boy singing "Tomorrow Belongs to Me" was a member of the Hitler Youth. Her face was unreadable when the Liza Minnelli character, Sally Bowles, decides to get an abortion, and Owen was so intent on watching her reaction to the ménage à trois that she caught him staring at her.

"What is it?" she asked.

Owen felt the beginnings of a blush around his ears and collar. "Nothing. I was watching for your reaction."

"Well, I'd be a poor doctor if I hadn't seen naked men before, and a poor nun if I thought a lot about it. Maybe I should be watching you?"

The blush escaped from under Owen's collar and covered his whole face. "No," was all he could think of to say.

Kate smiled at his embarrassment and waved it off. "Then let's both watch the movie."

Her face glowed with pleasure when Liza Minnelli lit into the title song, and she applauded the TV screen when it ended. "Wonderful movie," she said when the credits rolled. "Dark, for a musical, but wonderful."

Owen turned on the reading light beside the couch. The illumination cast shadows of himself and Kate on the rear wall that made them seem closer together than they actually were, two heads on a single body.

When the light came on, Kate pointed at the polished ebony cane hanging from the hall coatrack. "Where'd that come from?"

"Out in the garage. It was my dad's. He broke his leg once surveying roads. Next week it'll replace my crutches."

Kate took the cane from the rack, hefted it, turned it in her hands, then put the tip on the floor between her feet, rested both hands on the curved handle, and leaned forward so the cane jutted out at an oblique angle.

She held that pose for a few seconds, then brought the tip of the cane up to her cowl like a song-and-dance man tapping his straw hat, and began singing the title song from *Cabaret* in a low, throaty voice. She went through two choruses, then did a quick-time step, rapped the cane sharply on the floor, and sang out the invitation to "Come to the Cabaret."

The image of a demure nun belting out the cynical chorus of *Cabaret* was so incongruous that Owen laughed out loud and began applauding. "You'll never make the Kit Kat Club in that getup."

Kate rejoined him on the couch. "You don't think they'd take a singing nun?"

"Afraid you'd have to do a little more than sing to fit in."

Kate tilted her head forward and raised her eyebrows. "You mean those girls were, well, you know, professionals?"

"I don't think there's any doubt about it."

"Tsk-tsk. Another moonlighting option down the tubes."

"You're really good, you know. You could have been on the stage."

"Oh, sure. What time's the next one leave?"

"No, I'm serious. Do you regret not trying it?"

"Not as much as I'd regret not being a doctor."

Owen opened a subject he'd been avoiding. "You could have been a doctor without being a nun."

"That's not clear. I couldn't afford med school on my own. And then there was the Church."

"The Church. The Capital-C Church."

Kate reached forward and took a handful of popcorn from the roaster, then leaned back on the couch. Their shadows on the wall parted, then embraced. "Remember what you told me about choosing a college?" she asked. "About how you wound up at Marquette instead of Cal Tech?"

Owen smiled. "The nuns in high school told me I'd go to hell if I didn't go to a Catholic college."

"And you believed them?"

"No. I was pretty sure they were wrong. But I wasn't willing to run that big a risk."

"Well, it was pretty much the same with me and the convent. The nuns had been after me to join since the first grade."

"You and every other first-grader who could tie her own shoes and recite the Lord's Prayer."

Kate smoothed the folds of her habit. "This life has a lot to recommend it, you know. There's serenity. The chance to serve God in a focused way. The company of dedicated women, women I can look up to." She smiled and cocked her head. "Those nuns didn't exactly threaten me with hellfire. But they did let me know it would be hard for me to get to heaven if I denied my vocation."

"'Denied my vocation.' Those are words I haven't heard since high school."

"Well, they meant something to me then. That's really why I didn't go back to Cardinal Stritch after my junior year. I could see where we were going. You and I. And I wanted to go there. With you, I mean."

"So it wasn't the *Cabaret* curse that parted us. It just seems so..."

"Silly. I know. Go ahead and say it. But don't you see, you made the same kind of choice."

"But my choice wasn't as final as yours. I went from Marquette to graduate school at Cal Tech. You were stuck with your decision for life."

"No. That's not quite right. I stuck with my decision for life. There's a big difference."

"And you don't regret it?"

"Oh my, yes. Whenever I see my two cousins with their six children, or whenever the Pope issues statements making women second-class citizens. And, you might as well know, when I saw you standing next to that candy machine in the hospital."

Before Owen could respond, she added, "But anyone who's lived as long as we have is bound to have some regrets. To balance mine, there's the hospital. This county wouldn't have a hospital if it weren't for we nuns. We do everything from the laundry to the paperwork. And not a day goes by that I couldn't walk you through the corridors and point out ten lives that have been saved because the hospital's there. And a few souls as well."

"That's not a bad balance sheet."

"Neither is yours, if you look at it right. You regret being childless and divorced, but those two conditions are reversible. And you resent having to pry research dollars out of bungling bureaucracies."

"Did I say that?"

"Nearly every Wednesday night for the last month." She poked at the hint of a paunch that was beginning to puff out over Owen's belt. "But you're not starving. And every time you make a road safer or a bridge stronger, you're saving lives just as surely as we are at the hospital. Those lives don't just gather in corridors to be counted."

Kate rapped his cast with the ebony cane. "And in just a week you'll be free of that cast. I don't see that life's been treating you too badly." She did a quick drumroll on the turkey roaster with the tip of the cane. "'After all,'" she sang softly, "'life is a cabaret, old chum.'"

"I think that song's supposed to be ironic."

"Depends on the singer."

Kate stood and their shadows parted. "Well, I've got early rounds. Anything I can get for you before I go?"

"No, I'm fine. Thanks for coming."

"A pleasure. As always." She bent down and hugged him quickly, chafing his neck with the stiff bib of her habit. "See you next week."

OWEN SPENT HIS last mobility-impaired week getting ready to put Ken Kaylor's camera shipment to use. He edged his crutches sideways down the narrow aisle of the local hardware store and bought six rural mailboxes, along with the posts and angle irons needed to mount them.

As the store manager loaded the supplies into Owen's trunk, he said, "Not much building going on in the county lately."

"Must make it tough on your business."

"Puts the 'hard' in hardware, all right. Don't know that I've sold more than two mailboxes this past year."

Owen saw where the conversation was headed, but he didn't know what he was going to do when it got there. "Guess they just don't wear out."

"Some get vandalized. Used for target practice."

Owen shifted his grip on his crutches. "That right?"

The manager loaded the last of the mailboxes, slammed the trunk lid shut, and dusted off the front of his bib overalls. "You just bought out my entire stock of rube tubes. Mind my asking what you're going to do with them?"

At least he'd had a little lead time to prepare an answer. "My aunt runs a senior citizen's hospice on Possum Break Road. We thought we'd get some of the patients to decorate these mailboxes, paint patterns on them, maybe sell them for a profit. Even if we can't sell them, it'll be good therapy."

"Your aunt's Lizzie Neal?"

Owen nodded.

"She sure bought herself a peck of trouble. Still, you got to admire her for standing up to those developers. They come rolling in from out of state and roust people from their homes just so's they can build a mall with a bunch of Home Depots to roust the rest of us from our businesses."

When Owen didn't respond, he continued. "I tell you, I'd a sight rather see them use these mountains for mining coal. Course, I can't let my old lady hear me say that. She's in tight with those preservation people. They don't mind breaking down a mountain to get a shopping mall, but let somebody try to take a little coal out and their britches are all atwitter. Your aunt had the right idea, standing up to them mall maulers with a shotgun. Still, I think she might have fired a warning shot or something."

"I believe she did."

"Only trouble was, it caught Sam Mattingly head-on."

"She says she was just returning his fire."

"Hell's bells, a shoot-out between your aunt and Sam Mattingly ought to be about as lethal as a pillow fight at a school for the blind. I've had 'em both in my store. Neither of them can see what's on the top shelf. Your aunt must have got lucky."

"Or unlucky. She could spend the rest of her days in jail."

"I see what you mean." The man rapped lightly on the trunk of Owen's car. "Listen here. If those patients turn out some good-looking mailboxes, bring them around. I'll be happy to sell them for you."

Owen had a quick flash of Maggie Mason and Lizzie's other patients using their last days on earth to paint mailboxes, and his lie made him wince. "That's very kind of you," he said, without committing to anything.

On his way home from the hardware store, Owen stopped by the local office of the Department of Environmental Protection and copied down the location of all the mines and mining permits held by Mountain View Development, and its subsidiaries, and its sister companies.

Recalling his conversation with the hardware-store manager, he looked through the list and then asked the desk clerk whether anybody had ever applied for a permit to mine Dismal Mountain.

The clerk scratched at the gray stubble on his chin and disappeared into a back room. He returned ten minutes later with a puzzled look on his face. "I guess not. I thought somebody'd applied a year or so back, but I can't find any record of it. I must have disremembered." He shrugged his shoulders. "It's a moot point anyhow, you know. They're fixing to open a shopping mall there any day now."

Owen folded his list and tucked it in his pocket. "Yes, I know."

VERN EMBRY shuffled the stack of envelopes on his desk. He'd run them through the postage meter himself, so no one would ask any questions. But he hadn't mailed them yet. Twenty envelopes. Twenty patients who'd transferred from the hospital to Lizzie Neal's hospice.

Two months' worth of transfers. Some had died already, he knew. But some hadn't. It was a risk sending these bills out. That's why he hadn't done it, hoping against hope that Willis Grant's mall tenants would ante up their rentals. But that hadn't happened. And

Willis had just made it plain it wouldn't happen. Not this month. Probably not next month either.

Even if the patients didn't tumble to the overbillings, there was a good chance that Sister Mary would. She reviewed all their paperwork. And she was looking closer now, because of that damn dog. Grief counseling for a hound dog. No wonder she was suspicious. But those records had been corrected. Taken off the books. They weren't likely to happen again.

Vern evened the edges of the stack of envelopes. "What else can I do, Minna?" he asked the picture of his wife. The picture was silent, accusing. He'd thought of going over Willis Grant's head, but there was nobody higher than Willis in Mountain View Enterprises.

Maybe he should go to the police, tell them what he knew, let them sort it out. But he'd wind up implicating himself. After all, he was the one overcharging patients. What did it matter that he had Willis on tape encouraging him? He was the one responsible for the billings.

He wasn't responsible for the loan, though. He'd had nothing to do with that. The loan itself was Willis's doing. He'd taken money from a nonprofit hospital and channeled it into a profit-making venture. The IRS would probably like to know about that.

He remembered an article in the *Wall Street Journal*. Not more than a month ago. He'd clipped it out, in fact. It told about healthcare whistle-blowers, and how they could claim a piece of the money recovered as a result of their whistle-blowing. From fifteen to twenty-five percent of the total recovered.

He pulled the article out of his desk drawer. A man who worked for Columbia Healthcare had made ten million by blowing the whistle on his employer. And there were other examples. What's more, there was a law that kept employers from firing relators, the legal term for whistle-blowers. Relators. He liked that.

Maybe the employer wouldn't even have to know the identity of the relator. And an investigation of the loan wouldn't necessarily uncover his overbillings. Those were all backed by solid accounting records. And the unquestioning payments of the patients' survivors. And Medicare payments, of course. That made it a federal fraud. That could up the ante.

He reread the *Wall Street Journal* article. A mailroom supervisor in Illinois had gotten twenty-nine million from Health Care Services of Chicago. There were three cases mentioned. And the lowest of the rewards was ten million.

He'd start by telling the IRS about the loan. That was safe. If the investigation spread to the overbillings, that wasn't necessarily all bad. He had Willis on tape ordering him to do it. And the bigger the fraud, the bigger the reward.

Vern pulled a pad of yellow paper from his desk drawer. He'd write the letter out in longhand, then type it himself. It wasn't something he'd want his secretary to see. Or anyone else, for that matter. He wrote down the address of the regional IRS office, then followed with the appellation "Dear Sirs." Was that proper? he wondered. Or should it be "Dear Sir or Madame"? And should he send a copy to the state as well? Sure. Why not? He could mail both copies with the stack of patient billings.

KATE CALLED UNEXPECTEDLY the evening before Owen's casts were due to come off. It made him realize how happy he was simply to hear her voice.

"Just making sure you're all set for tomorrow," she said.

"I'm ready. I've rented *It's Always Fair Weather*."

"I don't know that one."

"Gene Kelly on roller skates. You'll love it. And I'm cooking salmon."

"I can hardly wait." After a brief pause, she said, "Listen, I've been meaning to ask. How's your mother?"

"Except for the side effects, she's fine. Chemo seems to be working."

"She didn't have a relapse or anything?"

"No. Nothing."

"That's very strange."

"What's strange?"

On the other end of the line, Kate's voice became muffled, as if she had lowered the mouthpiece to talk to someone else. Then it returned at full strength. "Listen, I've got to go. We'll talk about your mom tomorrow night. Sometime between the salmon and Gene Kelly."

THE CASTS CAME OFF the next day. The doctor removed the thumb splint and replaced the thigh-high cast with a shorter model that covered his left ankle and shinbone. But he could bend his knee, and the cast had a walking bar, so Owen felt free.

The first thing he did with his newfound freedom was to lay in a supply of groceries, including fresh salmon for his dinner with Kate. As soon as he got home, he put the salmon in a marinade of olive oil, garlic, rosemary, and thyme, and took Buster for a walk. Neighborhood kids had split the dog-walking chores while Owen was immobilized, and they came out to say hello in response to Buster's barking.

Owen stretched the walk with Buster, enjoying the cool fall air and the smooth, solid feel of his father's cane. A pickup game of touch football was in progress at a narrow creekside park, and Buster yapped happily along the sidelines, chasing the line of scrimmage up and down the field. Owen watched the game for a while, then took Buster and wandered away when an argument broke out over an out-of-bounds catch.

Back home, he took a hot bath, another pleasure denied him when he was encumbered by the heavier cast. The new, shorter model could be propped easily on the edge of the tub while he relaxed and pondered what he suspected and what he knew about the truck movements in Doubtful Hollow. He couldn't wait to see Kate and tell her what he thought was happening and share his plan for putting a stop to it.

He toweled off, dressed, and listened to a disc of Stephen Sondheim's *Follies* while he fixed a salad of green apple slivers, walnuts, Gorgonzola, bacon bits, and romaine lettuce. Then he set the table, lit two long, tapered candles, poured himself a glass of chardonnay, and waited.

And waited.

Kate usually arrived around six-thirty. When she hadn't shown up by seven-fifteen, Owen called Lizzie, who said Kate left the hospice at least an hour earlier. He waited another half hour and called the convent, thinking she must have stopped off and been delayed. The nun who answered the phone suggested he try calling Lizzie's hospice, saying Kate usually helped out there until fairly late on Wednesdays.

So she hadn't told the other nuns about her visits to a sick friend. Was she worried about appearances? Or was she worried that something might develop between them? Was she afraid he might chase her around the couch now that he had two reasonably good legs?

Didn't she trust him? He paced the darkened dining room, where the glow from the tapered candles caused his lone shadow to follow him along the wall. He scanned the intimate table setting, with the opened bottle of chardonnay resting in a silver ice bucket, snuffed the two candles with his wet fingers, and turned up the lights. What the hell had he been thinking?

She was a doctor, after all. There could have been some kind of emergency, on the road or at the hospital. He called the hospital and had her paged. When they failed to locate her, he left a message asking her to call if she showed up there.

He remembered her beeper. She'd given him the number, even though he'd never had any occasion to use it. He called it now and left his home phone number, then hung up and waited for her return call. Another half hour crawled past. Why hadn't she called? She knew he was expecting her. They'd talked just yesterday. There must be some simple explanation. If there was one, though, he couldn't think of it. He began to sense that something was badly wrong.

At nine-thirty, when she was nearly three hours late, he called the sheriff's office. A thick male voice with a pronounced twang suggested he wait until morning before filing a missing person's report.

"At least keep an eye out for her car," Owen pleaded. "Can you do that, at least?"

"Why? Do y'all think it's been stolen?"

"No. But I think there's a good chance that if we find the car, we'll find her."

Owen heard paper rustling at the other end of the line. "Can you give me a description of the car?"

"A black VW with the license NUN¢S. That's N-U-N, followed by a cents symbol and an S."

"We don't put cents symbols on license plates in this state."

Owen fought to control his voice. "Maybe she put a slash through the C herself, then. I don't know."

"That would be illegal."

Owen heard himself shouting. "Then find her and haul her in for defacing a state license plate."

"There's no need to take that tone with me."

"Oh, for Christ's sake. Let me talk to the sheriff."

"Sheriff Reader's gone home."

"Can you connect me?"

"That would be against policy."

"Look, I'm a friend of his."

"Sheriff's got a lot of friends. The really good ones have his phone number."

Owen remembered that the sheriff's mother had been a patient at Lizzie's hospice, and got Reader's home number from Lizzie, who by now was as agitated as Owen.

Thad Reader listened quietly while Owen explained the situation, laughed once at the license-plate mixup, and said, "You were right to call. I'll get my boys right on it. Stick close to the phone and let me know if she calls in."

Owen hung up. He couldn't shake the feeling that something awful had happened, but he didn't know what else he could do.

He nibbled at his salad, then covered it with Saran wrap and put it in the refrigerator with the salmon. His stomach wouldn't let him keep anything down.

He bounced a tennis ball off the stairwell until Buster tired of retrieving it, nosed the ball under the couch, and then rolled himself into a ball at Owen's feet. Owen couldn't remember a time when Buster had quit before he did, but the mindless repetition of throwing the ball was all he felt able to manage.

He couldn't concentrate enough to read, so he channel-surfed between Leno and Letterman, finally finding a cable channel showing Hitchcock's *Rear Window*. His own experience with a leg cast gave him a newfound sympathy for Jimmy Stewart's plight, but even speculating on how Stewart might have managed sex with Grace Kelly in his wheelchair couldn't keep Owen's mind off the silent phone in the next room.

He dozed fitfully, woke suddenly when he heard the phone ring, and stumbled off the couch to find Jimmy Stewart had answered it. It was Raymond Burr calling. By the time Burr made his menacing way to Stewart's door, Buster began barking and Owen heard a heavy knocking on his own front porch.

He turned on the porch light to see the sheriff standing, hat in hand, in the glare of the naked bulb. The garish light outlined the sagging pouch under his ill-fitting glass eye. His good right eye was bloodshot.

Owen opened the door and the sheriff stepped inside. He glanced at the intimate table setting and turned to face Owen. "Couple of neckers found the Sister's car on a path off Gobbler's Grade."

The sheriff shook his head slowly, and the glass eye seemed about to leave its socket. "There was a syringe on the seat next to her. Looks like she OD'd on something."

NINE

Untangling Webs

OWEN STOOD SILENT, uncomprehending. Not hearing, or not wanting to hear. Finally, he asked, "What did you say?"

The sheriff held his hat in front of him and gave it a quarter-turn, as if he were steering carefully around a tight bend. "She's dead, Owen. Sister Mary's dead. An overdose of some kind. It looks like suicide."

"Bullshit." Owen blinked and shook his head. "That's just bullshit. There's some mistake."

"There's no mistake. I saw the body." The sheriff reached out. "I'm sorry, Owen."

Owen batted away the sheriff's hand. "Calling it a suicide has to be a mistake. There's no way she's a suicide. Somebody did this to her."

"If they did, we'll find them."

"Bullshit. She'd never commit suicide. For a Catholic, that's a one-way ticket to hell. She put up with the Pope's prattle all her life. She'd never end it by doing the one thing that would wipe that out."

"Do you have a glass of water?"

Owen started for the kitchen, bobbing up and down on his walking bar. The bar caught on the sill of the dining-room door and he stumbled forward, steadying himself on a chair. He upended the chair against the table, knocking over the candlesticks.

"Maybe you better sit down," the sheriff said.

"Don't need to sit down."

The sheriff retrieved the upset chair and offered it to Owen.

"Don't want to sit here."

"We'll go back to the living room, then." The sheriff reached out for Owen's arm, but Owen shook him off, limped back into the living room, and smashed down onto the couch.

The sheriff went to the kitchen and returned with a glass of amber liquid, stopping on the way to set the overturned candlesticks upright. He handed the glass to Owen.

Owen sniffed at the glass. "Scotch."

"You look like you could use it."

Owen swallowed deeply. The liquor burned in his throat. "I thought you were the one who was thirsty."

"I got myself some water."

Owen stared straight ahead, glassy-eyed. "She didn't kill herself."

"I'll grant you, it's hard to believe."

"What are you going to do about it? Will there be an autopsy?"

"Of course. In cases like this, there always is."

"Let me know what it says. Let me know as soon as you know. I want to help."

"Best let us handle it. If she didn't kill herself, we'll find out who did."

Owen slammed his glass down, splashing liquor on the end table and his shirtsleeve. "She didn't kill herself. I just told you that. Listen to me. Listen to me. Somebody did this to her."

"Any idea who might want to kill her?"

Owen mopped up the spill with the dry side of his sleeve. "God, no. That's what we've got to find out."

"Right now I've got to find the next of kin. Know where they might be?"

"Her father's alive somewhere. The convent will know where. They're the ones to notify. Ask for Sister Regina Anne."

The sheriff put on his hat and pulled the chin strap tight. "I'm right sorry to be carrying this news."

"Oh, God. There's Aunt Lizzie, too. She'll have to be told."

"Your Aunt Lizzie?"

"Kate left her a little after six to come here. I've already worked her into a state with my calls. I'll get in touch with Lizzie. You notify the convent."

The sheriff stopped with his hand on the doorknob. "Tell Lizzie I'll want to talk with her tomorrow."

Owen finished the glass of Scotch. How long had it been since he'd tasted hard liquor? He thought of switching to wine or beer, but wine was for celebrating and beer was for relaxing. He needed something for grieving, something to blot out the pain, something strong for the call he had to make. He went to the kitchen, poured himself more Scotch, and returned to the living room sipping the burning liquor. He picked up the phone, then put it back on its cradle and set the half-empty glass of Scotch beside it. He slipped on a jacket, took his car keys off the hook under the mirrored coatrack, and went out into the cold night. There was some news that had to be delivered in person.

LIZZIE SAT AT the end of a long table in the hospice cafeteria. No one else was in the room, which was lit by a night-light in a socket three tables over. When Owen entered, she stood up and took two steps forward when something in his manner made her stop.

"She's dead, Lizzie," Owen said. "Kate's dead."

Lizzie swayed in the dim light and Owen clutched her to him. She gasped once against his chest. "Was it a car wreck?"

"No. They found her on Gobbler's Grade. Sheriff Reader says she OD'd on something."

"A drug overdose?" Lizzie pulled away from him. "A suicide?"

"The sheriff says that's what it looks like. But you and I know it can't be true."

Lizzie stumbled backward and sat down hard on the cafeteria chair. "Oh, Owen. She was bringing me morphine."

Owen stared in disbelief.

Lizzie waved her hand in front of her face. "Well, not for me. For the hospice. We're always on the ragged edge. It was one way we could save money."

"Where did she get the morphine?"

"When a patient on morphine dies, you're supposed to get rid of anything they haven't used. Flush it down the toilet. Then you sign a form saying you disposed of it." Lizzie shook her head slowly. "Well, Sister Mary found that wasteful, with us always needing help. She'd take the leftover morphine and bring it for our inventory."

"And sign a paper saying she'd destroyed it?"

"Yes, I suppose she'd have to do that. But Owen, honey, I never thought she might be using some herself."

"Don't be silly, Lizzie. Kate wasn't a drug user. She couldn't have been."

"But didn't the sheriff say she OD'd?"

"He said it looked like suicide. But you and I know Kate wouldn't take her own life."

Lizzie sat quietly. The dim night light etched deep creases in her face.

Owen felt a faint stirring of doubt. "We know that, don't we?"

"Just because she was Catholic?"

"There's that, yes. But mostly because we knew how strong she was in her faith. She was our friend, Lizzie. We knew her. She was no suicide."

"Owen, honey. A morphine overdose doesn't necessarily have to be a suicide."

"That's what I'm telling you. Somebody killed her."

"That's not what I meant. Morphine's tricky. It makes you woozy. Your heart slows and finally stops. It's pretty easy to lose track of how much you're injecting. I've seen it happen. It's why we don't let our patients control their own morphine drips."

"Are you saying Kate was an addict? A user?"

"That isn't what I said. I only meant that an overdose wasn't necessarily suicide."

"Do you have any evidence at all that Kate was using morphine?"

"None."

"Then if it wasn't suicide or an accidental overdose, somebody killed her."

"Who would do that?"

"That's what we've got to find out. Did she seem at all different when she was with you earlier tonight? Was there anything out of the ordinary?"

Lizzie stared into her black coffee mug. "No."

"What about the past month or so? Anything different or out of the ordinary?"

Lizzie looked up at him. "You." Her eyes flashed with reflected light. "There was you. You were different. Before you came, she'd stay late on Wednesdays. Helping me. Then we'd settle in right here. Or in the commons room. And just talk. We didn't do that after you got hurt. She was too anxious to go see you."

Owen knew the feeling. He'd shared it. He remembered how

eagerly he'd anticipated Kate's Wednesday visits, and the memory intensified his feeling of loss. Surely there was nothing between the two of them that could have caused a morphine overdose. He was angry with Lizzie for suggesting it. "Anything else? Anything she might have said? Anything different?"

"No. Just you."

"Goddamn it, Lizzie, there must be something else."

"I don't know, Owen. Whatever it was, I just don't know." Lizzie's head drooped as if she were trying to read the answer in her coffee grounds.

"Tell me something you do know, then. Tell me what really happened the night Sam Mattingly was shot at Cooter's Bend."

Lizzie's head snapped up. "How could that possibly have anything to do with Sister's death?"

"I don't know. But look at everything that's happened. Somebody tried to kill me. They're guarding Doubtful Hollow as if they were growing diamonds. Sam Mattingly was killed the night they started dumping there. And now Kate's been murdered."

Lizzie slumped back in her chair, taking her face into the shadows. Owen couldn't tell whether he was reaching her, but he plunged ahead anyway. "Now, some of this has to be connected. But I'm not likely to figure out how unless I know all the facts. And you've been holding out on me, keeping a piece of the puzzle all to yourself."

Lizzie's face emerged from the shadows, her eyes glazed with grief and lack of sleep. "Let me make a phone call."

"It's four-thirty in the morning."

"It'll be all right. I just need to talk to someone."

Owen shrugged and watched Lizzie retreat to her office. He'd thought a lot about how to approach his aunt tactfully, show her he knew she was lying, and persuade her to tell the truth. But he'd just been about as tactful as a tornado, browbeating her when they were both stricken with grief.

While he waited, he put fifty cents in the hospice vending machine and pulled the handle releasing a Milky Way bar. The bar fell into the delivery tray with a solid thunk that reminded him of Kate's "Miracle of the Milky Ways." He hammered the side of the machine for loosening the memory, wondering how many other inanimate objects would remind him of his loss. His loss. Jesus, what a selfish way of looking at her death.

"Hit it again for me," Lizzie said from the doorway. She switched on the overhead lights, pulled a key chain from her apron pocket, and unlocked a cabinet under the coffee machine.

"It reminded me of Kate," Owen said, feeling faintly foolish.

"Things have a way of doing that. After a while, you'll be glad they do."

Lizzie took a bottle of Scotch from the cabinet, filled two coffee mugs with the liquor, and handed one of the mugs to Owen. "Seems like you're a little ahead of me."

"I didn't know it showed."

"I've known a few Scotch drinkers in my time. You reek of it." Lizzie sipped at her mug, took a deep breath, and said, "Cooter's Bend happened just the way I told it—"

"Lizzie, you and I both know that's not true," Owen interrupted.

Lizzie held up her hand. "I'm not a vending machine, Owen. Don't hit me until you hear me out. It happened just the way I told it," she began again. "Except it was Bobby Ray did the shooting."

Fixing her eyes on the mug of Scotch, Lizzie filled Owen in on the events of that stormy night, beginning with the anonymous phone call. She told him how Bobby Ray had dropped her off and gone on to Cooter's Bend, and how she heard shots and hurried to the Bend to find Mattingly dead.

"So you see," she concluded, "I am responsible. I sent that poor addled man out there with a shotgun. I deserve whatever I get from the county."

"But you don't know it happened the way Bobby Ray told it."

"Oh, Owen. He's not bright enough to make things up. He's like a child in a lot of ways."

"But even a child will lie about who hit first in a fight. Are you sure Bobby Ray didn't panic and fire first?"

"I heard the shots. It sounded like more than one gun."

"But you're not sure who fired when?"

"No. But I believe Bobby Ray."

"But the sheriff found no evidence that anyone fired at Bobby Ray from the truck. So either Bobby Ray is lying or you've been set up."

"Set up for what?"

"I'm working on that. I'll know more when I find out for sure where those nighttime truck runs are going. In the meantime, I'd like to pass your story by a lawyer I know."

"Your ex-wife?"

"That's right."

"My lawyer thinks I did the right thing."

"It won't hurt to get a second opinion."

"I thought I was doing right, Owen. Even when it came to lying. But it keeps getting more and more complicated. What's that saying about a tangled web?"

Owen frowned and recited, "'Oh what a tangled web we weave, when first we practice to deceive.'"

Lizzie sighed. "Guess I just need more practice."

"No. I think we just need to start untangling the web."

Owen stood up. His head ached and his vision swam. As he fought to focus his watery eyes, he became aware for the first time that he'd been operating on little food and less sleep.

"You all right to drive?" Lizzie asked. "You're welcome to stay here."

"I'll be okay. It's not that far." Owen hugged his aunt. "I think I need to be alone."

He walked out into a cold darkness barely lit by a haloed half moon. As he fumbled the key into the car's ignition, a mixture of bile and chocolate rose in his throat. He opened the car door and leaned out, waiting for the release vomiting would bring. When it didn't come, he spit the mix of Milky Way and stale Scotch onto the frost-covered driveway.

The asphalt steamed where his spew dissipated the frost. He hung out the door, staring at the steaming pool, hoping for some sort of release from the evening's grief. When that didn't come either, he closed the door and cooled his sweating forehead against the window.

Too weak to turn the ignition key, he slumped forward against the steering wheel. Then he must have dozed off, because the next thing he knew, the moon had vanished and the sun was a thin promise behind a thick wall of hill-country fog.

OWEN ARRIVED HOME too tired to undress completely, or even to make it upstairs to his bedroom. He slept fitfully for four hours in the same downstairs room he'd used when the thigh-high cast had limited his movement. The makeshift bedroom opened onto the dining room, and the first thing he saw when he awoke was the table, set for two, with pinched-out candles and a silver bucket holding melted ice water and a wine label that had floated free of its bottle. In the cold light of day, it was a pretty sorry seduction scene. But he knew he'd never intended it as anything but a celebration between friends. He couldn't imagine that Kate would have seen it differently. And even if she had, she never would have driven five miles out of her way to Gobbler's Grade to fortify herself with morphine.

Owen put away the candles and ice bucket, showered, dressed, and called his ex-wife, who was just starting her day in her California law firm. "That nun I told you about. My friend from college? Someone killed her."

"My God!"

He supplied the few details he had, realizing in the process how little he had to go on. When he'd finished, he added, "That's not all. The accident I told you about. The one that put me in a cast? It was no accident. Someone tried to kill me."

"Why didn't you tell me?"

"I didn't want to worry you."

"By telling me now, with the body count rising, aren't you afraid I'll bypass worry and go directly to hysteria?"

"I hope not. I need your help."

After a short silence, Judith said, "There's more, isn't there?"

"There's more." Owen related his early morning conversation with Lizzie, when she admitted her confession was a lie.

"She's got a local lawyer? Someone I can work with?"

"She called somebody before telling me the truth. I gather it was her lawyer."

"Set up a meeting with Lizzie and her lawyer for late tomorrow morning. I'll fly out of here as soon as I can. If I can't make it all the way today, I'll come as far as Cincinnati and take the first flight in tomorrow. I'll let you know when to meet me."

"Will Lizzie still need a lawyer if she tells the truth? Won't she skate free? Isn't it Bobby Ray we have to worry about?"

"People retract confessions all the time. It doesn't usually get them off. Especially if the charge is murder. Most likely, the county will just bring separate charges against Bobby Ray."

"Didn't I read somewhere that 'The truth will set you free'?"

"It was Christ who said that. And look at what happened to him."

TEN

Videotape, Lies, and Sex

As SOON AS DUSK settled over the hills, Owen took Ken Kaylor's infrared lights and cameras and began installing them in rural mailboxes along the route he expected the yellow trucks to follow out of Doubtful Hollow. It was the first opportunity he'd had to set up the cameras since his cut-down cast had left him with enough mobility to negotiate the slopes next to the winding country roads. He'd looked forward to tracking the trucks electronically ever since Maggie Mason's joke about his ass-backward assumptions had left him thinking he knew what Mountain View was hauling out of the hollow under the cover of darkness. Kate's death, though, had lessened his fervor for the task. Now there were more important puzzles to ponder. Still, the job of plotting possible routes on his map of Mountain View's mine holdings and setting up the cameras gave him something to occupy his mind.

He installed the first camera on Possum Break Road in a mailbox that was so rusty and full of spiderwebs that it was obvious no one had checked it for mail recently. He labeled the tape and set the camera's sensor to record the time and videotape any movement on the road.

Rusting, abandoned mailboxes were more prevalent than he would have expected, and Owen managed to find four more along routes he'd marked on the map. One route he wanted to check, a little-used mining road, had no mailboxes at all. On another route, a stretch of highway edged with brand-new mobile homes, all the mailboxes were shiny and likely to be checked daily by their owners. On these two routes, he installed mailboxes from the local hardware store in places where they weren't likely to attract much attention.

He finished placing the sixth and last camera in a newly purchased mailbox along the deserted mining road just after ten o'clock. Mountain View Development had so many local holdings that six cameras wouldn't be enough to cover all the possible routes in a single night, but he expected to narrow the options and pinpoint the trucks' destination with no more than two or three nights of videotaping.

After adjusting the sensor on the last camera, Owen drove home and set his alarm for six in the morning. Judith had called from Cincinnati and would be arriving on the first commuter flight. Ordinarily, he'd look forward to seeing her, but Kate's death had drained him of all enthusiasm. He fell asleep wishing that the paths that would have to be traced to find her killer could be plotted as neatly as the truck routes on his geological survey map.

LIZZIE AND HER LAWYER were sitting in rockers on the hospice porch when Owen brought Judith in from the airport the next morning. When the lawyer, whom Lizzie introduced as Guy Schamp, stood to meet them, he surpassed Owen's six-foot height by at least four inches. He was slim and slightly stooped, either from age or from bending to make eye contact with shorter companions. Schamp's face was crosshatched with wrinkles, and a razor nick reddened the corner of one of the many tiny squares formed where the horizontal and vertical lines intersected. He wore a white panama hat and a white linen suit that was totally wrinkle-free, as if to compensate for his timeworn countenance. His eyes were slate-gray, with a perpetually amused expression that was accentuated by the horizontal wrinkles, and the hand he extended to Owen and Judith was delicate and neatly manicured.

After pulling up two more rocking chairs and inquiring politely about Judith's flight and the ride from the airport, Guy Schamp got right to the point. "Lizzie tells me y'all question our decision to make her the prime suspect in this here case." He spoke with a pronounced accent that married a soft Virginia drawl with the nasal twang of West Virginia's coal country.

The "y'all" Schamp was referring to included Owen out of politeness, but he was looking at Judith, his fellow lawyer, and she responded. "You know she's innocent. Why complicate the situation with lies? As an officer of the court, you place your standing in jeopardy, not to mention Lizzie's freedom."

Lizzie reached across to the arm of Schamp's rocker and covered his hand with her own. "Is that so, Guy? Could you be hurt by all this?"

Guy Schamp patted Lizzie's hand. "Not to worry. Your freedom's not at risk, and neither is my license." To Judith, he said, "Lizzie here could let her teeth rot and you couldn't find twelve people in this county who'd convict her of having halitosis."

Judith ran a hand through her brunette bangs. "That kind of clean-denture defense assumes you'll have a jury that knows Lizzie personally. But anybody who does will almost certainly be disqualified."

Guy leaned back in his rocker, extended his long legs, and crossed them at the ankles, exposing white linen socks embroidered with clock faces. "There's knowing and there's knowing. It's a small county. Everybody in it has an aunt or an uncle or a neighbor whom Lizzie has nursed through their last days on earth. You can't disqualify everybody in the county."

"But the sheriff has evidence that Lizzie was a quarter-mile away just before the shooting started," Judith said.

"Long as they're prosecuting Lizzie, they're not likely to use that evidence."

"Seems like you're taking a big chance," Judith continued. "The prosecution will say nobody fired at Lizzie. They'll argue she threatened publicly to kill the first man to drive a dump truck into Doubtful Hollow and went ahead and did just that. That's a charge of premeditated murder."

Guy rocked slowly while Judith was talking, then stopped to deliver his response. "Lizzie will say she was fired upon. The jury will believe her."

"But there's no evidence of it," Owen said.

"The jury will believe Lizzie," Guy repeated. "Not some young deputy who couldn't find shells that whizzed by and could have wound up half a mile away."

"Why wouldn't that same argument hold if you tell them the truth and give them Bobby Ray?" Judith asked.

Guy stopped rocking and said slowly, enunciating each word separately, "A...jury...will...believe...Lizzie." He shook his head. "They won't believe Bobby Ray. They'll see a dim, confused man who has to be constantly reminded which end is up. They'll assume he panicked and fired without provocation."

"Which could be what really happened," Owen said.

"No, it isn't what happened," Lizzie said. "I have to believe Bobby Ray."

Guy reached out and patted Lizzie's hand. "Of course you do, darlin'. You know and trust him. But a jury won't."

"So you think if you dangle just a little piece of the truth in front of them, a jury will snap at it," Owen said.

"But they'd choke on the whole thing," Guy replied. "Like the poet says, 'Too much truth is uncouth.'"

"Was it a poet or a lawyer who said that?" Owen asked.

"Poet wrote it, lawyers quote it." Guy smiled, accenting the rhyme.

"I'm sorry," Judith said. "I just don't buy it. You're saying the jury won't believe the truth, but will swallow a bigger lie you've concocted around a more attractive defendant."

"My dear," Guy replied, "you just flew in from California. Does the name O.J. Simpson strike a responsive chord in your memory?"

Judith bridled. "That was a sad day for our profession."

"I agree," Guy said. "But an instructive one. Believe me, the DA doesn't want to bring Lizzie here to trial. That's why he's agreed to all this delay. But he'd jump at the chance to convict Bobby Ray."

Owen could see that Judith was about to blow up. "Do we have to decide this now? The trial is still three weeks off. I'm working on something that might prove both Lizzie and Bobby Ray were set up."

For the first time, Guy Schamp stopped rocking when someone else was talking. "When will you have this evidence?"

"Could be as early as tomorrow. By the end of the week at the latest."

"If you're talking about tracking those trucks, all that will do is give someone else a motive," Judith said. "Nothing more."

"Even that would be a help," Guy said.

Judith shook her head. "You're saying you'll defend what you know to be a lie with a bigger lie. I don't see how I can be a part of a defense that has Lizzie confessing to something she didn't do."

"But my dear," Lizzie said, "I've already confessed."

"And we have no duty to the court to disclose a false confession," Guy said.

"But as lawyers, we can't put our client on the stand if we know she's going to commit perjury," Judith said.

"It may never come to that," Guy answered. "And you don't have to be a part of it. I can handle Lizzie's defense all by myself."

"You're willing to risk Lizzie's freedom on her clean dentures and your ability to charm a jury with your down-home twang?" Judith asked.

Guy smiled, then said without a trace of drawl or twang, "But my dear, I don't need the accent."

"So it's a put-on?" Judith said, half smiling. "Won't the poor hill-country folk on the jury be outraged to know you're mimicking them?"

"My dear, you misunderstand me. I'm not mimicking those poor hill-country folk at all. When I talk like this," Guy said in perfect, accent-free diction, "I'm mimicking you."

"THAT ARROGANT BASTARD," Judith exploded in Ruth's room following the meeting on the hospice porch. "He could be disbarred for what he's doing. And he's risking Lizzie's freedom."

"I can't believe Guy Schamp would put Lizzie in harm's way," Ruth said from her bed. "The two of them go way back."

"That condescending minor-league Matlock," Judith fumed. "'My dear' this and 'my dear' that."

"I don't know," Owen said. "I kind of liked him."

"That was obvious," Judith said. "You were no help at all. Going along with his big stall. Why didn't you fill me in on this guy?"

"I just met him for the first time myself."

"You could at least have told me what was going on." Judith refused to be placated. "But no. You spent the whole trip in from the airport talking about this murdered nun. You know what I think? I think you were in love with her."

"Judith!" Ruth said. "She was a nun."

"He's not denying it."

"It's silly," Owen said. "It's got nothing to do with what just happened."

"You haven't been straight with me," Judith said. "You could at least have backed me up. I felt like a fool down there on the porch. Why bring me all the way across the country if you weren't going to support me?"

"I missed you," Owen said. "I'd forgotten how sexy you are when you're mad."

"That kind of inane statement just makes me madder."

Owen squinted his eyes in an exaggerated stare. "You're getting madder without getting any sexier. Maybe I was thinking of someone else."

"Owen, what a thing to say," Ruth said. "Apologize to Judith."

Owen held up his hands in mock surrender. "I apologize. I was just trying to add a small laugh to our day." He backed away, reaching for the door handle. "You two have a nice visit. I'm going to find someone who appreciates my sense of humor."

"That might take a while," Judith said.

MAGGIE MASON WAS ASLEEP, her head nearly buried in the profusion of flowered pillows. Owen saw the sheet of notebook paper he'd left on her bedside stand and tiptoed over to look at it. Trucks had run in and out the last two nights. Last night, the first night he had cameras running, Maggie's wavering accountant's hand had written "2:45 a.m." in the column labeled "Out."

"They're running pretty regular again," Maggie said from deep in her pillows.

"Sorry," Owen said. "I was trying not to wake you."

"'S'all right," she said in a dreamy slur. "Always glad to see you."

"I had cameras out last night. Pretty soon I'll know exactly where they're going."

"It's a help, then?" Maggie asked, nodding toward the notepaper.

Owen clasped her thin hand. "It's a big help." He surveyed the stack of paperbacks on the nightstand. "Looks like you're almost through the Lewins."

"I've slowed down some. I like him, though."

"I'll bring you some Stephen Greenleafs. If you like Lewin, you'll like him."

Maggie patted his hand. "Got a joke for you." She motioned for Owen to come closer. "State trooper pulls over a pickup in Mingo County," she said in a low whisper. "Asks the driver if he's got any ID."

Maggie slumped back into her pillow. "Driver looks at the trooper, says, 'Bout what?'"

Her delivery of the punch line trailed off into her pillow, as if the effort had exhausted her. Owen was so concerned he didn't laugh.

"Get it?" Maggie whispered. "Any ID about what?"

Owen smiled and squeezed her hand. "I get it."

"Good," Maggie said. "That's good." She closed her eyes, murmured something unintelligible, and fell back asleep.

AT HOME THAT EVENING, Owen set up the TV monitor that Ken Kaylor had provided and began tracking the progress of the truck Maggie had heard at 2:45 in the morning. The camera on Possum Break Road had picked it up at 2:50. Ten minutes later, the truck appeared on the camera he'd installed in a mailbox beside State Route 85. Owen plotted its progress on the map he'd prepared. So far, it was following the same path it had taken that night over a month ago when he'd followed it in the Toyota.

After that, the truck dropped off his radar screen. It didn't show up on any of the cameras he'd planted farther along its potential route. He swore and checked his map. It could have taken either of two side roads after passing the camera on Route 85 before it would have appeared again on one of his tapes. He'd have to reposition a camera on at least one of the side roads. To be absolutely sure, he'd record traffic on both of them.

He explained the problem to Judith and asked if she wanted to ride along while he repositioned his cameras. She agreed, folded her glasses, returned them to their case, and dropped the case and her cell phone into a leather tote bag.

"I see you succumbed to some cell-phone salesman's pitch," Owen said.

"I haven't had a lot of other pitches lately. Besides, I couldn't live without it. Keeps me plugged in to the office."

"You see them everywhere. They tell me at Saint Vincent's that babies are being born with one hand on their ear."

Judith laughed. "Didn't you do a study for the CHP when cell phones first came out?"

Owen followed Judith out and locked the door behind them. He knew his mother always left it unlocked, but years of living in California and Washington had conditioned him to locking up. "Our cell-phone study was back in the mid-eighties. The Highway Patrol was worried that its nine-one-one lines would be clogged with Good

Samaritan calls if the phones became popular. And they weren't convinced it was safe to hold a phone conversation while driving."

Owen slid in behind the wheel of the car and fastened his seat belt. "Of course the manufacturers claimed that dialing a phone while driving was no more dangerous than tuning a car radio."

"And what did you find?"

"The manufacturers were right. Dialing is no more dangerous than tuning a radio. Trouble is, tuning a radio while you're driving increases your chances of an accident considerably." Owen switched on the car radio. "That's why I'm going to dial in some country music from Wheeling before we start out."

Judith put her hand on Owen's. "Leave it off. I want you to tell me again what you think is going on. It just sounds so crazy."

Owen let her hand rest on his for a few seconds before turning off the radio. "I know it sounds weird. But I'm pretty sure they're mining coal they already took out of Dismal Mountain."

"But why do it after dark?"

"For one thing, there's a court injunction against scalping a mountaintop for coal. Even if there weren't, they'd have to fill twenty three-ring binders with application materials and wait two years to get a permit."

"So they're just trying to get around the injunction and the paperwork?"

"It's more than that. To mine coal, they'd have to post a sizable bond and pay $250,000 an acre into a mitigation fund for the stream they buried in Doubtful Hollow. With all the debris they dumped there, I figure they're avoiding well over a million dollars in non-refundable penalties."

Owen pulled off to the side of the road, waited until there were no headlights in either direction, and retrieved the camera he'd installed in a rusted mailbox at the head of an overgrown gravel pathway. When he returned to the car, raindrops began to dimple the windshield. As he turned on the wipers, Judith asked, "Why wouldn't they have to pay the penalty anyhow? They filled up the hollow."

"Because as far as anyone knew, they were developing a shopping center, not mining coal. The penalties are only levied on coal miners."

"That seems like a pretty silly distinction. The critters they crushed in the hollow aren't likely to care what they did up on the mountain.''

"It gets even better," Owen said. "They're not only avoiding the penalties and the environmentalists, they're dodging the United Mine Workers as well. If I'm right, they're just picking up coal that they pulled from Dismal Mountain, trucking it to one of their other mines, and passing it off as coal from that mine. From the size of the cut, I'd guess the coal alone could be worth eight million."

"Enough to make it worth killing you for following their truck."

"This is Hatfield-McCoy country. People have been killed for a lot less."

"What would they do if they caught us videotaping them?"

The question stopped Owen cold. He'd been so caught up in his own calculations that he'd discounted the danger to himself. But he realized now that he never should have brought Judith along. "I think we're okay as long as they don't actually see us with the cameras," he said. "And installing the equipment and replacing the tapes is a quick in-and-out operation. If someone finds a camera during the day, they can't connect it to me. Even if they could, I can always claim they're part of a traffic-surveillance study like the one Ken and I worked on in Washington."

They'd be okay as long as no one saw them tonight, he thought. He'd just have to be extra careful when retrieving the last camera and installing the two he'd retrieved on the side roads. "When I'm sure where they're putting the coal, I'll bring in the sheriff. That should put an end to it."

"When will that be?"

"It shouldn't take more than another night or two of videotaping."

By the time Owen turned down the road to the mobile-home development where he'd installed a new mailbox, the rain was coming so fast the wipers couldn't dispose of it. The shiny metal homes reflected swimming patterns of silver light in the heavy downpour as he drove slowly past and turned onto a gravel road beyond the end of the development. He turned off the car's headlights, switched on a flashlight, and played the beam on a lone mailbox set at the end of the gravel lane on a knoll well back from the main road. "That's my mailbox and my camera."

"Why so high up?"

"I wanted it back from the main road, so I needed the elevation to be sure I'd catch all the traffic."

They waited and watched. There were no other cars on the road. Heavy rainclouds covered the moon, and the only lights shimmered from the distant windows of the mobile-home park.

"I'm going to get the spade from the trunk and bring in the mailbox and the camera," Owen said.

"I'll go with you. You'll need somebody to help keep the camera dry."

Owen used the spade as a cane to help the two of them struggle up the slippery slope to the mailbox. When they reached it, he disconnected the camera and infrared light and slipped them into Judith's tote bag. Then, with Judith making a tent of her raincoat, he attacked the base of the mailbox with his spade. While the rain made the leaves slippery underfoot, it hadn't soaked in deep enough to ease the spading.

He cleared the dirt from one side of the post supporting the mailbox, circled it with both hands, and wrestled it back and forth, trying to pull it free of the earth. His walking cast slipped on the wet leaves, but he clutched the mailbox to steady himself and could feel that his weight was about to slide the post free. Before that happened, a searchlight from the main road pierced the pelting rain and outlined Judith's billowing raincoat.

Owen grabbed Judith and tugged her out of the spotlight. They fell to the wet earth and scrambled away from the beam, slipping and sliding down the backside of the knoll.

"Y'all come back here!" an unnaturally loud voice boomed over the hillside.

Owen slid feet-first down the slippery hill, coming up short in a roadside ditch. He groped for Judith, found her hand, and limped away as fast as his cast would allow. The ditch deepened as they scuttled along it, and they were soon waist-high with the curving roadway.

The searchlight swept back and forth across the trees above them, moving slowly in their direction.

Owen spotted the lip of a corrugated metal culvert running under the roadway, and he pulled Judith into it just as headlights swept around a curve and lit up the ditch they'd been following.

The searchlight moved slowly from the ditch to the hill and back again, as if the operator knew what he was doing and had all the time in the world to do it.

They sat side by side in the tight cylinder, bent over with their chins nearly touching their knees. The ridges of the corrugated metal pressed into Owen's back, and the runoff soaked through the seat of his trousers. He put his arm around Judith, who shivered against him.

An amplified voice boomed, "Mailbox tampering's a federal offense, kids. Come on out now."

Owen could feel Judith relax beside him. "It's only the cops," she said.

"Come on out and we'll go easy with you," the voice boomed.

"Let's go on out," Judith whispered. "It's your mailbox, after all." Her lips grazed his ear as she spoke and she gave him a quick, reassuring hug. "What have we got to lose?"

"A night in jail and the whole county hearing about my videotaping," Owen said. "I say we stay put."

The sweeping searchlight crept closer.

"He's bound to find us," Judith whispered.

"Not if he stays in the patrol car. He'll pass right over this culvert. You can't see it from the road."

"But if he gets out of the car and looks in the ditch, we're dead meat."

"I'm betting he won't leave the car. The rain's on our side."

The searchlight swept the trees directly above them, and the car bumped over the culvert. They sucked in their breaths, but the car didn't stop.

Owen exhaled and nodded toward Judith's tote bag. "Give me your cell phone."

"Who are you going to call?"

"The cops." He dialed 911. When the operator answered, he said, "I'm at the corner of Gump's Grade and Highway 81."

The operator interrupted him. "What county is that, please?"

Oh, God, he thought. It's some sort of central operator for the cellular network. "Raleigh," he answered. "Please hurry."

"I'll connect you with the sheriff's office. Let me give you the number in case we're cut off."

The pelting rain reflected the searchlight's beams.

Two long rings carried over Judith's cell phone. Then a voice answered, "Sheriff's Office. Can I help you?"

"I'm at the corner of Gump's Grade and Highway 81. There's been a terrible accident. A truck and a sports car. You better get somebody here right away."

"Your name, sir?"

"Cummings. Edward E. Cummings." He tried to work some of the panic he felt into his voice. "Oh, God. It looks like they need help. Please hurry. I've got to go."

The patrol car continued down the road, sweeping the hillside with its searchlight. Owen entered the sheriff's number in the memory of Judith's cell phone in case he had to call back. The car stopped suddenly about a hundred feet beyond the culvert. "Maybe he just got the accident report," Owen said. They heard the car door open.

Judith squirmed against him. "Oh, shit. He's getting out."

A shortwave radio squawked through the pelting rain. They couldn't make out the words, but when the squawking stopped, the car door slammed, the siren began to blare, and the car sped back over the culvert and around the bend toward the accident intersection.

Owen patted Judith's shoulder and nudged her out of the culvert. "You get the car. I'll get the mailbox."

"Oh, for God's sake. Leave the mailbox. Let's just get out of here."

"We've got at least five minutes before he figures it out and comes back. They can trace the mailbox if they try. And my spade's still up there."

Judith pulled the hood of her raincoat up over her head. "You want to risk our necks for a twenty-dollar spade?"

"You'd risk our necks for a million dollars, wouldn't you?"

Water dripping from her nose, she gave him her "So what?" look.

"We're agreed on the concept," Owen laughed. "We're just a little far apart on the price. Are we going to stand here in the rain haggling over money?"

"You're getting off on this, aren't you? Go ahead, get your mailbox. I'll bring the car around."

Owen worked his way back up the slippery hillside in the driving rain, using low-hanging branches and slim tree trunks for handholds. He pulled the mailbox free of its loosened moorings, laid it across his lap with the muddy spade, and slid feet-first down the slope to Judith and the waiting auto.

Judith floored the accelerator as soon as Owen closed the Saturn's door, spewing mud and gravel in their wake as they slewed off the side road and sped past the trailer park.

Owen reached across and stroked her right hand, which clutched the steering wheel in a death grip. "It's all right, you can slow down. We don't want to attract any attention."

"Jesus Christ, that was really close." Judith's hazel eyes were wide and bright as the rain-streaked mix of light and shadow from passing street lamps played across her face.

Owen directed her to a little-used mining road, where he relocated the reclaimed infrared system in an abandoned mailbox. There were no other cars on the road, but the edge from their narrow escape added drama to the simple camera hookup.

The remaining camera installation went off without a hitch, but Judith was still keyed up on the drive home, drumming her fingers on the wheel, checking the rearview mirror, and overdriving her lights. Owen wanted to take her hand, try to calm her, but he didn't want her driving one-handed in her current state. His own high gave way to anger with himself for having been so careless as to expose her to danger.

Owen's funk deepened on their return home when he switched on the lights in his empty dining room and the bare table reminded him that the evening's activities left him no closer to understanding how Kate O'Malley died. He felt frustrated and angry.

Judith hung up her dripping raincoat and started to pull her damp sweater over her head. "I'll say this for you. You sure know how to show a gal a good time."

Sensing his mood change, she stopped with the sweater still clinging to one arm. "Something wrong there, crime-stopper?"

"I just feel like I'm looking for the wrong answers to the wrong questions in all the wrong places."

Judith pulled the sweater free of her arm. A damp vee at the neck of her blouse made the fabric transparent. She took a step toward him, focusing his attention. "Have you thought of looking upstairs in the shower?"

"What do you think I might find there?"

She began unbuttoning the damp blouse. "Me, if you're quick enough."

In bed afterward, they started slowly, nuzzling and kissing and fingering familiar places. As his desire mounted, Owen realized he'd forgotten how close passion could be to rage. And then he didn't care.

ELEVEN

If You Can't Solve It...

A RUMPLED QUILT trailed off the side of the bed and a pillow lay on the floor beside it, just out of reach. Owen retrieved the pillow and sat on the edge of the mattress. He was fluffing the pillow when he felt Judith's foot on his bare back.

"Morning," she said, kneading his backbone with her toes.

"Pillow was on the floor."

"So I see." Her toes worked their way down to the base of his spine. "That was quite a night."

Owen held up two fingers in a victory signal. "That would be our finest shower."

Judith laughed. "Where'd that come from?"

"Winston Churchill, I think."

"You know what I mean." Her toes started back up his spine. "Where'd all that come from?"

Owen covered his lap with the pillow. "I guess abstinence makes the heart grow fonder."

"For someone else, in my experience."

"Beg pardon?"

"Remember Jack Nicholson's joke in *Chinatown?*"

Owen's sleep-dulled memory churned slowly and conjured up an image of the actor's bandaged nose. "It only hurts when I breathe?"

"No. The one I had in mind was, 'Where'd you learn to screw like a Chinaman?'"

"Doesn't ring a bell."

"Man goes to his Chinese laundryman for advice on how to please his wife in bed," Judith started to explain.

Owen's sluggish memory caught up with the joke. "Oh, yeah. And when he applies the advice, the wife says..."

Judith joined him in repeating the punch line: "'Where'd you learn to screw like a Chinaman?'"

Owen laughed, turned quickly, captured Judith's bare foot, and began massaging it. "Are you saying you detected something of the Orient in my technique?"

Judith's eyes seemed to focus on something outside the bedroom window. "It's not that, exactly."

"What, then?"

Judith propped herself up on one elbow. The sheet fell from her shoulder, showing a discolored bruise at her collarbone.

"Did I do that?" Owen asked.

Judith touched the bruise tenderly. "I'm not complaining, mind you. I mean, that's the best sex we've had in years. It's just...you weren't yourself."

"I hope you're not implying the sex is worse when I am myself."

"That's not it."

"What, then?"

"I don't know where you were, but you weren't with me."

Owen reeled in the rumpled quilt. "Well, somebody sure as hell must have been here."

"You know what I mean. Your mind was somewhere else. With that woman, I think."

Owen shoved Judith's foot off his lap. "Oh, come on. That woman was a nun."

"I think I'm a little jealous of her."

"You don't think..." Owen's mind couldn't form the image. "Look. We were so far from..." He shook his head. "It never even came up."

Judith pushed at the pillow on his lap with her foot. "I surely hope not."

"We talked, is all. About our lives. What we believed. What we loved." He raised his hand to make a point and was surprised to find it trembling. "What we hoped for."

Judith slid forward, took the trembling hand, and rested her head on his shoulder. "I think that's what I'm jealous of."

THE HEAVY RAIN of the previous night had slowed to a steady drizzle by mid-morning when the postman made his rounds. Seeing Owen on the porch, he climbed the stone steps and bent to close his umbrella, dripping water from the clear-plastic cover of his blunt-billed cap.

He touched the cap with the tip of his furled umbrella. "Morning, Owen. How's your mom?"

"Doctor says the chemo seems to be working. He's pretty optimistic. I could be bringing her home in a month or so."

A smile creased the postman's face. "That's great news. Not many come back from Lizzie's."

"Mom may beat the odds."

"That's just great. How are her spirits?"

"Better than anytime since I've been back. You ask her, she says, 'I'm in good shape for the shape I'm in.'"

"That sounds like your mom, all right. Tell her I asked after her." He reached into his bulging mail pouch and handed Owen a sheaf of envelopes and folded magazines held together with a blue rubber band. "Just some bills, looks like, and a flyer from Dusty Rhodes. Best senator money can't buy. He's new since your time here."

"I heard one of his campaign songs. The takeoff on 'Country Roads.'"

"He's a pistol, Dusty is. A real throwback."

The wet leather smell of the pouch reminded Owen of rained-out baseball innings. "Still umpiring high-school games?"

"Gave it up five years ago. Seems like the kids and their parents wanted to argue every call from 'Play Ball' on."

"I remember one ball-four call that was worth arguing."

"You didn't complain at the time."

"I was shell-shocked. I'd just walked in the run that cost us the state championship."

"Still, you didn't raise a fuss. I appreciated that. And you won it all the next year."

Judith appeared in the doorway. Her feet were bare and she was wearing form-fitting jeans and a red plaid shirt knotted just above her navel. "I thought I heard you talking to someone."

"I don't know if you've ever met our letter carrier, Bill Farley," Owen said.

Judith shook Bill's extended hand. "Oh, yes. It was sometime ago, though. Your daughter was in one of Ruth's classes."

"That *was* sometime ago," Bill said. "Betty Lou's a freshman at Marshall now."

"That's right," Owen said. "Mom's been retired for nearly ten years."

"Doesn't seem that long," Bill said. "I'll be retiring myself soon."

"About time," Owen said. "Your eyesight's been bad ever since I was in high school."

Judith looked puzzled. "I must have missed a sentence somewhere."

"It's a long-standing quarrel," Bill said. "I have been wondering about my eyesight, though. I've started to see imaginary mailboxes."

Owen tried to keep his voice calm and reasonable. "Where do you see these mailboxes?"

"Well, there's just one, actually. I saw it yesterday out by Gump's Grade. All by itself in the middle of nowhere. Not even that close to the road."

"What makes you think it was imaginary?" Owen asked.

"When I drove by this morning, it wasn't there."

"You sure you had the right place?" Owen asked.

"Pretty sure. I poked around. It looked like someone had pulled out a post sometime recent."

"The Unabomber," Judith said. "Before they caught him, he experimented by blowing up rural mailboxes."

"But he wasn't anywhere near civilization," Owen said.

"Was there any debris around the spot?" Judith asked the postman.

"I didn't see any."

"Oh, come on," Owen said. "The Unabomber's in jail. What are you saying? That there's a copycat loose aping his warm-up routine?"

"I'm not saying anything," Judith said. "I just know that if I saw a strange mailbox in the middle of nowhere, I wouldn't go anywhere near it."

"But that's silly," Owen said.

"Better safe than sorry."

"If you really believe there could be a bomb, you ought to call the sheriff, at least," Owen said, watching for the postman's reaction.

"That could be embarrassing," Judith said. "I'd watch it from a safe distance for a week or so. If nothing happened, and there was no mail and no explosion, then I might mention it to the sheriff. Let him figure out why there's a mailbox in the middle of nowhere."

"That sounds like a better solution," Owen said. "What do you think, Bill?"

Bill was contemplating Judith's bare midriff. "Watch it from a distance. Yeah, that makes sense." He raised his gaze to her hazel eyes. "So. You two are back together?"

"We're working on it," Judith answered.

"Working on it," Owen echoed.

"That's great. That'll make your mom almost as happy as a clean bill of health." Bill reopened his umbrella. "Looks like the drizzle isn't going to stop. Can't let it stay me from my appointed rounds." He stopped on the bottom step and nodded to Judith. "Nice seeing you again. Don't forget to say hi to your mom, Owen."

Back inside the house, Owen couldn't contain an incredulous chuckle. "The Unabomber?"

"It was all I could think of. I didn't see you coming up with anything."

"Bill's no dummy. I don't think he bought it."

"He doesn't have to buy it. We're after reasonable doubt here. If he sees another one of your mailboxes, we want him to leave it alone for a while. Or if he can't do that, call the sheriff."

"Those damn mailboxes. So far, I've had to lie to the hardware store about rehabilitation, to the law about an accident scene, and now to the postman about imaginary bomb threats."

"You ought to be getting good at it."

"With any luck, we'll nail the truck's destination before I have to lie again." Owen leafed through the mail left by the postman. In addition to the election flyer, there were two bills, one from the telephone company and one from St. Vincent's hospital, a personal letter for his mother, a *Newsweek,* and an L.L. Bean catalog.

"Anything good?" Judith asked.

"Just a letter for Mom and some bills." He stuffed the letter in his side pocket and tossed the bills, unopened, on the marble-topped table beside the door. "I'll get to them the first of the month."

THE RAIN HAD STOPPED when Sheriff Reader knocked on Owen's door just before noon. Almost before he was in the door, Owen asked, "Do you have the autopsy results?"

"Not yet."

"But you'll bring them as soon as you get them?"

The sheriff fixed his glass eye on Owen. "Not so sure. You haven't exactly been forthcoming with me."

"What do you mean?"

"Got me a deputy, Hube Roberts. You talked to him the other night when you called us to report Sister Mary's disappearance."

"He was no help at all."

"I chewed him out a little for that. It's lucky for you I did."

"How so?"

"Hube was on patrol duty last night. Out around Gump's Grade he came across two teenagers vandalizing a mailbox." He shifted his gaze to take in Judith. "Leastways, he thought they were teenagers."

Owen groaned inwardly.

"Hube says he would have corralled them if the poet e e cummings hadn't called in a phony accident report up the road a piece."

"e e cummings?" Judith asked.

"Well, he gave his name as Edward E. Cummings. Course, he didn't identify himself as the poet. Too modest, most likely."

"Also too deceased," Owen said.

"Now, Hube's not the brightest bulb on the marquee. But he did take down the license number of a car parked near the scene of the crime. When he ran the plate and found the car belonged to the same man I reamed his ass about, he came to me."

The sheriff tucked his hat under his arm and sat down on the arm of the living-room couch. "Did me a little detective work. Somebody'd been up there on Gump's Grade stumping around with a walking cast, a spade, and a woman with a size nine boot."

"Eight and a half," Judith said.

"Noted." The sheriff looked from Judith's shoes to the stained heel of Owen's walking cast. "You want to tell me what's going on?"

Owen started at the beginning, explaining his theory that Mountain View Development was running coal they'd taken out of Dismal Mountain through one of their other mines under cover of darkness to avoid permit procedures, penalty payments, and union wages. He showed the sheriff his map of Mountain View's mining properties, then ran one of his late-night videotapes through the VCR.

"Pretty elaborate setup," the sheriff said, tapping the TV screen, which glowed with the frozen image of a yellow dump truck. "Why not just let me tail their trucks?"

"You tried that," Owen said. "They didn't come out. And even if they had, they wouldn't have dumped the coal if they saw you following them."

"Why only one truck a night?"

"My guess is that they're trying to limit the number of people involved."

"Take them forever at that rate."

"They think they've got forever."

The sheriff traced his finger along the map of mine holdings. "When will you know where they're dumping the coal?"

"I should have a sure fix the next time they go out."

"Let me know, hear?"

"I was planning to."

"Should have told me before you set up your cameras. Would have saved a lot of grief."

"I thought the fewer people that knew about it, the better off I'd be."

The sheriff tapped his badge. "That imply you don't trust your elected representatives?"

"I didn't mean it that way."

"Best you start trusting somebody besides yourself. Last time you lit out on your own, you wound up an air bag away from eternity."

Owen nodded.

"Lemme warn you, though. If my deputies get sent on anymore snipe hunts by e e cummings, T.S. Eliot, A.E. Housman, or any other writers with initials for a name, you're going to get a little private cell time to contemplate their collected works."

OWEN LEFT JUDITH talking with his mother in her hospice room and went upstairs to visit Maggie Mason and check on the previous night's truck movements. Maggie was asleep, and Owen was concerned to see that her stack of unread paperbacks was just as high as it had been during his last visit. When he checked the notebook paper on her bedside stand, though, he found she'd written "no trucks" in her log for the previous night.

Owen reported the lack of movement to Judith as they were driving Ruth to her chemotherapy treatment.

"You think they knew we were waiting to record them?" Judith asked.

"Let's hope they just got rained out."

"We should have taken a rain check ourselves."

Owen reached over and caressed Judith's hand. "I don't know. The post-event fireworks were pretty spectacular."

The maroon bill of Ruth's Cincinnati Reds' hat poked over the top of the front seat. "What's going on with you two up here?"

"Just a little hand-holding, Mom," Owen answered.

Ruth slid back into her seat. "About time."

OWEN SET ASIDE the dog-eared *New Yorker* he'd been reading in the clinic waiting room while they waited for his mother's treatment to end. "Mom's happier than I've seen her since I've been home. I think it's you."

"I think it's us," Judith said. "She likes seeing us together."

"You think she picked up on last night's activities?"

"Hard to misinterpret your fireworks comment."

"No, she just knows. She's got some kind of a built-in radar that tracks my semen output. When I was a teenager, I was always convinced she knew whenever I'd been masturbating."

"When you were a teenager, it would have been a bigger trick to know when you *hadn't* been masturbating."

Owen flung the *New Yorker* at Judith, but the pages rippled open and it fell to the floor halfway between them, causing the nurse at the reception desk to look up from her Rolodex. He retrieved the magazine, shuffled through the other periodicals on the waiting-room table without finding anything of interest, and slumped back into his chair.

When Owen had been silent for a long period, Judith asked, "Is something wrong?"

"It's this damn waiting. I can't track the trucks until they move again, and there's nothing to be done about Kate's death until the autopsy report's in."

"Kate. You call her Kate."

"It's her name."

"Everybody else calls her Sister Mary Perpetua. Or Sister Mary Perp."

Owen sighed, shrugged, and shuffled through the magazines

again, picking up a copy of *Computer Age*. "Know what?" he asked Judith.

"No, what?"

"When I was in graduate school, computer memories were just beginning to grow exponentially." He tapped his fingers on *Computer Age*. "It made a lot of things possible. You could beat a problem to death by looking at every conceivable answer. We had a saying, when problems got too big or cumbersome or had too many variables for a closed-form solution—"

"What's a closed-form solution?"

"One where you can work through the math and get a unique answer. Anyhow, the saying was, 'If you can't solve it, simulate it.'"

"And just how does that relate to our discussion of teenage masturbation?"

"We're going to simulate it."

"That should be interesting."

"You're being deliberately obtuse."

"Would you rather I be randomly obtuse? I don't have any idea of what you're talking about."

Owen stood up. "We're going to simulate the shooting at Cooter's Bend."

"Oh, well. That explains it."

Owen backed out of the waiting room. "Stay here. Wait for Mom. I'll try to be back before she finishes."

OWEN DROVE TO the hardware store, where he roamed the aisles, trying to find anything that might help with the simulation he had in mind. He finally purchased a stopwatch, a volleyball net, a roll of twine, and two flashlights with the largest lenses he could find.

As he paid at the checkout counter, the proprietor asked him how the painting went.

"The painting?"

"You know. Those mailboxes I sold you. Your hospice therapy."

"Oh, that." When did a lie finally come to rest, he wondered. "It was a disaster. Most of the patients were too sick to paint anything. Those who did try were so depressed all we got were a lot of black tubes."

"Well, I'm still game to sell the good ones."

Owen tucked the long, rectangular box with the volleyball net under his arm and picked up the plastic bag holding his smaller purchases. "Maybe for Halloween."

"I DON'T SEE WHAT you hope to learn from this playacting," Lizzie said.

Owen was driving the hospice van with Lizzie beside him in the front seat and Judith and Bobby Ray behind them. "I'm not sure myself," Owen said. "But you always learn something from a simulation. You learn something just setting it up."

"Like what?" Lizzie asked.

"Like what's important." He pulled the van off the side of the road onto a dirt turnaround. "This where you waited the night of the shooting?"

Lizzie pointed out a tree stump that cast a long shadow in the twilight. "My rocker hung up on the roots from that stump."

"Okay," Owen said. "I'm going to leave you here. Whenever you're ready, I want you to light out for Cooter's Bend. Try to move about as fast as you did the night of the thunderstorm."

Lizzie stepped down from the van. She was wearing the combat fatigues she'd worn on Owen's first trip to the hospice. "Will I need my shotgun?"

"Not just yet." Owen handed Judith the stopwatch. "You go with Lizzie. Time the trip from here to Cooter's Bend."

Judith took the watch and climbed out of the van to join Lizzie.

"Can I ride up front with you?" Bobby Ray asked.

"Sure, come on up," Owen said. "I need you to show me where you parked on the night of the shooting."

They drove a quarter mile up the winding road to Cooter's Bend, where Bobby Ray pointed out the window at a wide turnout. Owen pulled off the road and tried to follow Bobby Ray's finger. "Here?" he asked.

"Back up a little."

Owen backed up slowly until the van's rear bumper was about five feet from the first of several birch trees that stood between the turnout and a shallow creekbed.

"Right about here," Bobby Ray said.

"Headlights on or off?"

"Off."

"Did you wait in the van or outside it?"

"In the driver's seat."

Owen shut off the van's engine. "All right. Now show me where the truck was."

"At first? Or afterward?"

"At first."

Bobby Ray pointed up the road. "It come from thataway, then turned left into this here clearing."

Just as Bobby Ray stopped pointing, a Mercedes convertible swept around the curve toward them and made the left turn he'd just described. "Just like that," Bobby Ray said. "Wow. That was pretty good."

The Mercedes driver cut his engine, turned off his lights, and stepped out of the car, cradling a shotgun under his right arm.

"It's Mister Schamp," Bobby Ray said.

Lizzie's lawyer was wearing a corduroy hunting jacket with a leather patch on the right shoulder where the gun stock would rest. In the fading light of day, standing beside his tan convertible, he looked to Owen like an ad for *Town and Country* magazine.

"Nice car," Owen said.

"Thank you. It was my retirement gift to myself. I've had it almost twenty years."

"What about it?" Owen asked Bobby Ray. "Is he parked about where the truck was?"

Bobby Ray squinted as if remembering gave him a headache. "The truck was a lot longer. He pulled off far enough to clear the roadway."

"Can you pull forward a little?" Owen asked Guy.

Guy nodded, got back in his car, and inched it forward, leaving it parked at a forty-five-degree angle to the roadway.

"Is that about where the front of the truck was?" Owen asked Bobby Ray.

"That's about right."

"Lights on or off?"

"On. Shining past me into the creekbed."

Owen took a stick and outlined the location of the front and near side of the Mercedes, tracing a large L in the clay of the turnout.

"Better get that beauty out of the line of fire," Owen said to Guy.

"Gladly." Schamp drove the Mercedes forward and parked on the fringe of the turnout, about twenty feet from the hospice van.

Owen pounded one of the stakes for the volleyball net into the corner of the L he'd drawn around the Mercedes' original parking place. He was about to drive another stake beyond the tip of the L near the roadway when Lizzie and Judith, half trotting and half walking, rounded the bend beyond the hospice van.

Judith hurried over to Owen, breathing hard. She held up the stopwatch and panted, "Five and a half minutes." Then she bent double, straightened, and took two deep breaths.

Owen jotted down the time in his pocket notebook. "That feel about right?" he asked Lizzie.

Lizzie took off her camouflage hat and ran her hand through the wisps of gray hair that had worked their way loose from her bun. "I might have been a little faster back then. I was pretty excited."

Owen wrote "(minus ten percent?)" in his notebook and announced, "We'll say between five and five and a half minutes."

It was dark by the time Owen finished setting up the volleyball net along the long leg of the L he'd traced in the clay. He draped yellow sheets from the hospice over the net, then set up five folding chairs, seats outward, along the short leg of the L. He draped a yellow sheet over the chairs, and then set two large flashlights on the end chairs where the truck's headlights would have been.

Owen turned on the makeshift headlights. "All right, there's your truck."

"It's a volleyball net and a bunch of folding chairs," Bobby Ray said.

"Bobby Ray," Lizzie said. "Remember what I told you about simulation?"

"You mean it's like pretend."

"That's right," Lizzie said. "We're going to pretend that's a dump truck."

"All right, let's get started." Owen stationed Guy Schamp behind a tree near the headlights of the fake truck and sent Judith and Lizzie to opposite ends of the turnout to watch for traffic.

"Now, you said you were waiting in the van," Owen said to Bobby Ray. "What did you do when the truck pulled in?"

"I walked out to talk to them."

"With or without your shotgun?"

"With."

Owen handed Bobby Ray a shotgun from the back of the van. "What happened then?"

"They shot at me."

"How far did you get before they shot at you?"

"Ten, maybe twenty steps."

"Okay, take your shotgun and walk toward the truck."

"Right now?"

Owen pressed the button on his stopwatch. "Right now. Go."

Bobby Ray held his shotgun in both hands and took two tentative steps forward as if he were fording a stream. When he didn't sink, he walked more confidently toward the makeshift headlights and the draped sheets of the jerry-rigged truck.

Owen waited beside the van until Bobby Ray had taken fifteen steps. Then he switched on a small pocket flashlight, raised it once over his head, and brought it down quickly.

Guy Schamp stepped out from behind his tree and fired his shotgun in Bobby Ray's direction.

Bobby Ray turned tail and ran back toward the van, sliding feet-first to get it between him and the shotgun blast. "Jesus Christ," he said. "I thought this was supposed to be pretend."

"Most of it is," Owen said. "What happened next?"

"I sat here for a spell."

"Anybody say anything?"

"Not a word."

"Then what?"

"I peeked around the corner of the van and they shot at me again."

"Show me."

Bobby Ray peeked slowly around the corner of the van and quickly pulled his head back. As soon as he was under cover again, Owen raised and lowered his small flashlight once more and Guy Schamp answered with a shotgun blast.

Bobby Ray jumped when the shot rang out.

"What did you do next?" Owen asked.

"I shot back at the bastards."

"Okay. Wait till I say 'go' and do it."

Owen stood behind the van and waved his flashlight in a tight circle. First Judith, then Lizzie, answered by making circles with flashlights of their own, signaling that the road was clear in both directions.

"Go!" Owen shouted to Bobby Ray.

Bobby Ray jumped up, fired a shot toward the makeshift truck, and ducked back behind the van. His shot tore a low-hanging limb off the tree Guy Schamp was using as cover.

"I want combat pay for this, Allison," Schamp shouted from behind his tree.

"You should be paying me," Owen shouted back. "This is probably the most excitement you've had since you retired."

"Did I hit him?" Bobby Ray asked.

"Not so you'd notice. What happened next?"

"They fired more shots. Two, maybe three."

"Then what?"

"I shot back."

"All right, let's do it. Don't fire until I give the okay."

Owen stood and pumped his flashlight overhead twice. Guy Schamp fired off two rounds, his muzzle blazing in the dark.

Owen circled his flashlight, got answering circles from Judith and Lizzie, and tapped Bobby Ray's shoulder. "Go now."

Bobby Ray stood, took deliberate aim, and fired, shattering the flashlight simulating the truck's left headlight. "Got 'em," he shouted.

"Did you get 'em that night?" Owen asked.

Bobby Ray sat down behind the truck. "Not the headlight. But I heard glass shatter."

"When?"

"After my shot."

"Did they fire again?"

"Once, almost the same time I shot."

"Where were you then?"

"Behind the van here. Same as now."

"Did their shots come from the cab of the truck or outside it?"

"Outside it, I think. Over the hood, like."

"Then what?"

"The truck started rolling forward."

"Toward you?"

"Sort of. But then it veered into the creek."

"What did you do then?"

"I stayed put here. When I didn't hear nothing, I went to look."

"How'd you go? In a straight line?"

"Oh, no. I dropped down to the creekbed and went from tree to tree."

"Okay, show me." Owen checked his stopwatch. "First, though, show me how long you waited before you moved out."

Bobby Ray sat in the dirt behind the van, drumming on the stock of the shotgun with his fingers. After thirty seconds, he lifted his shotgun and moved from tree to tree until he reached the creekbed. At the edge of the creek he turned and moved upstream, still ducking from tree to tree and leveling his shotgun at an imaginary target.

Owen followed Bobby Ray until he stopped, then moved up behind him and switched on his flashlight. "This where the truck wound up?"

"Right here."

Owen swung the flashlight from the creekbed up to the turnout. Even after six months, he could still see broken bushes and mounds of spilled dirt that marked the path of the truck.

"Did you open the truck's door?"

"Jesus, no. I could see the guy was dead."

"And he was behind the wheel?"

"Oh, yeah." Bobby Ray shuddered. "What there was of him."

"Okay. I've seen enough." Owen climbed from the creekbed back to the turnout, waved his flashlight in two large circles, and shouted, "All ye, All ye, all out in free."

Judith, Lizzie, and Guy joined Owen and Bobby Ray at the van. "Pretty exciting stuff," Judith said. "Did you get everything you need?"

"Can we do it again?" Bobby Ray asked.

"Want to try shooting out the other flashlight?" Owen asked.

"I bet I could get it first try this time."

"I bet you could, too." Owen patted Bobby Ray's shoulder. "You did good, cousin."

Bobby Ray's smile lit up the darkness, then gave way to puzzlement when a siren sounded in the distance.

"Now that's a hell of a simulation," Lizzie said. "But your pretend cops are a little ahead of the timetable."

The siren grew louder, headlights swept around Cooter's Bend, and a patrol car with its flasher rotating screeched in alongside the makeshift dump truck. The siren stopped, a searchlight caught Owen and his cohorts in its beam, and Thad Reader's amplified voice ordered, "Just drop those shotguns right there, right now."

Guy laid his gun carefully on the ground, while Bobby Ray flung his away as if it were a snake.

The sheriff came forward slowly, his hand just above his unbuttoned holster. When he recognized Owen, he stopped and shook his head. "Might have known it would be you." He snapped his holster shut. "What is this? Another game of post office?"

"Just a little legal research," Guy said.

"Well, you've got the neighbors up in arms," the sheriff said. "They heard gunfire."

Guy nodded toward the gun at his feet. "I was shooting blanks."

The sheriff picked up the surviving flashlight from the near end of the makeshift truck and shone it on the shattered light at the far end. "Was it blanks that took out this flashlight and shot up this sheet?" He played the flashlight beam over the draped sheets, taking it all in. "This the way the truck was sitting when Sam Mattingly was shot?"

"That's the way it was, all right," Bobby Ray answered.

"For sure, that's the way it was," Lizzie added quickly.

The sheriff looked from Bobby Ray to Lizzie and back again.

"Don't you know how it was sitting?" Owen asked, hoping to distract the sheriff from Bobby Ray's answer.

"It was in the creek by the time I got here," the sheriff said. "Same as you, I thought," he added, looking at Bobby Ray.

"That's the way it was, all right," Bobby Ray repeated.

"We're about done here," Owen said. "We won't be shooting anymore blanks. I'm sorry if we disturbed the neighbors."

"Best you leave detecting to us professionals," the sheriff said.

"Just trying to help out where we can," Owen said. "Take the load off you so you can find Kate O'Malley's killer."

The sheriff's shoulders slumped visibly.

"You know something, don't you?" Owen said. "Did you get the autopsy results?"

The sheriff stepped away from his car's searchlight beam. "We got the autopsy results."

"Well?"

"You're not going to like them."

"It can't be any worse than not knowing."

The sheriff retreated toward his patrol car. "Can't we do this in private?"

Owen strode after the sheriff. "These people are my friends. Most of them were her friends, too."

The sheriff turned off the patrol car's searchlight, leaving its flasher as the only light illuminating the group closing in on him. "It was morphine," he said. "And there was more than one needle mark on her arm."

"What are you saying?" Owen asked. "That Kate was a user?"

"I'm just telling you what the coroner reported." The sheriff opened his mouth as if he wanted to say something, then closed it and shook his head from side to side.

"There's more," Owen said. "There has to be more. Was there any sign of a struggle?"

"No sign."

"But there's more," Owen insisted.

"There's more. But it gets worse, not better."

"How can it get worse?"

The sheriff sighed and scraped his boot along the dark clay. "Well, hell. It'll be all over the county by morning." He fixed his good eye on Owen. "Your nun friend was pregnant."

The rotating flasher turned the circled faces from cherry red to pale yellow and back again. Its insectlike whirr was the only sound in the quiet night.

Finally, Judith broke the silence. Her face flushed red and stayed that color as she glared at Owen and said, just loudly enough for everyone to hear, "You son of a bitch."

TWELVE

Last Kisses

WHEN THEY WERE ALONE in the car on the way home, Judith said, "You were right. You always learn something from a simulation."

Owen knew from the tightness in her voice where she was headed, but he answered with the logical response, "And what did you learn?"

"That you're a two-faced, two-timing, lying son of a bitch."

"No need to spare my feelings. Tell me what you really think."

"I think you're lower than snake shit."

"I don't suppose it would do any good to tell you I didn't sleep with Kate O'Malley."

"You already told me that. This morning. That's why I called you a lying son of a bitch."

"I didn't sleep with her." His mind couldn't form the image of the act he was denying.

"So we're talking another immaculate conception here? Funny, I must have missed the star in the East."

"All right. That's enough."

"I mean, don't you think we should alert the Vatican?"

Grief and rage mixed in Owen and he clenched the steering wheel to keep from lashing out. "I said that's enough. Drop it."

"To hear you talk about her, the church ought to be thinking canonization, at the very least."

"They don't canonize suicides."

"Kind of blew that pesky old chastity vow as well, didn't she?"

"Oh, yeah. Leap on that. Like you're an expert at keeping vows."

"That was years ago."

"I didn't check the statute of limitations. You're ragging me for something I didn't do. You ought to be willing to take a hit for something you did do."

"It's a matter of trust."

"Precisely. That's what I'm asking for. Just a little trust."

"How can I trust you? You lied to me."

Owen was so enraged and distracted he almost missed the turnoff to his mother's house. He screeched around the corner and slammed on the brakes. "I didn't lie to you."

Judith made no move to leave the car. "I'm not staying here. Not under the same roof with you. I can't trust you."

"Oh, for Christ's sake. This is crazy."

Judith clutched her shoulder belt with both hands. "You all but assaulted me last night."

The words stung Owen. "I thought that was mutual."

Judith slumped back against the passenger door. "I don't know you anymore."

Owen had never seen her like this. "Think about this," he said, as much to himself as to Judith. Choosing his words carefully, he pronounced them one at a time, trying to read her widened eyes. "Please." The eyes didn't react. "Stay." One blink, nothing more. "I need you."

Judith seemed to snap out of a trance. "You don't need me. Your mom's on the mend. Your aunt has Clarence Darrow's classmate for a lawyer. And you're about to blow the lid off this covert mining stuff. You don't need me."

Owen breathed a sigh of relief. He recognized this Judith. It wasn't easy to deal with her, but at least she was familiar. "It's not that simple," he said. "Something's going on. Lizzie was set up. Somebody killed Kate."

"Kate killed Kate. Are you in denial? She killed herself because you got her pregnant."

"I didn't get her pregnant. Goddamn it, why won't you listen to me?"

"Because nothing else makes any sense. If you didn't get her pregnant, then this woman you've been mooning over and everyone else admired was some kind of closet convent slut. How likely is that? If you didn't get her pregnant, who did?"

The question just fueled Owen's anger. "How the hell would I know? All I know is it wasn't me."

"This is where I came in." Judith opened the passenger door. "I'll get my things, call a cab, and find a hotel."

Owen watched from the car as she stormed up the stone porch

steps. He'd seen her this way before. No words of his would deter her. He had as much chance of changing her mind as of raising Kate from the dead.

THE FIRST THING Ruth asked when she got into the car the next evening was, "Where's Judith?"

"She decided not to come," Owen answered. "She didn't know Kate, and the idea of going to a rosary in her memory didn't appeal to her."

"Too bad they never met."

Owen didn't answer. They drove half the distance to the church in silence. Finally, Ruth said, "Well, are you going to wait all night to tell me Judith moved out on you?"

"Sounds like you already know all about it."

"She came to see me today. She was fixing to leave town."

Owen's stomach clenched and bile rose in his throat.

"Not to worry," Ruth said, touching his arm. "I talked her into staying. At least till this business with Lizzie is settled."

"I'm glad."

"I'd say you've got some fences to mend."

"More like a wall to tear down. She thinks I got Kate pregnant."

Ruth said nothing.

Owen glanced at his mother. A tear formed in the corner of her eye. "Oh, Mom. Don't tell me you think so, too."

"Owen, I'm your mother. I reckon I've felt every emotion there is toward you. I've felt anger, fear, hope, worry, and a hundred other things." She brushed at her eyelid with a fingernail. "Mostly, I've just been peacock proud. One thing, though, I've never been is ashamed. Not till now."

The words cut Owen deeply. "Mom, I didn't do this thing."

"Margaret Blair's boy, Mikey. He clerks at Angelo's Pizzeria. He says he saw the two of you holding hands. And Sister Mary was crying."

Owen struggled to remember. "She was crying about her mother's suicide, for Christ's sake. You don't get pregnant holding hands in a pizzeria."

"I know how people get pregnant, Owen. Lucky for you."

Owen shook his head. "How can you think I'd..." His mind wouldn't form the picture. His voice couldn't say the words.

"Truth to tell, it's a lot easier thinking it of you than thinking it of Sister Mary. I recall you had at least one girlfriend with a late period when you were still a teenager."

"You weren't supposed to know about that."

"I'm your mother, Owen. I know everything."

"Well, what you think you know about this is all wrong."

THE CHAPEL WAS packed with mourners. The four front pews on each side of the aisle were filled with black-robed nuns. Kate's body lay in state at the head of the center aisle, parallel with the altar railing. Two kneelers had been placed in front of the open coffin, and people had formed lines behind them to pay their last respects.

Owen and Ruth took a pew near the back, in two of the few spaces still available. People arriving after them stood in the side aisles and outer vestibule. Owen hadn't seen this many people in the church since he was an altar boy serving midnight mass on Christmas Eve.

He scanned the congregation. Many of the mourners looked familiar to him, older versions of regular mass-goers he'd known thirty years earlier. He wondered if these were the same people or their grown children. He also wondered if the father of Kate's child was somewhere in the crowd. If this were a movie, the guy would give himself away somehow. Throw himself on the coffin, overcome with guilt. So far, that hadn't happened.

The priest came to the altar wearing black vestments trimmed with gold embroidery. He knelt between Kate's coffin and the tabernacle and led the congregation in prayer. Rosaries rattled against the backs of pews as the mourners mouthed the familiar responses. Owen recited the once-familiar words like a mantra, without thinking, scanning the backs of heads, wondering if Kate's lover was mouthing the same words. Kate's lover. The thought stung him.

After the rosary, the priest faced the congregation and gave a short eulogy. Sister Regina Anne, the head of the convent, followed the priest to the pulpit and shared her memories of Sister Mary Perpetua, from postulant to nun. She was followed by Doctor Bake Morton, who read from index cards describing Sister Mary's life as a physician. All three focused on the joys of Kate's life, skirting the grim details of her death.

When the three prepared eulogies had been delivered, the priest

invited members of the congregation to come forward and share
their memories of Sister Mary Perpetua. A nurse went first, praising
Sister's bedside manner and citing samples of her healing humor.
As the nurse spoke, a procession of potential speakers lined up along
the communion railing so that they could follow one another to the
pulpit.

When the line of speakers had dwindled to half the length of the
communion railing, Owen rose from his seat. His mother reached
out for him, but he moved away, edged toward the center aisle and
started toward the railing, behind a postulant with her head bowed.
They were joined by a gray-haired woman Owen recognized as a
friend of his mother's. Owen couldn't remember her name, but he
nodded as she joined him in line. Instead of responding, she looked
down at the rosary beads she was working between her fingers.

Owen didn't know what he was going to say when his turn came,
but he trusted his instincts to find the right words. He could start by
listing her talents and all the things she could have done with her
life. Maybe he better not start that way, he thought. It implied the
convent was a bad choice. Well, what the hell. So far, none of the
speakers had mentioned her wonderful singing voice. Or her vol-
unteer work at Lizzie's hospice. So far, none of the speakers had
confessed to fathering her child, either. In fact, the only speakers
with the proper age and gender for fatherhood were Doctor Bake
Morton and the priest himself. And, except for Owen, there was no
one else waiting in the line who might qualify.

The postulant just ahead of him spoke haltingly of Sister Mary
as mentor, a shining example for the younger nuns. Owen listened,
readying his own speech. As soon as the postulant finished and
stepped down, the priest moved quickly to the pulpit and, looking
directly at Owen, said, "I'm sorry, that's all the time we have for
shared reminiscences. I would invite you all now to say your personal good-byes to Sister Mary."

The priest pressed his right hand against the black chasuble covering his heart and smiled down at Owen, giving him the "Father
Knows Best" look that all prelates seem to master. The woman
behind Owen made a barely audible noise that sounded like a slow
leak and went back to her seat. Owen turned and followed her,
feeling the eyes of the congregation boring into him with every step
he took.

Row by row, members of the congregation moved slowly to the

center aisle and formed two lines leading to the two kneelers in front of Kate's open coffin. Most of the mourners knelt swiftly, bowed their heads, made a hurried sign of the cross, and retreated quickly from the presence of death. Owen scanned the faces of the returning mourners, but none met his eyes.

Owen and Ruth were among the last to join the line of mourners. Only the two rows behind them and the four rows of nuns in the front pews remained when they reached the kneelers.

Owen knelt beside his mother. The gray pallor of Kate's face shocked him. The black habit and white bib framed her serene expression and accentuated the grayish tinge left by the embalmer. Jesus, Kate, he thought. I loved you. Why didn't you tell me? He rose unsteadily, walked around the kneeler, and stood in front of the open coffin.

A heavy black rosary was wrapped around Kate's folded hands. Owen reached in and took her hands in his own. Then he bent and kissed the still, gray lips. He was conscious of the strong scent of lilacs, and of a collective gasp from the nuns in the front rows.

Owen straightened and returned to the kneeler. Kate's rosary had left the imprint of three beads in the flesh of his palm. He rubbed the palm until the imprint disappeared. Beside him, his mother hid her eyes in steepled fingers.

VERN EMBRY WAS about to leave his office to go home when the phone rang. "Mr. Embry? Mr. Vernon Embry?" The voice was firm, commanding.

"Speaking."

"This is Special Agent Donald Kyle of the Internal Revenue Service."

Vern looked at Minna's picture and repeated the initials aloud. "IRS."

"That's right. We are in receipt of your letter of the twenty-eighth. These are serious charges you've leveled against your employer."

"I'm aware of that."

"Serious charges. With potentially serious repercussions."

"I'm aware of that as well."

"Yes, well. I'm not at liberty to speak as freely as I'd like, but you should be aware that we have had Mountain View Development under surveillance for sometime."

Vern wondered if that meant he'd have to share the reward. "I had no idea."

"Let me ask you, sir. Have you told anyone else about these charges?"

"No sir."

"That's good. That's very good. Now, Mr. Embry, I don't wish to alarm you, but the seriousness of your allegations, coupled with the findings of our own investigation, suggest that you could be in danger."

This call wasn't going the way Vern had envisioned it. "But I thought there were laws protecting my job."

"There are. And we're prepared to invoke them. But our current concern goes deeper than your job."

"Deeper? How?"

"We feel your personal safety could be compromised. We'd like to take you into our witness protection program as soon as possible."

"How would that work?"

"You will be fully briefed on the procedures."

"By phone?"

"In person of course. Leave your office as soon as possible. Go directly to your home. Pack a single suitcase, no more. Agent Thomas Wolfe will contact you there."

Vern took a circular band from his desk drawer, slipped it over the earpiece of his phone, and plugged the wire leading from the band into his tape recorder. "What about the reward?"

"Reward?"

"For being a relator."

"A relator?" There was a disturbing silence on the other end of the line. "Oh, yes, I see. As a relator, you'll be eligible for a percentage of the government's recovery, of course. I should tell you, though, that there are other claimants."

Vern's heart sank. "Other claimants?"

"As I indicated, we've been watching Mountain View Development for sometime."

"How many others?"

"I'm afraid I'm not at liberty to divulge that information."

The call was going from bad to worse. Vern decided to change the subject and test the waters a little. "What about my wife?" he asked, staring at Minna's picture.

"Your wife?" Another silence. "I'm sorry, your most recent return shows you to be a widower with no dependents. Has that status changed?"

"Excuse me?"

"Has your widower status changed? Do you have a wife?"

Vern winked at Minna's picture. "You must have misunderstood. I asked 'What about my life?'"

"You'll have to leave it behind, I'm afraid. Believe me, though, it's for your own good."

"That's a pretty big step."

"I realize that. Agent Wolfe will bring you to our office. We'll explain the program. The decision will be yours. If you decide not to relocate, we'll protect you as best we can in your current position."

"Protect me?"

"I don't want to alarm you, but we feel you could be in danger when this goes public."

"Why does it have to go public?"

"The court records in criminal proceedings have to be public."

Vern imagined Willis Grant's reaction. It wouldn't be pretty. "When can I meet your agent?"

"How long will it take you to pack?"

"Not more than an hour or so."

"Agent Wolfe will meet you at your home in two hours. And, Mr. Embry?"

"Yes?"

"Two things. First, I admire your courage in coming forward as you have. And second, I need to emphasize that you should discuss this conversation with no one. Do you understand?"

"I understand." Vern hung up, turned off his tape recorder, and put it back in his jacket pocket. He picked up his wife's picture. "Do you believe that, Minna? Man wants me to drop out of sight. I didn't think the IRS operates that way." He used his shirt cuff to polish the glass in the picture frame. "If that really was the IRS."

He kissed the picture and laid it facedown in his briefcase. "No matter who that was, we're going to have to leave town." He snapped the briefcase shut without taking anything more from his desk. The man on the phone was right about one thing. Wherever he was going, he'd have to travel light.

OWEN LED Sheriff Thad Reader about a half mile overland from the fire trail where he'd parked his patrol car. He stopped when his flashlight beam settled on a rump-sprung seat from an old pickup truck. The uprooted seat had been dragged to the center of a grove of elderberry bushes. Owen pulled off his backpack and dropped it onto the seat's peeling vinyl, then knelt beside it and pulled out a six-pack of Stroh's.

"All the comforts of home," the sheriff commented.

"If your home happens to be missing a TV, running water, and a refrigerator," Owen said. "I set this up earlier today. It can't be seen from down there."

He nodded down the hill to indicate the loading area and tipple of the Hash Ridge Mine, one of Mountain View Development's abandoned properties. The tipple overlooked a spur of the Norfolk & Southern Railroad.

Reader strained to make out the boxy shape of the tipple in the light of the waning moon. "We can't hardly see them, either."

"I'm going to fix that," Owen said. He handed the sheriff a beer and took two infrared spotlights from his backpack. He climbed the lower branches of an oak tree and aimed one of the spotlights at the base of the tipple. Then he climbed another oak and aimed the second spotlight at the mine face. He climbed down, used the remote to turn on the two spotlights, and took one of Ken Kaylor's infrared cameras from the backpack. Viewed through the camera lens, the work space below was as bright as day. Coal dust covered the asphalt loading area and clung to the surrounding bushes like black dew.

Owen handed the camera to the sheriff. "Take a look."

The sheriff sighted through the lens and whistled softly. "Sunlight bright."

He handed the camera back to Owen. "Tell me again why you think they're salting this mine."

"Last night my cameras picked up their truck going down Hash Ridge Run full and coming back empty. The mine hasn't had anybody working it for six months, but half the hoppers on that spur down there are full of coal."

"Coal from Dismal Mountain."

"By way of Doubtful Hollow. They've been running Dismal Mountain's coal through the Hash Ridge tipple because they couldn't get a permit to strip-mine the mountain."

"So they avoid permit fees and mitigation payments."

"And the UMW as well."

"Pretty slick." The sheriff popped open his can of Stroh's. "And what makes you think they'll run again tonight?"

"It's a nice night. They've been running pretty regular when the weather's good."

"What time did they dump last night?"

"In at three. Out before four."

The sheriff checked his watch. "It's just a little after one."

"They're not exactly punching a time clock. I wanted to make sure we got set up with plenty of time to spare."

The sheriff leaned back on the pickup seat, stretched his legs, and took a swig of beer. "Guess we better settle in."

Owen sat down beside him and opened a beer for himself. They clicked cans in the moonlight.

"You learn anything from that little charade at Cooter's Bend the other night?" the sheriff asked.

"Learned I'd like to see the truck Mattingly was driving."

"Thought you might."

"Can you arrange it?"

"I'll go with you. If memory serves, things don't quite line up the way they should."

"But you didn't check it out at the time?"

"Had me an uncoerced confession. Hardly seemed necessary to dot the i's and cross the t's." The sheriff sighted across his beer at Owen with his good eye. "Now, though, I'd be willing to bet that the person who confessed wasn't even at Cooter's Bend when Mattingly bought it. What do you think of that?"

"Sounds pretty complicated." Owen didn't like where the sheriff was headed, and decided to change the subject. "Anything new on Sister Mary Perpetua's death?"

"Got a pregnant nun with access to morphine who ODs on a back road. Far as I'm concerned, that's better than a duly notarized suicide note."

"So you're not investigating it?"

"Got better things to do with my time. So should you."

"It just doesn't add up."

"Maybe you just don't want it to."

"Why wouldn't I?"

"Try guilt."

"Bullshit. I didn't father that child."

"You want people to believe that, maybe you shouldn't have kissed her corpse in front of God and half the congregation of Sacred Heart Parish."

Owen slumped back into the pickup seat. "It seemed like the thing to do at the time."

They sat quietly for a while, listening to the chatter of locusts. The sheriff popped the top off a second beer, took a long pull, and said, "I kissed me a corpse once."

The flat statement jolted Owen out of his reverie. He looked over at the sheriff. "Vietnam?"

"You never went, did you?"

"No. I rode out a graduate-school deferment."

"Smart. I was teaching high school over in Mullens. History. Civics. Coached JV football. Marines came to the school recruiting our seniors. Made it sound so good I signed on myself and talked two of our football players into joining up."

The sheriff took another pull on the beer. "I was a supply officer. Rear-echelon stuff." He flicked his glass eye with his thumbnail. "Not far enough to the rear, as it turned out. Mostly, though, we sent supplies forward and bodies backward.

"I thought I'd get used to it. About halfway through my tour, though, I recognized the name on one of the body bags. Hampton Well beloved. Helluva name. Popped right out at me. One of the boys I'd recruited."

The sheriff shook his head slowly, but his glass eye stayed focused on the beer cradled in his two hands. "Boy'd been a tight end, six foot at least. But there was only about four foot of body in the bag. I knew better, but I opened the top to look. From his face, he might have been napping in the classroom." A dry, kissing sound escaped the sheriff's pursed lips. "You try not to think on death, but something draws your eyes to it."

"You never went back to teaching?"

"Figured I'd done enough damage to the next generation. The other boy didn't make it back either. They never found him."

"You weren't responsible."

"And you're not responsible for Sister Mary. People make choices. Sometimes even the right choices turn out bad." The sheriff took his gun from its holster and spun the cylinder. "Or leave you with a worse set of choices."

"Suicide isn't a choice she would have made."

"Neither was pregnancy, I should have thought." The sheriff broke open the chamber of his pistol and sighted through the barrel with his good eye.

"Expecting to use that tonight?" Owen asked.

"Never can tell. Been a while since I've had to. Just want to be sure the barrel hasn't healed up." He snapped the barrel back into place, returned the gun to its holster, unbuckled his gun belt, and pulled the holster onto his lap. Then he tilted his Mountie's hat over his eyes, slid down to a half slouch, crossed his arms, and said, "Wake me when the show starts."

THEY HEARD THE TRUCK before they saw it, a deep rumbling that shook the wooden piers supporting the dilapidated tipple. The sheriff jerked awake, and Owen trained his camera on the rutted approach road.

Gears grinding, the truck cleared a rise and loomed in the camera's viewfinder. Owen zoomed in on the front license plate, only to find it caked over with mud. The truck slowed to a near stop and a small, wiry man with a sharply pointed nose swung down from the passenger seat.

"Skeeter Dingess," the sheriff whispered. "He works for Letch Valence."

"Big surprise," Owen said. They watched as the small man windmilled his arms and pumped his grimy work gloves up and down in an attempt to guide the driver backing the load of coal up to the mouth of the tipple.

Owen adjusted the camera to get rid of the glare from the truck's windshield and handed it to the sheriff. "What about the driver? Recognize him?"

The sheriff peered through the lens at the night-lit scene. "Orry Estep. I'd know that bald top anywhere. Wind was right, we'd be able to smell him."

When the truck was positioned over the mouth of the tipple, Estep idled the engine, climbed down from the cab, and walked back to check the alignment. A burly, balding man with what was left of his dirty gray hair tied into a lank ponytail, he had cut off the sleeves of his denim jacket to reveal a bulging pair of coal-streaked biceps. He grabbed the trough at the tipple's mouth as if he wanted to tear it loose from its moorings and shouted something at Dingess.

The smaller man flinched and took two steps backward, as if he were trying to dodge the sound of Estep's voice.

Estep climbed back into the cab of the truck and, ignoring Dingess's hand wavings, pulled the load forward and backed it up once more to the tipple's mouth. Then he climbed down, rechecked the alignment and, evidently satisfied, shouted once more at Dingess.

The sheriff smiled. "Couldn't have moved it more than a mare's hair from the first position."

Estep returned to the cab, pulled a lever, and the truckbed slowly canted upward, disgorging its black load into the tipple's mouth. The first few coal lumps fell separately and skidded down the tipple's trough into the waiting hopper like the first drops of rain before a storm. Then the entire load tore through the tipple and thundered into the hopper. The tipple shuddered from its open maw to the rail tracks at its base and belched great plumes of coal dust.

Dingess backed away from the black plumes, waving his arms and coughing.

The sheriff strapped on his holster and nightstick.

"Going to do your duty?" Owen asked.

The sheriff squinted his glass eye. "My duty was protecting you. You look all right so far."

"Aren't you going to arrest those two?"

The sheriff gave a short, dry laugh and tapped his badge. "This here's an elective office I hold. Coal brings in three-quarters of my constituents' income. I'm not likely to last long as sheriff if I start arresting people for mining it."

"But they're breaking the state's laws."

"Bending them a little, maybe. Could be they even broke a few. But arresting those two good ol' boys down there won't get us much."

The sheriff snapped his holster shut and shoved it down on his hip. "Tell you what. You make a couple of copies of that videotape and tomorrow you and I will drive to Charleston, see the folks at the *Gazette* and the Department of Environmental Protection. They'll get you the action you're looking for."

THIRTEEN

Out of Sight

THE CHARLESTON *Gazette* broke the story under the front-page headline out of sight, out of mine, accompanied by a grainy picture made from Owen's videotape of Skeeter Dingess and Orry Estep dumping coal through the tipple of the Hash Ridge Mine. The story decried the environmental damage done to Doubtful Hollow, denounced Mountain View Development, and praised Owen, whom they identified as the grandnephew of Lizzie Neal and the man responsible for wresting damages out of Amalgamated Coal for its role in the dam failure that killed his father.

The Huntington *Herald Dispatch* chided the *Gazette* and other newspapers for their abrupt about-face from wholehearted support for the Dismal Mountain shopping center to near-universal condemnation when the development turned up coal. They characterized Owen in a single sentence as the "gadfly" who was responsible for driving Amalgamated Coal's jobs out of the county twenty-five years earlier.

Judith called to congratulate Owen on the success of his electronic vigil and his promotion to gadfly, which she viewed as a step or two above pissant. She hung up before Owen could persuade him to move back into his mother's house, or even to share a meal in neutral territory.

The local newspaper, the *Barkley Democrat,* put a picture of Maggie Mason on the front page above the fold and argued that the most serious offense of Mountain View Development was keeping her awake nights. In their view, the development company was entitled to profit from any incidental coal that turned up as part of its laudable and legitimate effort to build a shopping center. The continuation of the story on an inside page noted that construction delays continued to postpone the opening of the shopping center. A separate page-one article announced that the Candidate's Night scheduled for that evening would feature a debate on the Hash Ridge Mine's nocturnal windfall by the district's two state senate candidates, Democrat Elwin "Dusty" Rhodes and Republican Herbert Crane.

The *Wall Street Journal,* in an "Aside" on their editorial page, noted:

> The State of West Virginia cannot decide on an appropriate penalty for a contractor caught mining coal unearthed as part of a shopping-center development. The problem is a judicial injunction against mountaintop removal, a local euphemism for strip-mining. Representatives of the state's Division of Environmental Protection are trying to determine whether the coal was a byproduct of the commercial development, or the shopping center was a cover-up for an illicit mining operation. The absurdity of this chicken-egg controversy points up the futility of allowing left-leaning activist justices to set legislation through the liberal interpretation of federal statutes. Our sympathies are with the developer, who was caught black-handed. After all, a mine's a terrible thing to waste.

LIZZIE WAS SWEEPING the porch of the hospice when Owen arrived to take his mother to her chemotherapy treatment. "My nephew, the gadfly. Looks like you set all the mares' tails to swishing. You here for your mom?"

"Treatment time. How's she seem to you?"

"Lots better than the rest of my patients. What do her doctors say?"

"They say the treatments are working. But you'd never know it from talking to Mom."

"Chemo'll do that. It poisons the system. Your mom's not used to so much bed time. She'll come around." Lizzie flicked two golden maple leaves off the side of the porch with her broom. "While you're here, you ought to visit Maggie Mason."

"I came a little early to do that." Something in Lizzie's voice made Owen ask, "Is she all right?"

"She wouldn't be here if she were all right."

MAGGIE MASON'S EYES were closed and her frail hands were folded over a newspaper that lay on top of her flowered coverlet.

"Maggie. You awake?" Owen whispered.

"Just resting my eyeballs."

"How are you feeling?"

"Little tired." She lifted the newspaper a few inches above the coverlet. "Got my picture in the paper."

"I know. I saw it."

"Never had my picture in the paper." Her words were slow and measured. "Had my name in once, when I married the Mister. First time for a picture, though."

"It's a good picture."

"Waited till I was a size eight."

Owen didn't know what to say. He looked at the stack of paperbacks on the nightstand. "Can I bring you more mysteries?"

"No. Falling behind in my reading. Sleeping a lot."

"Anything else I can bring you?"

"Bless you, no. Want to thank you for the picture." She patted the newspaper. "And the paperbacks. And your visits."

"I should be thanking you. You helped me nail the truckers who ran me down."

Maggie let her left arm fall limply to her side. "You can thank me with a hug."

Owen bent forward, slid a hand behind her cotton print nightdress, and drew her upper body to him. He was surprised at how light she felt as he buried his head against her talcumed neck. He felt a dampness behind her ear where her cheek was pressed and realized that his eyes were tearing.

"I'll nap now," Maggie whispered as he lowered her back onto her pillow.

Owen moved toward the door. "I'll be leaving, then."

When he reached the door, Maggie spoke his name.

He stopped. "Yes?"

"It was nice meeting you, Owen Allison."

"It was nice meeting you, Maggie Mason."

As he descended the hospice stairs, Owen felt engulfed by futility. Maggie was dying. Kate was dead. His mother was fighting for her life. So much was out of his control. He tried to phone Judith to address one of the issues he could still do something about, but the motel said she wasn't in her room.

THE CANDIDATE'S NIGHT advertised in the *Barkley Democrat* was held in the gymnasium of the local high school. By the time Owen arrived, the bleacher seats along one side of the basketball court were filled, the court itself was packed with people, and teenagers were busy setting up extra rows of folding chairs in front of the bleachers. Guy Schamp's shock of straw-colored hair stood out above the crowd like a lighthouse beacon, and Owen joined him in the front row of folding chairs.

"Your little late-night foray got the candidates a full house," Guy said. "Everybody wants to see them walk a tightrope between the environmentalists and Big Coal."

On the narrow stage just in front of Guy and Owen, two wooden lecterns had been set up along a diagonal line that left them facing both the audience and a long table with three folding chairs. A lanky man wearing a polka-dot bow tie and a blue suit that failed to cover his shirt cuffs stood behind one of the lecterns, sorting through a pack of index cards.

"Herbert Crane," Guy whispered, nodding toward the man with the bow tie. "He kept quiet long enough to convince the local Republicans he was a staunch conservative. Actually, he just didn't have anything to say. Man's all hole and no coal."

"That doesn't disqualify him from public office," Owen said. "In fact, it might even help him get elected. What are his chances?"

"Slim to none."

"Why's that?"

Guy turned his head toward a tight knot of people clustered around a broad-shouldered man with the body of a football player a few years past his prime and an open, boyish face that could have been anywhere from thirty to fifty.

"Dusty Rhodes," Guy said. "Incumbent state senator with an eye on the governor's chair. Came out of nowhere eight or nine years ago and wants to follow in Jay Rockefeller's footsteps. I wouldn't bet against him, especially when all the Republicans can muster is Herb Crane."

Owen nodded. "I've heard Rhodes sing. On the radio."

Guy smiled. "You'll hear him sing in person tonight. Before the evening over, there'll be a spontaneous outpouring of demand for his talents. The state hasn't seen his like since Fiddlin' Bob Byrd. And Byrd stopped fiddling sometime ago."

"With his violin, anyhow."

"You got that right."

A tall, attractive woman with even features, gray-streaked brown hair that fell softly to her shoulders, and a knitted sweater-dress, adorned with Indian symbols, that dropped nearly to her ankles took the steps to the stage two at a time and knelt to talk to a man in the front row.

"Gail Meyers Connor," Guy explained. "She's head of the Society for Mountaintop Preservation. When your headlines shined a spotlight on this meeting and turned it into a full-fledged debate, she came down from Charleston and muscled her way onto the panel."

Gail Meyers Connor extended one arm, pointing toward a TV crew standing near the exit, and her flowing dress swept along the floor of the stage. The man she was talking to nodded and hurried off in the direction she was pointing.

"She looks like a woman used to getting her own way," Owen said.

"She is that. She's not bad, though. Some of these greenies are so blinkered about preservation, they'd have forced Michelangelo to put David's marble back in the quarry. Gail's not like that. You can talk to her." Guy smiled. "She don't always listen, but at least you can talk to her."

Owen pointed toward the three chairs behind the table on the stage. "Who are the other two panelists?"

"One's Walker Smith, head of the local Division of Environmental Protection. He's a good, solid government man. He was going to run the debate by himself until Gail showed up. I don't know who's filling the third chair. Probably got somebody from the coal companies to balance Gail. Doesn't matter who they got, really. It'll be Gail's show."

Walker Smith joined Gail Meyers Connor on the stage and invited Dusty Rhodes to join his opponent behind a lectern. Then he introduced Gail, as well as a man from Archway Coal, whose name Owen couldn't catch, and asked each candidate to state his opinion regarding the recent revelation that Mountain View Development was selling coal obtained in the course of the shopping-center construction.

Herbert Crane's position was clear. People needed coal, miners needed jobs, the state needed coal revenues, and Mountain View Development was well within its rights.

Dusty Rhodes was more circumspect. In his opinion, Mountain

View Development had found a useful loophole and exploited it. It was up to the legislature to decide whether to close the loophole, and up to the judiciary to determine whether Mountain View should be penalized for its actions.

Gail Meyers Connor addressed Herbert Crane, asking whether his views had been influenced by the sizable contributions he'd gotten from West Virginia's coal producers.

Crane blustered and answered that all West Virginia politicians, including his opponent, took money from the coal industry.

Dusty Rhodes smiled and interjected a comment before Gail could ask for a response. "That's true, Gail. My opponent took Big Coal's money and voted with them straight down the line in the house last term. I took half as much money and voted against them half the time in the senate. I figure if you can't take a man's money and vote against him, you don't belong in politics."

Someone in the audience twanged, "You tell 'em, Dusty," and the crowd applauded.

Gail waited for the applause to die, and then asked, "Mr. Crane, you say all the coal movement appears to be perfectly legal. Tell me, sir, if it's perfectly legal, why was Mountain View Development doing it in the dead of night?"

Herbert Crane's Adam's apple jumped up and down over his bow tie. He stared at his questioner like a cornered animal, finally saying, "I'm afraid I can't answer that."

Rhodes let his opponent sweat in the spotlight before saying, "I think we both know the answer to that, Gail. They were afraid people would jump to the conclusion that you're implying. Namely, that their chief purpose was to mine coal, not to build a shopping center."

"Isn't that a logical conclusion?" Gail responded. "After all, they've marketed thousands of tons of coal, but they haven't collected a single dollar of rent from the shopping center."

"Which hasn't opened yet."

"Still, nobody's shopping."

"As I understand it," Rhodes said, "the building contractors have been late in constructing the stores. Are you suggesting we start assessing penalties for broken contractor promises?"

"That might not be a bad idea."

Dusty grinned and pretended to take notes. "Be a real windfall for the state."

That answer garnered another round of applause. The advertised debate had devolved into a dialogue between the environmentalist and the incumbent senator. The moderator sat back and let the dialogue flow, and the other two people on the stage—the coal operator and the senator's opponent—appeared pleased to be out of the line of fire.

Gail continued. "By pretending to build a shopping center, the developers sidestepped a court injunction, dodged the miner's union, and avoided both a reclamation bond and mitigation fees of over one million dollars."

"One option the state has," Rhodes offered, "is to collect the mitigation fees after the fact."

"As I understand it, they've already mined at least three million dollars' worth of coal. Wouldn't that be like locking the barn after the horse is stolen?"

Rhodes smiled and appeared to consider the question. "More like collecting insurance on the lost property, I should think. It's all that could possibly be due the state, after all. The shopping center itself stands as the reclamation project the bond would have covered."

Guy nudged Owen. "Good answer."

"Your opponent claims all this activity is perfectly legal," Gail went on. "You characterize it as an open loophole. I ask you, shouldn't that loophole be closed?"

Rhodes tapped his upper lip with his forefinger, then smiled like a third-grader with the right answer and said, "Not necessarily. Loopholes are the lifeblood of politics. We politicians love opening them for friends and closing them for enemies."

Rhodes had been leaning with one elbow on the lectern. He suddenly dropped this friendly, bantering posture, gripped both sides of the lectern, drew himself up, and said, "We have laws, in my opinion, good ones, governing the filling of watersheds by any developer, whether he's drilling a mine or building a church. Mountain View Development abided by those laws. What you're calling a loophole, Gail, is the result of past legislation designed to assess monetary penalties against coal companies that strip our mountains and fill our hollows. We may not want to exact those same penalties from all developers."

"Why not?"

"Because it could stifle economic development. Coal companies can afford to pay the penalties as a cost of doing business. Other developers may not be able to.''

''Then they shouldn't be filling our hollows.''

Rhodes rapped the side of his lectern. ''This lectern is level because this stage is level. There are hills all around us. The state is built on a slant. This school isn't. In order to keep this school level, somebody had to dump some dirt somewhere. Should we have penalized them for that?''

''If they're upsetting the God-given contours of the land, I think we should.''

''Well now, Gail, I don't presume to know all God's plans, but I can't imagine he—''

''Or she,'' Gail interrupted.

Rhodes smiled. ''I can't imagine *he or she* wants West Virginia's schoolchildren to be sliding out of sloping seats just so we can preserve the lay of the land.''

Before Gail could respond, the moderator interrupted, saying, ''We seem to be drifting into issues of church and state here. Maybe it's time to take questions from the audience.''

Most of the audience members who responded to the moderator did not have real questions to pose, but rather gave rambling speeches that they turned into questions by asking the candidates, ''Don't you agree?'' when they had finished their discourses. A miner talked about the hardships of unemployment and the need for jobs; a woman announcing herself as a member of the Preservation Society complimented Gail Meyers Connor on her fine work and lobbied for stronger environmental laws; a helmeted bicyclist wearing spandex pants argued that all reclaimed coal lands should include bicycle paths. For their part, the candidates listened attentively and nodded agreement at the appropriate times. It was one aspect of campaigning that Herbert Crane appeared to have mastered.

When the moderator announced there was time for just one more question, a man behind Owen shouted out, ''Who's gonna win the election?''

Herbert Crane cleared his throat, cited polls that showed he was closing the gap separating him from Dusty Rhodes, and predicted that a lot of people would be surprised by the outcome of the election.

''I'm one of those people who's likely to be surprised,'' Rhodes said. ''Until tonight, I thought I had a pretty good chance. When I pulled into the parking lot outside and counted bumper stickers, though, I got the shock of my life. I counted seven for me, two for Herb Crane, and thirty for New River Gorge. It looks like New River Gorge will win by a landslide.''

In the general laughter that followed, the moderator rose to call the evening to a close. Before he could do so, a man holding a guitar jumped up on the stage, shouting, "Give us a song, Dusty."

The man held the guitar over his head and pumped it up and down like a weight lifter. In the crowd, people began to clap and chant, "Sing, Dusty, sing."

Guy nudged Owen. "What did I tell you? Spontaneous as a TV commercial."

Dusty took the guitar, slipped its strap over his shoulder, strummed a tentative chord, and favored the crowd with an "aw, shucks" smile.

The crowd cheered.

Rhodes leaned into the microphone and sang the opening lines of "Country Roads." The crowd's applause turned into rhythmic clapping. By the time Rhodes reached the chorus, singing, "West Virginia, Mountain Mama," the crowd was on its feet singing along.

On stage, Gail Meyers Connor swung her hips and clapped, her long sweater-dress brushing the floor with each dip of her shoulders. Walker Smith of the DEP clapped and sang, and the man from Archway Coal stamped his feet and clapped along. The only person on stage who didn't seem to be enjoying himself was Rhodes' opponent, Herbert Crane, who clung to his lectern with both hands as if the waves of enthusiasm from the audience might wash him overboard.

By the time Rhodes hit the second chorus, the crowd affirmed its pride of place by coming down hard on the words "West Virginia," stamping and shouting in time with the clapping.

Beside Owen, Guy Schamp clapped and smiled broadly. Owen looked around. Behind him, the crowd was chanting with the fervor of the newly saved at a revival meeting. Weathered faces forgot the problems of harsh mine work and harsher unemployment to clap and celebrate the winding roads of their home state. About halfway up the bleachers on the other side of the auditorium, Owen saw Judith, clapping and singing along. He tried to catch her eye, but her rapt gaze was fixed on the stage.

Rhodes ended the song by singing "Vote for me, Dusty Rhodes," and the crowd erupted in wild applause.

The moderator waited for the applause to die down and thanked everyone for coming, but no one was listening to him. People were already streaming toward the exits between the stage and the basketball backboards or moving aside the folding chairs to form small conversational knots. Owen picked his way through the departing masses, trying to reach Judith. He finally caught up with her at an exit near one end of the stage.

"Hey there," he called. In his hurry to catch up with her, he hadn't planned what he wanted to say. He was trying to come up with the words when a clump of people surrounded the two of them. Dusty Rhodes stepped forward from the center of the clump.

"You'd be the man of the quarter-hour," Rhodes said, extending his hand to Owen. "We owe you a vote of thanks for exposing this mess."

"Nice of you to say so," Owen said. "But it doesn't seem as if much will come of it."

"Oh, it will, it will. Believe me. I intend to introduce legislation closing that particular loophole."

"You didn't sound that certain about closing loopholes a little while ago."

"You say something like that in public and it becomes a promise. I need to work out the details and call in a few favors before I'm ready for that." Rhodes turned to Judith. "I don't make promises I can't keep."

Owen started to introduce Judith, but Rhodes waved him off, saying, "We met earlier, before I went on stage tonight."

"That was quite a show you put on," Judith said.

"Yes," Owen agreed. "I counted two quotes from Will Rogers, one from Woody Allen, one from Willie Brown, and the *Wall Street Journal*'s quote about a 'mine being a terrible thing to waste.'"

If Rhodes was perturbed by Owen's mild charge of plagiarism, he didn't show it. "I only steal from the best."

"Don't get me wrong," Owen added. "I agree with Judith. It was a pretty impressive performance. I certainly can't say the same for your opponent."

Rhodes looked around to see who was within earshot, then said, "My opponent's an idiot looking for a village. He'd let Big Coal strip the state. He doesn't understand you have to draw the line somewhere."

"I'm curious," Owen said. "Where'd you get your nickname?"

"My parents named me Elwin. When I went into politics, I tried shortening it to 'Win,' but 'Dusty' stuck. Anybody named Rhodes in this state is going to be nicknamed 'Dusty' or 'Lonesome.' It's almost a birthright."

"Why not 'Unimproved?'" Owen asked.

"Or 'Six Miles of Bad?'" Judith added.

Rhodes moved closer to Judith and ran his index finger down her bare forearm. "The two of you work well together."

Owen waited for Judith to say something, if only to acknowledge that they were a good team. But she just smiled at Rhodes and said nothing. Finally, Owen broke the silence himself, saying, "I thought maybe you were named for the old Giants' ballplayer."

"Hero of the fifty-six Series, you mean," Rhodes replied.

"I believe it was the fifty-four Series," Owen said.

"No, you're wrong. It was fifty-six."

Owen shrugged. "Well, it's your namesake."

A young woman pushed her way through the circle surrounding them. "Dusty, the TV people want that interview now."

Rhodes traced his finger down Judith's arm again and held out his hand. "You'll have to excuse me." He covered Judith's hand with both of his, then continued to hold her right hand with his left while he offered his right hand to Owen. "I hope to see you again," he said, looking from Owen to Judith. "Real soon."

Owen watched Rhodes cross the auditorium toward the TV reporters, then turned to Judith. "All right. Help me understand what just happened here."

"When he called you 'man of the quarter-hour,' I think he was referring to your fifteen minutes of fame. I don't think he meant it as a put-down."

"That's not what I meant and you know it. The man was hitting on you."

"He did seem to have awfully good taste. For a politician."

"And you let him."

"So did you. You seemed more interested in baseball trivia."

"He was wrong about the year."

"So you said."

Before Owen could respond, Sheriff Thad Reader joined them.

He tipped his hat to Judith, then took Owen by the arm. "Stop by my office tomorrow morning. I've set it up so we can take a look at Mattingly's truck."

"Great," Owen said. "Tell me something. What year was Dusty Rhodes' World Series homer?"

The sheriff frowned. "Fifty-four. Giants took the Indians apart. Rhodes' first homer came in the same game as Mays' catch. Helluva catch. Pretty dinky home run, though. Puny pop-up barely made the short porch at the Polo Grounds. Second baseman could have caught it if he hadn't run out of room."

Owen looked at Judith and asked, "Sure it wasn't fifty-six?"

"Nah. Fifty-six was Larsen's perfect game. Yanks against the Dodgers. Giants weren't even in the Series."

Owen raised his eyebrows and gave Judith an "I told you so" look.

Judith rolled her eyes and responded with a "big deal" look.

The sheriff raised both hands in mock surrender and backed away. "My police training in domestic disputes tells me I've just interrupted something here." He turned to Owen. "I'll see you tomorrow morning."

Owen watched the sheriff go, then said, "Fifty-four, not fifty-six."

"Oh, for Christ's sake. I don't get it. The man just mesmerized the audience, made several sensible proposals, and you're putting him down for not knowing the answer to some obscure Trivia question."

"It's not obscure. It's common knowledge."

"It's not common knowledge to me."

"I'm not surprised. You think third base belongs in the string section of a symphony."

"Actually, I've known since high school that third base is the final stage of foreplay. I'm surprised you think it's anything else."

"I can tell you're not taking this seriously."

"How can I? It's ludicrous. Let it go."

"It's not ludicrous. It's something anybody who calls himself Dusty Rhodes should know."

"Should know what?" Guy Schamp had approached from behind Owen.

"What year did Dusty Rhodes hit his World Series homers?"

"Fifty-four. Same year as Mays' catch."

Owen turned to Judith. "See? It's common knowledge."

Judith shook her head in disgust. "It must be some sort of guy thing." She patted Guy's arm. "No offense intended."

"None taken."

"If you'll excuse me, I don't have the time to wait while you conduct the rest of your exit interviews." Judith turned and walked back across the gymnasium floor.

"Was it something I said?" Guy asked.

Owen gave a quick account of his squabble with Judith, tracing it back to Rhodes' insistence that his namesake's home run happened in 1956.

Guy tugged at his lower lip. "One of the toughest trial lawyers I ever went up against would bait his conversation with little misstatements, just to see if you'd call him on them. And if you called him, how far you'd be willing to push it."

"Like a school bully testing how hard he could shove before you'd fight back."

"Something like that."

"But why would Rhodes bait me? I'm not running against him. I'm not even registered to vote in this state."

Guy took off his glasses and tapped an earpiece against Owen's chest. "Could be he calibrates everybody that way. Could be he's just keeping in practice. Could be you've got something he wants. Could be he figures to go up against you sometime in the future." He put his glasses back on. "Course, it could just be that he's not a baseball fan and really doesn't know it was the fifty-four Series."

Dusty Rhodes waved at Owen and Guy from across the auditorium. The TV cameraman was coiling his cable, and Rhodes had one hand on the shoulder of the young African-American woman who'd been interviewing him.

"Is the man married?" Owen asked.

"Wife's a psychiatrist in D.C. She shows up the last week of every election campaign. Word is, she really doesn't much like our fair state."

Rhodes leaned toward the interviewer, whispered in her ear, and pointed toward Owen and Guy.

"I don't think he wants for feminine companionship," Guy said.

The interviewer crossed the auditorium and introduced herself. "Senator Rhodes says you're the man who uncovered the mining operation," she said to Owen. "Mind if we interview you for TV?"

Owen shrugged. "Fine by me. I've already had eight minutes of fame, though. So you'll have to keep it under seven minutes."

The young woman didn't crack a smile. "We can do that." She straightened Owen's jacket and clipped a mike on his lapel. "With that cane, would you rather be sitting down?"

"Either way."

"Standing, then. I think the cane looks distinguished."

The interviewer ran through her instructions while the cameraman set up his equipment and adjusted the sound level. "Just look at me, not at the camera. I'll start with easy questions, ask you what made you suspect something fishy was going on, and see where it goes from there."

The cameraman indicated everything was ready.

"All right, let's go then," the interviewer said. "Doctor Allison, you were born here in Barkley, isn't that right?"

"That's right," Owen said. "And there's no need to call me doctor. You don't want your viewers calling on me for medical advice."

The interviewer smiled. "That's fine. We'll start again." She brought her microphone up to her mouth and then lowered it. "No, no. Look at me. Not at the camera."

Owen wasn't looking at the camera or at the interviewer. He was staring over the shoulder of the cameraman. Across the gym floor, Dusty Rhodes was leaving the auditorium. In one hand, he held a briefcase stuffed with papers. His other hand held Judith's elbow as he escorted her out.

FOURTEEN

Eyeball to Eyeball

As soon as he got home, Owen phoned Judith's motel room. When she didn't answer, he called again at ten-thirty and again at ten forty-five. He hadn't planned what he'd say to her. He just wanted to hear her voice, to know she'd made it back alone. When she still hadn't returned by eleven p.m., he left a message at the desk asking her to call him. The only plausible reason for continuing to call after eleven was the one he didn't want to acknowledge, his fear that she might become an intimate member of the group whose placards had dotted the auditorium that evening: VOLUNTEERS FOR DUSTY RHODES.

If Judith called back, he'd invite her to join him at the sheriff's office the next day to look at the truck in which Sam Mattingly had been shot. That would be his excuse for calling so late. Midnight passed without her calling back. Of course she might have returned and decided it was too late to call. He had no way of knowing. He had two beers to help him sleep, gave up waiting for her call, and finally went to bed at one a.m.

He tried to make his mind a blank, but it kept returning to those placards with a picture of Dusty Rhodes smiling over the word VOLUNTEERS and the image of Judith leaving the auditorium with the candidate. He tossed and turned for two hours, slept fitfully for two more, lumbered out of bed at five in the morning, and was at Lovisa's Café, across from the sheriff's office, when Bruna Lovisa opened its doors at six o'clock.

Owen had two cups of Bruna's hot cinnamon tea and picked idly at scrambled eggs until Sheriff Thad Reader pulled into the parking lot alongside his office. He left the café and intercepted the sheriff before he made it to the steps of the county building.

"Wasn't expecting you quite this early," the sheriff said.

"Early bird gets the worm."

The sheriff squinted at Owen with his good eye. "Looks like you're a man who's gotten a whole shovelful of worms already. They left tracks around your eyeballs. You stay up all night?"

"Might as well have. I hope it's not too early to see Mattingly's truck."

"It's not going anywhere. Just let me tell my office where I'll be." The sheriff climbed the steps and disappeared, then returned shortly with a ring full of keys and led Owen back to the patrol car.

Reader drove about two miles outside of town to a fenced-in area where dull, broken hulks of autos lined the narrow space between railroad tracks and a damp creekbed. The croaking of tree frogs rumbled up and down the creekbed.

"Pretty noisy for an auto graveyard," Owen said.

"Tree frogs in the morning. The sound of God farting."

Owen looked at the dank, stripped creekbed and the rows of rusted auto bodies. "If God has an asshole, we're not far from it."

The sheriff led the way down a tight, dusty path lined by the decaying remains of vehicles until they came to a locked cyclone fence encircled with bright yellow crime-scene tape. A grime-covered dump truck that had once been the color of the tape dwarfed the two other vehicles inside the fence, a blue Dodge Dart accordioned from a head-on collision and a wheelless patrol car sitting on cinder blocks.

The sheriff unlocked the fence gate, broke the yellow tape, and stood aside to let Owen enter.

Shards of glass still clung to the perimeter of the dump truck's shattered windshield. A length of red twine tied to the centerpost of the windshield had been threaded through the pockmarked steering wheel to the driver's headrest, which was torn and stained with reddish-brown blotches.

Owen photographed the shattered windshield and pointed toward the red twine. "That the trajectory of the shotgun pellets?"

The sheriff pursed his lips and nodded.

Owen positioned himself at the right front fender of the truck and sighted through the camera lens. "So the shooter stood about here?"

"Back a little. See there. Some of the shot spread and dimpled the hood."

Owen remembered that Bobby Ray said he hadn't left the cover of the hospice van until the truck was in the creek. He pointed over the hood to where the van would have been parked, well beyond the driver's side of the truck. "Strike you as strange someone would start from way the hell over there and walk all the way around the truck to shoot the driver from this angle?"

"In my experience, a man with a shotgun can go pretty much where he wants."

"You mean a woman with a shotgun," Owen said. "And she can't go wherever she wants if someone's shooting at her."

"There's no evidence any shots were fired from this truck toward the van."

"Even if you believe that, why would the shooter walk over here to the passenger side of the truck if there's no passenger? Why not just walk right up to the driver?"

"That's a good point. I wondered about that myself."

"When did you start wondering?"

"About the time I saw that little setup you rigged with the volleyball net and sheets."

"But not before?"

The sheriff bristled. "Look here, Owen. I had me an unsolicited confession. It was a cut-and-dried case. Still could be."

"I don't think so. Lizzie will plead not guilty. And Guy Schamp will shovel enough loads of reasonable doubt to bury the county's case."

"Let's stop fencing here, Owen. You and I both know Lizzie didn't shoot anybody. She's covering up for that slow-witted nephew of hers."

"She only thinks she's covering up for him. He didn't kill anybody either."

"Then who did?"

"Whoever rode the truck down to Cooter's Bend with Sam Mattingly. When they pulled in, the passenger fired a few shots, probably in the air, to keep Lizzie or Bobby Ray cowering behind the van, and then shot Mattingly from right about where I'm standing."

"Why shoot Mattingly? He's nobody important. Just an out-of-work miner."

"You don't have to be important to be a target. Somebody tried to kill me just for following a truck that looked about like this one right here."

"You think Mattingly got in somebody's way?"

"Don't you? Did he leave any people?"

"His wife Sarabeth."

"Did you talk to her?"

"Just to break the news about her husband's death."

"How'd she take it?"

"Like she'd been expecting it. She's a strong woman, but if it weren't for bad luck, she wouldn't have no luck at all."

"Can we talk to her? See what her husband might have been up to?"

"Now?"

"No time like the present."

THE BOXY HOUSE was one of three set well back from a potholed roadway. A row of plastic two-gallon milk cartons filled with murky water lined one side of a low porch that rested on a cracked foundation. The woman who came to the screen door might have stepped out of a Dorothea Lange dust-bowl photograph. She had a sallow, lined face that had once been pretty, framed by straight, gray-streaked brown hair, and wore a faded yellow print dress. Her feet were bare.

"Remember me, Sarabeth? Sheriff Thad Reader."

The woman unfastened the hook on her screen door, but made no move to open it. "You got more bad news to offload? Cause I've about had my fill."

"We just want to talk." The sheriff introduced Owen.

Sarabeth folded her arms across her chest. "You're kin to the woman that shot my Sammy."

Owen started to explain, "I'm Lizzie Neal's nephew, but—"

The sheriff interrupted. "We think there's a chance she didn't kill your husband."

"I heard she confessed," Sarabeth said through the screen door.

"We think she may have been covering up for someone," the sheriff said. "Can we come in?"

Sarabeth glanced back over her shoulder, sighed, and opened the door. "Come on ahead."

Owen and the sheriff entered the house and stood just inside the doorway. To their left was the living room, with a rocker, dilapidated couch, and a rabbit-eared TV. To their right was the kitchen. More water-filled containers lined the open wooden shelves above the sink.

"Got to apologize for my house. Went all to hell when they started blasting for that shopping center." She pointed to a broken window covered by a black Hefty bag. "Flyrock big as a football come right through that window. Lucky nobody was sitting near it. Only piece of good luck we had this year."

"The shopping center has to be a quarter of a mile away," Owen said. "And the flyrock still reached you?"

"Sounded like a hailstorm from hell sometimes. Other times the blast just shook the place up. Cracked our walls and broke our foundation. All but shut down our well. When it comes, what water we get now is puke yellow." She nodded toward the water containers over the sink. "I haul drinking water down from my sister's, but hers is none too good. Still use my own well water for washing, but it turns our clothes yellow."

"This all came from the blasting?" Owen asked.

"Yes sir."

"Can't you sue?"

"Takes money to hire lawyers. The Bellamys, next hollow over, tried it. Went into hock and lost anyhow."

Owen was stunned. "I can't believe it."

"Believe it," the sheriff said. "Big Coal rules these hollows."

"But these are shopping-center developers."

"Dynamite don't know the difference," Sarabeth said. "You light the fuse, you get the flyrock. Whether you're mining coal or setting up shops."

"Sarabeth," the sheriff said, "we came to ask you about Sam. How'd he seem in the time before he died?"

"How do you think? He'd been out of work for six months. He was a UMW steward, so he took it harder than most. Then the blasting turned our well sour and cracked our home."

"But he got work."

"Oh, yeah. He went to complain about the cracks and they took him on. He did a little loading and a little driving. But it didn't pay like mine work. Nowhere near." Sarabeth drew herself up to her full height. Her curled toes seemed to grip the warped wood flooring like talons. "Still, it was work. It kept him off the dole. And things were looking up."

"How so?" the sheriff asked.

"Day before he died, he stood right there in that doorway with a jar of moonshine in one hand, his lunch bucket under his arm, and a shine-simple grin on his face. Told me he'd finally picked his way into a paying seam.''

"What did he mean by that?''

"Don't rightly know. He was half pickled on moonshine. We finished off the jar and went to bed. Sweet Jesus, he was happy, though. Next evening, he was dead.''

"Would he have talked to any friends? Coworkers, maybe?''

Sarabeth shrugged. "Most of his friends were union men. This job wasn't union, so he didn't see much of them. Only coworker he ever talked about was the one who sighed him up. Skeeter somebody.''

"Skeeter Dingess?''

"Could be. Can't be that many people named Skeeter in this county.''

"Well, that answers all my questions.'' The sheriff turned to Owen. "Anything else you'd like to ask?''

Owen shook his head, started for the door, and then stopped. "There is one other thing, Mrs. Mattingly. I'd like to send a lawyer by to see you.''

"Mister, look around you. I'm dirt-poor here. I done told you I can't afford no lawyer.''

"This one wouldn't charge you.''

"Don't want no charity, neither.''

"Wouldn't be charity. If everything you say can be proven, the people who did the dynamiting will pay for your lawyer.''

"Well, then. Send him on.''

"It's a woman, actually. I'll send her on.''

"A woman lawyer?''

"That's right.''

"Well, don't that just beat all.''

BACK IN THE sheriff's patrol car, Owen's outrage spilled over. "How can you let that happen?''

"What do you mean, how can *I* let it happen?''

"You. The county. The state. The developers. It's shameful.''

"You'll get no argument from me.''

"I mean, I'm willing to grant you that you can reclaim the mountaintop and salvage the hollows. But how can you salvage what we just saw?''

"You're right. No question. But why yell at me?"

"Because you're here. Because you've been here. And because you're wearing that uniform."

"Guilt by association."

"I mean, my God. The last job I had in California, I was working with the Transportation Department to retrofit bridges so they could withstand heavier earthquakes. There was no blasting involved, just pile-driving and rivet-busting. Before they drove a single pile, though, they put strain gauges and vibration monitors on all the nearby buildings. If there were any homes or businesses that were likely to be shaken up, they went in and did advance surveys. Put together videotape records."

Owen's hands worked as if he were juggling invisible balls, and the words came tumbling out. "They didn't do all that just to be good guys. They knew they'd get their asses sued if they couldn't prove that cracks on people's walls had been there before the pile-driving started."

His hands dropped back into his lap. "But here, my God. There're broken windows, a cracked foundation, drooping floorboards, and a ruined well. And the woman believes she has no recourse."

The sheriff took his right hand off the steering wheel and raised it as if he were trying to stop traffic. "All right. All right. Calm down. You did what you could, promising a lawyer. Let's talk about what we came to find out. What happened to her husband?"

"We both know what happened to her husband. He was a UMW official. He saw what they were doing, taking coal from the shopping-center site and running it through the Hash Ridge Mine. They may have been more open about it when they were just starting out. Mattingly must have threatened to report them to the union."

"Maybe asked for a payoff to keep quiet."

"That's what he meant when he told his wife he'd finally hit a paying seam."

"So they killed him."

"They killed him. At exactly the same time Lizzie was making news by threatening to hold off the dumpers with a shotgun. That gave them a made-to-order fall guy."

"Fall guy. You said 'guy.' Does that mean you admit it was Bobby Ray, not Lizzie, at Cooter's Bend?"

"'Fall guy' is just an expression. Would you prefer 'fall person'?"

"I'd prefer the truth."

"The truth is, somebody from Mountain View Development shot Mattingly and pinned it on Lizzie. It's pretty slick, really. They get rid of a blackmailer and a vocal gadfly in the same move."

"Sounds convenient but far-fetched. What if Lizzie isn't out there with a shotgun?"

"Doesn't matter," Owen said. "They shotgun Mattingly anyhow and leave him in the truck. Lizzie's threat is on the public record, so she'll be your number-one suspect. Mattingly may have been dead when they brought him down the mountain. Was there an autopsy?"

"Man had half his face blown away."

"That was the window dressing. Was that what killed him?"

"According to the autopsy, yes."

"Who did the autopsy?"

"Doc Johnston's the acting coroner this month."

"Don Johnston?"

"You know him?"

"Crossed paths with him about a year ago. He was manufacturing fraudulent insurance claims. How'd he get to be coroner? Low bid?"

"Something like that. County pay scale being what it is, it's not exactly a sought-after position."

"So there's a chance he might have missed the real cause of death."

"If it was something other than a shotgun blast, yes. But we don't know that Mattingly wasn't alive coming down that mountain."

"Alive or dead, he wasn't alone," Owen said. "And whoever was with him knows how he died."

"And have you figured out who that was? Or is this where my police work starts?"

"Your police work starts with the people who knew about the truck movements. There's Letch Valence, and the two we video-taped the other night."

"Skeeter Dingess and Orry Estep. Skeeter's the place to start."

"He knew Mattingly."

"And he'll be the easiest of the three to crack."

"Can I come along?"

"I don't know. You might find my interview technique a little unorthodox."

"I haven't been a problem yet, have I?"

"No. In fact, you've been a marginal help." The sheriff laughed once, and his shoulder bounced against the seat belt. "What the hell, you can come along. We'll do it tonight, after dark. I know where to find Skeeter then."

Owen smiled at the grudging admission he'd been a marginal help. "Was it Doc Johnston who did the autopsy on Kate O'Malley?"

"I told you, it's his month."

"Any chance he screwed that up?"

"You're really reaching, Owen. It's one thing to miss a cause of death when a man has half his face blown away. It's another to misdiagnose a drug overdose."

"Maybe all he missed were signs that both victims had been manhandled."

"Why would anyone want to kill Sister Mary?"

"I don't know. I just know she wouldn't kill herself."

"Give it up, Owen. She was pregnant, and she had access to the drugs. It's a pretty clear suicide motive."

"Will you set it up for me to talk to Johnston?"

The sheriff shrugged. "It's your time you'll be wasting."

OWEN ARRIVED AT the hospice early enough to give himself time to visit with Maggie Mason before he took his mother to her chemotherapy treatment. Maggie's bed was empty, its coverlet turned down and neatly tucked at the corners.

Owen pounded down the stairs to Lizzie's office. He knew what had happened without asking, but he asked anyhow, hoping he was wrong.

"She passed yesterday afternoon," Lizzie said. "Right after you left. I think she was just holding on to see you."

Owen felt empty, sucked dry of emotion.

Lizzie handed him a shoebox. "She asked me to give you these."

Folded on top of the shoebox was the front page of the *Barkley Democrat* that contained Maggie's picture. The newspaper covered a box full of neatly packed paperback mysteries. Owen lifted out a handful and scanned the titles. Most of them were books he'd brought for Maggie to read. At the bottom of the box was a small plastic bag with a shiny gold ring and a photograph of a plump, healthy Maggie flanked by her two daughters.

Owen lifted the bag. "It's her wedding ring."

"She wanted you to have it. Everything else went to NOTIONS AND POTIONS."

Owen examined the ring. The inside of the band was inscribed *Faithful Forever—6/21/38.* "I can't take this. It should go to her daughters."

"They've been notified. They're both in California. I doubt that either one will come. Maggie said they'd gotten too highfalutin for her."

Owen leafed through the paperbacks. Most were his, but he found one of Maggie's, the Penguin edition of *The Adventures of Sherlock Holmes*. He took the book from the shoebox, along with the picture and newspaper page. "These are enough for me. Give the rest to NOTIONS AND POTIONS."

He hefted the plastic bag with the ring and handed it to Lizzie. "Hang onto this. If her daughters come for Maggie's service, see that they get it. If they don't, I'll be back for it."

Lizzie deposited the ring in her apron pocket.

Owen watched the ring disappear. "Look. It's a bad time to talk about this, but I just got back from examining Sam Mattingly's dump truck with the sheriff. There's a good chance we can prove Bobby Ray didn't shoot anybody." He went on to summarize their theory that Mattingly was killed to keep him from blowing the whistle on the illicit mining activity.

"Oh, my word," Lizzie said. "If only I'd been at Cooter's Bend instead of Bobby Ray, I might have seen what really happened."

Owen patted Lizzie's hand. "They might have shot you if you had. Let's forget about these 'what-ifs' and figure out where to go from here. Can you get Guy Schamp over here first thing tomorrow morning to help puzzle it out?"

"I can get him here right away."

"No. That won't work. I've got to take Mom to chemotherapy. And then the sheriff and I are going to call on a potential witness."

THE SHERIFF'S PATROL CAR ducked in and out of twilight shadows as he wheeled around a winding backcountry road unfamiliar to Owen.

"Why do they call him Skeeter?" Owen asked as the car approached a narrow switchback.

"Long, skinny nose he keeps sticking into other people's business, I reckon." The sheriff accelerated out of the switchback. "They called him Needle Dick in high school, till somebody figured out 'Needle Dick' Dingess was just a tad redundant."

"Skeeter's a definite improvement."

"He's the man we need to talk to, for sure. If he wasn't there when Mattingly's truck was loaded, he'll know who was."

The sheriff turned off the asphalt pavement onto a narrow gravel road. "One thing, though. Let me handle the questioning. Keep your mouth shut and your mind open. And whatever you do, don't laugh at him or me."

Owen laughed.

"Get it out of your system now. That's exactly what I don't want you doing when we're with Skeeter."

The sheriff pulled up in front of a rural mailbox. Two sets of parallel planks laid over muddy clay led from the mailbox to the sagging porch of a clapboard house. A stripped-down pickup truck sat beside the house, but the fading light was so dim that Owen couldn't make out the road the pickup had used to get there.

As they walked single-file over the parallel planks, they saw a dark shape move behind the screen door, which was held on by hinges fashioned from old tire scraps. The sound of clinking glassware came from inside the house. The sheriff paused and unsnapped his holster, then crossed the creaking porch and knocked on the screen door.

"With you in a minute," a voice shouted. The clinking sounds continued, then stopped, and Skeeter Dingess appeared in the doorway. His wiry frame was almost lost inside bib overalls that covered most of a grimy undershirt and bagged out over woolen socks.

Skeeter made no move to open the screen door. "What can I do for you, Sheriff?"

The sheriff pulled the door open and shoved his way past Skeeter into the house. "We're just here to ask a few questions. How about we sit a spell in your kitchen?"

"Living room's more comfortable."

"Kitchen will do fine."

Skeeter gestured toward three chrome chairs shoved under a stained Formica table. Owen sat down, but the sheriff moved over to the sink, where a white sheet had been draped over a shelf full of supplies. He pulled the sheet off the shelf to reveal two rows of mason jars filled with a clear liquid.

"Oh, shit," Skeeter said.

"Don't worry, Skeeter," the sheriff said. "I'm not after your supply of moonshine. What vintage is this?"

"Tuesday last."

The sheriff brought two jars to the table and placed them in front of Owen and Skeeter. Then he got three more jars and joined them at the table, sitting across from Skeeter. "Let's try it."

Owen knew his tolerance for moonshine was low, so he took his time unscrewing the jar lid and just sipped at the liquid, which burned his throat. At the same time, both the sheriff and Skeeter took substantial swallows from their jars.

The sheriff pulled a red bandanna out of his pocket and wiped his mouth. "Last Tuesday, huh? Helluva fine batch. The rat sure must have floated."

For Owen's benefit, the sheriff explained, "It's an old saying. 'If the rat floats, it's a good batch.'"

Owen stopped in mid-sip and returned his jar to the table.

The sheriff laughed. "Come on, let's drink up." He lifted his own jar to his lips and swallowed, then waited while Skeeter did the same.

The sheriff spread his red bandanna carefully on the table in front of him, weighting down two corners with the two extra jars of moonshine. He moved Owen's jar to cover the third corner, then took a healthy belt from his own jar and set it down on the fourth corner.

"Why don't you have another drink, Skeeter?" the sheriff said when the bandanna was in place. "We're here to ask you a few questions, and it's my duty to inform you that anything you say can be used against you."

"Do I need a lawyer?"

"You're welcome to one, of course. But I've got to warn you, if you were to make us wait while you get a lawyer, I might reconsider my position on that shelf full of shine. Might have to confiscate it."

"Ask away, then."

"Got to warn you about one other thing. Don't know whether you're aware of it or not, but my right eye here is glass." The sheriff flicked his thumbnail against his glass eye, causing a sharp click that made both Owen and Skeeter wince. "It's not good for much, except for one thing. It senses when there's mendacity in the air. You know what mendacity is, Skeeter?"

"Nope."

"Mendacity is lies. My glass eye senses when there's lies in the air. It cavorts something fierce when that happens. Rolls around, even bounces a little. I got to tell you, it's about as uncomfortable as burlap briefs."

Skeeter bit his lip. Owen did the same, mostly to help him keep a straight face.

"Deceit causes this eye of mine to bounce so bad that if I think I'm gonna be lied to, I just take it right out." The sheriff inhaled, pinched his glass eye between his thumb and forefinger, and pulled it from its socket. Then he set it carefully in the center of the red bandanna.

The glass eye stared up at Skeeter from its bright red resting place. He took a long swallow of moonshine.

The sheriff pulled a small tape recorder from his pocket, switched it on, and set it next to the bandanna. "Now then, Skeeter, for the record, your name is John Henry Dingess, known as Skeeter, is that right?"

Skeeter nodded.

"Speak up for the tape, please."

"That's right."

"And you heard me inform you of your rights, including your right to remain silent and your right to a lawyer, is that correct?"

"Yes."

"And you chose to go ahead with this interrogation?"

"That's right."

The sheriff pointed at his glass eye. "Now, just to help me calibrate this thing, I'd like you to lie to me. Understand?"

Skeeter nodded, looking at the glass eye.

"Tell me, Skeeter, is that moonshine strictly for personal consumption, or do you sell some of it?"

Skeeter stared at the glass eye. "Just for personal consumption."

The glass eye jiggled, then moved, almost imperceptibly, to a new position on the bandanna.

Owen struggled to suppress a gasp.

"Well, now, I guess that wasn't much of a lie," the sheriff said. "You must drink lots more than you sell off. You can see, though, how that little eye movement would be right uncomfortable if I hadn't taken it out.''

Skeeter nodded. "I can see that."

"Well, let's get back to it. Did you unload some coal from Dismal Mountain at the Hash Ridge Mine the other night?"

"You know I did. We made the newspapers."

"Been doing it for quite sometime?"

"Yes."

"Long as they've been blasting on the mountain?"

"Yes."

The glass eye sat motionless, staring at Skeeter.

"Did you help load the truck the night Sam Mattingly died?"

Skeeter glanced quickly at the glass eye. "No."

The eyeball bounced and rolled an inch along the surface of the bandanna.

"I'll ask you again," the sheriff said.

"All right. Yes. I helped load the truck."

"And did you ride down the mountain with him?"

Skeeter looked squarely at the sheriff. Owen followed his gaze to the empty eye socket. "No," Skeeter said, "I didn't."

"But someone did."

Skeeter's shoulders slumped and he bowed his head in a quick nod. "Was that a 'yes'?"

"Yes."

"Who was it, Skeeter?"

"I can't tell you that."

"Was it Orry Estep?"

"No."

The glass eye lay still.

"Was it Letch Valence?"

Skeeter focused on the eye and said, "No," as if daring it to move.

The eyeball jumped, danced, and nearly rolled off the table.

Skeeter shook his head. "All right. All right. Yes, it was Letch Valence."

"One more question. Did Mattingly seem all right when they started down the mountain?"

Skeeter appeared to be puzzled by the question. "Of course he was. He was driving. He wasn't all right when he hit the foot of the mountain, though. Not after Lizzie Neal got through with him."

"You're sure about that?"

"About what?"

"About Lizzie shooting Sam Mattingly."

"Hell, she confessed, didn't she? I mean, it's all over the county."

"Where was Letch Valence when Mattingly got shot?"

"I don't know. Ask him. Just don't tell him it was me that let on he started out with Sam."

"I'll try, Skeeter, but I can't promise anything." The sheriff looked at Owen. "Anything you'd like to ask while my little eye detector's out?"

"Was there anyone else on Dismal Mountain when you loaded Mattingly's truck?" Owen asked.

"No. Just the three of us." Skeeter snuck a quick peek at the glass eye, but it didn't move.

"So, if the word leaks out Letch was with Mattingly, there's only one place it could come from," the sheriff said.

"You just better not let it leak out, is all," Skeeter said, talking to the glass eye.

The sheriff shut off the tape recorder. "Okay, Skeeter. We're done here."

"You hear what I say about telling Letch?"

The sheriff picked up his glass eye. "Skeeter, I should tell you, there's some things inadmissible in a court of law in this country. Polygraph tests, for one. And hearsay evidence, and, you might as well know, my little eye detector here."

Thad Reader made a little flourish with the right hand holding his glass eye and returned the eye to its socket. At the same time, his left hand swept the bandanna off the table and stuffed it into his shirt pocket. Owen concentrated on the left hand and saw a washer tied to a long thread disappear into the folds of the bandanna.

The sheriff tapped his glass eye with his thumbnail. "I wouldn't want you to be fooled by the fact that the county's judges don't hold my eyeball in any greater esteem than they do a polygraph test. I know what you said here. And Owen here knows what you said. You know what you said, and we've got it all on tape. So don't even think about denying it."

"I won't, Sheriff."

Reader's glass eye popped out of its socket. He caught it waist-high and replaced it with a single motion. ''Now, why do I think you're lying?''

''I SEE WHY you wanted to wait until dark to interview Skeeter,'' Owen said as the sheriff wheeled his patrol car back over the winding rural road.

''That particular interrogation technique works best with little light and a lot of liquor.''

''Nice of you to warn him it wasn't admissible in court.''

''Just stating the fact of it.''

''I saw the washer when you put your bandanna away. How do you know when to jerk the thread and move the eyeball?''

''Intuition, mostly. Once a liar has seen the eyeball move, he can't help but sneak a peek whenever he lies. I just follow his own eyeballs.''

''What if you're wrong?''

''That's what the courts are for.''

''So Valence rode all the way down with Mattingly, planning to kill him.''

''With a shotgun, knowing Lizzie had broadcast statewide that she stood ready to shotgun anybody who tried to fill her creekbed.''

''And he saw Lizzie's van at Cooter's Bend and asked Mattingly to pull in.''

''Could be. Could be Valence killed or coldcocked Mattingly early on and drove down himself. Be a little easier.''

''In any case, it's time for us to go see Letch Valence.''

''Wrong. It's time for *me* to see Letch Valence. This is where you get off.''

''Why's that? I kept a straight face tonight.''

''It'll take more than a straight face and a little parlor magic with Valence. We're getting down to the short strokes. He could be dangerous. What's more, your great-aunt's still under indictment, and it doesn't look too good for me to be carting her nephew along when I go talk to a potential witness.''

''That didn't bother you earlier today when we looked at the truck. Or when we talked to Sarabeth Mattingly. Or just now.''

''Those visits weren't likely to blow up on me in court. You had a right to inspect the truck. And I sort of thought you might be able to help Sarabeth get some satisfaction out of the development company.''

"I still need to make that happen. What about Skeeter Dingess? Why'd you take me along tonight?"

Thad Reader took the washer from his pocket and lodged it over his glass eye like a monocle. "Tonight? Tonight was just showing off."

FIFTEEN

Whatever Remains

THE SUN HAD TAKEN the nip out of the fall air, and burnt-orange leaves covered the driveway of Lizzie's hospice when Owen arrived the next morning. Guy Schamp and Judith sat across from each other at the wrought-iron porch table, drinking hot coffee from mugs. On the table between them, the headlines of the *Barkley Democrat* announced HOSPITAL FACES BANKRUPTCY.

Owen had read the newspaper before leaving home. An IRS audit of a questionable loan had uncovered embezzling losses of a half million dollars that left Saint Vincent's Hospital unable to meet its debts.

Guy was discussing the hospital's situation as Owen climbed the porch steps. "Apparently the chief accountant, a man named Embry, went missing at the same time as the half million."

Lizzie appeared in the hospice doorway holding a pot of tea in one hand and two empty mugs in the other. "Would that be Vernon Embry?"

Owen took one of the empty mugs. "You know him?"

Lizzie filled Owen's mug with tea. "His wife Minna passed on here a year or so back. He seemed like a nice man."

"Embezzlers are invariably nice men," Guy said. "They seldom have money problems to make them grumpy."

"What'll happen to Saint Vincent's?" Judith asked.

"On the radio this morning, Dusty Rhodes was proposing to keep the hospital open by floating state bonds to retire the outstanding debt," Guy said.

"Now that's statesmanlike," Owen said. "Throw public money at a private problem to bail out a bad loan and paper over embezzling losses."

"It solves the problem," Judith said.

"The investors who made the bad loan will be more than happy to see it paid off," Owen said. "Probably happy enough to kick a little of that money back into Rhodes' campaign fund."

"It keeps the only hospital in the county open," Judith said. "And you don't know for sure that kickbacks are involved."

"I don't know for sure that the sun will come up tomorrow," Owen said. "But past experience makes it a pretty good bet."

"Now, children," Guy said. "We didn't come here to fight. Or to discuss Saint Vincent's Hospital. Owen, maybe you should tell us why you called this little meeting."

Owen reported on the previous day's activities, from the early morning dump-truck inspection to the evening's eyeball-to-eyeball confrontation with Skeeter Dingess. He described the shameful wreckage of Sarabeth Mattingly's home and concluded that her husband was killed by the person riding with him in the dump truck.

When Owen had finished, Guy Schamp clapped his hands silently and said, "You done good, Owen."

"And so did Thad Reader," Lizzie added. "I bet now he believes they fired on Bobby Ray."

"Actually, there's still no evidence of that," Owen said. "They could have fired blanks, though, the way Guy here did at the simulation. Or just fired into the air. There's evidence somebody did that."

"That was me," Lizzie said.

"Mattingly's killer could have done it, too," Owen said. "A few volleys in the air would have been enough to spook Bobby Ray."

"I can't believe Reader actually told the man his eyeball stunt wasn't admissible in court," Judith said. "What a hoot. I wish I'd been there."

"I tried to get you to come along," Owen said. "I left a message at your hotel the night before."

"I got in too late to call. And when I called back the next morning, you'd already gone."

"I stayed up late waiting," Owen said, and immediately wished he hadn't. "Where were you, anyhow?"

"Oh, gosh. Did I forget to fill in your sign-out sheet? How many demerits is that again?"

"Enough to ground you for the prom."

Lizzie stepped between Owen and Judith and poured more tea into Owen's mug. "What's the next step?"

"The sheriff is following up with Letch Valence today," Owen said. "I'd like to see if we can't do something to help Sarabeth Mattingly."

Owen sensed that if he told Judith he'd already volunteered her services to Sarabeth, she'd refuse to help, so he tried to frame the problem in a way that would make her want to offer assistance. "She's a woman without many resources, and she's really been victimized by the developers," he began, watching Judith for a reaction. When she didn't offer any, he continued. "It's an outrage what the blasting from the shopping center did to her house. They've ruined her well, cracked her foundation, broken windows—"

"How can they get away with that?" Judith asked.

"The mining companies have better lawyers," Guy said. "And the people in the hollows have been so beaten down by the system that they can't make it work for them."

"The state can reclaim the land, but they can't reclaim the lives," Owen said. "What Sarabeth needs is a good lawyer."

Judith stared at the hills beyond the hospice porch. "I'll go see her."

"That'd be great," Owen said.

"Don't sound so surprised," Judith said. "If I know you, you've already promised her my services."

"For a small contingency fee," Owen admitted.

"Let me know if I can help," Guy said.

"Thanks, but I think I can take care of it."

"Honey, you may know the law," Lizzie said, "but Guy here knows the local lawyers. Besides, you'll need somebody from the state bar on your team."

Judith smiled. "I appreciate your offer. I'll keep it in mind."

Owen could tell from Judith's smile and the tone of her voice that hell would freeze over before she'd accept Guy's offer. Still, he was so pleased just to have her agree to take on Sarabeth's case that he didn't pursue the matter.

"One other thing came up," Owen said. "There's a chance Mattingly was killed before the truck came down off Dismal Mountain and the coroner missed it."

"Who was the coroner?" Guy asked.

"Don Johnston," Owen answered. "I've run into him before. Shady lawyers were sending him accident victims for lawsuit-friendly diagnoses."

"They banned him from practicing at Saint Vincent's," Lizzie added.

"So it's not out of the question that he settled for the obvious cause of death and missed the real one," Owen said.

"My doctor friends used to say if you wanted to hide something from Don Johnston, all you had to do was put it in a medical textbook," Guy said.

"So we could attack him in court?"

Guy shrugged. "Might could do that. But you have to be careful. He's a sympathetic witness. Local jurors tend to believe him."

"With everything Owen found yesterday, you don't think they'll actually take Lizzie's case to trial, do you?" Judith asked.

"The DA still has her confession," Guy said. "They won't ignore that unless they've got an ironclad case against somebody else. It'd violate the wing-walkers' first rule."

"Which is?"

"'Don't turn loose the strut you're holding until you've got a firm grip on the next strut.'"

"And is a wing-walker what it sounds like?" Judith asked.

"Oh my, yes," Lizzie said. "Between the wars, flyers would barnstorm at county fairs. They'd always bring a copilot who'd walk out on the wings of their biplanes while they buzzed the crowd."

"It made a pretty good show," Guy said.

"Some would offer prize money to locals who'd try it," Lizzie said. "I mind one young buck from Barkley who went up and walked the wing of a yellow Sopwith Camel."

"I was young and foolish," Guy said. "Trying to impress a young lady."

Lizzie patted Guy's arm. "You did, dear."

"Lot of good it did me," Guy said. "Took me a while to learn the difference between courting death and courting women."

"One has a bigger downside," Owen said.

Guy smiled. "Be ungentlemanly to suggest which."

OWEN'S MOTHER HAD donned a blue-silk turban to cover her wisps of hair for the trip to the chemotherapy clinic.

"That's the third new hat in three days," Owen said as he held the car door for her. "Whatever happened to my Cincinnati Reds' number?"

"It's still around. I've been getting different ones from NOTIONS AND POTIONS. They've got quite a selection."

"Recycled," Owen said, and then wished he hadn't. He didn't want to think about the fate of the Notions and Potions donors.

"I'll be recycled myself soon."

Owen stopped at the end of the hospice driveway. "Is that what your doctors say?"

"Doctors. What do they know?"

"Anatomy, radiology, oncology. Quite a bit, actually. What does your oncologist say about you?"

"He says I'm improving. But he's not the one wearing haunted haberdashery."

Owen pulled out onto the winding access road. "You're improving. And you've got a new hat. I'd say things are looking up."

"Not for everybody. I saw Maggie Manson's housecoat in NOTIONS AND POTIONS."

"Maybe you should come home, Mom. Get away from all those reminders."

"Trust me, Owen. I'm not that improved."

"I can take care of you."

"I know you can. I'm just not ready." She reached out and touched the hand that held the steering wheel. "Your visits were good for Maggie Mason."

"They were good for me, too."

OWEN HAD MADE enough recent visits to the chemotherapy clinic to have memorized the magazines available in the waiting room, so he passed the time leafing through the Penguin edition of Sherlock Holmes that he'd taken from Maggie Mason's effects. He'd read most of Conan Doyle's books when he was in high school, and had enjoyed the PBS series starring Jeremy Brett as Holmes, but he found he had little desire to reread the original stories, fearing he'd find them too contrived.

Now he scanned the pages, seeking out the parts he'd always enjoyed most, those snatches of dialogue in which Holmes imperiously explains his methods to Watson. An exchange from "The Sign of Four" jumped out at Owen. In one of his lectures to Watson, Holmes says, "When you have eliminated the impossible, whatever remains, *however improbable,* must be the truth." Conan Doyle had italicized the words "however improbable," but Owen's eyes kept returning to the word "impossible."

For him, it was impossible that Kate O'Malley would have killed herself. Or, in the improbable event that she were pregnant, doubly improbable that she wouldn't have told him. He snapped the book shut, rose, and walked down the hall to his mother's treatment room. Ruth was asleep, so he mouthed the words, "I'll be back," to the nurse adjusting her IV tube.

In the treatment room next to his mother's, a man who couldn't have been much older than Owen sat hunched over an empty gurney cart, sobbing. A woman ran her hands through his hair while a chubby teenage boy wearing a backward baseball cap stared out into the hallway. The boy caught Owen's eye and they both looked away, embarrassed.

Owen hurried back down the hallway and out into the sunshine. Fighting death was a losing battle. It was time to start fighting the living.

He found Bake Morton on the slim balcony outside Saint Vincent's doctors' lounge. The glowing stub of a cigarette threatened to ignite his walrus mustache, and his baggy green scrubs didn't fit him any better than they did the day he operated on Ruth Allison.

"I need to talk to you," Owen said.

"I've got rounds in ten minutes."

"This may not take that long. Can we go somewhere private?"

Morton took the cigarette from between his clenched teeth, squinted through the smoke, and ground the stub underfoot. "Let's go to my office."

He led the way in silence, ushered Owen into his office, then closed the door and stood beside it, as if he didn't want anyone blocking his exit route. "I've seen the oncology reports. Your mother's making remarkable progress."

"This isn't about Mom."

"What, then?"

"It's about Kate O'Malley."

Morton's face hardened. He leaned back against the doorjamb and rested the heel of his hand on the doorknob.

"I know you were her friend," Owen said. "I think it's impossible that she committed suicide."

"Morphine's a tricky thing. She might not have meant—"

"Forget that. Did you have any inkling she was using morphine?"

"Of course not. But the police found needle marks."

"Sister Regina Anne told me Kate gave blood every chance she got. Most of the nuns did."

"That just explains the needle marks. What about the pregnancy?"

"I think that's just as impossible."

Morton lowered his glasses and peered over their frame. "But the autopsy report showed—"

"That's what I want to talk to you about. How much trouble would it be to fake an autopsy report?"

"Depends on who's reviewing it. But why would anyone want to?"

"To cover up a murder."

Morton left his station by the door and settled his bulk on the edge of his cluttered desk. "You think Sister Mary was murdered? Why?"

"I haven't quite figured that out. This embezzlement that just surfaced. Didn't she work with the accountant, Embry?"

"Every Tuesday. She went over the hospital's accounts."

"Maybe she stumbled onto something that made her a target."

"Could be. But there's still the pregnancy."

"That's what I'm asking you. How would you fake that?"

"And what I'm asking you is 'Why?'"

"Because no one's going to ask many questions if a pregnant nun kills herself. The sheriff's told me twice it's better than a notarized suicide note."

"Who did the autopsy?"

"Don Johnston."

Morton stared at Owen, saying nothing.

"What?" Owen asked.

"Don Johnston is a prime cock-up. Sister Mary had him barred from practicing in this hospital."

"So he had a motive."

"For killing her? Hardly seems likely. He's been barred from here for the past two or three years, and it barely put a dent in his practice."

"But he might be willing to fake autopsy results."

"He'd be the guy I'd ask if I wanted it done. Hell, he's so sloppy, you might not have to ask."

"Sloppy implies he'd miss something. In this case, he found something that couldn't have been there."

"The pregnancy, you mean."

"How could he fake that finding?"

Morton pursed his lips. His mustache bobbed up and down. "He made a living finding injuries that weren't there, for insurance claims. Easiest way to fake a finding is just lie."

"Just lie?"

"Just flat-out lie."

"If he lied, the only way to find out the truth would be to exhume the body."

Morton frowned and shook his head. "Not necessarily."

"There's another way?"

"No. I mean exhumation might not tell you anything. If I was a coroner who wanted to lie about a pregnancy, I'd dispose of the organs before burial."

"Oh, God." Owen's stomach clenched and his mind rejected the image that Morton's comment called up.

Seeing Owen's distress, Morton said, "Course, Johnston might not have been that thorough. He's not the sharpest scalpel on the instrument tray."

"Look, this is a potential murder case. Surely he'd have to back up his findings somehow."

"Seems logical. But it's a little out of my field. Still, it wouldn't be too hard to fake some evidence."

"How would you do that?"

"Get the blood work and slides from sections of the uterus of a pregnant woman and substitute them for Sister Mary's."

"If you do that, though, the DNA of the substitute slides wouldn't match the rest of the workup."

"I doubt anyone would check. If you thought they might, just take everything from the pregnant subject."

"Would that subject have to be dead?"

"Not necessarily. But it wouldn't be too tough to find autopsy slides from a dead pregnant woman. The state requires us to keep autopsy records for at least five years."

"But the substitute slides wouldn't match Kate's DNA. So if there's something on record—"

"Or if you exhumed the body."

Owen winced. "We keep coming back to that. I hope that's a last resort."

A nurse opened the office door. "Bake, we're waiting."

"With you in a minute."

The nurse nodded and stepped outside, closing the office door behind her.

Morton rose from the edge of his desk. "I'm sorry. I've got to go. Look, this is all a little out of my line. But we've got a good pathologist on the staff here. His name's Howard Sussman. If you clear it with the sheriff, I'll ask him to review Sister Mary's autopsy reports."

"That'd be great."

"If you're right, the only way to prove it may be to recover her remains. Better find out how to do that."

Owen nodded, although he dreaded the task.

"This all seems so far-fetched. You sure it's worth it?" Morton asked.

"She didn't commit suicide. She couldn't have been pregnant. It's impossible. You know it and I know it."

Morton followed Owen out of the office, then took his arm before departing down the hall. "Look. I owe you an apology."

"What for?"

"For taking all this at face value. For believing the gossip."

"Forget it," Owen said. "You sure as hell weren't alone."

OWEN STOOD ON the hospital steps. In the field next door, orderlies were furling up the volleyball net after their lunchtime game. A pretty young nurse stubbed a cigarette under her shoe and joined a white-robed nun on her way back to work. Visitors streamed past him on their way to the bedsides of loved ones. The threat of bankruptcy hadn't slowed the pulse of the hospital.

The scene before him hadn't changed much in the thirty years since he worked here. But he had. Instead of following the nurse back into the hospital for the afternoon shift, he was thinking about exhuming the remains of a friend. How could he even consider digging up Kate's body? He couldn't imagine doing it. He forced himself to disengage his feelings and apply a little Holmesean logic. If Kate wasn't pregnant, she almost certainly wasn't a suicide. And if she wasn't a suicide, somebody murdered her. If the way to expose the murderer was to dig up Kate's remains, he couldn't imagine not doing it.

"YOU WANT TO do *what?*" the sheriff asked.

Owen hung his cane on the lip of the Formica tabletop and slid into one of the corner booths at Lovisa's Café. "It's a last resort. It may not be necessary. Before it comes to exhumation, I want to get an independent pathologist to check your coroner's findings."

The sheriff slid along the plastic surface as if he wanted both to make room for Owen and to distance himself from Owen's request. "Where did all this come from?"

"I've done some checking. It's not that tough to fake autopsy results. And Kate O'Malley had barred your Doctor Johnston from practicing at Saint Vincent's."

"Will you for Christ's sake quit calling him *my* Doctor Johnston? And why would he want to gin up fake autopsy results?"

"To cover up Kate's murder."

"And Sister Mary was murdered because?"

"There's a good chance she stumbled onto the embezzlement scheme."

"And what's the connection between the embezzler and Doctor Johnston?"

Owen frowned. "I haven't figured that out yet. Maybe it was just money."

The waitress appeared at the head of their booth, took a pencil from the bun of her hair, and licked the tip with her tongue. The sheriff ordered a cheeseburger with fries and a beer. Owen's stomach was still churning, so he made do with chicken soup, dumplings, and a glass of 7 Up.

When the waitress had gone, the sheriff said, "Owen, I've got to say you're operating more on blind hope and coincidence than on any kind of hard evidence."

"Humor me. Let Doctor Sussman check the autopsy findings."

"I can do that."

"And tell me whose permission I'd need to have the body exhumed."

"The DA could order it on my say-so. But I won't say so. Not without a lot more than you're giving me."

"Who else might ask for it?"

"Parents, or a surviving spouse."

"Her mother's dead. Her father's still alive, but they fell out when she entered the convent. As far as spouses go, she was a Bride of Christ."

"You come up with his signature, I'd honor it."

"In case I can't swing that, is there anybody else?"

"Head of the convent could request it."

"That'd be Sister Regina Anne?"

"She's the Mother Superior. But I can't imagine she'd be any easier to convince than I am."

"I'm hoping it won't come to that."

The waitress returned with their drinks. Owen sipped his soft drink, then asked, "What did you learn from Letch Valence?"

The sheriff picked at the label on his beer with a ragged fingernail. "Getting information out of Letch is like mining coal with an emery board."

"Could he account for his whereabouts the night Mattingly died?"

"Claims he was playing poker. Gave me the names of five cronies."

"That should have set off your eye detector. Did you check it out?"

"So far, the buddies I talked to back his story."

"But they're his buddies."

The sheriff nodded. "Every last mother's son works for Letch's security outfit."

"Can you crack their stories? We know he started out with Mattingly."

"He even denied that at first. Then he changed his story to say Mattingly dropped him off at the game."

"He's lying."

"I think so, too. But it will take more than my glass eyeball to prove it." The sheriff took a long pull on his beer, then grimaced as if it had left a bitter taste. "Speak of the devil."

Owen heard a familiar voice and turned to look. Letch Valence stood in the open doorway with Orry Estep. The crisp October air chilled the café.

"Estep's one of his alibis," the sheriff said.

Valence spotted the sheriff and started toward their booth, talking in a voice that could be heard by everyone in the café. "Say, Orry, hear the one about the fellow who banged a nun?"

Estep grunted.

"He was feeling a little superior."

Estep frowned.

"Get it? The nun was a Mother Superior."

Estep's frown stayed put. The joke still appeared to be beyond him.

"Never mind," Valence said. He gestured toward the corner booth where Owen and the sheriff sat. "These fellows get it. The bearded one's a nun-banger from way back. How about it, Allison? What's it like to get in the habit?"

Owen reddened.

Valence leaned over their table. His forearm brushed Owen's cane and knocked it to the floor. "Scuse me. I'm a little clumsy this evening."

Valence's breath smelled of stale beer and onions. Owen clutched the edge of the booth to keep from lashing out.

"Seriously, though, Allison. What's it like to bang a nun?"

Owen slid out of the booth and knelt to retrieve his cane.

"I mean," Valence continued, "like, did she shout 'Jesus, Mary, and Joseph' when she came?"

Owen balanced his weight over his bent knees, closed his hand in a forehand grip just above the rubber tip of the cane, and brought it up from the floor as if he were lobbing a tennis ball. He did it automatically, flicking his wrist to impart topspin just as the cane handle connected with Letch's crotch.

Valence screeched and dropped to his knees.

Owen sprang up, shifted to a backhand grip, and was about to drive Letch's head cross-court when Thad Reader grabbed the handle of the cane.

"That's enough," he said.

Valence rolled onto his side and curled into a fetal position, tucking his chin against his collarbone and clutching his genitals.

Owen bent his knees to hit the lower target, but the sheriff gripped the cane handle tightly.

Orry Estep stepped over Valence and hit Owen solidly in the solar plexus.

Owen's breath wooshed out. He released the cane and stumbled backward into the restaurant booth.

The sheriff brought the cane down sharply on Estep's wrist. "I said that's enough."

Estep screamed in pain.

Owen gasped for breath, making rattling noises deep in his throat.

Valence lay on his side, whimpering. He regained his voice first. "Dead man," he squeaked. "You're a dead man, Owen Allison." He used Orry Estep's leg to pull himself up to a kneeling position. "Count the hours, motherfucker. You're a dead man." His voice was an octave high.

The sheriff stepped between Owen and his wounded tormenters. "I'd call this little set-to a draw. If either of you has any thoughts of continuing it, you should know that if this man Allison gets so much as a nosebleed in my county, I'll lock you both up till you're older than Job's dirt. I don't give a shit if you've got the entire Mormon Tabernacle Choir swearing they were playing poker with you."

Valence pulled himself upright with the help of Estep's uninjured arm. "Look to yourself, lawman. That badge isn't a shield."

The sheriff unpinned his badge and examined it closely. "By God, you're right. It's no shield." He laid it on the Formica table. "Would you like to try taking me on without it?"

Valence and Estep exchanged glances, turned in tandem and limped out of the restaurant, leaning on each other for support.

Owen sucked in his breath. "Jesus, I don't think I've hit anybody in anger since the third grade."

"How'd it feel?"

"I don't even remember the kid's name."

"No. I mean how'd it feel just now?"

"I don't remember much. It was like I blanked out. I could have killed him."

"Just as well I stopped you. You'd best be careful, though. Valence will try to make good on his threat, and I can't protect you round-the-clock."

"Why talk about protecting me? He's the one who just limped out of here."

The sheriff handed Owen his cane. "I wouldn't count on using this again. Valence isn't dumb. Next time he won't be standing in front of you, unarmed, telling recycled nun jokes."

SIXTEEN

In God We Trust

THE NEXT MORNING'S MAIL brought two catalogues, the phone bill, and a flyer with the now too familiar face of Dusty Rhodes. The election was only two weeks away. Owen took a certain satisfaction in tearing Rhodes' flyer up into small pieces before depositing it in the wastebasket with the catalogues.

He tucked the phone bill under his arm, picked up the other bills that had accumulated on the marble-topped table next to the front door, and retreated to the breakfast room, where he heated a fresh pot of water for tea and settled in to pay the month's bills. He'd taken out a joint account with his mother at the Matewan National Bank and it gave him an eerie feeling to see Ruth Allison's name and address with his own name in the upper left-hand corner of the checks. It was the first address he'd ever known, and the joint account made him the executor of his mother's estate. A premature executor, if Bake Morton was right. Maybe even an unnecessary executor.

He'd paid Appalachian Power & Light and Bell Atlantic when he opened the bill from Saint Vincent's Hospital. The bottom line of the invoice showed that his mother's insurance had covered the entire amount, so that nothing was owed. He was about to move on to the water bill when an entry in the string of figures caught his eye. In addition to the usual indecipherable stream of charges, the hospital had invoiced his mother for a four-night stay. But he knew that she had spent only two nights there following her operation. He examined the rest of the charges more carefully. There were entries for a list of medicines he couldn't confirm or deny, and a charge for a service abbreviated G. Con., which the fine print on the reverse side translated as "Grief Counseling."

Grief counseling. No one had counseled him, and the only other person who might have received such counseling was his mother. As long as she was alive, though, there was no need to grieve. Pre-need grief counseling for the soon-to-be-deceased seemed a little too avant-garde for West Virginia.

Grief counseling. The phrase triggered his memory. He could hear Kate's laughter, then her concerned voice on the telephone. He hurried to the phone and dialed Sheriff Thad Reader.

"Lemme get this straight," the sheriff said after listening as Owen's story tumbled out. "Yesterday you thought Sister Mary was murdered because she worked with an accused embezzler. Today you think she was killed because you were overcharged on your hospital bill. Jesus, I can hardly wait for tomorrow's theory."

"No, listen." Owen backed up and tried to explain again. "The last time I heard from her, the day she was killed, she called me to ask if my mother had gone back to Saint Vincent's. I think she reviewed our bill, knew we were overcharged, and saw some sort of a pattern."

"What sort of pattern?"

"I remember her telling me about a dog whose owner had been charged for grief counseling."

"A dog?"

"A dog. It was a mistake."

"I'd hate to think they did it deliberately."

"But it was the same kind of mistake that showed up on our bill. I think they were systematically overcharging some people."

"What people? Anyone with dogs or mothers? That covers a lot of territory."

"I don't know for sure what people they were targeting. Most likely anybody with high insurance coverage—they'd be less likely to notice. But I'm pretty sure Kate figured it out and confronted this man Embry."

"And he killed her so he wouldn't have to stop charging dogs for grief counseling?" The sheriff's voice was still skeptical. "I knew Vern Embry. He didn't strike me as a killer."

"Did he strike you as an embezzler?"

There was a short pause on the other end of the line. Then the sheriff said, "What do you want from me?"

"Come with me to the hospital. Help me to convince the nuns to let me look at their books. I'd bet my life Embry overcharged a lot more people than Mom and some dog owner."

"The IRS is all over the hospital's books. You'd just be one more fly on the dunghill."

"The IRS doesn't know what to look for."

"And you do?"

"Kate did. I'm hoping she left a trail."

"You sure don't mind living dangerously. Last night you took a cane to Letch Valence's crotch. Today you expect to talk your way past a bunch of nuns who think you drove their favorite sister to suicide—just so you can show up some IRS agents."

"That's one way of looking at it."

"What'll you do for an encore? Swan-dive naked off the bridge over New River Gorge?"

"That still the highest in the country?"

"Last I heard."

"Well, stick around. The day's young yet."

SISTER REGINA ANNE'S face was composed of sharp angles and the narrow, vertical facets of a Giacometti sculpture. Clear blue eyes softened the effect of the hard surfaces framed by her white cowl. The eyes looked out at Owen and the sheriff from behind the broad oak desk of the chief hospital administrator.

"You feel that Vernon Embry was systematically overcharging our patients?"

"That's right, Sister," Owen answered.

The nun pointed a long, thin finger at the bill for Ruth Allison's hospitalization, which rested on the center of the oak desk. "On the strength of this single bill?" She looked at Thad Reader for confirmation.

The sheriff shrugged.

Owen nodded emphatically. "That, Sister Mary's phone call, and the bill for canine grief counseling."

"The curious incident of the dog that didn't bark," Sister Regina Anne said.

"Excuse me?"

"I was quoting Sherlock Holmes. Forgive me, but your inquiry seems as arcane as his investigations. In my experience, if a dog's not barking, there's a good chance it doesn't exist or there's nothing to bark at. I'd be very surprised if this hospital ever billed anyone for canine grief counseling. If we had, I can assure you I would have heard of it before this."

"I'd like a chance to pursue the possibility," Owen said. "If we could just see Sister Mary's personal effects."

"Her personal effects." The corners of the nun's mouth extended a little, without quite turning up into a smile.

"That's right."

"Mister Allison, Sister Mary Perpetua took a vow of poverty. There were no personal effects."

Owen slumped back in his chair. Under Sister Regina Anne's composed gaze, he felt as if he'd just misspelled a simple one-syllable word in the first round of a spelling bee.

Seeing Owen's disappointment, Sister Regina Anne spread her palms outward like a medieval madonna dispensing blessings. "A few books and compact discs are all she left behind. We donated them to your aunt's hospice. I'm sure that's what Sister Mary would have wanted."

"I'm sorry. I should have realized." Owen was reluctant to come away empty-handed. "Look, Sister. I hadn't intended to bring this up, but we feel there's a good chance Sister Mary's autopsy results were misreported."

"Misreported?"

"Look here, Owen," the sheriff said. "There's no need to go into that."

Owen ignored the sheriff. "We think she was murdered, and the pathologist fabricated evidence of pregnancy to cover it up."

Sister Regina Anne frowned. "Who was the pathologist?"

"Doctor Donald Johnston."

The nun's eyes appeared to focus inward, giving nothing away. "Mr. Allison, you seem to see evil everywhere. In Vernon Embry. In Doctor Johnston. So far, I've heard little to substantiate your views."

"It's not that I see evil everywhere, Sister. It's that I see only good in Kate O'Malley."

The nun's blue eyes locked onto Owen's. "In Sister Mary Perpetua, you mean."

"Of course."

"And how can I help you?"

"In order to prove that the autopsy was bogus, we may have to exhume Sister Mary's body. I understand you have the authority to order that.''

Sister Regina Anne blinked once and uttered a soft sound that was somewhere between a sigh and a moan.

"That may not be necessary, Sister,'' the sheriff said. "We've got your pathologist, Doctor Howard Sussman, working on the autopsy findings right now. We won't know what's needed next until he reports in.''

Owen waved off the sheriff. "We pretty much know what he'll find. Either Johnston was so dumb he lied outright and buried the evidence, or he was smart enough to fabricate consistent documentation. Either way, we'll need the body to prove him wrong.''

Sister Regina Anne held up her hand, palm outward. "Gentlemen, there's no need to argue this point with me. Sister Mary is with her God. I trust they've sorted it all out by now. I see no need to dig up...'' she hesitated, then added, "past scandals.''

"But you could clear her name,'' Owen said.

"Sister Mary's name needs no clearing in the eyes of God, or in the eyes of those who knew her. You said yourself you saw only good in her.''

"But the rest of the county thinks—''

Sister Regina Anne held up her hand again. "Ask yourself whose name you're worried about clearing, Mr. Allison. Suppose you go through with this grisly charade and find Sister Mary was not carrying a child. Imagine the headlines. NUN NOT PREGNANT. Hardly page-one news. I doubt we'd make the news at all. It's not exactly 'man bites dog.' It's not even 'dog bites man.' More like 'dog doesn't bite man,' I should think.''

"But if we can prove she wasn't pregnant, it's not likely she committed suicide. Knowing that could help us find her killer.''

Sister Regina Anne fixed her eyes on Thad Reader. "Isn't that your province, Sheriff?''

"It certainly is.''

"Then I will defer to you in this matter. If you feel the preponderance of evidence dictates that Sister Mary's remains should be disinterred, so be it. But you'll have to order it yourself, because I'll not be the one to request it.''

"I understand completely, Sister.'' Reader shot Owen a "shut-the-hell-up'' look.

"Will that be all?'' Sister Regina Anne asked.

The sheriff got up to leave. Owen stayed put, reluctant to give up. It occurred to him that he'd been wrong to ask about Kate's personal effects. "Sister Mary must have had an office."

"Of course."

"Could we see it?"

"I'm afraid all her medical records are confidential."

"But she helped with the financial records as well."

"Ours is a small hospital. We all have extracurricular duties."

"Surely those records aren't confidential."

"No. In fact, they're being reviewed as we speak."

"Where did she work on them?"

"Where? Why in the small office adjoining Vernon Embry's. It held a part-time assistant when we could afford one."

"Can we see the office?"

"I don't see why I should deny you that." Sister Regina Anne rose, adjusted the rosary hanging from her belt so that it would clear the oak desk, and beckoned for them to follow.

In the hallway, she said to Owen, "Your mother has been a good friend to this hospital. I pray for her daily."

"Your prayers must be working. She seems to be recovering nicely."

"I've been praying for her soul, actually. But we take what we can get."

Sister Regina Anne stopped and unlocked a small office that held a metal desk, a file cabinet, and two battered metal chairs. She gestured toward the desk. "I hope you find what you're looking for."

The empty office was spare and forbidding. All the metal surfaces were bare. The desk's "In" and "Out" baskets were empty. The sole ornament on the walls was a wooden crucifix.

The sheriff nodded toward the crucifix. "What are we looking for? A sign from God?"

"Either that, or evidence that Kate was on to this Vern Embry." Owen opened the top left-hand drawer of the desk. Loose pens rolled and rattled over scattered paper clips.

The wide middle drawer of the desk held an oversized ledger. The left-hand pages of the ledger were dated and filled with entries that Owen assumed must correspond to the hospital's accounting codes. The right-hand pages included handwritten lists of issues to be discussed with Vern Embry. Owen recognized the open, expan-

sive handwriting as Kate's. It reminded him of the one letter she'd
sent him the summer before she went into the convent, the single
response to all his otherwise unanswered correspondence. He still
had the letter, stored with his other college memorabilia in a black
footlocker at his mother's house.

A square sheet of paper from a doctor's prescription pad had been
used to mark the last page of entries in the ledger. The sheet held
eight names neatly lettered in alphabetical order, from Akers to
Waldron. The second name on the list was Ruth Allison's.

"Find something?" the sheriff asked.

"I think so. Look here. Akers was the name of the man whose
dog triggered the counseling bill. My mom's name is here, too.
Recognize any of the others?"

The sheriff examined the prescription sheet. "Bauer, Bigwood,
and Moore all died recently. Within the past two months. I don't
know any of the others."

"I'm betting they all died recently. And were well-insured. Do
you know any of them well enough to call their families and ask a
few questions?"

"I know Bauer and Bigwood. What should I ask?"

"Ask them to check their hospital bills. Meantime, I'll call Lizzie
and see if she recognizes any of the rest of this list. The hospital
hands a lot of its terminally ill patients off to her hospice."

There was no telephone in the small outer office, so the sheriff
left for his squad car while Owen used the phone in the inner office
that had belonged to Vern Embry. While talking to Lizzie, he examined the office, trying to imagine what kind of man would occupy
it. There were no pictures, no plaques, no framed diplomas. Even
though investigators must have searched it thoroughly, not a ledger
or a book appeared out of place. It was the office of a hyper-neat
nobody. A hyper-neat nobody who might have killed Kate
O'Malley.

Thad Reader returned just as Owen was saying good-bye to his
aunt. As soon as Owen hung up, the sheriff said, "Well, you called
it. Dave Bauer says they tacked two extra days onto his brother's
stay. Says they never noticed it because it was covered by insurance.
Same with B.J. Bigwood's widow. I couldn't get through to the
Moores, but my office is working on it."

"Aunt Lizzie says two of the other three died at her hospice.
Both came from Saint Vincent's, and neither lasted more than three

weeks after arriving. Insurance covered their entire hospice stay. So everybody on the list was well insured and either dead or dying when they left the hospital.''

"Except your mom."

"They probably targeted everybody released to the hospice. Lizzie usually only takes people who don't have long to live. She just took Mom as a favor to the family."

"That means they must have hit lots more than the eight names on Sister Mary's list." The sheriff shook his head. "Don't see that I have the manpower to sift through the books trying to find the rest."

"You don't need to. The IRS is already auditing the hospital's books. Let's just tell them what we've found out."

"And let our tax dollars work for us."

"Death and taxes. It's a natural." Owen closed the accounting ledger. "We better tell Sister Regina Anne what we've found."

"She's not a woman I'd want to see unhappy."

"Better unhappy than uninformed. She's not a woman you want to keep secrets from, either."

"THEY COVERED themselves pretty good. We didn't get a whiff of any of this." Tom Parker, the chief IRS auditor, pointed at Owen's hospital bill with a pen so well-chewed that all the nourishment had long since left it. "Now that we know what to look for, though, we'll send letters to all the patients that fit the profile."

"The patients that fit the profile are mostly dead," the sheriff said. "Better get in touch with their survivors."

Parker stared at the sheriff over his bifocals. "That's what I meant, of course."

"I still can't believe Vernon Embry could be responsible for any of this," Sister Regina Anne said. She sat at the head of one of the four rectangular tables that had been shoved together in the center of the hospital's conference room.

"Son of a bitch had us all fooled," Willis Grant said. "Excuse me, Sister." The head of Mountain View Development sat at the other end of the table configuration, wearing a dress shirt with notches cut in the short sleeves to accommodate his bulging biceps. The display reminded Owen of the Reds' Ted Kluszewski, who used to slit his sweatshirt sleeves so his massive shoulders could intimidate opposing pitchers.

"What I don't understand," Owen said, "is how Embry personally benefited from any of this. After all, the overcharges just went into the hospital's coffers."

"Which the son of a pup looted to the tune of a half million dollars," Grant said, flexing his muscles so that the anchor of a Marine Corps tattoo peeked out under his left shirtsleeve. "He overcharged, lined his own pockets, and then panicked and disappeared when the auditors showed up."

"Well, that's all pure speculation, of course." The IRS agent pointed at the stacked accounting ledgers with the chewed end of his pen. "With what you've given us here, we should be able to fill in a lot of the blanks."

"Will that be all, then?" Sister Regina Anne asked.

"For now, Sister." The IRS agent addressed Owen and Thad Reader. "Thank you for bringing this to our attention."

Owen held the door open for Sister Regina Anne. As they were about to leave, Tom Parker took off his bifocals and tilted them toward Thad Reader. "See you alone a minute, Sheriff?"

Reader stayed behind while Owen, Sister Regina Anne, and Willis Grant left the room. Grant huffed off down the corridor without a word, evidently angry at being excluded from the auditor's invitation to the sheriff.

Sister Regina Anne watched Grant disappear around the corner. "I just can't believe what that man said about Vernon Embry is true. Not to mention your theory that he killed Sister Mary."

"The alternative is to believe that Sister Mary was pregnant and killed herself."

"Pregnancy speaks to a sin of passion. A hot sin. The other, murder, is so cold-blooded. I find it easier to understand the hot sin."

"How's that?"

"Experience, I guess. Over the years I've seen several of the nuns in my charge succumb to that particular hot sin. Does that surprise you?"

"Only in the case of Sister Mary."

"Sister Mary had a mind of her own. She questioned so much.

It's often the brightest of our sisters who find themselves entangled. And I've seen many more devout than Sister Mary renounce their vows of chastity. It makes me think Napoleon was right."

"Napoleon Bonaparte?"

Sister Regina Anne cocked her head and smiled. "He said he liked convents, but he wished they wouldn't admit any women under fifty."

Owen smiled too and was about to reply when Thad Reader came out of the conference room into the hallway. Seeing both Owen and Sister Regina Anne smiling, the sheriff said, "Looks like I missed something."

"Just discussing the proper age for entering the convent," Owen said.

The sheriff chuckled. "No offense, Sister, but anything under forty's a waste."

Sister Regina Anne pursed her lips. "I'd say you definitely have a Napoleonic complex."

Thad Reader drew himself up to his full six feet of height. "I thought that had to do with being short."

"There are lots of ways to be short," Owen said. "You can be short of temper, short of cash, short of stature—"

"You can stop right there," the sheriff interrupted. "You wouldn't want to embarrass the good Sister."

"Why should she be embarrassed by your shortcomings?" Owen asked. "What did the IRS man have to say?"

"He apologized for not being more forthcoming while the audit was still going on. That was the word he used, 'forthcoming.' Don't think I've ever heard anybody say it out loud before. Said he'd be able to tell us more when they finish with the books. One thing he wanted to clear up right away, though, was Vern Embry's role in all this."

"Oh, dear," Sister Regina Anne said.

"Well, the money's missing all right. And Embry's missing as well. But Parker couldn't say for sure that Embry took the money. One thing he knew for certain, though. Embry didn't spook and run when he heard the auditors were coming, like Grant suggested."

"How can Parker know that?" Owen asked.

"Because it was Embry who ordered up the audit."

IN THE SHERIFF'S patrol car on the way home, Owen said, "Sister Regina Anne doesn't think Vern Embry could be an embezzler, let alone a murderer."

"She tends to overestimate the good in everyone. It's an occupational hazard."

"In your occupation, you overestimate the bad. What's your take on Embry?"

"I wouldn't have pegged him for a killer, but Sister Mary's dead. The money's gone. Embry's gone. He left just after Sister Mary died. She was clearly on to his game. That's a load of circumstantial evidence. He may not have done anything, but he's the first guy to look for."

"Still, it's not like an embezzler to order up an audit. What if he's just a fall guy?"

"We still have to find him."

"Can you nail down the last time he was seen? And get me a description of his car?"

"Sure. But I've had an APB out ever since the money turned up missing. Nobody in West Virginia or the surrounding states has seen his car. Even if he's a fall guy, he's long gone. If the law in five states can't find him, how do you expect to?"

Owen smiled. "Just tell me what kind of a car he was driving. I may not be able to find him, but there's a good chance I can tell you which way he went."

JUDITH CALLED ALMOST as soon as Owen arrived home. Her voice was breathless, excited. "Quick, turn on your TV. Channel Three."

Owen carried the phone into the living room and switched on the TV. The image of Sarabeth Mattingly shimmered onto the screen. She was standing in her kitchen, in front of a row of water-filled milk containers, and talking about her failed well. The camera dollied in until her face filled the screen. Then it backed away, leaving Sarabeth's frozen close-up as a portrait behind a pert brunette anchorwoman.

The anchorwoman shuffled papers professionally and announced that, "As a result of today's negotiations and the promise of a *Sixty Minutes* investigation, Mountain View Development will be making full restitution to Mrs. Mattingly and her neighbors. We asked State

Senator Dusty Rhodes to comment on his victory for our cameras."

Owen was stunned. How did this get to be a victory for Dusty Rhodes? But there the man was on the screen, walking down the muddy street in front of Sarabeth Mattingly's house, holding a large hunk of flyrock in his hands and addressing the camera.

"It's not enough just to make restitution to Sarabeth Mattingly and her neighbors," Rhodes said. "We must be sure that this travesty will never be repeated."

The camera closed in on Rhodes' face and was rewarded with an earnest stare. "To make sure that this doesn't happen again, I intend to introduce legislation giving the Department of Environmental Protection the power to handle claims such as these expeditiously, without litigation."

The camera pulled back to take in the hunk of flyrock held by the senator. Rhodes shifted it from hand to hand, and Owen found himself hoping he'd drop it on his foot. "The legislation will also set more stringent limits on blasting," Rhodes said when the camera returned to his face. "We intend to establish procedures for advance testing so that any blast-caused failures of wells and foundations can be documented, and the owners reimbursed."

Rhodes paused. "After all," he concluded, "it's a lot easier to reclaim land than to reclaim lives."

"Asshole," Owen blurted at the TV. "Those are my words. Where do you get off using my words?"

"Owen?" Judith's voice came faintly over the telephone, which he'd jammed against his hip. He'd forgotten she was on the line.

He raised the receiver to his ear. "I'm here."

"Isn't it great? Mountain View is scrambling to fix everything before *Sixty Minutes* comes with its camera crews. And the legislation's just what you suggested."

"Oh, yeah, it's great all right," Owen said without much conviction. "How the hell did Rhodes get involved?"

"I needed somebody from the West Virginia bar."

"I thought you were going to use Guy Schamp."

"Are you kidding? Guy Schamp could never have gotten these results. He'd still be swapping war stories with Mountain View's attorneys. He certainly never could have hooked us up with *Sixty Minutes*. My God, we'd have been lucky to get radio time on a late-night talk show."

Owen knew he ought to be happy that Sarabeth Mattingly was

getting restitution, but he still felt an uneasy sense of betrayal. Because he couldn't begin to match Judith's enthusiasm on the phone, or even appreciate it, he just said, "You can tell me all about it at dinner," and made arrangements to meet her at Lovisa's Café.

JUDITH POINTED A FORK holding a crouton and two leaves of lettuce from Lovisa's house salad at Owen. "What difference does it make who gets credit for it? Sarabeth and her neighbors are getting their homes fixed."

"I just feel like Rhodes is using us." He was careful to say "us" instead of "you."

Judith swallowed the forkful of salad. "Using us how?"

"He's a politician. He's riding the goodwill from this bout with Big Coal to get himself reelected. With any luck, the *Sixty Minutes* segment will air just before the election."

"What do you care? You're not running against him."

"I just don't trust him, is all."

"Why not? He's clearly been on the side of the good guys in sticking it to Mountain View Development, first for using its shopping center as a front for mining coal, and now for the damage it did with its blasting."

I'm afraid he might be sticking it to more than Mountain View Development, Owen thought. But he couldn't bring himself to say so out loud. After all, he had no evidence but his own paranoia. Instead, he said, "He only stuck it to Mountain View Development after we showed the world what they were up to."

"Give him credit for taking the right side at least. There'd be more political contributions if he sided with Mountain View."

"But more votes in opposing it."

"I give up." Judith wiped a fleck of salad dressing from the corner of her mouth. "What about you? You said you might have some big news."

Owen told her about Saint Vincent's billing practices and his suspicion that Kate O'Malley had been killed because she'd stumbled onto the hospital's overcharging scam.

"So you're convinced that your friend was murdered," Judith said when he finished.

"I'm almost sure of it."

"I'm sorry, Owen. I'm sorry she's dead and I'm sorry I accused you of fathering her child. I should have trusted you."

"I guess it did look bad for the home team." With all the talk of trust, he was glad he hadn't hinted that Judith might be too close to Dusty Rhodes.

"So tell me," Judith said, as if she'd read his mind, "aside from the fact that he's a politician, what do you have against Dusty Rhodes?"

Trust, Owen reminded himself. Just let it drop. But he answered, "I don't know. You tell me. Should I have something against him?"

Judith looked puzzled. She bit her lip and stared over his shoulder. He didn't know how to interpret her response. "Judith?"

"You better turn around slowly," she said. "There's a man behind you pointing a gun at your head."

SEVENTEEN

Brier-Patch Bargains

OWEN TURNED CAREFULLY in his seat. Letch Valence leaned on the edge of the booth, holding a revolver that was almost completely concealed by the leather jacket slung over his arm. The exposed barrel of the revolver pointed directly at Owen.

Time slowed, then stopped.

Valence puffed his cheeks and made a quiet popping sound, then stretched his lips into a tight smile. "Little preview of coming attractions. Just showing you how easy it's gonna be."

Time slipped slowly into gear. Owen was conscious of his own breathing. Somewhere behind him, silverware clanked.

"Wait a minute," Judith said. "Are you threatening this man?"

"What's it to you?" Letch asked.

"I'm his lawyer. I want to be clear on what's happening here."

Valence let the gun dip. It wavered in his hand, exposing more of the barrel. "This don't concern you. Butt out."

Judith brought her yellow tote bag up and laid it on the table. Her right hand was inside of it. "Are you threatening *me* now?"

"You got something in that bag?" Valence asked. "Take your hand out real slow. And it better be empty."

"You are threatening me."

"Judith, for Christ's sake," Owen said. "Leave it alone."

"That's good advice, lady." Valence turned the barrel toward Judith. The covering jacket slid back to his wrist, exposing the full length of the revolver.

Judith took her empty hand out of the tote bag. "I just want to be clear about this." Her voice was strained and, Owen thought, unusually loud. "Are you just threatening the two of us with that gun, or are you threatening everybody here in Lovisa's Café?"

At the table behind them, a small red-haired boy stared at Letch's exposed gun with the rapt attention first-graders give to Saturday-morning cartoons, TV shoot-outs, and open wounds. Across from the boy, a woman in curlers blurted, "My God, it's a gun. Run, Johnny, run."

Johnny looked from Letch to Owen and back again, not wanting to leave or have the channel changed. The woman lurched from her chair, grabbed the boy by the hand, and bolted for the door.

"I think *they* felt threatened," Judith said.

Valence waved his gun in small, tight circles. "I wasn't threatening them."

A murmur moved in waves through the café. Most of the diners headed for the exit doors, leaving a trail of discarded napkins in their wake. An older man in blue overalls ducked under his table for cover. The few remaining customers sat still, transfixed.

"Everybody here in Lovisa's Café seems to feel threatened," Judith said.

Valence stuffed the revolver inside his belt and donned his jacket. "I'm not threatening anybody but you."

"But you are threatening us," Judith said. "Both of us."

Valence zipped his jacket up halfway, then leaned forward to give Owen and Judith a look at the revolver. "That's right, lady. You're the lucky ones."

Sheriff Thad Reader came through the doorway with his pistol leveled. Two deputies followed him in, their guns drawn.

Valence quickly finished zipping up his jacket.

"What the hell's going on here?" the sheriff asked.

Judith pointed at Valence. "This man's been threatening us, Sheriff. You'll find a gun under his jacket."

Valence crossed his arms. "I was just joking around, Sheriff. I never threatened nobody."

"His threats were quite clear." Judith reached into her tote bag and pulled out her mobile phone. "Your operator should have a record of what he said."

Valence stared at the exposed phone. "That's been on the whole time?"

"That's what brought us here." The sheriff reached out, unzipped Letch's jacket, and removed the revolver from his belt. "Got a permit for this?"

"Course I do. I need it for my business."

Judith waved her mobile phone. "What part of your business involves threatening innocent diners?"

"Just keep pushing, lady," Valence said. "Just keep pushing and you'll make the same list as your client here."

"Now that sounds a lot like another threat," Judith said. "Where do we go to press charges?"

"Jail's just across the street." The sheriff took Letch by the arm and handed him over to the two deputies. "Take Letch here across and book him."

"Should we cuff him?" one deputy asked.

"Not unless he gets ornery. If he does that, though, you've got my permission to shoot him somewhere nonfatal but unpleasant."

"You'll be sorry you ever met me," Valence snarled at Owen.

"I'm already sorry," Owen answered.

The two deputies flanked Valence and led him out of the café. The sheriff watched them leave. "That's two nights in a row Letch has left here with his tail dragging because of you," he said to Owen. "If I were you, I'd find someplace else to eat tomorrow night."

"Can't you keep him locked up?" Judith asked.

"Wish I could, but he'll make bail and be out by morning."

Patrons began filtering back into the café. As they came through the door, they glanced at Owen and Judith and then looked quickly away, like rubberneckers passing a car wreck.

"He's not going to be a happy camper when he gets out," Judith said.

"Did you have to provoke him when he was holding a gun on me?" Owen asked.

"I was trying to get his threats on the public record. If he didn't shoot you when he first pulled his gun, I didn't think he'd shoot at all."

"But the way you were provoking him, he might have shot me anyway."

Judith smiled and patted Owen's arm. "I guess I was willing to take that chance. We're just lucky you'd programmed the sheriff's number into my phone the last time we needed it."

"The night you were wrestling mailboxes," the sheriff said.

"Your folks responded pretty well that night, too," Owen said.

The sheriff touched his hat brim. "That's the good news. The bad news is that Letch isn't your only problem. They're moving your aunt's trial up."

"She's innocent and you know it," Owen said. "Why would they move the trial up?"

"*Sixty Minutes.*"

"*Sixty Minutes* is covering Big Coal and Sarabeth Mattingly," Owen said. "What's that got to do with Aunt Lizzie?"

"Your aunt confessed to killing Sarabeth's husband. Nobody wants to have to explain to Mike Wallace why her husband's confessed killer is running around loose."

"So the DA would rather lose the case than go after the real killer?"

"He'd rather be seen on national TV prosecuting somebody's ass than sitting on his own. It's his fifteen minutes of fame. By the time he loses, the TV cameras will be long gone."

Owen shook his head. "I don't believe it."

"Believe it," the sheriff said. "Justice isn't so blind she doesn't want to look good on TV."

"We'll have to get together with Lizzie and Guy," Owen said to Judith. "Are you up for that?"

"I doubt that Guy will want me. I ought to be getting back to California anyway."

"Forget about Guy," Owen said. "I want you."

"Then I'll stick around. I guess I owe you that much for taunting the man with the itchy trigger finger."

"Don't let Owen give you grief over that," the sheriff said. "You saved his sorry ass."

GUY SCHAMP PEERED OVER his bifocals from a chair on the porch of Lizzie's hospice. "We could always object to moving the trial date up, but the judge has already been pretty liberal in extending it. I think it's time to fall back on every lawyer's last resort."

Lizzie set a tray of four steaming mugs on the wicker table next to Guy. "What's that?"

"The truth."

Lizzie laughed. "That's what Judith here has been suggesting for weeks."

Judith allowed herself a tight smile, nodded, and poured cream into her coffee.

"Thanks to Owen here, we know a lot more about the truth than we did before." Guy raised his mug in a salute to Owen. "Even though the truth Lizzie tells will leave Bobby Ray exposed, we can point enough fingers at Letch Valence to drown a jury in reasonable doubt."

Guy blew softly into his coffee mug. "Course, it would help a lot if the sheriff could break Letch's alibi."

"He's working on it," Owen said.

Lizzie moved behind Owen and Judith and rested her hands on their shoulders. "The two of you have been such a help. And not just with my case. There's Sarabeth Mattingly, too. I hear Dusty Rhodes taking all the credit, but we know who really got the well dug and the water hauled."

"There's at least one part of the deal that smells of Dusty," Guy said.

"What's that?" Owen asked.

"The lack of punitive damages. All he asked for was a straight one-for-one reimbursement. A well for a well." Guy shook his head. "Hell's bells, juries nowadays hand out damages that make Midas look like a piker. Woman gets millions from McDonald's for spilling hot coffee on her own crotch. Another woman in Philly gets a million for a CAT scan that she claims blotted out her psychic powers. You can't tell me old Dusty couldn't have stuck Mountain View with a couple of million in damages for drying up Sarabeth's well and cracking her foundation."

"That would have required a jury trial," Judith said. "Dusty thought it best to avoid dragging it out and get everything patched up as soon as possible."

"Sure would have been a shame if it dragged on past the election," Guy said. "Or if it was still up in the air when the *Sixty Minutes* cameras show up."

"You're being too hard on Dusty Rhodes, Guy," Lizzie said. "He's been good for this state."

"He's been good for Dusty Rhodes. He sets himself up as the champion of the people, but he's as deep into Big Coal's pockets as any of our politicians. The Mattingly case is a good example. He takes credit for sticking it to Mountain View, when he actually got the absolute minimum for his client."

"Not the minimum," Judith said. "He could have come away with nothing."

"In this county?" Guy snorted. "Not a chance. A bought-off jury of Mountain View stockholders would have had a hard time bringing a verdict against Sarabeth and her neighbors."

"That wasn't the way Dusty Rhodes saw it," Judith said.

"Course not," Guy answered. "Dusty's a master at setting up what my law professors at Harvard used to call false dichotomies. He only shows you two possible outcomes and hides any other options that might bite the hand that's really feeding him.

"Here in West Virginia, we call them brier-patch bargains. He did the same thing when Owen here caught Mountain View mining their shopping-center site for coal. Dusty held up two possibilities: let Mountain View off scot-free, or fine them the fees they would have owed if they'd gotten mining permits in the first place."

"What's wrong with that?" Lizzie asked.

"He could have fined them more, hit them with damages, or even barred them from getting anymore mining permits. Smaller companies have been hit harder for lesser offenses. If you limit the fines to the fees they would have owed anyhow, there's no penalty to keep them honest in the future." Guy smacked his hand hard against the side of his wicker chair. "Old Dusty slapped their wrist but managed to make a noise like he was coldcocking them."

"So he gets votes from the little guys and money from the big guys," Owen said.

"Man's slicker than snail tracks on a marble floor," Guy said.

"What about his plan to bail out Saint Vincent's bankruptcy?" Owen asked.

"It keeps the hospital afloat, so it's probably a good deal for the county," Guy said. "But it's a better deal for the shopping-center investors. By floating bonds to pay off Saint Vincent's debt, he props up some private asses with public funds."

"So Willis Grant won't do time for arranging that shady loan?" Lizzie asked.

"As a nonprofit, maybe Saint Vincent's shouldn't have been speculating in local real estate. But loaning money to a sister company isn't exactly illegal, so there's no way Willis will wind up in jail." Guy shrugged. "There's been enough bad press so the board will boot him out. But they'll call it early retirement and give him a golden parachute and a fancy retirement dinner."

Owen shook his head. "It's the American way."

"Old Willis has got more sand than cheap concrete," Guy said.

"He used the hospital's money to fund a losing real estate deal, salted coal profits away in a separate company, and stands to walk off even wealthier because the county can't afford to let the hospital fail."

"He couldn't have planned it better," Lizzie said.

"*Somebody* couldn't have," Guy corrected her.

"Not Willis?"

"I'll grant you Willis is not as dumb as he looks, but he's not a whole lot smarter, either," Guy said. "Took somebody sharper than him to set this up. Be interesting to see who holds the purse strings on Mountain View Enterprises. I'll bet you'll find a passel of Dusty Rhodes' campaign contributors."

Judith clanged her mug down on the wrought-iron table. "I've heard about enough of this gratuitous Rhodes-bashing. You and Owen are like two Monday-morning quarterbacks grousing after a win because your team didn't run up enough points to cover the spread. Well, guess what, fellows. There was another team on the field keeping the score down. It was Big Coal. And until Dusty Rhodes came along, that team had been damn near undefeated. You said so yourself, Guy, when Owen first told us about Sarabeth. Remember what you said? 'Big Coal rules these hollows.'"

"Judith's right, Guy," Lizzie said. "The Bellamys in Blair Hollow lost their home when they went to court over blast damage."

"So Dusty deserves a little credit for breaking Big Coal's winning streak," Judith said. "And I frankly don't see what any of this has to do with the strategy for Lizzie's trial."

"My apologies." Guy lowered his shock of sandy hair in a mock bow. "You're right of course. To review, we'll be following the biblical strategy laid out by Saint John in chapter eight, verse thirty-two."

"And that is?"

"'You shall know the truth. And the truth shall set you free.'"

"THAT ARROGANT BASTARD," Judith fumed in the car on the way back. "He acts as if the truth is his personal plaything, to trot out whenever it suits him."

"He views it as a strategic option, is all," Owen said.

"Just one of many options."

"I kind of like him."

"You would."

Owen smiled tightly. "What did you think of his take on Dusty Rhodes? That he's a closet crony of Big Coal, rigging legislation to limit their liabilities."

"That's horseshit."

"But a lot of his campaign contributions come from coal."

"Oh, don't be so naive. Most of the nation's electricity comes from coal. You grew up here. One third of this state's wealth comes from coal. Damn near all the money in this county comes from coal. Guy Schamp didn't get that cream-colored Mercedes defending people like Sarabeth Mattingly. You can bet Big Coal paid for a good share of his retirement. What you're hearing when he attacks Dusty is the righteousness of the repentant sinner."

"You've got to admit, though, that Rhodes' brier-patch bargains leave him looking like a man of the people without really nailing the mine developers."

"I'll give you a brier-patch bargain." Judith imitated Guy Schamp by drawling out the word brier so it rhymed with far. "One option is 'shut up and drive.'"

"What's the other option?"

"Drive and shut up."

SHORTLY AFTER Owen returned home, the sheriff's patrol car appeared in front of his house. Owen met Thad Reader on the porch. "We've got to stop meeting like this. The neighbors are starting to talk."

"Maybe I should cuff you or kiss you. Give them something to talk about."

"Don't bother. What they don't know won't hurt me."

The sheriff sat down on the porch swing. "Doc Sussman turned in his report." He handed Owen a folder with several neatly typed sheets. "Brought you a copy."

"And?"

"If Doc Johnston was faking it, he did a pretty good job. There's a slide in his autopsy report that definitely came from a woman six weeks pregnant."

"But was that woman Kate O'Malley?"

"Only way to know for sure is to dig up the good sister, run a DNA match."

"Shouldn't we make sure all the autopsy slides came from the same person before we do that?"

The sheriff nodded. "Doc Sussman's doing that. He sent them off to the FBI lab for a matching test."

"How long will that take?"

"Could be a couple of weeks. Lab's right here in the state, courtesy of Senator Byrd, but there's a long line ahead of us. Lots of demand, what with people wanting to overturn old convictions or get new ones."

Owen hefted the report. "What's Doc Sussman think?"

"He thinks the slides will match."

Owen slapped the report against his free hand. "Shit."

"But even if they do match, Sussman thinks we ought to test them against Sister Mary's DNA."

"Why's that?"

"Doc Johnston's reputation, mostly. He's about as reliable as a stopped watch. He once diagnosed an eight-month pregnancy as gas on the stomach."

"Bet the baby was a cute little fart."

The sheriff frowned. "That's my punch line."

"Yours and about three million high-schoolers."

"Well, it could have originated with Doc Johnston. He actually did misdiagnose an eight-month pregnancy. Sussman says the only way he'd spot a six-week pregnancy in a dead nun is if someone told him where to look and what to look for."

"You'd think he'd at least know where to look."

"Point is, it would be easy to miss, and Doc Johnston has already logged more misses than a blind goaltender."

"Sounds like you're ready to take the next step even if the lab reports show the autopsy slides match."

"And have the body exhumed, you mean?"

Owen still found it difficult to think about disinterring Kate's body. He just nodded.

"I'll order it. I'll need a judge's signature, but I should be able to get that."

"But we're looking at a two-week wait for the current DNA test. And at least another two weeks for the next batch. Isn't there some way we can speed up the process?"

"We could pay a visit to the good Doctor Johnston."

"Think he'd fall for your little eye detector?"

"The good doctor's a man of science. I don't think the eyes have it this time." The sheriff smiled and rose from the porch swing. "I've done a little homework, though. There might be other ways to bluff him."

FROM EVERYTHING HE'D HEARD about him, Owen expected Doctor Donald Johnston to be a ferret-faced little man with bad teeth and dirty fingernails. Nothing could have been farther from the truth. Seated in his office in a spotless white lab coat, Johnston looked more like Doctor Marcus Welby from the TV show Owen used to watch with his mother. Robert Young with a neat gray mustache. The man's countenance and bearing exuded confidence and competence. Owen had to keep reminding himself that the competence, at least, was nowhere to be found beneath the confident facade.

"Thank you for seeing us on such short notice, Doctor," the sheriff began. "We just want to talk a little about your autopsy of Sister Mary Perpetua."

The doctor nodded gravely. If the prospect bothered him, he didn't show it.

"This pregnancy thing was a big surprise, her being a nun and all," the sheriff said. "How'd you come to check for that?"

Johnston flashed a "Doctor Knows Best" smile. "Well, I knew the circumstances of her death and wanted to be as thorough as possible."

"It couldn't have been obvious," the sheriff continued. "I mean, with her only six weeks gone."

"No, but the trained eye learns to recognize certain abnormalities. And the samples I took bore me out."

Owen could understand why the doctor was in demand as a witness for personal-injury lawyers. His demeanor and delivery were convincing, even though Owen was sure he was dissembling.

"Here's the thing," the sheriff said. "Being a doctor, you probably know this. Nuns have a higher-than-average risk of uterine cancer. It's God's way of saying, 'Use it or lose it.'"

The doctor just nodded. Not giving anything away. Not even a smile.

"Because of this higher risk," the sheriff went on, "Sister Regina Anne orders regular exams for all her nuns. Sister Mary Perpetua had hers recently and it didn't show any pregnancy. How would you account for that?''

The doctor's eyelids flickered, as if he'd flinched faster than the eye could follow. "As you yourself observed, it's difficult to detect a pregnancy at such an early stage. Perhaps the examining physician missed it.''

"Could be. Hardly seems likely, though." The sheriff made a show of tilting his Mountie's hat back and scratching his thinning hair. "Something's sure screwy somewhere. So what we did, see, was have Doctor Sussman over at Saint Vincent's check your autopsy results. You know Doctor Sussman?''

The doctor nodded. A bead of sweat appeared between his close-cropped mustache and his upper lip.

"Well, Doctor Sussman said the autopsy slides came from a pregnant woman, all right. But we've still got this contradiction, see, between the results of your autopsy and Sister's uterine exam.''

The sheriff took two folded forms from his breast pocket. "So here's what we decided to do. What I've got here is a release to exhume Sister Mary's body.''

The sheriff kept the release forms folded. Owen knew they hadn't been signed.

The doctor licked the bead of sweat from his upper lip. "Why would you exhume her body?''

"So we can get this pregnancy thing resolved," the sheriff said. "Here's what I think might have happened. Maybe you made a mistake. Maybe you mixed up Sister Mary's slides with somebody else's. You think that might have happened?''

The doctor's cheeks reddened. "Absolutely not.''

"Because, you know, right now I might be able to understand a mix-up like that. If we have to dig up Sister Mary's body, though, and find out she wasn't pregnant..." The sheriff walked around the doctor's desk and put one hand on the back of his leather swivel chair. "Well then, I wouldn't see it as a simple mistake any longer. More like a conspiracy to commit murder.''

The doctor leaned away from the sheriff. "How's that?''

"If Sister Mary wasn't pregnant, it's not likely she was a suicide either. So your mistaken autopsy looks like part of a cover-up. Makes you look like part of the conspiracy.''

Squeezed between his chair and the desk, the doctor said, "My autopsy wasn't mistaken. And you won't learn anything by exhuming the body."

"Why's that?"

"I'm afraid I destroyed the uterus. Along with the other internal organs."

Owen winced.

"Well now," the sheriff said. "Doc Sussman and I talked about that eventuality. He said it might be difficult to verify a six-week pregnancy once the organs start to deteriorate. Now you're telling me the organs aren't even with the body?"

"That's right."

"Doc Sussman said we shouldn't worry, even if the organs deteriorate. One thing he can do if we exhume the body, you see, is check Sister Mary's DNA against the DNA of those slides you filed with your autopsy report."

The doctor slumped down in his leather chair. After a long silence, he said, "It's possible I confused the slides."

"Just possible, not for-certain sure?" The sheriff stood erect to give the doctor breathing room. "Speaking hypothetically, Doc, what would make you do a thing like that?"

"Overwork."

"Wouldn't have anything to do with the hundred grand that showed up in your bank account a week ago?"

The doctor slumped still more and whispered, "Oh, Jesus."

"Now I'm gonna ask you some more questions," the sheriff said. "You answer them to my satisfaction, I might be able to see that you don't spend the rest of your days in jail. You understand?"

The doctor nodded.

"Before I ask, it's my duty to tell you that you have a right to a lawyer, or to remain silent, and that anything you say can be taken down and used against you. Is that clear?"

"It's clear, yes. Just ask your questions."

"Was Sister Mary pregnant?"

"No."

"So you added that false information to the autopsy report?"

"Yes."

"Did you add anything else?"

"No."

"Did you leave anything out?"

The doctor closed his eyes and sighed. "Yes."

"What did you leave out?"

"There was tape residue on her wrists and mouth."

Anger welled up in Owen. "So she was bound and gagged."

From behind the doctor's chair, the sheriff signaled Owen to keep quiet. "And you saw fit to suppress this evidence?"

The doctor clenched his jaw and nodded.

"Why? If you were so thorough as to find a phantom fetus, why leave something out?"

The doctor shrugged and seemed to shrink still lower behind the desk. "I got a call."

"A call?"

"A voice offered me a hundred thousand dollars to report what I reported."

"Did you recognize the voice?"

"No."

"Man or woman?"

"Man."

"Old or young?"

"Don't know."

"I've got to tell you, Doc, your answers are starting to slip below the 'satisfactory' level."

"I couldn't tell about the voice. It was disguised somehow."

"What else did the voice say?"

The doctor lowered his head and muttered into his chest. "He knew things."

The sheriff cupped his hand behind his ear. "Speak up there, Doc. What things?"

"Things that got me removed from the staff at Saint Vincent's. Things that Sister Mary promised she'd never reveal."

"But the caller knew these things."

"He threatened to make them public if I didn't go along."

"So you lied in the autopsy."

"I lied. But Sister Mary had no right to tell those things to other people. She said if I resigned, she'd never tell anyone."

"What else do you remember about the call?"

"Nothing. Nothing else."

The sheriff slid a pad of yellow paper across the desk blotter. "Write it all down. Then sign it."

While the doctor was writing, the sheriff paced up and down in front of his desk. "I'll try to keep you out of jail, Doc. But you're never going to practice medicine in this state again. On your own or in a hospital. If I see you within ten feet of a stethoscope, or catch you consorting with shyster lawyers or insurance companies, you're going to find your ass behind bars.''

The doctor laid his pen beside the yellow pad. ''You can't do that. You can't stop me from practicing. You're not the state board. You're not the AMA.''

''As far as you're concerned, I'm the state board *and* the AMA. A Motherfucking Avenger, that's what I am. Now, did you lay that pen down because you're done or because you wanted to argue about acronyms and debate my jurisdiction?''

''I'm done.''

''Then sign it.''

The doctor signed the pad and slid it back to the sheriff.

The sheriff picked up the pad, read the statement, and handed it to Owen. ''I'll tell you something else, Doc. I'm going to get Sister Mary's killers. When I do, if I find you've been holding anything out on me—anything you don't want to tell or can't remember— you'll spend the rest of your life in jail.''

''I've told you everything I know.''

''You better hope so. You better think hard about that phone call. Remember everything that was said between 'hello' and the hang-up click. Make sure you squeeze all the juice out of it. Because if I find so much as a dribble that went unreported, I'll see you get the same treatment as the killers.''

The doctor slumped forward. Sweat stains under the arms of his white smock reached halfway to its belt loops.

IN THE SHERIFF'S squad car on the way back, Owen was irate. ''That son of a bitch. He's as guilty as the killers. How can you let him go free?''

''I may not,'' the sheriff answered. ''For now, though, the promise of freedom may prod his memory. I want to be sure I get everything he's got to give.''

''How'd you find out about the hundred grand?''

''Barkley's a small town, Owen. A hundred grand in cash sets tongues wagging. An experienced crook would have deposited it in dribs and drabs in separate accounts.''

''And that stuff about uterine cancer. Where'd that come from?''

"Sister Regina Anne called me. She remembered the nun's regular checkups and thought it might help."

"If it's true Kate's exam showed she wasn't pregnant, though, there's no need at all to recover her body."

"It's true. The exam showed she wasn't pregnant, but the results are over two months old. And a pap smear and physical exam wouldn't necessarily detect an early pregnancy anyhow."

"I didn't know that."

"Neither did I. Apparently the good doctor wasn't too sure of it either."

Owen laughed. "So you bluffed Johnston."

"With a few trimmings."

"Couldn't have happened to a more deserving guy. If we've got a pap smear, though, can't we get Kate's DNA from that? Without disturbing her remains?"

"We don't need to, now that we've got the good doctor's testimony."

"Are you satisfied he had nothing to do with Kate's death?"

"Not entirely. The killers had to get their morphine somehow. I think everything he's told us is straight, though. And we may still get more out of him."

"Be interesting to know who else besides Kate knew why Johnston was kicked out of Saint Vincent's. What do you suppose they were trying to keep secret?"

The sheriff shook his head. "When you think about all of Johnston's foul-ups that are common knowledge, I'm afraid to ponder what he wants to keep secret. I'm more interested in who else knew about it."

The sheriff pulled up in front of Owen's house. "I'll work on finding Johnston's mysterious caller. In the meantime, I've got that description you wanted of Vern Embry's car." He reached into his pocket and handed Owen a slip of paper with the words "Blue Chevy Cavalier," along with a license number. "Damned if I know what good it'll do you."

"Maybe none. But there's a good chance Embry left a recorded trail."

BACK IN HIS HOUSE, Owen broke out the videotapes he'd used to track Mountain View's late-night truck runs. Vern Embry had disappeared the same night Owen had videotaped the dump truck's trip to the Hash Ridge Mine. He found six blue Chevys on the first tape he reviewed, but none of them were Embry's. It had been a lot easier tracking an outsized yellow dump truck. It stood out in the flow of traffic, while the Chevys blended in.

He finally found the first trace of Embry's blue Chevy after three hours of watching cars follow one another on the TV monitor. It was traveling north on Possum Break Road, on the same tape that later recorded the first sighting of Mountain View's dump truck. The search for the next sighting of Embry's car took almost as long. It hadn't turned down the road to the Hash Ridge Mine with the dump truck. And it hadn't followed the Route 187 continuation of Possum Break Road.

Owen finally located the Chevy again on another tape. It was four in the morning, but what he saw made him so excited he called the sheriff's office right away and left a message. "Vern Embry didn't leave town alone. In fact, he may not have left town at all."

EIGHTEEN

Where the Sun Never Shines

OWEN STOPPED AT the Department of Environmental Protection for some information as soon as the local office opened and then showed up at the sheriff's office with his tapes, VCR, and TV monitor just after nine o'clock the next morning. He set the VCR and monitor up on a pale-green table in the sparsely furnished interrogation room.

"You've got to see this," he told the sheriff. "The night Vern Embry disappeared, I had tapes tracking Mountain View's trucks."

"The same tapes that led us to the Hash Ridge Mine?"

"That's right. I searched through all the tapes I recorded the night he disappeared. Here's what I found." Owen put a tape in the recorder. The monitor showed a string of cars following a rural road.

"Not much plot so far," the sheriff said. "No sex, either. And it's way too slow for a chase scene."

A blue Chevy crossed the screen. Owen stopped the tape, then reversed it frame by frame until the license plate was visible. "It's Embry's Chevy."

"Where is this?"

"Possum Break Road. Just after nightfall."

Owen backed the tape up a little more. The windows of the car were blank. "It's the wrong angle," he explained. "There's too much glare to see inside."

"No plot, no sex, no cast of characters. Suppose it is Embry. How do we know where he's going?"

"I had my cameras set up to find out which of Mountain View's mines was being used as a dump for the Dismal Mountain coal."

"So?"

"So the Chevy didn't show up again on any of the main roads I was taping. But look at this." Owen took the tape from Possum

Break Road out of the recorder and replaced it with another. The monitor showed a narrow gravel road with no traffic.

"No plot. No sex. No cast. Now there's not even any action," the sheriff shook his head. "I don't think we're looking at Oscar material here."

"Just wait."

The blue Chevy appeared on the screen. Owen froze the tape. "There's not so much window glare at this angle." The dark outlines of two heads could be seen against the front-seat headrests. "Two people in the car. Can't tell who they are, though."

"We'll put the FBI crime lab to work on the tape."

"You may not have to."

"Why not?"

"I told you. Just wait."

Owen let the tape run. No more vehicles appeared on the screen. "Where is this?" the sheriff asked.

"Crawley Creek Road."

"Not a road I'd choose for a getaway."

"I don't think Vern Embry chose it either."

Before the sheriff could respond, a black Jeep appeared on the screen, going in the same direction as Embry's Chevy. Owen stopped the tape and backed it up frame by frame to pick up the license plate. "Plate belongs to Letch Valence. I got a good look at it back when he was trying to run it up my tailpipe."

Owen let the tape run. The road was empty again.

"Not exactly rush-hour traffic," the sheriff said.

"It gets more interesting." Owen fast-forwarded the tape. "This is two and a half hours later."

The monitor showed the empty gravel roadway. Then the Jeep appeared, traveling in the opposite direction. Owen froze the tape. Two heads were visible through the Jeep's windshield.

"Jeep carried one man in, brought two out," the sheriff said. "Chevy ever come out?"

"Not while the camera was running."

"Plot's picking up. What's on down the road?"

"You can get all the way to Contrary if you keep winding across the mountain. But it's the long way around."

"Taking Crawley Creek Road to Contrary would be like going twice around your asshole to get to your pecker. Anything on the road before Contrary?"

"Crawley Creek Mine. That's the reason I set the camera up where I did. It belongs to Mountain View."

"Are they working it?"

"Not anymore. I stopped at the local DEP office on the way over. The mine's been shut down for five years." Owen unrolled a set of engineering drawings. "They had a map of the tunnels, though. Two years ago they hired a contractor to install drainage as part of a statewide reclamation project."

"And you brought these plans because you think you can find some coal Mountain View left behind?"

"I brought these plans because I think we'll find Embry's Chevy in one of their tunnels."

The sheriff reached into his pocket, pulled out his key ring, and twirled it around his finger. "Worth a shot."

Owen started to gather up his videotapes.

"Leave the tapes here," the sheriff said. "With no sex and no name stars, I don't think we can open nationwide. But we should be able to arrange a short run at the county courthouse."

"IT'S AS IF the mountainside healed up," Thad Reader said. "If it weren't for the tipple and the rail tracks, you'd never know there was a mine there."

Reader had parked next to the dilapidated tipple that had once fed the railhead of the Dismal Fork Mine. Rail tracks ran from the tipple through an overgrowth of wild grasses, ironweed, and goldenrod into the side of the mountain.

"Don't want to drive through those grasses," the sheriff said. "My muffler could start a fire that'd clear out the hollow." He handed Owen a flashlight from the glove compartment and took a portable searchlight from his trunk. Then the two of them followed the rails through the tall grasses to the boarded-up mine entrance.

Weathered planks hung vertically from the main beam over the mouth of the mine. Flush at the top, the planks had rotted at the bottom from contact with the damp earth, making the entryway look like a dental nightmare. Two longer planks had been nailed in a V over the vertical members, but the right arm of the V had been pulled off, along with several of the planks it had once joined, leaving a gaping hole in the mine entryway.

Owen played his flashlight on the hole left by the few remaining planks, which hung loosely from the overhead beam, marked with the faded imprint of the missing crosspiece. "Not exactly inviting."

"Could use a welcome mat and a few flowers. We tried to interest Martha Stewart in serving on the Mining Reclamation Committee, but she declined."

"Decorators are just like policemen. Never there when you need one."

"Ain't that just the way of it, though." The sheriff switched on his searchlight and led the way into the mine.

Owen felt a stab of dread. Until now, he'd been riding the adrenaline high that accompanied detection and discovery. Suddenly the road to discovery was taking him into the bowels of the earth, where the folk song warns that it's dark as a dungeon and the sun never shines. The sheriff was about to disappear into the blackness. Owen trained his flashlight on the sheriff's back, shoved aside his apprehension, and followed him in.

The mine's entryway was a corridor just wide enough to accommodate the coal carts that followed the rail tracks in and out. And wide enough to accommodate an automobile, Owen thought, although there was no sign that one had passed through recently.

Sunlight squeezing through the slits left by the missing entrance planks followed them nearly twenty feet down the corridor and then petered out. About ten feet farther on, the mine widened into a brown-walled anteroom with a low, wet ceiling supported by a small forest of stunted wooden beams.

Owen played his flashlight on the gray-brown walls. "No wonder this mine's abandoned. Anybody can see there's no coal here. The walls are all brown."

"It's rock dust. They spread limestone dust on the walls because it doesn't ignite the way coal dust does." The sheriff directed his searchlight beam to a black slash that looked like tarpaper poking through torn wallpaper. "You can see the coal seam there, where a hunk of slate fell away."

The rail tracks they had followed through the entry corridor dodged the wooden beams and disappeared into the center-most of five dark tunnels leading off the low-ceilinged room. While the sheriff directed his searchlight beam from one tunnel entrance to another, Owen shone his flashlight on the plans he'd gotten from the local DEP office. The plans looked like the imprint of a square waffle iron, showing a honeycomb of crisscrossing tunnels. The tunnels farthest from where they stood had been colored with a red cross-hatching and marked UNSAFE.

"Looks like the middle shaft with the rail tracks is the longest," Owen told the sheriff. "And it's one of the few that's still open all the way."

"Let's try it, then." The sheriff focused his searchlight on the center shaft and walked along the rail spur to its entrance. About twenty feet into the tunnel, another shaft met theirs at right angles.

"Where are the supporting beams?" Owen asked.

The sheriff shone his searchlight on the column of coal at the intersection of the two shafts, which measured twenty feet on a side. "They gouge out these shafts with continuous mining machines and leave enough coal in the columns to support the roof." The sheriff's searchlight sought out a metal plate in the damp ceiling. "They strengthen the ceiling with those roof bolts."

"It's been a while since I've been in one of these," Owen said. "Twenty-five years at least. I'd feel a lot better if I could see a few support beams."

"Now that it's all mechanized, they don't generally need support beams." The sheriff shone his searchlight down the side shaft, picking out a floor-to-ceiling wooden skeleton that looked like four ladders tied together. "When they think the ceiling might not hold, they strengthen it with those columns. They call them 'cribs.'"

The sheriff turned his searchlight back down the main shaft. "For the most part, the coal columns are all the support they need. When they're ready to pull out of a mine, they start from the back and harvest the coal in the columns. That's why that red area on your map is labeled UNSAFE."

Owen followed the sheriff with his flashlight. The crisscrossing beams of their two handheld lights pierced the blackness of the shaft, which soon funneled down so that neither the sheriff nor Owen could walk upright. Owen hunched down and played and played his flashlight beam on the parallel rails, picking his way over the cross ties.

"Look over here," the sheriff said, aiming his searchlight beam at the narrow space between the right rail and the shale wall. The beam picked up the faint outline of mud-caked tire tracks. "Somebody's been here recent. They tried to cover their tracks, but that one must have been under a little bit of water."

"Embry's car, probably," Owen said, pleased to have his logic validated, and relieved that they weren't likely to have to explore the other pitch-black tunnels.

A skittering noise came from the other side of the shaft. Owen swung his flashlight in time to catch the tail of a large gray rat as it scampered away toward the mine entrance.

"Miners used to say, 'When the rats leave, you leave,'" the sheriff said. "They can sense a cave-in coming."

"That rat just left. Should we follow it?"

"It didn't leave it because it sensed a cave-in. You scared it."

"I'd say the scaring was mutual."

"Let's keep going. We're onto something here. I can feel it. I can smell it." The sheriff stopped and sniffed at the heavy air in the tight tunnel. "Smell that?"

Owen inhaled the dank odor. "Smells just like a moldy cellar to me."

"No. I smell gas."

"Not methane, I hope." Owen knew that methane loosed by mining could cause major explosions.

"No. More like car exhaust. It's faint, but it's here."

They pressed on into the constricting darkness, following the rail spur. Owen had to hunch his shoulders and bend his knees with each step to keep his head clear of the damp ceiling.

The crisscrossing flashlight beams picked up a makeshift barrier formed by two toppled crib ladders, weathered planks, and a knee-high mound of shale and debris. A wheelless coal cart was propped upside down against the mound.

Owen had been counting his steps and measuring them against the length of the shaft in the plans he carried. "The shaft shouldn't end this soon."

"It doesn't." The sheriff yanked the broken coal cart away from the barrier and kicked out at the wooden cribs. The nearest crib splintered and gave way, raising a cloud of black dust from the debris pile.

Beyond the makeshift barrier, their flashlight beams glared off the chrome fender and tailpipe of a blue Chevy Cavalier. A garden hose led from the tailpipe through the window on the driver's side, where a man's head was visible.

Owen trained his flashlight on the barrier while the sheriff splintered the second crib and knocked aside the remaining planks. He used the last plank to level the mound of debris, raising more black dust and clearing the way to the blue four-door coffin.

The Chevrolet had been driven as far as it would go into the mine shaft, so that there was barely any room between the car and the lowered ceiling. The sheriff worked his way between one gray-brown wall and the driver's side of the car, while Owen edged along the passenger side. He had just focused his flashlight beam on the pallid profile of the seat-belted driver when the sheriff cracked open the car's front door.

A fetid stench like sour milk, car exhaust, and rancid meat assaulted Owen's nostrils. The pungent odor drove him backward, and he stumbled onto the overturned coal cart, fighting nausea.

The sheriff's voice echoed off the tunnel walls. "It's Vern Embry, all right."

Owen sat on the overturned cart and ducked his head between his legs. He heard a scuffling noise and felt the sheriff's hand on his back.

"You all right?" the sheriff asked.

"Smell got to me."

"Never quite get used to it. Somebody rigged it to look like a suicide."

Owen swatted at the hose leading from the car's exhaust. "What kind of a suicide barricades himself in a mine and erases his tracks before sucking on an exhaust pipe? Who are they kidding?"

"Whoever did it didn't want him found anytime soon. So long as he's missing, he's the prime suspect in a half-million-dollar theft."

"Which somebody else has pocketed."

"The longer it takes to find him, the easier it is to sell the suicide story. A few years from now, nobody'd notice that his tracks were erased. Likely they might remove the barricade, too. You and your videotapes screwed up some careful planning."

The sheriff took his cell phone from his pocket, flipped it open, and punched a button. When nothing happened, he punched it again, then shrugged and snapped it shut. "Won't work here in the mine." He pocketed the phone. "I want to take a last look before we go out and call in the crime-scene folks. Don't go anywhere."

Owen wasn't sure his wobbly legs would let him stand. "I'll stay if you insist. I was thinking of going off to look for Becky Thatcher, though."

The sheriff opened the car door as far as he could. "Who?"

"Tom Sawyer's girlfriend. Wasn't she lost in a cave?"

"Oh, yeah. But Tom found Injun Joe instead."

"Native American Joe. I don't think you can call them Injuns anymore."

The car horn honked. Startled, Owen rose six inches off the coal cart.

"Shit. Sorry," the sheriff called. "Not much room here."

Owen put his head back between his legs. He didn't know whether it was the smell itself or what he imagined was causing the smell that was making him nauseous.

The car door slammed and the sheriff appeared beside him holding a small tape recorder. "Look what I found in Embry's inside pocket." He rewound a short length of tape and pushed PLAY.

They heard the hum of a car engine. Then a car door opened and a muffled voice said, "Don't turn the ignition off. Suicides can't turn the ignition off when they're done."

Owen raised his head. "That sounds like Letch Valence."

A second, clearer, voice answered, "I'll turn it back on when I get this tape off his wrists. Otherwise, the fumes'll get me, too."

The sheriff rewound the tape a little more. The engine's hum still dominated the recording. Then an unfamiliar voice said in a shaking half-whisper, "They're outside waiting, the vultures. They think I'm praying. Well I am. I'm praying they don't find my pocket recorder."

"Jesus Christ," the sheriff said. "The man recorded his own murder."

Owen felt the same mixture of fascination and horror he remembered as part of an accident team listening to the cockpit recorder of a doomed aircraft.

"Man brought me here calls himself Wolfe," the voice continued. "Showed me ID that said he was with the IRS. Other man's Letch Valence. Followed us out in his Jeep. Sounds like he's running things. He's not. Man behind this...is Willis Grant."

There was a pause, followed by a short, soft bleat. Then the voice went on. "Grant forced me to overcharge patients. He knew things. About Minna's insurance. Sister Mary found out. I told Willis. Wanted to quit."

The voice was slowing, slurring, as if he were talking under water.

"Ordered IRS audit. Willis found out...somehow...sent Wolfe...not IRS...slow down."

A sudden sharp intake of breath, and the voice dribbled away to a whisper. "Slow down, Minna. I'll catch up."

Except for the steady hum of the car engine, the tape was silent.

The engine continued to hum for a long while. Then a car door opened and they heard Letch Valence saying, "Don't turn the ignition off."

The sheriff switched off the recorder. "That's where we came in."

"They taped his hands. Just like Kate's."

"Didn't bother to tape his mouth, though."

Owen flashed his light around the tight, damp blackness. "Who'd hear him if he screamed? What was that he said near the end? Slow down...something?"

"'Slow down, Minna.' Minna was his wife. She passed a few years ago."

Both flashlights spotlighted the silent recorder. A timber creaked somewhere near the mine entrance.

Owen swung his light in the direction of the sound. "What was that?"

They heard a skittering noise, and the sheriff's searchlight picked up a large gray rat. The rat rose up on its haunches, frozen by the beam. Then it scampered past them, disappearing under the Chevrolet.

"Oh, shit," the sheriff said. "Something scared it our way." He began running toward the mine entrance. "Come on."

Owen rose to follow, not quite comprehending.

The sheriff's searchlight beam jounced off the scarred brown walls as he hurried, hunched over, picking his way between the rail ties. He had just reached the anteroom when the outer corridor exploded.

NINETEEN

The Weeping Madonna

THE BLAST ECHOED down the corridor and drove the sheriff backward, his arms flailing.

The ceiling shook and the tunnel rumbled as the shock subsided. Owen hurried to the sheriff, who lay flat on his back, covered with dirt and powdered coal dust. "You all right?"

The sheriff pulled himself up to a sitting position, trying to flex the fingers of his left hand. "My wrist took a pretty good whack."

Owen retrieved the sheriff's searchlight and handed it to him. "Can you move your fingers?"

The sheriff pressed his left wrist against his chest and used his right hand to shine the searchlight on the entry tunnel, which was filled with shale and loose chunks of limestone. "Fuck my fingers. The entrance is shot to hell."

They crossed the anteroom and played their flashlight beams on the entrance. Only six feet of the corridor remained. The rest was clogged with rubble. Owen calculated that the rubble blocked at least twenty-five feet of what had been the entryway.

"Don't suppose there's a back door to this place?" the sheriff asked.

Owen's senses shut down for a few seconds. Finally, he answered the sheriff. "They didn't build it with one."

The sheriff massaged his left wrist with his right hand. He winced and shook his head. "Shit. Shit. Shit."

"Let me look at your wrist."

"Fuck my wrist. We've got bigger troubles. Goddamn Letch Valence. Had to be him."

"Must have followed us."

"Probably been trailing you, waiting for his chance."

"Or they could have rigged an alarm, somehow, to let them know when visitors showed up."

"Whatever they did, it's left us up shit creek."

"Who knows we're here?" Owen asked. "Did you call your office?"

"Yeah, I called them."

"Well then, won't they come here looking for us?"

"Last location I reported was Crawley Creek Road."

"But not this mine?"

The sheriff shook his head.

"Was that good police procedure?"

"What the fuck do you know about good police procedure? For your information, this here mine is private property. What we did could be construed as breaking and entering."

"We had the videotape records. Don't they give reasonable cause for search?"

"If we come out with Embry's body, yes. Nobody'd say a word. I didn't want to have to justify B and E if we didn't find it."

"Well, we found it."

"Now the trick is getting it out." The sheriff set his searchlight on the floor and squatted on his haunches. Lit from below, he looked like a character in a silent horror film. "What about you? Anybody know you were coming here?"

Owen shrugged. "Nobody."

"All right. When will you be missed?"

"I was supposed to pick my mother up for chemo this afternoon." He imagined his mother waiting at the hospice, then phoning her home, finally calling a cab. How long would it take for her to report him missing? "What about your office? We left the videotapes there."

"The tape in the monitor shows Crawley Creek Road, but nobody's likely to put that together with this mine."

"What about your patrol car?"

"We might get lucky there. But I wouldn't count on it. It's out of sight of the road, and the road doesn't carry much traffic. Anyhow, there's a good chance Valence will have moved it." The sheriff stood up, causing his shadow to stretch to the tunnel ceiling. "Like I said, we're up shit creek."

Owen stood to join the sheriff. "Let's look around. Maybe we can find a paddle." He tried to keep his voice steady, to project an optimism he didn't feel.

They set out to explore the dark labyrinths of the interior tunnels. The right-most tunnel constricted to a tight crawl space after about five hundred feet. The next tunnel over once went deeper, but was clogged with rubble. They turned and started back toward the anteroom when Owen's flashlight flickered.

"Turn that damn thing off," the sheriff said. "What the hell are you doing, wasting batteries? We only need one light on this mission."

"Sorry. I didn't think—"

"Neither did I. We've got to start thinking, though, if we want to make it out of here alive."

Owen turned off his flashlight and followed the sheriff in silence. The bar on his walking cast was caked with mud, and he could feel the sweat soaking his undershirt as he labored to keep up with the sweeping searchlight beam.

At the intersection of two tunnels, the beam silhouetted a broken-handled pick leaning against the coal-support column. "First ray of hope I've seen," the sheriff said. "Maybe we can dig ourselves out."

Owen hefted the pick. Its metal head was still solidly attached to its broken and splintered handle. He forced the handle through his belt and began walking down the tunnel.

"Where you going?" the sheriff asked.

The question confused Owen. "Just getting back to our search."

"Not that way," the sheriff said, swinging his searchlight down the adjoining tunnel and spotlighting their muddy footprints. "This is the way we came."

"Jesus," Owen said. "All these tunnels look alike."

The sheriff took the pick from Owen and slashed a horizontal gash in the wall of the tunnel they'd just traversed. Then he scratched two diagonal lines to turn the gash into an arrow. "That'll tell us we've been here," he said. "Christ. How can we hope to find our way out if we can't even find our way back?"

The center passage with its rail tracks bore deeper into the mountain than any of the other tunnels, extending at least a thousand feet beyond Embry's Chevrolet before choking off. For the length of that thousand feet, all the side tunnels leading into the center passage had been marked as UNSAFE on Owen's map. A few of the side tunnels had crude cardboard DANGER signs tacked over them. Others bore no warnings at all. Some tunnels had collapsed entirely, squeezing shards of wooden supports into the main corridor like severed limbs. Others appeared clear.

The sheriff shone his searchlight down one of the apparently clear passages. "Maybe we ought to check this out."

"Better not. Map says it's unsafe."

"Looks okay from here."

"It's not worth it. It doesn't go anywhere."

"We can't afford to leave anything unchecked."

"We can't afford to go into the tunnel. For one thing, it could collapse. For another, we don't know it's ventilated. Ever hear of the black damp?"

"It's what miners call oxygen deprivation."

"Right. There's no warning. You just feel dizzy, keel over, and die. Let's at least check out all the open tunnels first."

Reader handed Owen the searchlight. "You think you know where we should go, you lead."

Owen saw the way the sheriff held his left wrist pressed against his breastbone. "Is your wrist all right?"

"Will you quit worrying about my wrist? That fucker Valence has left us buried under a mountain of coal. Try worrying about that."

Stung, Owen pointed the searchlight down the rail lines and started back toward the anteroom.

In three more hours of exploring, they covered the two other open tunnels leading from the anteroom and found, in addition to the broken pick, a torn sleeping bag filled with rat droppings, a roll of blasting wire, two coal carts with three wheels between them, and the contents of Embry's trunk, which included a jack, a screwdriver, a spare tire, strapping tape, a coiled clothesline rope, two flares, and a suitcase full of clothes and shaving gear.

"He must have thought he was leaving town," the sheriff said, snapping the suitcase shut.

"He did leave," Owen said. "I just hope we don't follow him."

They sat on the trunk of Embry's car while Owen fashioned a crude splint from strapping tape and splintered crib wood and immobilized the sheriff's wrist. Then they headed back down the main tunnel toward the anteroom and the collapsed entryway.

In the anteroom, Owen shone the searchlight up the long metal air shaft leading to the surface. "At least we won't suffocate. All the main tunnels vent through clear shafts. We better not stray too far from them, though."

The sheriff peered up the main vent. "Not big enough for Santa Claus. Guess we can write off Christmas this year."

Owen sat back against a pillar and cradled the searchlight between his legs. If we're not out by Halloween, he thought, we'll have a good start on skeleton costumes. But he kept the observation to himself.

The sheriff paced along the rail line, causing his searchlight-cast shadow to leap from the wooden pillars to the gray-brown walls and back again. "There's no way we can get out of this ourselves. We've got to find some way to contact the outside world." He took his cell phone out of his pocket. "I'm going to walk around with this, see if there's anyplace it works."

Reader reached between Owen's legs and picked up the search-light. "Mind if I take this?"

"And leave me here in the dark with the rats? Why should I mind?"

"Come on along, then."

Owen's back and neck ached from walking lopsided on his cast and hunched over to clear the low ceilings. He waved the sheriff off. "Go ahead. I'll just sit here and hold up this pillar. I've got the flashlight for emergencies."

"Its batteries are about to go. Better not use it too much."

"Blaze a trail on the coal columns. And don't try any of those abandoned passages. I don't want to have to hunt for your body in the dark."

"You sentimental fool. You do care after all."

"Don't flatter yourself. It's the searchlight I'll be looking for."

The sheriff made an arc on the ceiling with the searchlight beam. "I won't be long."

"Good luck." Owen didn't think there was a chance that the phone would work anywhere in the mine, but he didn't want to squelch the sheriff's hopes. It was a long shot, but their lives were likely to depend on long shots. He watched the searchlight beam grow smaller and smaller as the sheriff disappeared down the main tunnel, leaving him alone in the dark.

It was a dark like he'd never known. Not the dark of a moonless night, when the eye adjusted and shapes still shifted and moved, but a deep, shadowless dark, a limb-amputating dark that left him no sense of his own boundaries.

He'd never thought much about his own death, but he never imagined it would come this way, blind to the world, caught in a dark trap with tons of coal and rock where the sky should be. It was like getting an advance tour of your own tomb.

Jesus, he had to stop thinking that way. It's not a tomb until you're dead, and we're not dead yet.

He couldn't see the rubble in the entrance tunnel, but he tried to visualize it. At least twenty-five feet of crumpled mountain blocked their way out. He didn't think they could dig through it. That meant they had to make outside contact. But how?

Smoke signals? Who'd see them? Maybe they could use the blasting wire to rig an antenna for the sheriff's cell phone. He tried to remember what he'd learned about broadcast frequencies and wavelengths in college, but he hadn't been particularly interested at the time and the intervening years had wiped it all out.

He felt a pang of hunger. He'd missed both breakfast and lunch. Usually, it wouldn't bother him. If he was noticing it, though, it must be well past dinnertime. He guessed it must be at least seven-thirty in the evening. He switched on the flashlight, which had just enough power to illuminate his watch. It was only four in the afternoon.

The surrounding darkness had upset his internal clock so that he couldn't sense what time it was. He was like a novice pilot in bad weather who couldn't tell up from down without a clear horizon line. He shut off the flashlight and let the darkness envelop him. Better get used to it.

He sat alone in the dark, his back against the wooden pillar, trying to keep his mind free of dread and reset his internal clock by guessing when an hour had passed. He came up ten minutes short with his first guess. Where the hell was the sheriff? He should be back by now. It hadn't taken them much more than three hours to explore every open passageway. Maybe Reader was poking his nose into the abandoned tunnels. He'd wanted to try them the first time through.

Or maybe the black damp got him. It wouldn't be a bad way to die. Quick and painless. Just drop and doze. A lot better than slow and painful. Which is what they were facing.

Owen's stomach growled. It had to be well past dinnertime. He fought the urge to use the flashlight to check his watch again. Wait at least an hour. How long should he wait before he went looking for Reader? How could he look for him, anyway? Reader had the only reliable light. What if he didn't come back?

Owen's left leg began to tremble. It had trembled uncontrollably when they put him to sleep before they set it. He thought then he was fighting the anesthetic, afraid he might not wake up. He leaned forward and pushed both hands down on his thigh. Why was it trembling now?

He released the pressure on his thigh. He couldn't see his cast, but he could feel it flopping about like a gaffed fish. As if it wasn't a part of him. Stand up, he told himself. Stand up and put your weight on it. As he struggled to put his right leg under him and stand, he heard the rumble of a car engine.

The roar grew louder, and the Chevy's taillights appeared, backing out of the main tunnel.

Owen's leg stopped trembling. He edged behind the pillar so he wouldn't be run over.

The sheriff backed the Chevy along the rail tracks into the center of the anteroom, where he parked and swung the door open. "Couldn't get the phone to work, so I tried my luck with this here car."

"Wasn't it out of gas?"

"There's a little left. Either they didn't restart it after Embry died or the engine just stalled out."

"So we've got gasoline."

"Better yet, we've got headlights, radiator water, and a place to sleep."

"What'd you do with the previous driver?"

"Left him as an offering for the rats."

"That's not funny."

"Do you see me laughing? Tell you what's really not funny. I listened to the rest of Embry's tape." The sheriff pulled the tiny recorder from his shirt pocket. "Couple more tapes in with Embry's shaving gear. He'd been getting the goods on Willis Grant for several weeks. Thought he was going into the witness protection program. It's all on the tape. Guy came to his house posing as an IRS agent."

"He must have suspected something, or he wouldn't have been taping it."

"I don't think he was sure he was in trouble until the guy asked him to turn down Crawley Creek Road. Embry objected and the guy pulled a gun."

"That's not necessarily a dead giveaway. The IRS has been robbing people for years."

"Not at gunpoint." The sheriff shook his head. "Letch Valence showed up once they got to the mine here. What an asshole. He took the last hour of Embry's life telling him what a fool he was to think he could bring down Mountain View Development. Bragging on how well-connected they are. Told Embry he never had a chance."

"I've heard Valence gloat. Embry probably welcomed the carbon monoxide."

The sheriff tapped the recorder. "It's tough listening to the tape. After hearing it, though, it'll be a pleasure to bring Letch Valence in for good and all."

"We've got to get out of here first."

"I've got a few thoughts on that." The sheriff disappeared into the main tunnel. He reappeared about ten minutes later, pushing a reconstructed coal cart. The cart wobbled along on three wheels, but didn't leave the rails. Inside the cart was the broken pick they'd found on their first trip through the mine.

The sheriff hefted the pick. "We're going to dig ourselves out while we've still got the strength."

"What do you mean, 'we'? I see only one pick."

"I've thought of that." The sheriff popped open the Chevy's trunk and rummaged through it, retrieving a screwdriver from the spare-tire well and a pair of leather gloves from the suitcase. He used the screwdriver to pry a rear hubcap off the Chevy. Then he put the gloves in the hubcap, raised it overhead with his good hand like a waiter balancing a tray, and carried it to Owen.

The sheriff bowed deeply and handed over the hubcap and gloves. "Your shovel, sir."

Owen took the hubcap, pulled on the gloves, and helped the sheriff push the three-wheeled cart up to the wall of rubble that blocked their exit.

The sheriff swung his short-handled pick at the center of the wall.

"Not that way," Owen said. "It's at least twenty-five feet and we'd need pillars and beams to shore up the tunnel."

The sheriff gestured toward the anteroom. "Lots of pillars and beams back there."

"Even if we could manage it, I wouldn't know which ones to pull out. And the thought of playing pick-up-sticks with hundreds of tons of rock overhead doesn't appeal to me."

"Where do we dig, then?"

"Out the top." Owen took the searchlight and pointed it at the seam in the ceiling where the cross-bracing was still intact and the wall of rubble began. "The blast didn't damage that cross-bracing. Let's start pulling the rubble away from that seam."

"Won't the mountain just replace whatever we take out?"

"It has to run out sometime. There's a pretty good system of trees and roots over our head. If the blast didn't damage that cross-bracing, it probably didn't loosen a lot of dirt above it. We just have to take out whatever's higher than the ceiling between us and the entryway."

"That could be a lot."

"Like you said, there's no backdoor."

The sheriff swung his short-handled pick at the top of the wall of rubble just ahead of the surviving cross beam. A chunk of shale tumbled down the sloping wall to the floor of the tunnel. The cavity it left was filled by two smaller black clods. "Your turn."

On the other side of the tunnel, Owen took his hubcap and scraped at the seam, dislodging a flow of black dirt. More rubble filled the void.

The sheriff began swinging his pick in rhythm, causing a small avalanche of black chunks to tumble to the tunnel floor. Coal dust swirled around them. Owen scraped at the seam for a while, then took his hubcap and filled the coal cart with the rubble they'd dislodged. He pushed the cart along the rails into the anteroom, dumped it against the wall, and then rejoined the sheriff.

They worked nonstop for what felt to Owen like three hours. When he checked his watch, though, he found that only two hours had passed.

Seeing Owen check his watch, the sheriff asked, "Got an appointment?"

"Just wondering if it was quitting time."

"Best keep at it. If you ain't ruptured yet, you ain't doing your share," the sheriff said, exaggerating his normal twang.

Owen went back to work with his hubcap, scraping down rubble and loading the coal cart. The sheriff's face, arms, and clothes were covered with a fine black sheen. From the powdery patina on his own clothes, Owen knew his face must match the sheriff's.

After what seemed to Owen to be another hour, the sheriff stopped swinging his pick. "We're wasting batteries. Think we could do this in the dark, just turn the light on to mop up?"

Owen shrugged. "I'm game to try it."

Reader turned off the searchlight and Owen began scraping at the seam with his hubcap. Rubble tumbled past him, now and then bouncing off his toes. Although the sheriff was only two arm lengths away, Owen couldn't see him. But he could hear the steady rhythm of his pick. The air felt heavy and hard to breathe.

Without any trace of light, Owen felt the need to talk, to establish contact. "Imagine doing this for a living?"

The sheriff matched his responses to the swing of his pick.

Thwack. "They got machines." *Thwack.* "That do it now."

"Before the machines, I mean. Just picking at a black wall for eight hours a day, inhaling all this dust."

Thwack. "Took a special breed." *Thwack.* "Ever know any?"

"Knew an independent miner over in Contrary. Stonewall Jackson Hobbs. Feisty, hardheaded, peacock proud."

Thwack. "Used hard and used up." *Thwack.* "They gutted the mountains."

Thwack. "For out-of-state owners." *Thwack.* "Now welfare guts them."

"Between the machines and the litigation, it's got to be tough."

Thwack. "Hard to find work." *Thwack.* "Harder to find hope."

The sheriff switched on the searchlight and glared up at the overhead seam. "The mountain fills it as fast as we take it away." He turned the beam on the tunnel floor. They were ankle-deep in rubble. "Maybe we best clear away this mess and call it a night."

OWEN STRETCHED OUT in the backseat of Vern Embry's Chevy, leaving one door open to allow him to extend his long legs. All the scraping and hauling had left his neck and shoulders stiff, and he twisted and turned, trying to find a comfortable position. He was just as happy that the sheriff had taken the front seat, which had recently served as Embry's next-to-last resting place. The lingering smell of car exhaust reminded him of Embry and turned his mind to thoughts of death.

He'd seen a lot of death lately. There was Kate, bound, gagged, and dispatched by morphine. And Maggie Mason, joking about getting down to a size eight. And now Vern Embry, whose recorded death haunted him. In the end, Embry had hallucinated. Maggie, too, had hallucinated during one of his visits.

Could he expect to hallucinate? Would that be one of the signs? He turned on his side, feeling the grit on his clothes soil the Naugahyde seat cover. What had these people left behind? Kate had nothing and left nothing. Maggie left two estranged daughters, a newspaper clipping, and an unclaimed wedding ring. Embry left a suitcase and that damned and damning recording.

Not much to show for three lives. But he wouldn't leave much more. He'd always wanted children, always assumed that they would come eventually. He had to stop thinking about death and dying. Get a grip. Concentrate on something else. He tried naming the Cincinnati Reds' lineups from 1960 on, and fell asleep before he got to the championship teams of the early '70s.

He slept fitfully and awoke in the all-encompassing dark. For a moment, he experienced the unsettling horror of not knowing where he was. Then he remembered, and the horror settled in.

The sheriff snored softly in the front seat. Owen slid quietly out of the backseat, felt on top of the car for the sheriff's searchlight, aimed it toward the car's rear bumper, and turned it on. Then he sat with his back against the bumper and unrolled the maps he'd gotten from the Department of Environmental Protection.

He took the measurements of the now-clogged entry corridor from the plans, then turned them over and sketched two parallel lines representing the corridor on the back of the plans. He topped the two parallel lines with a triangle representing the mountain that had existed before the explosion. Then he measured off the twenty-four feet of corridor that had been obliterated by the explosion and dropped the overhead triangle representing the mountain into it, so that he could calculate the amount of dirt and slag that sat above the seam they were trying to clear.

He estimated that they'd have to remove roughly a thousand cubic feet of dirt and slag to free themselves. At the rate they were going, that would take four days.

Four days. Could they last four days? He was certain their flashlight batteries wouldn't hold out that long. Maybe, if they dug in the dark, and used the car headlights when they needed to, the light would last. But could they dig for four days without food? Were his calculations right? Had they made a mistake somewhere? He'd become so accustomed to calculators and computers, it was hard doing the math by hand.

He stretched his legs out in front of him, pressed his ankles together, and stared down at his muddy feet. The athletic sock covering his cast was just as black as his soot-covered shoe. He'd have to rework his calculations, try some different assumptions about the slope of the mountain.

He glanced at the slate wall pressing in on him. There, in the center of the wall, was the image of a white-robed nun.

"Kate?" he said aloud.

Was he hallucinating? In the time it took to ask that question, he recognized the phantom for what it was, the retinal image of the soot-black feet he'd just stared at. He could blink and make it disappear, but he tried not to.

Eyes wide open, he watched as the image started to fade. Then it began to weep.

He stood and walked over to the wall. The image had vanished, but the tears remained.

He touched the sweating surface. An underground stream had worked its way through a crease in the layers of shale. Rivulets etched in the wall below the crease told him the stream had been there for some time. But he hadn't noticed it before.

The flesh on his arm prickled under the layers of coal dust. It was a sign from Kate. It was an old stream, a retinal image, and a trick of the mind, but it was a sign from Kate.

He watched the groundwater trickle along the base of the wall. Where was the water going? If it was a sign from Kate, what the hell did it mean?

Owen returned to the plans he'd dropped when he went to examine the apparition on the wall. They'd re-rolled themselves into a cylinder beneath the Chevy's rear bumper. He unrolled the plans and studied them in the glare of the searchlight. And the meaning of the sign became clear.

He banged on the front door of the Chevy. The sheriff stirred. White eyes appeared in the coal-black planes of his face.

"Wake up," Owen shouted. "I know how to get us out of here."

The sheriff stumbled out of the car, rubbing his eyes.

Owen unrolled the plans on the hood of the Chevy. "A contractor filed these plans four years ago when they put in a drainage system as part of a statewide reclamation project. The legislature didn't want these old mines flooding."

"So?"

Owen pointed to a series of alternating long and short dashes. "So there's a drain at the end of the right-hand tunnel."

"How'd we miss it?"

"The tunnel shrinks down to a tight crawl space at the end. We didn't go back into it. That's where the drain comes in, though. They picked the shortest distance to daylight—about sixty feet."

"Hope the drain's a little wider than that straight line."

"The plans call for a sixteen-inch pipe. It'll be a tight squeeze, but it's as close to a backdoor as we're going to get."

They hurried down the right-most tunnel. Just before it ended, the ceiling squeezed down to a three-foot clearance. Owen wriggled in, tracking ruts in the mud with his elbows and knees. "Here it is."

The sheriff's searchlight lit up a half-circle of steel pipe. "Nobody's going to fit into that."

"No. It's a full sixteen inches across. They came in a little low when they drilled in from outside." Owen scooped out a handful of mud. "We just need to widen the mouth."

The sheriff disappeared and returned with the broken pick and hubcap they'd used to dig the night before. Owen scooped out muck with the hubcap while the sheriff used the pick to widen the crawl space. When the mouth of the pipe was fully exposed, the sheriff laid aside his pick. "I'll go first."

Owen looked at the sheriff. An ex-football coach, his shoulders and thighs bulged as if he were still wearing pads. "You may be a little too broad to fit, and your wrist is taped up."

"But you've got that half-cast on your leg." Reader stripped off his grimy uniform shirt, exposing an undershirt ringed with a coal-dust collar. "Only one of us really needs to make it out."

Owen slid feet-first out of the crawl space. "You're welcome to try."

The sheriff's head and shoulders disappeared into the crawl space. Owen could see his hips twist and his knees struggle for purchase in the mud. Massive grunts accompanied each thrust of his buttocks.

After five painful minutes, the sheriff backed out of the crawl space. Both of his undershirt sleeves were torn, and one shoulder was rubbed raw and bleeding. "Christ, it's like trying to screw a Coke bottle. Even if you can do it, it's no damn fun." He slid past Owen until he found room to sit upright. "All right. You try it."

Owen nodded toward the sheriff's torn undershirt. "The curse of a manly physique."

"Luckily, you won't have that problem." The sheriff reached out and knocked twice on Owen's cast with his wrist splint. "I think you're gonna make it." He backed away and found standing room. "Wait a minute before you go in."

The sheriff followed his searchlight out of the tunnel. Owen stripped off his shirt and ran his hand over the bottom of the drain. Murky water trickled along the curve of the steel pipe.

The sheriff returned with Vern Embry's suitcase and a coiled length of clothesline rope. He knelt in front of the crawl space, opened the suitcase, and pulled out a neatly folded undershirt.

Owen almost laughed. "The last thing I need right now is a change of underwear."

"You'll need this," the sheriff said. "Give me your arm."

Owen extended his left arm and the sheriff wrapped the folded undershirt around his elbow. Then he secured the shirt with strapping tape, fashioning a makeshift elbow pad.

"Other arm," the sheriff said, tearing off lengths of strapping tape with his teeth.

"That's the roll of tape they used on Embry. Isn't it likely to be evidence?"

"We got enough evidence in the tape recorder to fry Valence and see that Grant simmers in prison for the rest of his days. We just need to get out to use it." The sheriff taped up a second elbow pad, then rigged kneepads from folded boxer shorts. "Embry'd be glad to know we're putting his legacy to good use."

Owen started to duck into the crawl space, but the sheriff grabbed his arm. He made a noose of the clothesline rope and looped it around Owen's waist. "It's gonna be tighter than a gnat's navel in there. You get stuck, yank twice on this. Maybe I can help pull you out."

Trailing the clothesline rope, Owen wriggled into the crawl space and clasped the searchlight over his head with both hands like a Jedi knight wielding a light saber. Then he thrust the light into the drainpipe and shoehorned his shoulders in after it. Both shoulders scraped the sides of the pipe, but he was able to squirm forward on his knees and elbows.

By the time he'd wriggled far enough to get both feet into the tunnel, he saw a slanting shaft of light ahead of him. He stopped, swore aloud, and jerked twice on the rope around his waist. Then he pushed himself backward as the sheriff pulled on the rope.

As soon as his hips cleared the mouth of the pipe, he turned on his side so he could shout out to the sheriff. "Stop tugging on the rope. You're about to take my pants off."

"Problems?"

"The good news is, I can see the light at the end of the tunnel. The bad news is, it comes in checkerboard squares. There's an animal grate blocking the mouth of the pipe."

"Shit. Hold it there a minute." The sheriff's legs disappeared from Owen's view, and he heard him clomping off down the corridor.

The sheriff returned with a screwdriver. He ducked his head into the crawl space and handed the tool to Owen, whose torso was still in the drainpipe. "Take Embry's screwdriver. Maybe you can pry the grate loose from the inside."

Owen stuck the screwdriver under his belt. "Give me your cell phone, too."

"Good idea." The sheriff handed the phone into the drainpipe.

Owen stuffed the phone under his belt as well. "What's your office number?"

"Punch MEMORY, then ONE."

Owen wriggled ahead until both feet were in the drainpipe. Then he pulled himself forward on his elbows, dragging his legs behind. Sixty feet, he thought. The distance from the mound to home plate. How many times had he felt small enough to crawl that distance?

He raised his buttocks and tried to push forward with his knees, but his hips caught on the drainpipe wall. Most of his progress would have to come from his elbows. He crept forward, scooting on his forearms and lifting his tailbone tentatively, like an injured inchworm.

After about ten feet, a raised seam in the pipeline rubbed his shoulder raw. He shrugged past it and scraped along another ten feet, when he encountered another protruding seam. Two more seams tore the flesh from his shoulders before he reached the animal grate at the mouth of the drainpipe.

The sunlight streaming through the grate blinded him temporarily. He crept forward, his eyes squinting against the light, and pounded the grate with the butt of his flashlight. It didn't budge.

Beyond the grate, limestone strata stepped down about twenty feet to a gravel road, where a rusting pickup raised dust as it bounced along. A teenager sat in the bed of the pickup. Owen thought for a moment the teen was waving at him, then realized he was just exposing his bare arms to the air flowing over the truck's cab.

Owen pried at the grate with Vern Embry's screwdriver, but it held fast. He took the sheriff's cell phone from under his belt, extended the antenna, and stuck it through the grate. "Please, God, I need a little help here," he prayed as he punched in the sheriff's office number.

There was a long pause, followed by a short ring. Then a live male voice said, "Sheriff's office. Can I help you?"

Owen sighed. "Boy, can you ever."

TWENTY

Coming Clean

THEY HEARD THE MACHINES long before they saw them. First a faint drone, then a chugging clatter, and finally a thundering roar as a backhoe bucket ripped through the entryway ceiling. The bucket was pink, with fierce eyes painted on either side of threatening yellow teeth. The fearsome countenance was a welcome sight, but not nearly so welcome as the sunlight streaming in behind it.

Two men in silver space suits slid through the slim opening left when the backhoe removed a mouthful of debris. One poked at the air with a steel rod, while the other offered oxygen and bottled water to Owen and the sheriff.

Owen inhaled the fresh air and let the water cascade past his parched lips, splash down his throat, and trickle over his coal-blackened beard. Then he sat on the fender of the Chevy while two backhoes gobbled up the remaining rubble blocking the entryway.

When the entryway was clear, the two spacemen led Owen and the sheriff out into the sunlight. They stepped onto a widening path between two walls of debris that ended in a semicircle of vehicles and sawhorses linked by yellow crowd-control tape. The vehicles included an ambulance, two patrol cars with their lights flashing, and a yellow van bearing the insignia of WSAZ-TV.

Crowds of people packed into the spaces between the vehicles began to cheer as soon as they caught sight of Owen and the sheriff. As the two men approached the parked vehicles, a young blonde woman led a TV cameraman forward and thrust a hand microphone at the sheriff, who dodged around it to talk in private with one of his deputies and two ambulance attendants.

The blonde interviewer turned from the sheriff to Owen, who waved her off. He'd spotted Judith and his mother behind a taut yellow tape stretched between a sawhorse and the TV van. Before the deputy assigned to crowd-control could stop him, Owen breasted the yellow tape like a winning sprinter and carried it into the crowd to hug Judith.

When they finally broke the hug, Owen became conscious of the crowd's clapping and the TV camera pointed at the two of them. Judith's blouse was covered with coal dust, and the right side of her face was jet-black. Owen dropped her hand, turned to his mother, and blackened her with a second hug.

As Ruth Allison clutched Owen, he could feel her tears against his cheek. When she released him, though, she said in her best finger-wagging voice, "How many times have I told you not to play in abandoned mine shafts?"

Before he could answer, the blonde TV interviewer shoved her microphone into Owen's face and asked, "How does it feel to be freed from that black pit?"

Owen smiled. "After a day and a half in an underground tomb, I feel like Lazarus."

The interviewer frowned and dropped her microphone to waist level. "The department store?"

Ruth laughed.

Owen continued to smile. "No. The biblical Lazarus. He was—"

Sensing something was wrong, the interviewer cut short Owen's explanation by reclaiming the microphone and saying, "We understand there's a body still inside the mine. Can you confirm that for our viewers?"

Owen closed his fist over the microphone ball and swung it aside. "You'll have to get that news from the sheriff."

Over the shoulder of the interviewer, past the cameraman, Owen could see the sheriff directing a deputy and two paramedics into the mine shaft. As the paramedics headed into the mine carrying a folded stretcher, the sheriff turned and approached the cameraman.

Owen removed his hand from the microphone. "Here comes the sheriff now."

Glad to be released from Bible Class, the interviewer turned her back on Owen and directed her cameraman to film the approaching sheriff.

The sheriff stopped, mopped his brow with a handkerchief that left a swath of white skin showing above his coal-caked eyebrows, and began answering the interviewer's questions.

From where he stood on the fringe of the crowd, Owen could

hear snatches of Reader's answers. "Yes, there is a body in the cave." "Identification will have to wait until next of kin had been notified." "Apparently died of asphyxiation." "We'll know more after the coroner has a chance to examine the body."

The paramedics emerged from the mine carrying a stretcher that held Vern Embry encapsulated in a body bag. The interviewer cut short her questioning, took her cameraman's arm, and tugged him toward the ambulance so they could capture the loading of the body for the evening news.

The sheriff watched the interviewer position herself in the frame with the paramedics and the ambulance. "Woman's got the persistence of a palsied woodpecker."

"Roughly the same IQ, too," Ruth said. "Imagine not knowing who Lazarus was."

"She knew he founded department stores in Columbus and Huntington," Owen said.

"Was that before or after he rose from the dead?" the sheriff asked. He watched the interviewer address the camera. "Kinda cute, though. I've got deputies who aren't much smarter, with half her drive and none of her looks. I tell you, I'd trade a couple of them for her, even up, and throw in a patrol car or two."

The sheriff nodded toward a slim deputy with a hawk nose lounging against his patrol car and chatting with two women standing just inside the police cordon. "Speaking of my deputies, see that dandy on crowd-control over there? That's Wes Waldron. He's the one who took your call from the drainpipe."

"I won't soon forget," Owen said.

"Tells me he hasn't been able to find Letch Valence. Evidently Valence has gone to ground."

"Did Valence have something to do with all this?" Judith asked.

"All this and more."

"And he's still loose? Oh, Owen."

"What about Willis Grant?" Owen asked.

"You're gonna love this," the sheriff said. "Wes thought Grant was too important a personage to pick up on your say-so alone, so they haven't touched him."

"What's to keep him from following Valence into hiding?"

"They did put him under surveillance at least. Wes figures he's not likely to go anywhere, though. Tonight's his retirement dinner.

The board cut him a sweetheart deal and they're holding a roast and naming a hospital wing in his honor.''

Owen shook his head. "Man bankrupts the hospital and they're naming a wing in his honor.''

"Man bankrupts the hospital, kills two people, and embezzles a half million dollars, and he's a hero to the public,'' the sheriff said. "I'm in the wrong damn business.''

"The public doesn't know about the murders and embezzling,'' Judith said.

"They know about the bankruptcy. They'll know about the rest soon enough,'' the sheriff said. "I'm going to get my wrist fixed and pick Grant up myself. If I hurry, I can bring him in just before he gets to his dinner.''

"You say the dinner's a roast?'' Owen asked. "Where everybody makes jokes at the expense of the guest of honor?''

"Homage disguised as public humiliation.'' The sheriff spat on the ground. "Just another feather in our murderer's cap.''

"You'll have to really hustle to get your wrist fixed and arrest Grant before the roast.'' Owen checked his watch. "Maybe you shouldn't be in such a hurry. You've got him under surveillance. Why don't we take our time, get cleaned up and go to his dinner?''

"And join in the public homage?''

"It was the humiliation I had in mind. Strikes me nothing's likely to be more humiliating than a public arrest.''

WHEN THE BATHWATER turned the murky gray of mine runoff, Owen drained the tub and refilled it with water as hot as he could stand, adding his mother's bath salts until the bubbles skimmed the rim of the tub. The operation was complicated by the need to keep the cast on his left leg dry. He propped it on the edge of the tub and sat back, letting the hot water engulf him and rinse the coal dust from his pores.

The foot of the cast was caked with grime and his protruding toes were black with soot. He leaned forward and tried to clean his toes with a washcloth, but they were just out of reach. He raised his cast from its haven on the side of the tub in an effort to bring his toes within reach, but his tailbone slid forward and he went under.

He came up sputtering and swearing, and his flailing arms knocked the plastic shampoo bottle halfway across the bathroom floor. He swore at the bottle, too far away to reach, and at his cast, which had taken a ducking when he slid underwater.

"What's going on in there?" Judith called.

"Nothing." His voice betrayed his frustration.

Judith cracked open the bathroom door and poked her head in. "Need help?"

Owen waved at the shampoo bottle and his damp cast. "Can't reach anything."

Judith came into the bathroom. She still had on the blue jeans she'd been wearing when Owen was freed from the mine shaft, but she'd changed to a clean tank top. She replaced the shampoo on the lip of the tub, then perched next to it, took Owen's cast in her lap, and began applying a washcloth to his grimy toes.

"They tell me some people find toes erotic," she said.

"If you're one of them, there are five more somewhere under these suds."

"I'll pass. You can reach those yourself."

She wrung out the washcloth. "I was really worried about you. When you didn't show up for your mom's chemo, I thought that man Valence had gotten you."

"He almost did."

"He's still loose. Maybe you ought to leave town. Go back to California."

"Mom needs me."

"I can take care of your mom for a while. She's feeling lots better."

"She's my responsibility. Anyhow, Valence has bigger worries than me right now. The sheriff wants him for murder."

"Letch Valence didn't strike me as a real clear thinker. He may not set his priorities the way you would." Judith lifted the cast from her lap. "Best I can do. You really ought to get that cast replaced. It's crumbling and starting to smell."

"Aren't we all?"

"Speak for yourself." She laid the cast on the edge of the tub. "Anyplace else you can't reach?"

"There's this spot right in the middle of my back."

Judith smiled and slipped off her sneakers. "Scoot forward a little."

She rolled her jeans up above her knees and stepped into the tub, straddling Owen from behind. "Water's hot."

"I like it that way."

She slid down to sit on the edge of the tub, pressing her knees against Owen's shoulderblades. "Now, where's that pesky spot?"

Owen relaxed against her knees. "You may have to hunt for it."

She ran the damp cloth over the nape of his neck and then began kneading his left trapezius muscle through the cloth. "Is it there?"

"I'm not sure. Keep that up a little longer."

She shifted to the right trapezius. "How about there?"

"You're getting warmer." He tilted his head to give her more room to work. "In the mine, I was thinking I'd really like to have children."

Judith stopped kneading his neck. A trickle of water from the cloth ran down his spine.

Owen broke the silence. "It's not as if we haven't discussed it before."

"That was half a lifetime ago. Before the divorce."

"I'm feeling lucky to have any lifetime left."

"We'd be starting pretty late."

"It's not even five-thirty."

She flicked the top of his head with the washcloth. "You know what I mean. I'm pushing forty. You're forty-six. That's pretty late."

"Better late than neutered."

"Jesus. Be serious a minute."

Owen felt her knees pressing against his shoulder blades. "What makes you think I'm not serious?"

"I mean, we still have issues to settle between the two of us. And now you're talking about three of us?"

"Or more."

"Oh God, Owen. I really need to think about this."

Owen grabbed Judith's ankles, pulled her legs apart, and slid backward, sloshing a wave of water between them. Then he tilted his head back into her soaked tank top and looked up into her startled hazel eyes. "While you're thinking, could we maybe practice a little?"

THE PRIVATE DINING ROOM of the Frederick Hotel had a placard posted on each side of the door. The placard on the left announced retirement roast and bore Willis Grant's name and a picture of his bullet head.

On the other side of the door, a placard chipped and creased from too much handling bore the picture of an aging actor raising two bushy gray eyebrows and a stubby cigar. The picture's caption announced:

YOUR EMCEE
DUANE "DROOPY" TALES
APPALACHIA'S ANSWER TO GEORGE BURNS

"Somebody should tell him George Burns is dead," Judith said. She'd changed into black pants and a gray blouse and stood with Owen in the hotel lobby watching diners arrive to attend Willis Grant's retirement dinner.

"I'm sure he knows. He's old enough to have been around before Burns met Gracie Allen."

"Who is Droopy Tales, anyhow?"

"When I watched him, he was Appalachia's answer to Howdy Doody. We had only three TV channels when I was growing up."

"Is this going to be one of those 'how tough I had it as a child' stories?"

"Only if you'll stop interrupting long enough for me to tell it. After school, we had three viewing choices: The Mickey Mouse Club, Howdy Doody, or Droopy Tales. Droopy broadcast out of the local Huntington station, so I tended to watch him."

Owen remembered the younger edition of Droopy Tales, wearing an outsized tuxedo jacket that dragged the ground behind him as he half-strutted, half-stalked around the stage, raising and lowering his eyebrows and flicking cigar ashes at the camera. Later, in college, when he first saw a Marx Brothers film, Owen thought Groucho had copied Droopy's walk. By the time he'd seen all of the Brothers' films and committed their best bits to memory, he realized it was the other way around. Droopy had copied Groucho.

"He was no spring chicken when I was growing up," Owen said. "The man must be at least seventy-five."

"Didn't George Burns live to be a hundred? Maybe that's the comparison Tales is advertising."

"In Appalachian years, he's already got Burns beat."

A young man in a tuxedo standing at the entry door asked Owen, "Excuse me, sir. Will you be coming in? The dinner's about to start."

"We're waiting for someone."

The sheriff came through the hotel's revolving door with three uniformed deputies trailing after him. He saluted Owen and Judith with a hand encased in a fresh white cast, conferred with the deputies, and sent them to stand somewhere near the banquet room's exit doors. Then he offered Owen and Judith each an elbow and led them through the main entrance to the festivities.

"Excuse me, but do you people have tickets?" asked a man guarding the entrance.

The sheriff waved him off. "It's all right, son. We're part of the entertainment."

THE BANQUET ROOM was set up with a series of round tables accommodating eight to ten diners. Owen counted ten full tables as he, Judith, and the sheriff took over an empty table in a corner well removed from the raised podium set against the far wall.

Willis Grant sat at one end of the long table that commanded the podium. He'd taken off his jacket and was talking loudly and gesturing with his beefy arms to communicate with the occupants of the round table nearest him.

A stocky, middle-aged woman with silver-gray hair sat at the other end of the podium table. From the way she ignored Grant's loud conversation, Owen assumed she must be his wife.

The center chair at the long table was occupied by a man who looked old enough to be the father of the aging actor in the entryway photo. Owen revised his estimate of Droopy Tales' age upward by ten years.

A thin man with close-cropped hair and a goatee sat between Droopy Tales and Willis Grant's wife. The sheriff identified the man as Gerald Elmer Reynolds, board chairman of Mountain View Enterprises. The chair between Droopy Tales and the guest of honor was empty.

A waitress brought three fried chicken dinners and set them in front of Owen, Judith, and Reader. The sheriff picked up a drumstick and began eating it with his fingers. "Never thought I'd see the day when the Frederick Hotel's chicken would look good to me. After our time underground, though, this seems like a veritable feast.''

Droopy Tales waited until the waiters began serving dessert and then rose to address the crowd. After alternately encouraging and disavowing their applause, he said, "The man we're honoring here tonight needs no introduction...because you wouldn't know who he is even if I told you." The wispy gray eyebrows shot up and his cigar did a little dance beside his mouth. The audience took this as a cue to laugh.

Tales milked the laughter, then cleared his throat and said, "But seriously, folks, Willis Grant is the kind of man who brings laughter and happiness whenever he goes." The eyebrows shot up again, the cigar danced, and Tales repeated the punch line. "That's *whenever* he goes. Get it?"

At the end of the table, Willis Grant roared and slapped his thigh, and the rest of the audience laughed along with him.

Tales held up both his hands, palms outward, as the laughter died down. "Joking aside, folks, it's hard to overstate what Willis Grant has done for this community." He paused. "Hell, it's hard to understate it." Tales chomped on his cigar and pretended to sift through a sheaf of papers. "In fact, I can't find anything to say about it at all.

"So help me out here, folks. We all know Willis Grant's reputation. Just to get us started, I'd like to ask anyone who's ever been screwed by Willis to stand up."

Amid a smattering of nervous laughter, a blowsy blonde woman with a cantilevered bosom stood and waved.

"Obviously a plant," Judith whispered. "Nothing about her is real."

"Oops, is my face red," Droopy Tales said. "I meant to ask anybody who's been screwed *over* by Willis Grant to please stand up. Let's try it again. Anybody who's been screwed *over* by Willis Grant, please stand up."

One or two men at a front table stood up. They were joined by two or three others scattered around the room. Then, as the audience caught on to the joke, half the diners were standing and laughing. Willis Grant doubled over and slapped the head table with his meaty palm.

"That's it, that's it. Now you're catching on," Droopy Tales said into his microphone. "You're gonna be a great audience and we're gonna have a lot of fun tonight, I promise you.

"Here's how it's gonna work. Those of us here at the head table are going to tell a few stories about our guest of honor. Then, when we're done, we'll put a mike down in front so you all can add your two cents worth."

"That'll be our cue," Owen whispered to the sheriff. "Did you bring the tape?"

The sheriff patted his pocket. "Brought a copy. Original's in my evidence locker."

"Then," the emcee continued, "if Willis has been a good sport through all this, we'll let him have his say. Give him his day in court, as it were."

Owen smiled and repeated, "As it were."

"Prophetic," the sheriff said.

"I almost feel sorry for the poor schmuck," Judith said.

"Don't," Owen said. "You haven't heard the tape. He's behind at least two murders. There's Kate O'Malley and Vern Embry for sure, and probably Sam Mattingly as well."

Grant's wife Verna stood up briefly to say, "I'd like to tell you an interesting story about Willis, but he's so boring I can't think of one. I can tell you this, though. If the doctors at Saint Vincent's ever give me a month to live, I'd want to spend it with Willis. It'll seem like a hundred years."

Grant frowned through his wife's speech, then laughed when Tales, eyebrows dancing, said, "How about that, folks? Willis and Verna have been together for six happy years. And six out of thirty ain't bad."

Then the board chairman of Mountain View Enterprises read from a prepared script that reflected little credit on Willis Grant and even less on the preparer. After everyone at the podium had their say, Droopy Tales acknowledged the empty podium chair by saying, "We had hoped our state senate candidate Dusty Rhodes would join us tonight, but he's busy campaigning."

"Not like Dusty to pass up a crowd this size," Thad Reader observed. "It's almost as if he knew the guest of honor's going down in flames."

"He's wrapping up some *Sixty Minutes* stuff," Judith said.

Owen wanted to ask how Judith knew what Rhodes was doing,

but the sheriff tapped his arm and nodded toward two waiters who were installing a microphone in front of the podium. "Get ready."

Tales reached into his vest pocket and pulled out a yellow sheet of paper. "Even though Dusty couldn't be here, he did send our guest of honor a telegram. He asked me to read it, knowing how Willis here struggles with literacy."

The crowd, conditioned to laugh at any stab at Grant, hooted while Droopy Tales solemnly donned a pair of bifocals. Tales cleared his throat to quiet the diners and read the telegram. "'Dear Willis, congratulations on your retirement. You're truly an inspiration to us all. If you can make it to the top, anybody can.'"

The crowd roared and clapped as Droopy Tales pocketed his bifocals and the telegram.

"Now we come to the audience-participation portion of the evening," Tales said. "I see we've got the microphone installed. Anybody who wants to can step right up and share a Willis Grant story with us. Come on, now. Don't be shy."

A short, balding man seated at the table nearest the podium stumbled over his chair in his haste to get to the microphone. He arrived at the mike just ahead of Owen, who stood aside and waited while the man launched a rambling discourse about Grant's magical ability to turn a bankrupt hospital into a shopping center and an unopened shopping center into a coal mine.

Grant scowled at the mention of the hospital's bankruptcy, and held the scowl as the speaker concluded by clutching the mike and saying, "I'll say this for you, Willis. Success hasn't changed you. You're still the same mean son of a bitch you always were."

As the crowd laughed, Willis Grant replaced his scowl with a frozen grin and nodded to the speaker, who relinquished the microphone to Owen.

"My name's Owen Allison," Owen said into the mike.

A puzzled frown flitted across Willis Grant's face before the frozen grin returned.

"The previous speaker mentioned Mr. Grant's coal mines," Owen went on. "Well, Sheriff Thad Reader and I just spent a little time in one of those mines. You can watch us coming out on the evening news later tonight.

"We went into the coal mine looking for Vern Embry. You all know Vern Embry. He disappeared about the same time a half million dollars went missing from Willis Grant's hospital."

Grant blanched visibly. Droopy Tales' eyebrows danced as he nodded encouragement.

Out of the corner of his eye, Owen could see uniformed deputies stationing themselves at each exit. "Well, we found Vern Embry. What was left of him. He'd been in the mine a little too long. We didn't find the missing half million, though."

A smattering of nervous laughter ran through the audience. Owen could feel the tension building in the room. He held up Vern Embry's tape recorder. "What we did find was this tape recorder. Vern Embry managed to record his final words."

Owen held the tape recorder up to the microphone and pushed PLAY. Vern Embry's voice filled the room. "The man behind my murder...is Willis Grant."

When Owen had anticipated this moment in his mind, he imagined the audience would react with stunned silence as the forces of law and order advanced to arrest Willis Grant. Instead, the audience erupted in laughter. They thought it was a put-on, a staged part of the roast. But Willis Grant wasn't laughing. He recognized the voice.

The voice on the tape continued. "Grant forced me to overcharge patients. He knew things." Laughter was drowning out Embry's last words. Owen switched off the recorder and waited for the laughter to die down. When the room was relatively quiet, he announced, "I believe Sheriff Thad Reader has something to say."

While Reader shouldered his way past the people waiting in line to speak, Droopy Tales bounced his eyebrows, jiggled his cigar, and said, "Is this great, or what?"

Reader took the microphone from Owen. "Willis Grant, I'm here to arrest you for conspiring to murder Vernon Embry." Again laughter erupted. The sheriff ignored it. "You have the right to remain silent..."

Owen turned and watched the audience as the sheriff read Grant his Miranda rights. Half the crowd was laughing uncontrollably. The other half sat in uncertain silence.

When the sheriff finished reading Grant his rights, he advanced on the podium, joined by two deputies. The deputies flanked Grant, who rose and shambled off between them with Reader following.

The laughter turned edgy and was about to die when Droopy Tales stood and said, "How about that, folks? Let's hear it for the sheriff." Then he raised both hands, wiggled his fingers like quotation marks, and winked as he repeated, "...the sheriff."

Led by Tales, the audience started applauding. As the sheriff reached the exit, he turned, touched the tip of his Mountie's hat with his cast, winked back at Tales, and followed his captive out the door.

Owen left the microphone, threaded his way through the applauding audience, and took Judith by the arm. Just as they were leaving, Droopy Tales took over the microphone to announce, "You can come back now, Willis. We're not done with you yet."

Owen held the door open for Judith. As he did so, he heard Tales' voice turn plaintive. "Willis?"

Owen swung the door shut and breathed in the cool mountain air.

Judith turned to walk toward their car. "Wait a minute," Owen said. "I better give the sheriff his tape back."

They'd left through the hotel's main entrance, while the sheriff and his deputies had taken Willis Grant out a side door. Owen took Judith's hand and they rounded the corner to see Grant arguing with the two deputies.

Out of view of the dinner crowd, Grant had turned obstreperous. His curses carried a block down the near-deserted street. Neither of the deputies appeared to want to manhandle their prominent prisoner, who swore and pounded on the roof of the squad car.

Finally, as Owen and Judith approached, the sheriff said, "Fuck it. Cuff him."

The taller of the two deputies took Grant by the arm and spun him around so that he faced Owen and Judith. Seeing the two of them, Grant swore again, jerked free of the deputy, and lunged for Owen's throat.

The sheriff moved quickly to intercept Grant. As the three men came together, a gunshot exploded in the night air.

TWENTY-ONE

The One-Eyed Trust

THE SHERIFF GRABBED Willis Grant and threw him to the pavement.

Owen stood frozen for a second. Then he clutched Judith and pulled her down to the sidewalk. A second shot rang out, chipping the curb.

They scrambled for cover behind a parked patrol car. Another shot shattered the patrol car's window.

The sheriff lay motionless in the street, covering Willis Grant with his body. Blood pooled on the asphalt beneath them.

Owen edged around the bumper of the patrol car. After the next shot, he'd try to pull the bodies back out of the line of fire. Before that could happen, the sheriff rolled off Grant, tucked his knees under him, and sprang for the cover of the patrol car.

Grant lay motionless on the pavement, bleeding from his mouth and chest. He looked as if he'd never move again. The two deputies returned fire with their pistols from behind a car parked two spaces away.

The sheriff rose to his knees, opened the door of the patrol car, crawled in under the steering wheel, and radioed his office. Then he took the shotgun from the clamp next to the passenger seat, slid back out, and joined Owen and Judith on the curb. "Riot squad's on the way."

A shot punctured the patrol car's tire, which exploded with a loud pop.

"Shots are coming from the third floor of that theater across the street," the sheriff said.

"The Keith-Albee," Owen said. "I used to usher there."

"What's on the third floor?"

"Just offices and storage when I worked there. It wasn't a multiplex then, though."

The crowd from the dining room had collected behind the hotel's revolving doors. When the next exchange of shots ricocheted off one of the door's glass panels, the watchers screamed and everyone vanished inside.

"How many ways in and out?" the sheriff asked.

"Two fire exits on either side of the main screen open into the alley behind the theater. Then there's the front entrance beyond the box office."

"What about the roof?"

"Fire escape in the rear alley gets you there."

"Can you reach it from inside?"

"Don't think so. There's one other entrance. Theater used to be a vaudeville house. The basement's honeycombed with old dressing rooms and tunnels. One of the tunnels comes up where the stage door used to be, in a store in the mid-block arcade."

"What store?"

"Thirty years ago, it was Van's pinball parlor. After I quit ushering to play baseball, we used to sneak into the theater through Van's shop and the underground tunnels."

"Think you could find your way back in?"

"You're not going to take Owen into that theater?" Judith said. "Surely someone else must know about those tunnels."

"I don't have time to advertise for help. And Owen's the one they're shooting at."

"Grant's the one bleeding in the street. Why do you think they're shooting at Owen?"

"Grant's down in the street, but they haven't stopped shooting. Look around you. You see anybody else who's been getting death threats?"

"So you think Letch Valence is the one shooting at us?"

"He's the one who's been making the threats."

A black-and-white police van, siren blaring, rounded the corner and pulled up in the middle of the street, directly in the line of fire. The van afforded the sheriff additional cover, and he took advantage of it by pulling Willis Grant's body back onto the sidewalk and conferring with the deputies who'd been returning fire.

"Keep him busy," the sheriff said. "We're going to cover the other exits. Meantime, don't let anybody out."

"What happens when one of the features ends?" the taller deputy asked.

"People can watch the credits and clean up the spilled popcorn. I don't give a shit. Just don't let anybody out. City cops should be here soon. They can help you keep order. This isn't going to last more than ten minutes."

The sheriff pounded on the side of the van. The rear door facing the theater swung open, affording more cover from the sniper's bullets. The sheriff raised his shotgun barrel toward the open door. "Get in," he shouted to Owen and Judith.

They scrambled into the rear of the van, and the sheriff jumped in after them. A bullet pinged off the rear door just before he pulled it shut, and the van rolled away.

Two men and a woman wearing helmets and flak vests over their uniforms sat on a bench on one side of the van. All three cradled shotguns between their knees.

"You must be the riot squad," Judith said.

"Honey, we're the riot squad, the color guard, and the school safety-patrol liaison," the woman answered. "Wherever the day takes us."

"Pull into the alley behind the theater," the sheriff said to the driver. Then he rummaged through a bin under one of the side benches and found two flak vests. He pulled one over his head and handed the other to Owen.

Owen took off his sport coat, donned the vest, and buttoned his coat over it.

The sheriff took a shotgun off the rack on the wall separating them from the driver and handed it to Owen.

"Oh, God," Judith said.

"I've never used one of these," Owen said.

"I can't let you go in unarmed," the sheriff said. "Would you rather have a pistol?"

"Never used one of those either. It's bound to be easier to carry, though."

"Now there's a solid reason for a choice of weapons," the sheriff said. He took a pistol from the rack, loaded it, and handed it to Owen.

"I still don't see why he has to go at all," Judith said.

"He knows the way."

"I'll be all right." Owen hefted the pistol. "Valence is the man that killed Kate. If he's doing the shooting, I want to help get him."

"You already got the man that ordered the killing. Isn't that enough?" Judith said.

"I want the man that ordered it, the man that did it, the man that covered it up, and anybody else in the chain," Owen said. "Besides, so long as Valence is loose, I'm a walking target."

The van stopped and the doors opened. They were in the alley behind the theater. The sheriff assigned the female and one of the two male deputies to watch the two rear exits and the fire escape. Then he ordered the remaining deputy and the driver to accompany Owen and him into the arcade.

"You should be all right here in the van," the sheriff said to Judith. "We won't be long."

"Take all the time you need," Judith said. She hugged Owen. "For God's sake, be careful."

The sheriff led Owen, the deputy, and the driver to the arcade entrance. "I don't think there's a place called Van's here anymore."

"His pinball machines would be antiques by now," Owen said. He stopped halfway down the row of shops. "This is it." Van's had become a snack shop called "Nuts to You."

The sheriff and Owen stood aside while the driver went to work on the store lock. "Many people know about this entrance?" the sheriff asked.

"About half my high-school class."

"Letch went to high school here in Barkley. It'd be a fool's game for him to be shooting at us without planning a way out. I'm guessing this is the way he'll come."

The driver looked up from the lock and shrugged. The sheriff nodded impatiently, and the driver broke one of the glass door panels with the butt of his gun, reached through, and unlocked the door.

Owen led the way to a fire door at the back of the long, narrow store. The door was locked, and the sheriff motioned for the driver to try his luck.

"Wait a minute," Owen said. He went behind the counter. There, hanging on the same peg under the cash register where Van had kept it, was the key to the fire door.

The door opened onto a small landing flanked by shelves holding cartons of candy bars and cans of nuts. Beyond the landing, concrete steps led down to a dark tunnel.

Owen started down the steps. He stopped halfway and handed his cane back to the sheriff. "Let's leave this behind. It's just extra noise."

"Can you make it without the support?"

"Long as I don't have to run very far."

"If we have to run, we're all in deep shit."

The sheriff propped the cane beside the doorway. "What about lights? Can you find your way in the dark?"

"That's the way I always snuck in."

"That's the way we'll do it, then." The sheriff stuck his flashlight into his hip pocket. "We'll go in quiet as mice in sweat socks. Anybody's in there, I want to surprise him before he surprises us." To the driver of the van, he said, "You wait here. Once we're in, close the door and lock it just like we found it. If anybody but us tries to come out, be prepared to shoot."

The driver nodded.

The sheriff looked from Owen to the remaining deputy. "All right, then. Let's go."

Owen continued down the stairs into a narrow concrete tunnel. As the sheriff and the deputy entered the stairwell, the driver closed the door behind them. The tunnel was dark, but it was the darkness of a familiar room, not the terrifying blackness of the Crawley Creek Mine.

Owen pointed the sheriff's pistol at the ceiling, like the thousands of movie actors he'd watched, and put his free hand on the concrete wall.

The tunnel soon branched in two directions. Owen knew that the right branch dead-ended in a dressing room where the theater manager used to entertain his lady friends. It was the corner where they had to be the most careful when sneaking into the movies.

Owen turned left and hurried down the corridor. The years melted away, and he was sneaking in to watch *Butch Cassidy and the Sundance Kid,* with Bobby Bauer and Bob Ruddle close to his heels.

Bobby's Keds always squeaked on the concrete. Owen stopped to listen. He couldn't hear the sheriff or his deputy. Maybe he'd gotten too far ahead of them.

His up-pointed gun reminded him of Paul Newman before the final shoot-out in *Butch Cassidy.* That didn't turn out well, he remembered, and he decided to wait for the sheriff.

The sheriff caught up and whispered, "Don't get so far ahead."

"Left at the next turn," Owen whispered. "It takes you through the men's lounge into the theater."

The sheriff nudged him gently. "Lead on."

Owen hurried ahead and quickly arrived at the next corner. He'd told the sheriff to turn left, but now he wasn't sure. Was that the right way? One direction led to the ushers' dressing room, the other to the men's lounge and the theater.

He turned left and was blinded by a flashlight's glare. From behind the flashlight, Letch Valence's voice said, "Well, well. It's bargain day."

Owen barely had time to wonder what good it did to have his pistol pointed straight up when a muzzle flashed, a shot echoed, and a sharp blow to the chest emptied his lungs and sent him reeling backward. He landed hard on his back, cracked his head on the concrete, and dropped his pistol.

He lay still, trying to clear his head, as the flashlight danced closer. "Two for the price of one," Valence said, leveling his rifle.

A second shot echoed in the tunnel. Valence's flashlight clattered to the floor. He half turned to face the sheriff, who was pointing a smoking shotgun at his chest, and then fell across his flashlight.

"I warned you about getting too far ahead." The sheriff straddled Owen and helped him up. "You were moving like you were afraid you'd miss the main feature. You're just lucky Letch aimed low enough to hit your vest."

SUNDAY MORNING'S newspapers characterized Willis Grant as a prominent civic leader accidentally cut down by sniper fire. The alleged sniper, Letch Valence, was in turn shot and killed by Sheriff Thad Reader after Valence opened fire on a small party of police officers attempting to arrest him.

There were several quotes from the sheriff, whom the newspapers reported as having attended a dinner honoring Grant at the Frederick Hotel. None of the newspapers mentioned that the sheriff's role in the festivities was to arrest Grant for conspiracy to commit murder. This inconvenient fact had escaped most of the dinner attendees, who thought the sheriff was part of the roast. As a result, the canned newspaper obituaries simply listed Grant's long history of civic service and highlighted his recent position as president of Mountain View Enterprises and head of Saint Vincent's Hospital.

The news of the shooting consumed four pages of the *Barkley Democrat,* three pages of the *Huntington Herald Dispatch,* and two pages of the *Charleston Gazette.* None of the pages even hinted that Willis Grant was anything less than a model citizen.

Why hadn't the sheriff set the record straight, Owen wondered. Was he just unwilling to speak ill of the dead? He certainly had nothing good to say about Letch Valence, who the papers reported was evidently trying to carry out a death threat made several days earlier against Barkley native Owen Allison.

Owen took some small satisfaction in the fact that the news of the shootings had driven Dusty Rhodes off the front page. Dusty more than made up for his short absence from the spotlight during the evening's edition of *Sixty Minutes,* however. With a little over a week left before the election, the national TV news magazine hailed Rhodes as a crusading congressman fighting to save West Virginia from the vested coal interests intent on destroying the state's streams and mountain vistas.

Owen and Judith watched in Ruth Allison's living room as Rhodes was shown talking with displaced constituents, hefting fly-rock, surveying mountain streams, pointing at a map, and promising legislation that would limit Big Coal's stranglehold on the state's resources.

Sarabeth Mattingly was shown watching muddy water pour from her kitchen faucet and talking about the cracks in her foundation. Although a voice-over explained that her husband had been killed by a protester, Lizzie wasn't named and the DA was denied his fifteen minutes of fame for her prosecution. Instead, the interviewers had a field day pillorying coal company representatives, who were shown grimacing and flinching before they answered questions about stopping streams and destroying the state's natural beauty.

The governor, in particular, came off badly, being characterized as a "former coal company executive" who had received a half million dollars from Big Coal during his last campaign.

"Dusty Rhodes got nearly a half million himself, but they're not mentioning that," Owen said. "And they don't show Rhodes sweating any questions, either. They just play his prepared sound bites straight."

On the TV screen, the governor was backpedaling, saying the state had to wean itself from its dependence on coal. "It's not generally known, but our state has more Ph.D.s than coal miners," he announced.

"At the rate they're shutting down mines, it won't be long before the state has more governors than coal miners," Owen said, talking to the TV screen.

"Whose side are you on, anyhow?" Judith asked.

"I'm not on anybody's side."

"But you're against Dusty Rhodes. It almost sounds like you're jealous of him."

The observation stopped Owen cold. "Why would I be jealous of Rhodes?" he asked, trying to keep his voice level.

"Because he's there on nationwide TV taking bows for saving Sarabeth Mattingly and getting credit for policies you suggested."

"That's got nothing to do with it. I'm happy you followed up with Sarabeth, and I certainly didn't have a patent on any of those policies. I just don't trust him."

"You weren't in a position to make those policies work. He was, and he's doing it."

"How could I be jealous of that? More power to him." It was true, Owen thought. He didn't envy Rhodes' success as a politician. And it didn't bother him that the congressman took full credit for ideas that may or may not have been his. He knew exactly what he had against Rhodes. But he wasn't about to tell Judith he hadn't trusted her either.

THE NEXT MORNING, Dusty Rhodes reclaimed half of the *Barkley Democrat*'s front page with a legislative proposal to render eighty percent of West Virginia's mountain peaks off limits to mountaintop removal. The sacrosanct peaks in southern West Virginia's coal country were mapped on the second page of the newspaper. Owen recognized the map as the one Rhodes had used as a prop in his *Sixty Minutes* appearance the night before. It was the same base map Owen had gotten from the Department of Environment Protection in order to plot Mountain View's holdings.

Reactions from the coal industry and its environmental attackers were predictable. A spokesman for Dome Coal protested the taking of some of their properties as unconstitutional, even though Rhodes' bill provided for the use of severance taxes to purchase any currently held properties at fair market value. Environmentalist Gail Meyers

Connor complained that eighty-percent protection was insufficient, since it still left twenty percent of the state's irreplaceable peaks exposed to mechanical rape.

Owen was about to move on to the sports section when the pattern of protected peaks stirred his curiosity. He retrieved the plot he'd made of Mountain View's properties and compared the two maps. Not a single one of Mountain View's holdings was affected by the proposed legislation. Somehow, Rhodes had managed to take eighty percent of the area's peaks out of play without affecting the properties of one of the largest local mining companies.

OWEN SHOWED UP at the county courthouse just before lunchtime. Lizzie's trial was still in the jury-selection phase, and Guy Schamp was questioning a retired schoolteacher who sat primly in the jury box wearing a cotton print dress. Guy took his time, drawling his questions, joking with the woman, and finally accepting her as a potential juror.

The DA took over the interview, asking question after question in a disinterested monotone before determining that the teacher's brother-in-law had spent his final days as a patient at Lizzie's hospice. At that point, the DA asked that the potential juror be excused for cause.

The judge excused the schoolteacher and then consulted his watch and declared a lunch recess. The teacher, clearly disappointed, flounced down from the jury panel and left the courtroom ahead of the trial teams and remaining jurors.

Owen waited for the defense team at the door of the courtroom. He kissed Judith, hugged Lizzie, shook Guy's hand, and asked how the trial was going.

"Painfully slowly," Judith said.

"The DA kind of lost interest when he didn't make *Sixty Minutes*," Guy said. "Now he can't seem to find any jurors who haven't had a friend or relative in Lizzie's care. My guess is, this won't last much longer."

"He'll try to cut a deal?" Owen asked.

"The only deal we'll take is dropped charges," Guy said. "Now that Valence is dead, your friend the sheriff is revisiting his alibis for the night Mattingly was shot. If Valence's cronies don't stand by their stories, we can generate enough reasonable doubt to stop this trial before the jury is impaneled. Lizzie here's going to walk.''

"Right now I'm going to walk over to Lovisa's for lunch," Lizzie said. "Will you join us, Owen?''

Lovisa's was bursting at the seams with lunchtime patrons, but the proprietor had saved a corner table for Guy's party. As they sat down, Owen showed Guy a copy of the morning paper, folded to display the proposed map of protected peaks. "Seen this?" he asked.

"Oh, yes," Guy said. "Good old Dusty is proposing to make the legislature the gatekeeper for eighty percent of the state's mountain-tops. It'll take a sizable load of campaign contributions to get the politicians to back off and revise the list when the first twenty percent is mined out.''

"That's a pretty cynical view," Judith said. "If you read the article, you'll see that both Big Coal and the environmental lobby hate the legislation. As far as I'm concerned, that's a sign it's a pretty good law.''

"That's a curious criterion for a good law," Guy said. "Damn near everybody hates the alternative minimum tax, the three-strikes law, and the designated-hitter rule, and they're still pretty crappy pieces of legislation.''

"Not everybody hates the legislation Rhodes is proposing." Owen unfolded his map of Mountain View's holdings. "What would you say the chances are you could set aside eighty percent of the peaks in coal country and not hit a single one owned by Mountain View?''

"About the same as your chances of pissing in an open field and not getting the ground wet," Guy answered.

"Well, that's exactly what Dusty Rhodes has managed to do," Owen said.

Guy examined the two maps. "Sure gives Mountain View a leg up on the competition. That's pretty blatant, even for Dusty.''

"Not so blatant," Owen said. "He'd never expect anyone outside Mountain View to have a map like mine.''

"So Rhodes' legislation is lining somebody's pockets," Lizzie said.

"I'd like to know whose pockets are being lined," Owen said. "Who owns Mountain View Enterprises?''

"The usual suspects, I imagine," Guy said. "I believe most of it's held by a private trust."

"Can you get me a list of the top shareholders?" Owen asked.

"You're asking me to pierce the corporate veil?" Guy drawled out the word "veil," giving it two syllables.

"My goodness, you make it sound almost obscene," Lizzie said.

Guy dabbed at his mouth with his napkin. "At my age, the most I can do is *sound* obscene. I rely almost exclusively on aural intercourse." He laid the napkin on the table and said to Owen, "I'll make a few inquiries when we're finished in court. Stop by my office tonight."

GUY SCHAMP'S SPACIOUS office was packed with the accumulation of over a half-century of legal practice. A rolltop desk overflowed with papers, and the parquet floor had been turned into an obstacle course by a barber chair, a rolling file cabinet, a leather sofa holding a postal basket filled with mail, four leather-covered swivel chairs, a conference table, a sculpted wood rocker, and a wooden clothes tree topped by a dented miner's helmet.

One wall of the office was filled from floor to ceiling with law books. The other three held Guy's Harvard law degree and framed photos of Guy with Harry Truman, Adlai Stevenson, John Kennedy, Jimmy Carter, and several governors. Two black-and-white snapshots held a place of honor above the rolltop desk. One showed Guy in the cockpit of a World War II P-40 Warhawk. The other displayed a lanky young man leaning against the strut of a biplane and talking to a slim, pretty woman in a nurse's uniform.

Owen waved at the framed photos of former governors and ex-presidents. "Pretty impressive cast of characters."

"Kennedy is the only one I knew at all well," Guy said. "The rest is just advertising."

"And the nurse in the snapshot. Is that Aunt Lizzie?"

Guy smiled. "Oh, yes. That was the day I did my wing-walking act, trying to impress her."

"She looks pretty impressed. You made a handsome couple."

"The war separated us. We never quite got back together."

The regret in Guy's voice made Owen want to change the subject. "Did you manage to track down Mountain View's chief shareholders?"

"I did. Seventy-five percent of Mountain View Enterprises is owned by a blind trust, the Canaan Valley Trust."

"And who owns the trust?"

"Strictly speaking, that information isn't supposed to be available. The public record just gives the name of the lawyer administering it." Guy leaned back in his chair, clasped his hands behind his head, and cocked an elbow at one of the walls full of pictures. "One of the nice things about living to be my age is that a whole lot of people owe you favors. I just called in a few."

"And?"

"The Canaan Valley Trust is just another name for Dusty Rhodes."

"So he's proposing legislation that funnels money into his own pockets."

"He's not supposed to know he owns Mountain View Enterprises. That's why they call the trust blind."

"How do we know he didn't peek?"

"We don't. What you've got in this blind trust is an instrument with a politician at one end and a lawyer at the other. It stands to reason that whatever's in the middle is likely to be as crooked as a dog's hind leg."

"So the information could easily leak?"

"Like a colander."

"Suppose we shine a light on all this? Let the voters know what's going on."

"Dusty will claim he didn't know his trust held Mountain View's paper."

"But it stinks. And the stench should be enough to overwhelm his disclaimers."

"So you want to go after Dusty Rhodes?"

"Why not? It's a clear conflict of interest."

Guy leaned forward in his swivel chair. "Let me tell you a little story about Dusty Rhodes. He first surfaced here in the state about twelve years ago. Came here from Maryland pushing a scheme called 'pump storage.' Ever hear of it?"

Owen shook his head.

"There's a good reason you never heard of it. Way the scheme worked, you'd turn one of West Virginia's valleys into a man-made lake. Then you'd pump lake water uphill during the night when electricity is cheap, hold it in another man-made reservoir, and release it during the day to generate electricity at peak-load rates.''

"Unless somebody figured a way to pump the water uphill with no energy loss, I don't see how it could be economical.''

"It's one of those schemes dreamed up by so-called experts that leave the average man scratching his head.''

"I'm scratching mine right now.''

"Dusty had a lot of believers, though. Land developers, Appalachian Electric, the coal industry, the legislature. They all wanted to make it work. He bought up a lot of land cheap over in Eden Valley. Sold it to a developer promising him it'd be prime lakeside property once pump storage got started.''

"How'd the environmentalists react?''

"Like Dusty'd proposed to flood the Sistine chapel. They claimed he'd be ruining both the valley and the highlands. Managed to jam the process up with environmental-impact reports and got some WVU professors to study the power-generating prospects for the legislature.

"Well, the WVU study said the average man was right to be scratching his head. As a power-producing scheme, pump storage made about as much sense as tying a bunch of hamster wheels to a generator. Their report and the environmental obstacles killed the project deader than last week's roadkill.''

"But Rhodes still pocketed the profits from his bone-dry lakeside property.''

"You bet. The developer who'd bought the property came after him in court, claiming he'd been duped. Threatened to expose some backroom political deals if Dusty didn't make him whole.''

"What happened?''

"Dusty backed and filled, trying to stall until the developer choked on his legal fees. Week before the trial date, they found the man hanging from his chandelier. Dusty parlayed his profits into some other real estate deals and a state senate seat. Left a whole passel of bodies strung out behind him and never looked back.''

"What's your point?''

"Point is, going after Dusty Rhodes is a little like entering a pissing contest against a fire hose.''

"Are you saying you're afraid to go after him?''

Guy hooted. "Me? Afraid of Dusty Rhodes? Hell, son, I was warning *you*. Dusty doesn't scare me.''

Guy stood up and leaned against the rolltop desk. "Look here. At my age, every sunrise is a blessing. Except for missing out on the only woman I ever loved, life's been good to me. You get past eighty-five and if they haven't found a spot on your lung or a lump in your prostate, you're uncommonly blessed. What the hell do I care if Rhodes comes after me? Dusty Rhodes may be a threat, but he's in line behind prostate cancer, heart failure, and diabetes. I say fuck him, and the focus groups he rode in on."

"So what do we do to nail him?"

"We engage the power of the press." Guy flipped through his Rolodex. "Might as well start with the *Barkley Democrat*. They've got at least an hour before they wrap up tomorrow morning's edition." He picked up his phone and punched in the number, then put his hand over the mouthpiece, listening for the ring. "The *Democrat* used to be a helluva paper when Charley Peters ran it. His son runs it now. A chip off the old block, but still just a chip." He took his hand off the mouthpiece. "Junior? This is Guy Schamp. If your dad was still around, I'd say 'stop the presses.' I know y'all don't say that anymore, but I want you to listen up. I've got some hard news for tomorrow's paper."

TWENTY-TWO

A Poke in a Pig

THE *BARKLEY DEMOCRAT* printed a map of the peaks that Rhodes' legislation proposed to put off limits, superimposed on a plot of Mountain View's holdings, all under the headline RHODES CONFLICT OF INTEREST?

Where'd the question mark come from, Owen wondered. Of course it's a conflict of interest. Give the headline an exclamation point if you feel like punctuating it.

Rhodes' printed retraction was predictable. His money was in a blind trust. He had no idea of how it was invested. Somehow, the trust had been breached by political enemies.

Owen caught up with the Huntington and Charleston papers while waiting out his mother's chemotherapy treatment at Saint Vincent's. The out-of-town papers had the same mixture of tentative charge and glancing countercharge as the *Barkley Democrat*. Nobody was calling Rhodes a crook. Not even his opponent, who demanded a thorough investigation. Nobody questioned Rhodes' claim that he didn't know where his money was invested.

Owen had expected more of a fuss. It had seemed like a much bigger deal the night before, when he and Guy were calling in the news. Last night they felt like West Virginia's answer to Woodward and Bernstein. In the light of day, the newspapers' need to present both sides made him feel more like a campaign flack whose latest press release had been undercut by a salvo from the opposition's publicity team.

He returned the newspapers to the rack in the waiting room and went off to find Sister Regina Anne.

He found Saint Vincent's head nun wheeling a hamper full of dirty linen up a long incline to the hospital laundry. Owen hung his cane on the side of the hamper and helped with the pushing. "When I worked here, the orderlies did this job."

"They still do. But we're shorthanded, so we try to rotate everyone through the different chores once in a while." She grimaced as the rolling hamper bounced over a crack in the pavement. "These menial jobs keep us reasonably humble. I can complete my daily prayers in four round-trips, so that these uphill runs are a kind of pious workout."

They shoved the load up a ramp and through a pair of swinging doors into a steaming room where a sweating laundry worker exchanged their hamper of soiled linen for a similar hamper filled with freshly laundered and folded sheets and pillowcases.

"Let me take it," Owen said. He guided the rolling hamper back down the outside ramp. "Did Sister Mary Perpetua do this?"

Sister Regina Anne walked alongside the hamper. "Oh, my goodness, no. She was on the professional staff."

"I wanted to ask you about her. She had Doctor Don Johnston removed from the staff here."

Sister Regina Anne pursed her lips. "That's right."

"For some sort of unmentionable transgression."

Sister Regina Anne shot him a look that would have withered a hardwood forest.

"Don't worry. I don't want to know what he did. What I'm curious about is this. If it was so bad, why didn't she take it to the state board?"

"We discussed that. We felt the state board was likely to close ranks and shield its own member."

"What made you think that?"

Sister Regina Anne frowned. "Tradition." She joined Owen in pushing the handle of the hamper. "Sister Mary also felt that some of the details would reflect poorly on Saint Vincent's. She wanted to make sure the man would never practice here again, so she struck a deal."

"She wouldn't tell if Johnson left the staff."

"Exactly."

"And did anyone else know what Johnston had done to get the boot?"

"I hardly think so. Sister Mary was a woman of her word."

"Did you know?"

"Not the details, no."

They had reached the main hospital. Sister Regina Anne guided the hamper inside to the service elevator. "These go to the second-floor linen closet."

While they waited for the elevator, Sister Regina Anne said, "Sister Mary wanted to be sure that even if she left the staff, Doctor Johnston would never practice here again. So she wrote the incident up and sealed it in Johnson's personnel file."

"Who had access to that file?"

"No one. Well, I did, of course. And Willis Grant, I suppose. God rest his soul. But he rarely took an interest in personnel decisions."

"He may have taken an interest in this one. Someone used the incident sealed in that file to blackmail Dr. Johnston into falsifying Sister Mary's autopsy."

Sister Regina Anne unlocked the linen closet. "Oh, my. But why?"

"To cover up the real reason for her murder. That she'd discovered Grant's overcharging scheme."

They had begun unloading the fresh linen from the hamper onto the closet shelves. The nun stopped suddenly, holding an armful of folded sheets. "I thought Vernon Embry was responsible for the overcharging."

"Grant was behind it. And the embezzlement as well. He blamed them both on Embry."

"And you say he used the sealed personnel file to persuade Doctor Johnston to cover up Sister Mary's murder?"

"If he was the only one besides you with access to the file, that's almost certainly what happened."

"So if Willis Grant was covering up Sister Mary's murder, it's safe to assume he was in some way responsible for it."

"The sheriff has evidence suggesting that's the case."

Sister Regina Anne took a folded pillowcase from the hamper, pulled it taut and examined it closely. "And to think that the entire convent spent the morning mass praying for the repose of Willis Grant's soul." She shook her head and hung the offending pillowcase on the side of the hamper. "It's unchristian of me, I know, but I hope the man rots in hell."

"I'm not up on heavenly balance sheets, Sister, but I'm guessing it'll take more than one convent mass to save Willis Grant's soul."

They finished shelving the laundry and Owen said, "I've got to get back to my mother. Thank you for your time."

"I should be thanking you."

Owen patted a stack of fresh sheets. "I enjoyed doing it. It took me back to my youth."

"No. I mean for clearing Sister Mary's name."

The nun backed the hamper out of the linen closet and locked the door. "I didn't think it mattered," she said. "What the world thought, I mean. Those of us who knew Sister Mary were sure the allegations had to be false."

She pushed the hamper down the hall to the elevator. "But no matter how strong your faith, doubt can eat away at it. It's like a tiny pinprick that causes a small tear in a fabric." She held up the rejected pillowcase, poked her finger through a hole, and threw it into the just-emptied hamper.

She wheeled the hamper into the elevator. "You want to believe. But the evidence seems against you. You start to question. You say to yourself, 'What if?' You find you're not a hundred-percent sure. So many of our beliefs turn on faith. If the fabric tears in one spot, it must be weak in others as well."

The elevator reached the ground floor, and Owen started to leave. Sister Regina Anne took his arm. "But you were sure. You knew Sister Mary was innocent. You never doubted. And you showed us the way. God bless you for it."

OWEN FOUND HIS MOTHER in Dr. Bake Morton's waiting room, looking flustered and worried. "Doctor Morton wants to see both of us," Ruth said. "He's hinted he wants to cut back on chemotherapy. I think he's going to recommend we start palliative care."

Owen's heart sank. He'd been around the hospice long enough to understand that "palliative care" was a euphemism for "It's all downhill now. There's nothing we can do but make you comfortable." He took Ruth's hand. "You don't know what he wants, Mom. Maybe we're just behind in our bill payments."

As he had in their first conference, Bake Morton slumped in his chair, lowered his head, and mumbled through his walrus mustache as if he were addressing the fingers laced across his ample stomach. "As I told you," he began, "I want to reduce your chemotherapy treatments. We'll continue to monitor your CA-125 levels carefully. It's one of the few reliable blood markers we have.''

Owen marveled at Morton's lack of expression. He knew from informal chats in the doctors' lounge and from Kate's stories that the man could be funny and responsive. The stomach-directed monotone must be some sort of defense against the bad news he generally had to deliver.

"Your levels have stabilized," the doctor droned on, "but I need to warn you there's a very good chance of recurrence."

"Recurrence?" Owen sat straight up and interrupted. "Why are we talking about recurrence? What about palliative care?"

Baker looked up and raised his eyebrows, creating two bushy arcs that matched his mustache. "Why on earth would we be talking about palliative care? Your mother's CA-125 levels are quite low. She has nothing to worry about—for now."

Owen looked from Doctor Morton to his mother. "Let me understand this. Mom? You've beaten the twenty-percent odds?"

Ruth looked stunned. "Is that true?" She asked the doctor, "Why didn't you tell me?"

"I thought I was telling you."

Owen left his seat and hugged Ruth, half lifting her out of her chair and dislodging her striped stocking cap.

"To be fair," Morton said, "we're never really sure about these things. And this sort of cancer quite often recurs. But I'm quite confident we can cut your chemo dosage in half."

"My God. My God." Ruth fumbled with her stocking cap. "I was so afraid. I almost didn't try it."

"But you did," Morton said. "And you definitely appear to be out of the woods—for now."

"You keep tacking 'for now' onto your prognosis," Owen said.

"That's all we can say, for now." Bake Morton smiled, elevating the ends of his mustache. "That's all anybody can ever say, really."

THE SHERIFF'S PATROL CAR was parked in front of Lizzie's hospice when Owen and Ruth returned. On the hospice porch, Guy, Lizzie, Judith, and the sheriff stood around a tub packed with ice, soft drinks, and individual cartons of milk and juice.

"Looks almost like a celebration," Owen said. "What happened to the trial?"

"Letch's death improved his cronies' memories of the night Sam Mattingly was shot," Thad Reader said. "Orry Estep even remembered that Letch had come late to that night's poker game, and that he didn't bring a car with him."

"He did bring a shotgun, though," Guy added. "When the DA heard that, he dropped his charges against Lizzie."

Ruth hugged Lizzie. "That's wonderful." Then she retrieved an orange soda from the tub, pulled the tab, and toasted the crowd. "It's a double celebration. Doctor Morton just gave me a clean bill of health."

"For now," Owen added.

Lizzie clapped her hands, then hung her head in mock dejection. "Means I'll have to kick you out, gal. Healthy folk like you could give my place a bad name. The government starts growling if my patients hang on too long without dying."

"You can't mean that," Judith said.

"Oh, yes." Lizzie shook her head. "Some hospices have actually lost their funding because their patients didn't die fast enough. Can you believe that?"

"I'll happily give up my spot," Ruth said.

"I can take care of you at home, Mom," Owen offered.

Lizzie took Ruth by the arm. "There's no hurry. You're not on my books, anyhow. What the government doesn't know won't hurt us."

Owen took the sheriff aside. "Nice job of police work, cracking those alibis."

"I was due. I'd blown a few lately. Remember that voice on Embry's tape that identified himself as an IRS man named Wolfe?"

"I won't soon forget that tape."

"I assumed it was some kind of alias. Turns out it really was a tax man named Wolfe. State tax man, anyhow."

"No wonder his credentials convinced Embry. They were real. Did you arrest Wolfe?"

"Didn't figure it out in time. Didn't figure it out at all, actually. Had it handed to us. When Wolfe didn't show up for work this week, his landlord checked and found him dangling from a light fixture."

"Lot of that going around. I just heard about a similar suicide."

"Think they're related?"

"The other one's twelve years old. Anyhow, the state tax connection explains how they knew Vern Embry had ordered an audit."

"Ties up one loose end."

"I just tied up another," Owen said. "Sister Regina Anne told me Kate had written up Don Johnston's offense and sealed it in the hospital files. Willis Grant had access to those files."

"So Willis had blackmail ammo."

"Along with a half million in embezzled funds to buy off Johnston. He got him cheap at a hundred grand."

"Kind of makes you sorry old Willis caught a bullet. Been nice to see him try to explain all this."

"Be nice to see him exposed for the prick he was," Owen said. "The papers still treat him as a civic leader and the nuns are praying for his soul. Why didn't you tell the world what was on Embry's tape?"

"So long as Wolfe was still loose, I wanted him to think he was safe. Be easier to track him down, I thought. Turned out to be a lot easier than I imagined."

"I think you owe it to Embry to release his dying words."

"I always intended to. You have any other advice on how I should do my job?"

"Funny you should ask."

"My question was sarcastic."

"So was my answer. Got a minute?"

"Walk me to my car." The sheriff shook hands with Guy, waved at Lizzie and Ruth, and descended the porch steps.

"I don't think I was Valence's target Saturday night," Owen said. "At least not at first."

"Your ex-wife thought Grant was the target. You saying you agree with her?"

"Grant's the one Valence hit. If Valence was planning to shoot me, he was at the wrong window. I only turned onto that street to see you. And we didn't even decide to go to the roast until the last minute. It was Grant's roast. Grant was the target."

"If he was after Grant, why'd he keep shooting after he got him? He might have gotten away clean if he hadn't stayed there at the window."

"He kept shooting because I happened along. In the tunnel, Valence crowed about it being a two-for-one day."

"Why shoot Grant?"

"To keep him quiet."

"We had all the evidence we needed to hang Valence without Willis Grant."

"Valence didn't know that. But I don't think he was only trying to protect himself."

"Who, then?"

"Someone higher up. On Embry's tape, Valence bragged about how well-connected they were."

The sheriff unlocked his car and stood with one arm draped over the open door. "Does this higher-up someone have a name that you're willing to share?"

"Who stood to gain the most from all this?"

"Let me rephrase that. Do you have a name you're willing to share sometime today?"

"Who owns sixty percent of Mountain View Enterprises? Dusty Rhodes."

The sheriff laughed. His keys clanked against the car window. "Come on. Be serious."

"I am serious. Everything that's happened, the shady loan, the overcharging, the midnight mining, all benefited Mountain View Enterprises. And Mountain View Enterprises is Dusty Rhodes."

The sheriff stared at the woods behind the hospice and tapped his key against the car window. Finally, he shrugged. "It's all circumstantial. There's not a shred of evidence linking Rhodes to any crime."

"That's because everyone under him is dead."

"Shit flows downhill."

"But the money flows uphill. He's at the end of every payoff."

"If having politicians pocket payoffs were evidence of murder, we'd have to arrest the entire legislature."

"Look, I just thought of this. Rhodes heads the Senate Tax Committee. He probably knew your man Wolfe."

"Even if he did, we're still talking circumstantial evidence." The sheriff slid behind the wheel of his patrol car. "Seems like you've got a real hard-on for Rhodes. I understand you and Guy surfaced this conflict-of-interest story." He started the engine. "Give me a call when you've got some hard proof to go with your hard-on. In the meantime, your best chance to get at Rhodes is to vote against him on Tuesday."

"Can't. I'm registered in California."

DUSTY RHODES CALLED a press conference on election eve to respond to the conflict-of-interest accusations surrounding his latest legislative proposal. Owen watched with Guy and Judith in his mother's living room as Rhodes, facing a camera positioned over the shoulders of two news commentators, led off with a prepared statement.

"This is as much of a surprise to me as it is to you," the candidate said. "When I took office, I put all my investments into a blind trust. I had but one stipulation for the administration of that trust. Namely, that they invest primarily in West Virginia equities. I believe in this state.

"Because of that stipulation, it's not surprising that legislation proposed by me would affect properties held in my trust. Because the trust is blind, though, and the money was invested without my knowledge, I had no way of knowing whether my legislation would affect my holdings favorably or unfavorably."

"Anyone who believes that would buy the New River Bridge with up-front cash," Owen said to the TV set.

"Somehow, my political opponents managed to break the seal on the blind trust," Rhodes continued. "Now everyone in the state knows how my money was invested. And now I know. But I didn't know before the seal was violated and the news broke."

Dusty paused, looked down at the table, inhaled deeply, and stared hard at the camera. "I trusted the system. Somehow, the contents of my trust were leaked to the press. I assure you, I fully intend to investigate the source of that leak."

"You do that," Owen said.

"In the meantime," Rhodes continued, "because I do not want my candidacy for the state senate to be tainted by any doubt or innuendo, I have withdrawn the proposed legislation."

Guy clapped his hands once and leaned forward. "You've got to hand it to him. The man's a master. It's another Brier-patch Bargain."

"How so?" Owen asked. "Sounded like standard-issue bullshit to me."

"Think about all the things he could have done," Guy said.

"He could have done nothing," Judith said.

"But that might leave him vulnerable tomorrow," Guy said.

"He could have divested his trust of the Mountain View holdings," Owen said.

"But that would leave him poorer," Guy said. "And he could have added Mountain View properties to the off-limits list, but that would defeat the purpose of the legislation. Instead, he withdraws the legislation."

"Doesn't that leave him poorer, too?" Owen asked.

"Tell you what's going to happen," Guy said. "The legislation will resurface after the election, sponsored by one of Rhodes' cronies. There'll be a few negligible Mountain View holdings added to the off-limits list, but nothing they'll miss."

"And they'll be well compensated for the holdings," Owen said.

Guy shook his head, smiling. "You've gotta love the man. He's got more nerve than a toothache."

On the TV screen, the commentators were following up with questions, giving Rhodes the chance to elaborate on points he'd already made.

"Will voters really buy this performance?" Owen asked. "We caught him with his hand in the till."

"Not quite," Guy said. "The till is open. And the money's earmarked for Rhodes' pockets. But the blind trust makes it look like somebody else is making the transfer. Dusty's hands look clean."

"They're about as clean as a coal miner's in mid-shift," Owen said. "This whole blind-trust thing is a transparent dodge. It's like hiding stolen loot with a neighbor when the cops come to search your house."

"I don't know," Judith said. "You can't prove he knew about the trust's investments. And even if you could, I doubt that you'd cost him many votes."

"I suppose you'd vote for him," Owen said.

"I think I would. I imagine most of the female population would."

"Why? Because he's good-looking and can carry a tune?"

"No. Because his opponent's a dunce with delusions of mediocrity. And because Dusty's on record as being pro-choice."

"Pro-choice? For Christ's sake. What's that got to do with this election? I'm as pro-choice as the next man, unless the next man happens to be a woman. But we're talking about a vote for a state senator. Rhodes could believe in forcing chastity belts on teenagers or sacrificing firstborn females. Who cares about his thoughts on reproductive rights? He's never going to be in a position to vote—" Owen stopped in mid-rant.

Judith was smiling her "gotcha" smile.

Owen slid back into the couch. "Oh, I see. You were just jerking my chain."

"Well, your chain's been dangling pretty far out lately," Judith said. "I've never seen you so worked up about an election."

"Rhodes is getting away with murder. Almost literally," Owen said. "And we've shown the world he's using his position to line his own pockets. But the two of you are telling me we haven't hurt him a bit?"

"Hurt him?" Guy chuckled. "Hell, we probably helped him. You didn't see his opponent anywhere on TV tonight." Guy stood and patted the top of the TV set. "I'm afraid all we managed to do was get Dusty a half hour of prime TV time the night before the election."

DUSTY RHODES WAS winning sixty-two percent of the vote when Judith got tired of waiting for his opponent to concede and went to bed. "Herbert Crane didn't have a clue about how to run a campaign," she said from the staircase. "It's not surprising he doesn't know how to end one."

Owen hung on, more out of habit than hope. He never left baseball games before the last out. As a boy, he knew that the record for ninth-inning runs was twelve, Giants versus Reds, 1961. Whenever the Reds were behind in the ninth, he kept hoping for a new record. The statistician in him knew better, but the fan in him enjoyed watching the game, so he always hung on to the bitter end.

He wasn't enjoying tonight's game at all. He'd felt certain that their conflict-of-interest revelations would sink Rhodes' campaign. Instead, it just gave the candidate more TV exposure.

Owen knew the way Bob Lemon, Cleveland's pitcher, must have felt when Dusty Rhodes' namesake dumped his cheap home run into the short porch at the Polo Grounds to win the first game of the 1954 World Series.

Off the bat, it would have looked like an easy pop-up. Certainly no threat. The second baseman was even chasing it. Lemon would have waited on the mound as the right fielder drifted over, then watched helplessly as he ran out of room and the ball dinked in for a 255-foot home run.

A photographer had followed Lemon off the field, probably hoping to get a picture of dejection, like Ralph Branca slumped on the bench after serving up Bobby Thompson's homer. Instead, Lemon threw his glove at the camera. That was the picture that made the papers, the glove in the foreground, about to hit the lens. An angry Lemon in the background.

On TV, Dusty Rhodes the candidate had increased his lead by two percentage points.

Owen knew exactly how Lemon felt. It was definitely glove-throwing time. He sailed a pillow at the smiling TV image of Dusty Rhodes. "I'm going to get you, you son of a bitch. This isn't over."

There was a knock at the door. Guy Schamp stood in the doorway, holding a bottle of red wine. "Thought you might need some company."

Owen stepped aside. Guy headed for the kitchen, found a corkscrew, and returned with two full glasses. "It's a flinty little Merlot with a nice ironic aftertaste."

"Does it go with beer and popcorn? Because that's what I've been having."

"It goes with beer, popcorn, dejection, and defeat."

"Then it's just what I need."

They clinked glasses. "How're you feeling?" Guy asked.

"Hosed."

"Fire-hosed in a pissing contest. Can't say I didn't warn you."

On the TV screen, Rhodes was pushing toward sixty-five percent of the vote.

"We didn't hurt him a bit," Owen said.

"If we did, he hid it well." Guy sipped his Merlot. "Maybe I should tell you the story of Rafe Caughlan."

"Who's that? Somebody else Rhodes left dangling in his wake?"

"No. This was way before Rhodes' time. Caughlan was sheriff over in Mingo County, back when being sheriff carried a lot of patronage jobs. He was running for reelection, and everybody figured he had it made."

Guy smiled over his wineglass. "Then his opponent came up with a Polaroid of Caughlan having sexual congress with a pig."

"This is a joke, right?"

"No joke. Caughlan was a country boy. No accounting for tastes."

"Well, half the county saw the picture and the other half heard about it. Looked like Caughlan had about as much chance as a celluloid print of 'The Ten Commandments' at the Hell Multiplex.''

Owen laughed.

"This was back when election day was serious business. Big holiday, with bunting and downtown parades. Kiwanis, Elks, marching bands, convertibles with the county coal queen and her attendants. Well, the last majorette had passed the bandstand and folks were fixing to pack it in when somebody pointed back down the street.

"There, walking along at the tail end of the parade, was Rafe Caughlan."

"All by himself?"

"Not quite. He was leading the pig on a rope. Pig cleaned up real nice. Had a red ribbon around her neck. Rafe marched her right past the bandstand."

"This has got to be a joke."

"No joke. We're talking Mingo County here. Caughlan won by four votes. And the pig wasn't even registered."

Owen laughed out loud. "What's your point?"

"Well, there are lots of lessons we can learn from this." Guy held up his index finger. "First, like Yogi Berra says, it ain't over till it's over."

Two fingers went up. "Second, West Virginians will almost always vote for a rapscallion. Especially if he's running against a Republican."

Guy held up three fingers. "Third, and most important, there's a lot more pig-fuckers out there than anybody realizes. And damn near all of them vote."

TWENTY-THREE

Going Home

THE HUNTINGTON-ASHLAND AIRPORT sat on a ridge that had been leveled to make room for the runway and control tower. Owen and Judith were the only two people in the waiting area, which looked out on the runway through a floor-to-ceiling plateglass window. Except for a stray baggage cart that cast a long shadow in the morning sunlight, the tarmac was empty.

"You're on some kind of a vendetta," Judith said. "There's absolutely no proof linking any of the murders to Dusty Rhodes."

"Follow the money," Owen said. "It leads to Rhodes."

"It leads to a blind trust that was out of his control."

"I think there's damn little in this state that's out of his control."

Judith paced between two empty rows of formed-plastic chairs. "I don't get it. You're the last person I'd expect to buy into a conspiracy theory. I've heard you pooh-pooh them hundreds of times. I even know your three-pecker theory by heart." She stopped pacing, faced Owen, and recited, "'If you take any three bureaucrats, or politicians, or petty crooks, there's only one chance in sixteen their peckers will all point the way you want them to.'"

"One chance in eight," Owen said. "To get one chance in sixteen, you'd need four conspirators, assuming peckers are only bi-directional. The more you have, the tougher it gets. And it's probably sexist to assume they're all male."

"Whatever. It's your theory, not mine. And it's even less likely that they'll all be able to keep their mouths shut."

"Especially if they're not all male."

"Now who's being sexist?"

"Look, I never said I thought Rhodes was the head of some vast conspiracy."

"But you're trying to find evidence linking him to at least three different killings."

"No, I'm not. All the mouths that might link Rhodes to those murders have been shut. Permanently. I don't think is any evidence. In fact, I seriously doubt whether he ordered any of the murders." Owen paused, thinking. "Except maybe Willis Grant's."

"Then what's this vendetta all about?"

"He created the climate that made the killings possible. He provided the protection that made Grant and Valence think they could get away with murder. You should have heard Embry's tape. Valence was frothing at the mouth about how well-connected they were."

"Did he mention Rhodes by name?"

"No."

"Then what makes you think he was their connection?"

"I told you. Everything that happened, from the initial loan to the legislation he proposed, put money in his pocket."

A small twin-engine turbo prop landed and began taxiing toward the gate.

Judith began pacing again. "Oh, God. It's a puddle jumper. I hate flying in small planes this time of year." She stopped suddenly, turned her back on the runway, and pointed a finger at Owen. "Listen to me. I know Dusty Rhodes. I've worked with him. Those laws he proposed are good for this state. I don't think there's a chance in hell you're right about him."

She put both hands in front of her and pushed downward, like a conductor trying to quiet a crescendo. "If you're not right, you're wasting your time staying here to poke around. And that time you're wasting is time we could be spending together in California."

"I still need to be here to get Mom through the rest of her chemotherapy."

"Let me finish. If you're wrong, you're wasting your time. And mine. But suppose you're right. If you're right, you're going up against someone who's killed at least three people without leaving a trace. Let me tell you, love, you're overmatched."

"You underestimate me."

"I don't think so. Look, I'm not trying to minimize what you've just done. My God, in the space of two months you've exposed a mining scam, solved two murders, freed your aunt, got the law to fix Sarabeth Mattingly's well, and suggested we start a family."

Owen tilted his head and put on an "aw, shucks" smile. "If it weren't for that damn Kryptonite, I would have nailed Rhodes by now, too.''

''Be serious a minute. In the process, you've had to crawl away from a head-on collision, a mine explosion, and a point-blank shooting. You've been pretty damn smart. But you've also been pretty damn lucky.''

''Maybe the two go together.''

''The game you're playing, you only need to be unlucky once. You're pushing your luck fantasizing about revenge against a man who's either totally innocent or, if he's not, will kill you in a heartbeat. If you're right about Rhodes, your kind of smarts won't help you a bit.''

Judith raised her hands, then let them drop to her sides, exasperated. ''I repeat, you're overmatched. You're just too nice a guy. You're so nice, you never even had the nerve to ask me if I slept with Rhodes.''

There it was, out on the table. ''Did you sleep with Rhodes?''

''No.''

''Would you tell me if you had?''

''No.''

''Why not?''

''Because I love you. And because I wouldn't want to add anymore fuel to your revenge fantasy.''

''Wait a minute. You think some part of my revenge fantasy is the need to avenge your honor?''

''My honor's my own concern. But yes, it crossed my mind. I've never seen you go after anybody the way you're going after Dusty Rhodes.''

''I'm going after Rhodes because Kate O'Malley would still be alive if slime like Grant and Valence didn't think they had a 'Get Out of Jail Free' card from somebody higher up.''

The PA system announced Judith's flight, and a ticket attendant showed up to stand by the glass door leading to the tarmac. Owen took his cane in his left hand and stood up, then lifted Judith's carry-on bag with his right hand. ''Looks like you're the only passenger.''

Judith started for the glass door, then stopped and stared beyond the ticket attendant. ''Is that the pilot wheeling the steps over to the entry hatch?''

''That must be the copilot. I think that's the pilot loading your luggage.''

"God, I hate this."

"Oh, I'd say he knows what he's doing. He got your bag onboard with one clean swing."

"Didn't Marshall lose its entire football team at this airport?"

"That was a long time ago. It was a dark and stormy night. And they were landing, not taking off."

"But they were in a bigger plane."

"They had to be. That plane you're going up in would barely hold a two-person volleyball team."

"You know just what to say to make me feel better." She turned and kissed him. It was a quick, preoccupied kiss. A worried kiss. "The minute your mom finishes chemotherapy, I want you to be on one of these planes to California."

"Are you kidding? These planes aren't safe."

The ticket attendant rolled her eyes. "Our planes are quite safe, ma'am."

"Tell her," Owen said. "How many passengers did you lose just last week?"

The attendant bridled. "Sir, this airline has never lost a plane."

"Well, maybe *lose* was the wrong word," Owen said. "You always know where the pieces are, I suppose."

"Ignore Mr. Smarty-Pants here," Judith said. "He's at least as much of a white-knuckle flyer as I am. He's only sounding off right now because he's staying behind."

"That's true," Owen admitted.

Judith turned and took her carry-on from Owen. "Take care of your mom. Then come home to California. Don't tangle with Dusty Rhodes. Promise?"

"As soon as Mom's off chemo, I'll be heading home. I promise."

Judith handed her ticket to the attendant, walked to the plane, and climbed the three steps to the open hatch. Then she turned, waved, pointed at the knuckles of the hand clutching her carry-on, and mouthed the word "white."

Owen waved back, then watched as the plane taxied to the runway, gathered speed, and took off, disappearing between two tree-covered peaks. He turned and walked out the airport door to his car. Heading home, he thought. He'd just promised to take a plane home. But it felt like that was where he was going now.

OWEN SHOWED UP at Lizzie's hospice with two cylindrical hatboxes under his arm and Buster circling his feet.

The old man rocking on the hospice porch in faded blue pajamas and tattered slippers had been in the same chair on Owen's first visit and on most of his visits since. He was as much of a fixture as the wooden rockers and potted geraniums. "How're you doing, Lucas?" Owen asked as he climbed the stone steps to the porch.

"Pretty good for somebody whose innards empty into a plastic bag." The old man stopped rocking. "You bring a ball for that pooch?"

Owen reached into his windbreaker pocket and handed Lucas a worn tennis ball. The old man raised it overhead, causing his pajama sleeve to droop below his knobby elbow. At the sight of the upraised ball, Buster took off down the driveway.

The rocker pitched forward, and the bony arm catapulted the ball past Owen's car. Buster caught it on the first bounce and returned it to Lucas's lap. "Excellent," Lucas said.

Lizzie appeared in the doorway. "Thought I heard Buster. Your mother will be ready to go in a few minutes, Owen. She's just saying her good-byes." She held the screen door open and eyed the two hatboxes, which bore the red-and-blue stripes of the exclusive Banning Emporium. "Been shopping?"

"Thought I'd get Mom a new hat to help her celebrate." Owen opened the top hatbox to show Lizzie a bell-shaped, mauve cloche.

Lizzie nodded her approval. "Pretty stylish. Course, that's what I'd expect from Banning's. What's in the other box?"

"It's empty. Thought I'd fill it with a hat from NOTIONS AND POTIONS."

"Well, aren't you the discerning shopper. Come right this way and let me show you our fall collection."

Lizzie stepped aside and Owen went ahead of her into the living room, with its racks of donated clothing and tables full of memorabilia. "Mom seems to like wearing hats from your collection. She calls them 'haunted haberdashery.'"

"It's a good thing, I think. Somehow it keeps the memory of the previous owners alive."

Lizzie stopped at the tin cash box sitting on the table nearest the door. She lifted the change tray, reached under it, and held up a plastic bag containing a gold wedding band. "That reminds me.

Neither of Maggie Mason's two girls thought enough of their mother to show up for her funeral. She'd want you to have this."

Owen took the plastic bag. He remembered the inscription, "Faithful Forever," inside the ring. "I don't know, Aunt Lizzie. This will just collect dust in a drawer somewhere."

"Better your drawer than mine. You're younger. The memory will last longer."

Owen pocketed the ring and moved on to the table containing a selection of donated, abandoned, and bequeathed hats that included three knitted stocking caps, a pillbox hat from the '60s, a turban, and a visored creation made of cut-up cans of Stroh's beer.

Lizzie modeled the turban.

"Mom's already got a turban."

"Oh, yes. It was Dorothy Bauer's." Lizzie picked up one of the knitted caps. "Can I interest you in a stocking cap? Christmas is just around the corner."

Owen shook his head. None of the hats was quite right. It was starting to seem like a dumb idea. His eye drifted to the next table over, which was labeled odds and ends. Someone had covered a striped railroad engineer's cap with old campaign buttons and small gold figurines from a charm bracelet.

Owen picked up the cap. The campaign buttons ranged from GIVE 'EM HELL HARRY TO VOLUNTEERS FOR DUSTY RHODES, and included VOTE STEVENSON and IMPEACH THE COX SACKER. The gold charms included a donkey and an elephant, as well as a miniature map of West Virginia, a tiny flag, and a United Mine Workers insignia.

"Timeless," Lizzie said. "It'll never go out of style."

"I wonder," Owen said. "Can it be altered?"

Lizzie frowned. "I'd have to speak to the milliner. What'd you have in mind?"

"Got a safety pin?"

Lizzie reached into her apron pocket and handed Owen a safety pin.

Owen took Dusty Rhodes' campaign button off the hat. Then he fished Maggie Mason's wedding ring out of his pocket and pinned it through the tiny holes left by the campaign button.

Lizzie nodded approval. "Just the right touch. Your mother will love it."

"I think so, too." He opened the empty hatbox and placed the engineer's cap inside. "I'll take it."

Owen took the two hatboxes to the table containing the tin cash box. Next to the cash box was a display of used CDs. The first disc in the display was the original cast recording of *Cabaret*.

Owen picked up the CD. "Sister Regina Anne said she donated Kate O'Malley's personal belongings to your hospice. Was this hers?"

"I'm sure it must have been. And if it isn't, I will personally guarantee you it sounds just like her copy."

Owen smiled. "Sold. What do I owe you for the hat and the CD?"

"My goodness, Owen. Consider them a gift. After all, I owe you my freedom."

"You don't owe me anything. Besides, you've been taking care of Mom all these weeks."

"I just do that so you and Buster will visit from time to time."

As if on cue, Buster burst through the door, skidded to a stop in front of Lizzie, and nosed the tennis ball so it landed at her feet. Lizzie turned her back on Owen and bent to pick up the ball. As she did so, Owen emptied all the bills from his wallet into the cash box.

Lizzie tucked the tennis ball into her apron pocket. "Not in the house, Buster."

Owen picked up Buster and ruffled the black-and-white hair over his eyes. Then he pocketed the *Cabaret* CD and picked up the two hatboxes. "Come on, Buster. Let's go find Mom."

"The two of you make a pretty good team," Lizzie said. "You've got change coming, you know."

"Take it off Mom's bill."

Owen carried Buster up the stairs and down the hallway. The door to his mother's room was open. Ruth's back was turned as she bent over an open suitcase on the bed. She was wearing the same stocking cap she'd worn on her last visit to the doctor.

Owen knelt quietly and released Buster, who jumped onto the bed beside the suitcase.

As Ruth turned, Owen stood and knocked twice on the open door. "Come on, Mom. We're going home."

Irene Marcuse

The Death of an Amiable Child

AN ANITA SERVI MYSTERY

When Manhattan social worker Anita Servi stumbles over the body of an elderly female outside her apartment, she recognizes her as Lillian, the homeless person who spent occasional nights in the hallway and whom some tenants call the "lady of the landing."

Though the woman's death is ruled accidental, Anita digs deeper into Lillian's murky past and makes some stunning discoveries. As Anita uncovers the shocking answers, the dark and dangerous face of a killer emerges, determined to make sure Anita takes the truth to her grave.

"A vibrant milieu, a caring and determined protagonist, and a deceptively simple plot result in a winner."
—Library Journal

Available September 2002
at your favorite retail outlet.

WORLDWIDE LIBRARY®

WIM433

THE GOOD AND THE DEAD

A BEN NEWMAN MYSTERY

True-crime writer Ben Newman has a talent for re-creating murder, though until now he's viewed homicide only as an outsider looking in. But suddenly bodies are turning up in his suburban Philadelphia hometown. And he knows each and every one of them—they were all classmates at the same elementary school.

What secrets lie behind the innocent facade of childhood in this small, tightly knit community? As corpses and old memories come to light, Ben is reconnecting with the past...and getting worried about his own future.

SEYMOUR SHUBIN

"Shubin keeps his winning streak going..."
—Tony Hillerman

Available October 2002 at your favorite retail outlet.